JUST A KISS

"You guard your moods as if they were a rope that could hang you."

Her eyes flew open. *What did he mean?*

"I feel sometimes I could guarantee your complete cooperation in everything I demanded if only I knew your secrets."

He did *know them, or at least the most important one. He knew about the murder. That was what he was saying, wasn't it?*

As his mouth descended, she removed her arm's barrier and did as he indirectly demanded. She kissed him.

His fingers crept along her collarbone, feeling his way to her neck and throat. His hand was cool against her warm skin and when he touched her so delicately, she had to struggle to remember he was blackmailing her.

His tongue soothed her lips.

He massaged the cords of her neck. "It's just a kiss."

And William the Conqueror was just a bastard.

Books by
Christina Dodd

Coming Soon

ONE KISS FROM YOU

CHRISTINA DODD

A Well Pleasured Lady

AVON BOOKS
An Imprint of HarperCollinsPublishers

This is a work of fiction. Names, characters, places, and incidents are products of the author's imagination or are used fictitiously and are not to be construed as real. Any resemblance to actual events, locales, organizations, or persons, living or dead, is entirely coincidental.

AVON BOOKS
An Imprint of HarperCollins*Publishers*
10 East 53rd Street
New York, New York 10022-5299

Copyright © 1997 by Christina Dodd
Cover art by Fredericka Ribes
Inside front cover art by Elaine Duillo
Library of Congress Catalog Card Number: 96-95483
ISBN: 0-380-79089-0
www.avonromance.com

First Avon Books printing: August 1997
First Avon Books special printing: March 1997

Avon Trademark Reg. U.S. Pat. Off. and in Other Countries, Marca Registrada, Hecho en U.S.A.
HarperCollins® is a trademark of HarperCollins Publishers Inc.

Printed in the U.S.A.

20 19 18 17 16 15 14 13 12

With gratitude and admiration,
I dedicate this book
to my editor, Carrie Feron,
who gave birth to Charlotte,
then rose like a Phoenix to
buy this book sight unseen.
You're a woman of strength, fortitude,
and vision.

Acknowledgments

My thanks:

To Heather MacAllister, Jolie Kramer, and Susan Macias for giving me their expert help in plotting this book. Who would have thought a story would come out of all that shrieking?

To Susan Wiggs, Joyce Bell, Barbara Dawson Smith, and Betty Gyenes, who took me to their collective bosoms and who fearlessly give me their opinions no matter how much I sulk.

Especially thank you to Connie Brockway, who reads chapters when asked and brainstorms titles with rare skill.

Chapter 1

Scotland, 1793

As usual, everything was going perfectly.

The kitchen buzzed as the servants prepared for their visitor. The French chef brandished a spoon and barked commands. His minions stirred, ground, and tasted. The maids swirled in and out, showing their serving outfits and receiving approval from the dour butler. Even Bronson's faded eyes sparkled as he chose wines appropriate for such a distinguished personage as Sebastian Durant, Viscount Whitfield.

In the midst of the turmoil, the turnspit sat, his nose pressed to the chilly pane, watching for the outrider. When he called, "Miss, he's comin'!" the hubbub died.

Everyone looked to Mary Rottenson. She poured boiling water into the teapot, then set it on the tray of artfully arranged biscuits and cakes. Smiling at her staff with a confidence now intrinsic to her, she said, "You've all done well, and I have every faith in you. You know if you need me, you have only to call."

A sigh of collective relief breezed through the kitchen. She wanted to laugh at their silliness, yet like soldiers on a battlefield, they wanted their commander's encouragement before they moved into action.

"Carry on," she said as she picked up the laden tray. Behind her, the clamor rose once more.

Ten years earlier, she wouldn't have believed directing the operations of a country manor could give her a sense of satisfaction. No frivolous dream or grand emotion could compete with the gratification of knowing each servant respected her.

Tremayne was stationed outside the library. There Mary paused and waited for his report. "I built up the fire, miss, and took in extra candles. And . . ." The footman shuffled his feet as if he were guilty of some breach of manner.

"Yes?"

"I moved some furniture."

Startled, she asked, "Why?"

"M'lady told me to."

Automatically Mary reassured him. "Then you have done as you should."

A good housekeeper always encourages her underlings.

He gave a grin and nodded. "That's what *I* thought."

And thinking wasn't what he did well, Mary knew. "Would you knock for me?"

He did, then opened the door when Lady Valéry called.

As Mary glided into the book-studded room, she moved silently.

A good housekeeper is unobtrusive.

Just as Tremayne said, furniture had been shifted. Lady Valéry's usual chair had been turned sideways to the fire. Two other chairs formed a triangle, and the tea table had been placed between Lady Valéry's chair and one of the others.

Not only had the furniture been moved, but an extra chair had been pulled up. What did it mean? Who would the other visitor be? Why hadn't she been informed? Mary hadn't prepared the proper amount of bedchambers, and she almost stepped back out the door to instruct a maid to do so.

But Lady Valéry called, "Come in, child, and put that heavy tray down."

The elderly woman stood beside the bookcase wall, fingering the bindings on her favorite books. Her short, plump figure retained none of the grace that had once made her the toast of London society and enthralled two husbands, but her smile, when she used it, shed such warmth that those around her thought themselves blessed. That smile had given Mary the nerve to approach her ten years ago, and the kindness that the smile represented had made her Lady Valéry's devoted attendant.

Placing the tray on the table, Mary said, "Lord Whitfield's carriage has crossed onto the estate. He'll be here within the half hour." She closed the heavy drapes, trying all the while not to look out. The winter sun had begun its early descent behind the brae. Curls of mist rose from the cold ground and sank from the bruised skies. Everywhere outside, light was dying, fading, slipping into the oblivion of night, and darkness had the ability to shake Mary's composure as nothing else could.

Hadden was out there, but Hadden relished the night. Hadden claimed to find comfort in the distant light of the stars or in the suffocating closeness of the fog. Hadden never cried at the bone-chilling loneliness of the soul, and he never got lost. Never. Never.

Hastily she turned away from the gathering desolation and her own disquieting despair. Collecting her composure, she assured herself her weapons had been placed throughout the comfortable room. Candles and fur and good food soothed with their abundance. Lady Valéry had seated herself, and Mary moved until she stood behind the tea tray.

"Why don't you go ahead and pour?" Lady Valéry rested her hands palm-down on the silk-covered arms of her chair. "And while you're serving, pour a cup for yourself."

Mary paused warily. She had never been invited to take tea with Lady Valéry. Silently, she recited one of the tenets that ruled her life.

A proper housekeeper never presumes upon her relationship with her employer.

Lady Valéry said, "Sit as you pour. Serving tea to her social equals is a fitting occupation for the daughter of Charles Fairchild of the Sussex Fairchilds.''

Mary didn't need to be told again to sit. She barely made it to the chair before her knees gave way.

The daughter of Charles Fairchild. No one knew that. No one. Silly Guinevere Mary Fairchild had disappeared from the face of the earth ten years ago. Now there was only a housekeeper.

Lady Valéry reached across and patted her hand. "You're looking rather pale. Surely you knew that one day the truth would come out?"

No. No, she hadn't known that. Mary Rottenson had taken Guinevere Fairchild's place, and Mary had been so different—solemn where Guinevere was lighthearted, responsible where Guinevere was flighty—that after the first few years, the fear of exposure had faded.

"When did you find out?" Her voice sounded odd to herself—calm, as always, but higher—and she tried to still the leap of panic. The position of housekeeper required control, which she'd won in hard-fought battles with herself, and carried a mantle of power, which she now wore with ease.

Lady Valéry gestured, a sweep of the hand that showed her instinctive domination. "That doesn't matter. What does matter is that my godson is coming to see, not me, but you."

Pressing her trembling knees together, Mary asked, "Why? Is he coming to . . . arrest me?"

Lady Valéry burst into open, hearty laughter. "It's

not a crime to be a Fairchild, although perhaps Sebastian would try to convince you otherwise.'' Then she stopped laughing and observed Mary with such acute interest, Mary wanted to squirm. ''Why would anyone want to arrest you, my dear?''

Mary lowered her gaze and shook her head.

''Were you truly twenty when you begged me for a position?'' Lady Valéry asked.

What was the use of lying now? ''Sixteen,'' Mary admitted.

''A very young sixteen.''

''Yes.'' Looking back, Mary could easily see that. Sixteen, desperate, without a farthing to her name and a little brother to support. ''I wonder that you made me such a generous offer.''

''My housekeeper was aging and wished to go live with her son. You were obviously a lady, and I thought I saw, beneath the youthful flurries, signs of promise. Signs of . . . maturity.''

''Oh, yes,'' Mary whispered. ''I had begun to mature.'' Maturity had been shocked into her in one dreadful episode that had left her scarred and fearful, and every time that young girl, that Guinevere Fairchild, popped up, Mary had ruthlessly suppressed her.

One's mind boggled when one contemplated the lackwitted things wild Guinevere Fairchild might say—or do.

''I wondered then what had caused you to flee England, but you were so reserved about your past.''

Mary said nothing.

"As you still are," Lady Valéry acknowledged with a smile, reassuring Mary of her continued good humor. "You should be aware that Sebastian is very interested in the daughter of Charles Fairchild."

A good housekeeper is always calm.

Having her true identity revealed was not necessarily a disaster, Mary reminded herself. Perhaps Lord Whitfield didn't know . . . everything. Carefully she relaxed her tense shoulders and strove to look normal. "May I ask why, my lady?"

"To beg a service which only you can render."

Mary had heard much about Lord Whitfield in her sojourn as Lady Valéry's housekeeper. She knew he was a powerful man, in business and in politics, and she didn't believe he would travel from London to beg anything from anyone.

"He wanted to tell you himself, but I thought it would be cruel to spring so much on you at once, and in front of him, too. In front of a stranger."

"Thank you for your thoughtfulness." Mary badly wanted that cup of tea now, but she didn't trust herself to pour it without spilling, so she sat as still as she could. "What service does Lord Whitfield require?"

Lady Valéry's warm hand slipped away from Mary's. She tried to speak, but the right words seemed to have escaped her. An ominous sign, Mary thought, for Lady Valéry specialized in knowing what to say and how to say it gracefully. She could have taken her place among the rulers of the world. But rulers were men.

Lifting one finger, Lady Valéry said, "Listen."

Mary heard the clomp of boots across the wooden floor, the deep resonance of a man's voice. Lord Whitfield had arrived, and Lady Valéry sighed in a manner that could only be relief. Mary's premonition of disaster deepened.

The library door flew open and a large man, still wearing his hat and muffler, stepped into the doorway. "My dearest godmother!" His black cape formed wings as he flung his arms wide, and when Lady Valéry rushed to him, he enfolded her like a great bat capturing its prey.

Rising to her feet, Mary averted her eyes. Lady Valéry greeted Lord Whitfield with all the abandon of a mother greeting her long-lost son. Surely she wouldn't want Mary observing such a tender reunion.

"Step back," Lord Whitfield commanded Lady Valéry.

His incisive tones brought a tingle to Mary's already jangled nerves. Had she heard his voice before?

"Let me look at you," he said. "Ah, I see no signs of this old age you claim which has brought a dearth of elegance and wit in London."

"Flatterer." Lady Valéry laughed, a light chime of joy. "It's what I like about you. Come and warm yourself."

"Gladly. 'Tis a damn cold exile you've chosen for yourself, my lady."

Mary gestured to Tremayne, and he entered and assisted Lord Whitfield out of his outer garments.

She still hadn't looked at Lord Whitfield. She couldn't. Not yet.

One of the maids whisked in and handed Mary a new pot of steaming tea. "Supper in an hour," Jill whispered.

Everything was proceeding on schedule. Everything in Valéry House was the same. Everything, and nothing.

"Tell Cook to proceed," she said to the wide-eyed maid, and the girl bobbed a curtsy before she carried the cooling tea out of the room. Tremayne shut the door behind her, leaving Mary alone with Lady Valéry and Lord Whitfield.

Hoping to blend with the shadows, Mary stepped behind the tea tray. Moving with a clock's oiled precision, she set out the teacups—three, for she conceded she must do as Lady Valéry required—and lifted the teapot to pour. She'd performed the safe, nameless role of housekeeper for so long, it was like a second skin to her, and she slipped into it effortlessly, feeling a sense of relief as that personage called Lady Guinevere Fairchild made way for Mary Rottenson.

Lord Whitfield had moved toward her, but she kept her eyes cast down as befitting the housekeeper. He moved closer, insistently, demanding by his presence that she receive him. He blocked the light of the candles and the warmth of the fire, but she pretended to be brave and held out the full cup for him to take.

His hands reached out and grasped the saucer—and she recognized the scar that slashed four fingers on the right hand.

It was him. It was him.

The hot pool of liquid never wavered as she gave up the cup. After all, Mary had spent the last ten years training herself to be the perfect housekeeper, and she refused to let the sight of a man's hands overset her— not even the man who could identify her as a murderess.

Chapter 2

Ever so slowly, Mary lifted her gaze and met his eyes. Gray eyes. Cold eyes, as chill as the mist outside. Hastily, she looked away.

It was him. She'd last seen him at night. The lights from the stable had faintly lit the yard, and she'd prayed that he couldn't see the bloodstains on her gown or the dirt on her hands. That time she'd been unable to look him in the eyes, so she'd fixed her stare on his hands—scarred, but strong and capable of tying a noose around her neck—then she'd focused on his lips.

The lips were the same. Broad, smooth, stretched over sharp white teeth that shone bright against his swarthy complexion. As he took the cup of tea, his smile deepened, and it reminded her of a street dog who had cornered an unwary kitten.

Her pulse sped up a bit—well, really, how many

women faced their executioner without a tremor?—but she efficiently poured the second cup of tea.

Surely he wouldn't recognize her. She had changed immeasurably. She'd covered her curly blond hair with a servant's mobcap. She'd exchanged a youngster's daring flare for fashion for an adult's dull good sense. She'd defeated the parade of volatile emotions that had led her into disaster. That, more than anything, marked the difference between the hopeful girl she had been and the responsible woman she had become.

Then he said it. *"I remember you."*

She froze. Hot mahogany liquid filled the delicate cup and overflowed onto the saucer, then onto the tray. Lady Valéry gave a cry and Mary came to her senses. Hastily she placed the teapot onto the hot pad and reached for the towel she always carried.

A good housekeeper is prepared for any emergency.

As Mary blotted the overflow, she was gratified to note she hadn't fainted or cried out, or even changed expression. Quite an accomplishment for a woman waiting to be accused and arrested.

He sipped his tea and observed her closely. "You're Charles Fairchild's daughter."

Stunned, for she expected something considerably more dramatic, she looked him full in the face. "Charles Fairchild's—" Her finger came in contact with the bulging silver side of the teapot, and she jumped as the skin seared. She stifled the urge to stick the burn in her mouth to cool it.

A competent housekeeper never shows emotion.

"Here." He grasped her wrist and guided her hand into the cream pitcher. "Milk's good for a burn."

As her fingers disappeared into the cool cream, Mary tried to think what a proper housekeeper would do in these circumstances. For once, her mind failed her. She couldn't leave her fingers in the pitcher. How improper.

Yet he held her as firmly as a shackle, and she couldn't struggle. How undignified.

So she stood there staring at his hand wrapped around her wrist and wondered why fate had decreed she had to see his hand, or him, ever again.

She wouldn't have thought it possible, but he looked even more menacing than he had ten years ago. Beneath his finely crafted frock coat, his shoulders rippled with muscle. His black hair, well streaked with silver, was long and pulled back with a simple ribbon. The style accentuated the harsh lines around his mouth and eyes and stripped his broad face of any of the softness a fashionable cut would have provided.

"Good heavens, Sebastian, I already told her we knew, and I'm glad I did." Lady Valéry sounded stern. "You frightened her half to death."

Using her most sensible tone, she replied, "I was only startled, ma'am. You have a most aggressive attitude, Lord Whitfield."

Lord Whitfield rocked back as if amazed by her accusation, but his faint, mocking smile let her know she hadn't fooled him. "I have a most *aggressive* curiosity, Miss Fairchild."

Chilled, she wondered—how much *did* he remember of those long-ago events?

"So you do, Sebastian." Lady Valéry's plucked brows rose in delicate inquiry. "Do you expect me to put that cream in my tea now?"

"Her hand is clean." Lord Whitfield lifted Mary's wrist and used his handkerchief to wipe the white film off her finger. "It feels better now, doesn't it?"

Mary hated to admit it, but the pain had almost vanished. "Yes, thank you, sir." She wanted away from him. He stood so close, his legs brushed her substantial skirt, pressing her petticoats against her legs, and he took up all the air to breathe. That had to account for the faint ache in her lungs, that sensation of constriction in her throat.

She didn't want to ask the question, but she knew she must, and vigilantly she framed the words. "Have we met?"

"I knew your father."

He hadn't answered her question, but Mary's nerve failed her. Was it possible he hadn't recognized her, or was he toying with her? She wanted to peer into his mind, and at the same time shied away. She wanted to interrogate him, and at the same time feared his responses.

She wanted to run.

She wanted out of this room, and she said, "If I may, I'll return to the kitchen and fetch a fresh tray."

"No, you may not. You'll sit down right there and tell me what you're doing in Scotland."

His deep, slow, soft tones brought forth rough emotions she thought long buffed away, but she displayed her thoughts and feelings for no one. She simply stood, one hand limp at her side, one hand allowing his brisk ministrations.

"You'd better sit," Lady Valéry said. "Sebastian is not easily refused."

Lord Whitfield tossed his limp white handkerchief onto the tea tray where it immediately soaked to a soggy brown.

Mary glanced toward the farthest stool in the dimmest corner, but Lord Whitfield pointed at the chair that faced the fireplace. "No, girl, sit there."

A good housekeeper does as instructed.

Her rigid corset would keep her from wilting beneath his interrogation, and vigorous self-training kept her spine from touching the chairback.

Lady Valéry, she was distressed to see, concealed a smile behind her fan.

"Look at me, girl," Lord Whitfield instructed. "I want to see your face."

The trouble with that, of course, was that she would have to see his face, too. *But a good housekeeper keeps the guests happy.*

Lifting her head, she stared straight at him and refused to let him intimidate her. Of course, it could have been easier. He stood when she sat. He observed her closely when she much preferred to be invisible. He blocked warmth and light with his mere presence.

"Yes, you *are* Charles Fairchild's daughter," he

said with evident satisfaction. "You have his look—except he never eyed anyone so coldly. Where did you learn that trick?"

She thought of several replies, all impertinent, and discarded them.

Somehow Lord Whitfield must have known, and his voice grew gentler. "Want to tell me to knock off, do you? Well, you can't, you're the housekeeper. What's your name?"

In as courteous a tone as she could manage, she said, "Mary Fairchild, at your service."

"Miss Guinevere Mary Fairchild," Lord Whitfield corrected. "It is still 'Miss,' isn't it? You haven't wed as an escape from this onerous position, have you?"

"It is not onerous at all." Mary spared a smile for Lady Valéry. "I'm honored and grateful—"

But Lady Valéry interrupted. "I told you not to use that word. You're not to be grateful to me."

"I treasure your kindness, then," Mary answered.

"You've more than repaid me." Lady Valéry's long nostrils pinched, her eyelids drooped, but beneath the leathery skin, Mary could see a resonant beauty still. "Do you think I don't know how many of my guests have tried to steal your services? Just last month my own sister tried to bribe you into returning with her to England."

How had Lady Valéry found out? Mary wondered. She frequently seemed omniscient, but she had never inquired about the events that had driven Mary to Scotland. That, more than anything else, explained

Mary's unwavering devotion. "I have no wish to work for anyone else."

Lady Valéry opened the drapes, glancing out the large windows at the last swirl of fog to be seen before night fell over the Scottish Lowlands. Leaning closer to the fire, she spread her veined hands. "It would be warmer in England."

Warmer? Yes, they'd burn Guinevere Mary Fairchild alive in England.

Lord Whitfield smiled again, gloating as if he scented vulnerability. "Charlie was always loyal, too."

He still watched her with that unnerving stare, but Mary was thankful that he'd changed the subject. In her own way, Lady Valéry was as stubborn as Mary.

"But a wastrel, of course." Lord Whitfield sighed as if in sympathy. "He left you penniless, didn't he?"

Abruptly, mightily furious, Mary rose to her feet in one smooth movement and started toward the door.

She didn't know why she was angry. Men had said worse things to her in her tenure as housekeeper. But this man with his judgmental air grated, and she lost her valued self-discipline.

Then his arm wrapped around her waist and he spun her so she faced Lady Valéry.

Mary got the impression Lady Valéry's interest verged on voyeuristic.

Then Lord Whitfield adjusted Mary, fitting them like two spoons in her own well-kept silverware drawer, and all else fled her mind. No one had dared hold the grande dame of housewifery for years upon years.

Did he understand what he dared? Did he realize the impact of one strong male body against her flesh where only the winds of desolation had swept? She wanted to strike out at him, to box his ears or pull his hair, anything to make him feel the pain of the constant, bone-chilling loneliness she'd accustomed herself to.

And learned to live with.

He spoke in her ear, and the warmth of his breath intruded on her, too. "Too much pride, too, just like Charlie."

She shuddered. How dared she even contemplate the ache of her isolation? She was the housekeeper, a nobody . . . a murderess. And of all the people in the world, she had to allow this man every liberty he desired.

His hands moved slowly away from her, releasing her with the care of a parent who any moment expected his toddler to flee into the arms of danger. Just as slowly, she stepped away.

He was looking at her. She could feel his gaze almost as clearly as she had felt his grip. Her skin still burned. Her bones still ached. Tears pressed against the back of her eyes, and if she returned his gaze, she feared he would detect them.

Instead, walking on wobbly feet, she navigated the short distance to her chair. She wouldn't rise again. She was a fast learner, and that brief contact had taught her she didn't want Lord Whitfield touching her.

He seated himself. His fingers templed before his chest and his elbows rested on the arms of the chair while he studied her.

Apparently, chasing women and subduing them was nothing unusual for him. *She* wanted to lift her hands and check her strictly restrained hair to see if tendrils had escaped. She wanted to rub her finger, which still stung, and the places where he'd touched her, which still throbbed from his oppressive hold.

But she didn't. *A housekeeper didn't fidget*—especially when a man was about to destroy everything she'd worked to build. "How did you know my father?"

"We were neighbors once," Lord Whitfield said. "And he was kind to me."

Kind? Yes, that described her father perfectly. He was also loyal and proud and a wastrel, just as Lord Whitfield had said. She'd loved her father, worshiped him, and in his joyous, thoughtless way he'd infected her with his philosophies and ruined her life.

She didn't like to remember her father.

"You are the stillest woman I've ever met." Lord Whitfield studied her more, drawing her into the clasp of his gaze. "I wonder why."

Because the hunted always take refuge in stillness. Mary fought dueling urges—she wanted to close her eyes against him. At the same time she needed to watch him. Without moving, he seemed to be circling her, looking for a vulnerable spot to attack.

"And silent, too." He tapped his fingertips together as if in thought. Turning to his godmother, he asked, "Discreet?"

"Very." Lady Valéry no longer smiled behind her fan. She no longer smiled at all, and Mary began to sense the earnestness of Lord Whitfield's intent. Of Lady Valéry's intent, also?

In deference to Lady Valéry's serious demeanor—surely she wasn't curious on her own behalf—Mary asked, "What help could Charles Fairchild's daughter render to you, Lord Whitfield?"

He said, "There is a lady, a very beautiful, intelligent lady, who was the mistress of several of our revered government leaders. She had a great deal of influence on them, which she used wisely, but unwisely, she recorded all in her diary."

Mary found her attention straying from him to Lady Valéry. A half smile hovered around her mouth, lighting, then flitting away like a butterfly.

"The diary was stolen by those who wish to use it for ill, and in the process the beautiful lady will be harmed."

A combination of dread and inevitability mixed in Mary, and she wanted to scream at him to get to the point.

But a housekeeper never shows impatience.

"The beautiful lady could pay money to these scurrilous rogues and they promise they will return the diary, but she fears—and I agree—that that is unlikely. Yet if she doesn't pay, the diary will be published, and with it her chance for discretion and anonymity.''

The room was silent except for the crackle of the flames. The faint scent of smoke lingered in the air, and Mary thought incongruously that she must have the chimney cleaned. Carefully she avoided the realization that made her stomach twist in dismay. The realization that the diary Lord Whitfield sought was . . .

She looked straight at Lady Valéry. ''It's yours, isn't it?''

''Yes.''

It was only a whisper of sound, but to Mary it cracked like the closing of irons around her wrists. For Lady Valéry, she would do anything.

As she struggled to retain her composure, to remain for this time, at least, the calm and efficient Mary Rottenson, Lady Valéry made her way to the door. Opening it, she spoke to Tremayne. Returning, she seated herself as calmly as if she hadn't just given another direct order and circumvented the chain of command Mary had so carefully set into place.

When had Mary's life careened out of control? She stared directly at Lord Whitfield, blaming him. ''This sounds like the beginning of a fairy tale to me.'' Her voice cracked. ''One in which danger looms.''

''Yes,'' Lord Whitfield admitted. ''But the publication of such a tale will shake the very foundation of the government. Since the French have beheaded their king, we fear a similar uprising in England.''

"French barbarians," Lady Valéry exclaimed in disgust. "They made poor King Louis pay for the sins of his fathers."

"It is a bloodbath over there." Lord Whitfield faced Mary squarely. "I don't know if you've heard the tales of whole families going to the guillotine. Women, children, the French peasants don't care. They chop off their heads with unvarying fervor."

"We're in Scotland, not Utopia," Lady Valéry said. "We hear the stories here, too, and I hear more than others. After all, my dear duc de Valéry was French."

"An unfortunate business development for you, this revolution." Sebastian flicked an imaginary piece of lint off his buckskin trousers. "You have lost the income from Valéry's lands, have you not?"

"I'm not destitute yet," she snapped. "I still have the income from Guldene. And doesn't the possibility of government overthrow affect your business, too, Sebastian?"

She mocked him, but Sebastian answered steadily. "There is that."

Lady Valéry faced Mary squarely. "For me, it's more than just the government. It's the careers that will be ruined, the lives destroyed. I'm not ashamed of my past. If I had it all to do again, I would repeat every last, delicious moment. But I made a point of being circumspect. No one was ever hurt when I took my pleasures. Now someone, some wretch, threatens to destroy my accomplishments."

"Accomplishments?" Mary asked faintly.

"Accomplishments," Lady Valéry declared firmly. "Furthermore, I'll not sit by and watch while the men I loved, and their families, are tortured by scandal."

Mary looked at the lady who had saved her life and Hadden's. Trapped, she asked that lady's godson, "What has this to do with me?"

Lord Whitfield settled back, slouching in his chair like an insolent youth. "I've traced the diary to Fairchild Manor."

Mary's blood chilled, then warmed with a surge of pure hostility. "Are you accusing me of stealing it, then sending it to the Fairchilds?"

As a reply, he placed his finger in front of his lips as a parade of servants entered the room. Jill brought a new tea tray, another took the old one away, another brought firewood and stoked the fire. They kept their eyes decently averted, but Mary knew they observed her sitting, speaking with Lady Valéry and her guest. Mary could imagine the speculation in the servants' hall. Worse, she could imagine how astonished they would be if she shouted at that smug brute who lounged in his chair.

She'd found safety and refuge in this place, and if it were up to her, they would never know she had been born to the English aristocracy. If it were up to her, tonight would be nothing more than a nightmare.

Jill came close to Mary and leaned toward her ear. "Shall we serve supper at the appointed time?"

"At the same time," she said firmly.

"And should we set an extra place?"

Mary turned her head and stared in surprise. "For whom?"

"For you."

Mary's scowl made Jill straighten hastily. "We'll serve two for dinner," she said coldly.

Jill curtsied and scurried from the library while Lord Whitfield watched. After the door clicked shut he said, "It's a perfectly natural question. The girl didn't deserve to be reprimanded."

"That was hardly a reprimand." Mary spaced her words. "But housekeepers don't eat with the gentry."

"Such a little prig. You didn't get *that* from Charlie."

She hated to hear him talk about her father almost as much as she hated to be compared to her father. Coldly she repeated her question. "Are you accusing me of stealing that diary?"

"Who else would know where it was but the housekeeper?"

"I am not a robber." A murderess, but not a robber.

"You're the first Fairchild who could claim that distinction, then."

His cynicism infuriated her, and all the more for knowing that her father had indeed been accomplished at "picking up a little something" when he needed.

"Enough!" Lady Valéry held up her hand. "As you very well know, Sebastian, the diary was stolen over a year ago." Turning to Mary, she said, "It was during the entertainment I arranged for that horny old bastard.''

"The French ambassador?" Mary clarified.

"The very same." With a half smile, Lady Valéry arranged the rings on her fingers, and Mary knew Lady Valéry had more than a few fond memories of "the horny old bastard." "Someone removed one of my jewel boxes. It contained nothing that would interest an accomplished thief—a few lesser pieces of jewelry, an ivory fan—but the working on the box was quite lovely."

"My lady, why didn't you tell me?" Mary asked.

"My dear, I haven't had enough house parties for you to know, but something always disappears, and usually several somethings."

"Oh." So others like her father did exist. Mary burned with the shame of knowing such improprieties had occurred in *her* well-run household. "Forgive me. I didn't realize . . ."

Lady Valéry waved Mary's perturbation away. "The French are notoriously light-fingered, and their servants learn to steal in their cradles. I thought—I hoped—the thief would toss the diary without realizing the value of the contents, and when so much time had gone by, I believed myself safe."

Mary knew that in Lady Valéry's eyes, she had been exonerated.

"That letter was quite a shock," Lady Valéry finished.

"What letter?" Mary asked.

"The blackmail letter." Lady Valéry dusted her

fingers together as if the mere mention made them feel dirty.

"Does your housekeeper know anything about *that?*" Lord Whitfield doubted Mary in every way. He'd made it clear before; he showed it now with that nasty half smile and his skeptical tone of voice.

"I have free access to everything here!" Mary wanted to convince him of her innocence in this matter, at least. "Why would I have stolen a diary when I could have had jewels?"

"The diary is worth more than the crown jewels." He stood, and Mary shrank back. He observed and found her guilty, she was sure, but he did no more than remove his jacket. Such informality was his right, of course. This was his godmother's home, and he remained decently covered by a double-breasted waistcoat. His white shirtsleeves covered his arms, but somewhere during the journey he'd untied his cravat, which hung in limp strands around his neck. Slowly he pulled it away and tossed it over an ottoman with his jacket.

Mary's fingers itched to pick up his apparel and hang it on a hook, but she subdued her housekeeperly instincts.

He sat once more, sideways in the chair, and hooked one knee over the wooden arm.

To Mary, schooled to rigidity, his sprawl bespoke a lack of respect, almost . . . intimacy. She glanced at Lady Valéry, but Lady Valéry seemed affectionately amused at his discourtesy.

"There's to be a house party at Fairchild Manor," he said.

She took a long breath and with a courtesy born of desperation, said, "There is always a house party at Fairchild Manor."

"I haven't been invited," he said.

"Do you think I have?"

"Of course not. The Fairchilds don't know where you are." He observed her closely. "I wonder why."

Panic writhed in the pit of her stomach. She'd trained herself to listen when the occasional guests visited, and never had she heard the name of Guinevere Mary Fairchild mentioned as a fugitive from justice. But this man seemed to be demanding that she revive Mary's vanished spirit, and with it, the specter of disgrace, imprisonment, and death. She scarcely unclenched her jaw as she replied, "I can be no help to you. When my father died, we begged my grandfather for help and he refused us. There's no reason for the family to welcome us now."

"Us?"

Funny. She was usually more discreet. "Hadden and me. My brother and me."

"So Charlie had an heir."

He made a statement, but it sounded as if he were musing, or worse, remembering, and she didn't want that. Not if he truly didn't remember that night. "As I said, the Fairchilds would not welcome me."

Clearly he realized her discomfort, but this was a man who liked to have the upper hand. He relaxed back into the upholstered Chippendale chair.

She comprehended his scheme. Thinking her uncowed by the threat of arrest, he threatened her with himself. Beneath the thin white linen of his shirt, she could see a thatch of dark hair over a well-muscled chest, and his shoulders resembled a prize-fighter's more than a nobleman's. His hands, she'd already noted, and his face . . . well, she'd seen executioners less austere.

Yes, he was threatening her.

"I can't help you."

"But you must, my dear. Half of the ton has been invited, including some very powerful men. I have no doubt the exchange of diary for money will occur during the party."

Mary winced.

"I'll use you as a distraction while I search for the diary, and that distraction will be a pervasive one."

Oh, she would be a distraction, all right. Especially if one of the nobles at the house party recognized her.

"I assure you, I've anticipated every possible obstacle."

"*Every* obstacle?"

"You see"—he leaned forward, his eyes as gray and cold as the night fog she feared—"you are going to be my betrothed."

Chapter 3

"*Don't be absurd.*" Mary had seen Trouble before without putting a name to him. Now she knew; the name was Sebastian Durant, Viscount Whitfield. With forced composure she said firmly, "I have no intention of masquerading as your fiancée."

"If I might speak?"

Mary started. Lady Valéry had been so silent, she had almost forgotten her presence. And—*regardless of the circumstances, a good housekeeper never neglects her mistress*. "Please, Lady Valéry. I'm sure you will be the voice of reason."

"My dear, the idea might sound absurd. It certainly sounds so to me." Lady Valéry fixed her godson with a regal look. "But perhaps we should listen to Sebastian's entire scheme. Our primary goal, after all, is to recover the diary."

"Our goal?" Mary questioned faintly. She wanted to implore Lady Valéry to see sense. Instead, she looked at Lord Whitfield and found him staring as she convulsively crumpled the bell of her woolen skirt in her fists. She hadn't even realized what she was doing. When had he so undermined her poise?

Stretching out her fingers, she forced them to remain at rest.

But apparently she'd betrayed too much. He laughed, a harsh bark of ruthless mirth. "Of course she'll go as my fiancée. It is the only possible plan."

Clearly it was up to Mary to be the voice of reason. "The Fairchilds won't let me in the door," she replied.

"They will now." Lord Whitfield put his hand on his heart. "I fear, Miss Fairchild, I must offer my condolences. Your grandfather, the marquess of Smithwick, last year passed from this earth to another, better place."

I hope they kindle the fire hotter just for him.

Mary's memory of Fairchild Manor consisted of nothing but shame, incredulity, and a deep, biting anger at the man with malice-filled eyes. His long finger had pointed the way to the door, and when she hadn't believed his indifference, he'd had her thrown out.

"Has the lecherous old villain gone at last? Good riddance, I say," Lady Valéry exclaimed, echoing Mary's thoughts.

Mary had kept secret the memory of the tall, sophisticated man who'd called himself her cousin. When her grandfather had disappeared back into his study, he'd stopped the eviction process and flung a handful of money at her. That money had been her nest egg. It had taken her and Hadden as far as Scotland when the time had come to flee.

"Such a lack of charity," Sebastian chided Lady Valéry. "But yes, the old marquess is dead, and his son has inherited the title, the entailed lands—and damned little else."

"Wasn't there money?" Lady Valéry asked. "I cannot believe there was not! There was always so much, and after your father—"

"There was money," Sebastian said smoothly, "but for reasons only Lord Smithwick understood, he chose not to leave it to his son." He hesitated as if he wished to say more.

Mary could contain herself no longer. "It is most peculiar *I* had heard nothing about his death."

What did Lord Whitfield see when he looked at her? The anger, the resentment, the bitter scorn she felt for all the Fairchilds? The family consisted of four great-uncles, brothers of her grandfather, and Bubb Fairchild, her father's brother and the new marquess. None of them had tried to help her when she'd taken custody of her brother. None of them cared for anything but their own worthless hides.

Sebastian spoke with exaggerated patience. "You live in the wilds of Scotland. The Fairchilds live in the south of England. You've changed your name and your appearance—"

She jumped. "My appearance? What makes you say that?"

He swept her with a look. "I never saw a Fairchild

who looked anything less than gorgeous, and *you* look like a housekeeper.''

Thank you, kind sir. But she didn't say it.

And in truth, she was relieved he meant nothing more.

''Most important, the new marquess hasn't been seeking you,'' Sebastian said. ''Why should he? Bubb Fairchild was frightened of his father in life, and indignant at his death. How will he maintain the family without the blunt to do so?''

''Do you suspect him of having the diary?''

''Of course. I suspect every Fairchild.'' Sebastian squeezed the arm of his chair as if he could squeeze the life from the polished wood. ''Ah, Miss Fairchild, wouldn't you like to see your uncle squirm?''

The trouble was, she would. She would like to see all the Fairchilds squirm. Yet she snapped, ''You mistake indifference for interest.''

''Mary!'' Lady Valéry sounded appalled, but she watched as if diverted by the byplay. ''If you don't wish to do this, say so, but don't compromise your dignity.''

Whitfield took his godmother's hand. He kissed the freckled knuckles and murmured, ''Hush, dear. I'll handle this. I promised I would.''

Lady Valéry tilted her head, watching her godson as if he were a charming scamp rather than a pitiless savage, and Mary did see how he might have fooled his godmother. He represented the symbol of sincerity in a carefully-wrought French painting. His eyes glowed. His lips smiled, not in amusement, but to coax a similar reaction from his godmother. He held his extended hands cupped upward as if to catch the blessings she would rain on him.

Acutely aware of his charm and power, Mary feared him—in all his guises.

Floundering now, she tried to redeem herself. "I'll do whatever needs to be done, Lady Valéry, but it just seems that you, Lord Whitfield, are better equipped to gain entrance to Fairchild Manor than I."

"Perhaps we should look at this another way." He smiled invitingly. "Think of the family's consternation when they find their long-lost niece is already betrothed."

"Why should they care?"

"If I were to speculate, I would have to say that since the marquess's death, each and every Fairchild has been given a mission—to wed money." For a man who smiled often, Lord Whitfield gave no impression of warmth or amusement. "Even now, I would guess, they are regretting the loss of you as another lure. The family will believe you to be just like them—charming, convivial, beautiful—"

"Shallow, vindictive, frivolous, treacherous," she finished for him.

He sat back in a hypocritical exhibition of wonder. "You *did* meet them, didn't you?"

"Quite," she said.

"But they were not all . . . vindictive," he admitted. "Or treacherous."

She wanted to ask who he meant, but he returned to the subject with relish. "The Fairchilds would expect you to be one of them."

"They will try and separate us, and why not? It will be immediately obvious that we are less than fond."

"Will it?" He lifted one finger and caressed his lips in a manner Mary found highly suggestive. "I suspect we can convince them we are . . . lovers."

Lady Valéry had been watching them with the fascination of a playgoer, but now she interrupted. "You'll convince them of no such thing! You'll not ruin her reputation, Sebastian, not when she's been living with me all these years."

"She is going, my lady. She has no choice." He had gone from superior to overbearing to ruthless in the space of a single conversation.

"Somehow you'll force me?" Mary asked.

"Not at all." His street-dog smile made her want to arch her back and claw at his face. "Your father was the Fairchild without treachery. Are you going to tell me you *haven't* inherited that loyalty from him?"

"I have inherited nothing from my father," she said fiercely. "My loyalty is my own."

Sitting up straight, he became in expression and manner a courteous stranger. "Then I'll have to speak to your brother. Perhaps I can convince *him* to accompany me."

A shiver worked its way up Mary's spine. This man, talking to Hadden? Offering him a chance to go to England? Then interrogating him as he interrogated her?

Not that Hadden was simple. No, indeed, Hadden could be—should be—studying at the university. But he was open and unsophisticated, and Mary cringed at the thought of the information he would artlessly reveal.

She recognized defeat when it stared her in the face, and so rose with what dignity she could maintain. "When did you wish to leave, my lord?"

"Tomorrow," he said.

"Don't be ridiculous, Sebastian," Lady Valéry said. "She can't make herself ready overnight."

"How much can she have to pack?" he demanded impatiently.

"She has to organize the staff for her absence."

"She won't be coming back."

"Won't be coming back?" Mary cried.

He said simply, "Fairchilds don't work as housekeepers."

"He's right, dear." Lady Valéry smiled at Mary. "Much as I hate to lose you, I'm afraid our cozy arrangement is over."

Mary felt the carefully built foundation crumbling beneath her feet. "But what will I do? Where will I go?"

"The Fairchilds will welcome you this time, I assure you," Lord Whitfield said.

Mary wanted to shriek. Didn't he understand anything? *"I* don't want the Fairchilds. I don't want to know them, and I certainly don't want to live with them.''

"You'll always have a home with me," Lady Valéry soothed her. "If not as my housekeeper, then as my friend." Mary wanted to babble her thanks, but predictably, Lady Valéry wasn't interested. "You'll have to make arrangements with Hadden. Will you bring him?"

"Of course not!" Too emphatic, Mary realized, and she fought to tone down her consternation. "There's no need for him to leave here."

"Hadden's a young man," Lady Valéry pointed out gently. "Perhaps he'll have some thoughts of his own."

Mary shook her head. "He likes it here. He'll be satisfied to stay."

"How old is he?" Sebastian demanded.

Mary didn't even turn her head and look at him when she answered. "Nineteen."

"Your brother must be a dull youth if he's content to remain in the lowlands of Scotland."

How obnoxious this Lord Whitfield was! She'd never be able to convince anyone she loved him. Never. Never. As evenly as her temper would allow her, she answered, "Hadden is much given to adventure, but unlike some youths, he can find it in places other than the stewpots of London."

"A direct hit," he murmured, and clapped his hands softly. "Brava!"

Mary turned her back to him. "When should I be ready to leave?" she asked.

"Time *is* of the essence, especially if one of the guests will be purchasing the diary." Lady Valéry tapped her fingers together. "Would it be possible for you to be ready to leave in two days time?"

"As you wish, my lady." Mary curtsied to Lady Valéry, wheeled and bowed stiffly to Sebastian, and walked toward the door.

Lady Valéry waited until the door shut behind Mary before rising to stand beside him. "What a vulgar exhibition that was. I would have never told you who she was if I had known you were going to approach her so crudely."

She waited while he weighed his answer, and knew a sense of satisfaction. Sebastian still respected and feared her. Now in her seventies, she hadn't cared when her beauty faded, when wrinkles had formed around her eyes and she'd had to resort to plucking stiff hairs off of her chin. But she had minded, greatly, being excluded from the conferences of the powerful.

A man, regardless of age, merited respect. A woman, especially an elderly woman, merited only a pat on the head and a bowl of sops. It was another of life's injustices, and the one she'd had most trouble adjusting to.

Placing her finger on his cheek, she turned his head toward her. "*I* will go with you to the Fairchilds' as Mary's chaperone."

"Chaperone?"

His chin dropped, and she pushed it shut with a click of his teeth.

Indignantly, he asked, "Do you think me so lacking in control I would dishonor that woman?"

"No. I think you so lacking in control you would seduce that woman." She pressed a kiss on his forehead. "It is, after all, my diary we seek to recover. I'll accompany you when you go, or you'll not take my housekeeper at all."

"You know I have no reason to be fond of a Fairchild."

He defended himself hotly, and Lady Valéry knew she had stumbled on the truth. Mysterious Mary Fairchild tantalized Sebastian.

"And she is a true Fairchild." Clearly, he hated the ardor that burned in him against his will. "One has only to look at her to know."

Now confident of her scheme, Lady Valéry walked to the door and opened it. "Oh, my dear one, how long will you carry this grudge against them?"

"How long will Fairchilds exist on this earth?"

As she left him, she chuckled.

She hadn't been so entertained in years.

Chapter 4

Mary stared at the candle she'd set in the kitchen window. She was too numb with worry to pray and too used to the anxiety to pace. She simply waited. The wooden table before her had been washed so many times through the years it was smooth to the touch, bleached almost white and bowed in the center where the most scrubbing had been done. The clock ticked on the mantel. The fire flickered in an ever lowering ebb, and the darkness pressed in on her.

He would be all right. He was always all right.

As the hour struck midnight the door opened and Hadden swept in on a restless drift of fog.

"Sister, you shouldn't have waited up." Her little brother had taken to Scotland with a boy's innocent pleasure in the open spaces and mighty storms, and as he walked the countryside he'd grown strong and hardy. Now he smelled like moist air and heather, and his eyes sparkled with excitement as he leaned over and bussed her on the cheek. "I never get lost, you know that."

She slipped the napkin off a tray and pointed to the array of bread and cheeses protected beneath. "I thought you might be hungry."

He snorted. "Which I could have fetched myself. Dinna fash yourself."

"I truly don't believe it is proper to use the Scottish dialect . . ." He grinned at her, and she realized he was teasing her. With a smile, she slapped at his arm. "So I waited up for you. I don't like the dark. It's just silliness." Then she couldn't help adding, "Much like your mission."

He paused in the act of tearing a chunk of bread from the loaf and gave her a warning look.

"Did you get some of them to talk to you?" she asked.

He stared at the bread in his hands, then put down the remains of the loaf. "Naturally. They *like* to talk to me."

"I suppose they do. Who else would listen to them blathering about the old ways?"

He picked up a piece of cheese and laid it on his bread, then took a bite.

She should keep quiet. She knew she should. He showed more restraint than she did about this, their greatest conflict, but still she nagged him. "If you must listen to those useless stories, I don't know why you can't do it in the daytime."

He deliberately finished chewing before he answered. "The poor folk of Scotland work for a living, that's why. The only time they can talk to me is at night." Then his control broke. Slapping his palm on the table, he said, "Since Culloden, the old ways are dying. Half of the people emigrated from the Highlands, and thousands of years of tradition are being swept away by the English and their bloody superior justice. I don't see why you can't understand that. We've discussed this a hundred times—" He stopped and took a breath. "Is this why you stayed up? So we could quarrel?"

He was resentful, and she couldn't really blame him. All their lives she been there, encouraging him, helping him, praising him as the smartest, the most talented, lad in the world. Only now she found herself at odds with him, and what could she do about it? He was nineteen. He'd been taller than she for six years. His shoulders were broad, his legs long. His deep voice sounded so much like Papa's, she had only to close her eyes to return to an earlier time—and that was the problem, really.

She tried to smile and patted the seat of the chair beside her. "Actually, tonight I waited for a different reason."

He glowered. "What?"

"I don't know where to start." She pressed her palms together. "I'm going to England."

"To England!" For a single moment she saw his yearning for adventure. Then concern replaced it. "Why?"

What should she tell him? How should she tell him? "It's all so odd, Hadden."

She seldom dithered, and he realized it, for his eyes narrowed. Putting down the bread, he grasped her hand. "What has happened?"

"That man who came tonight."

"Lord Whitfield?" Hadden's grip tightened until the knuckles ground together. "Did he assault you?"

"No!" Horrified by his conclusion, she cried again, "No, of course not! Lady Valéry would never have allowed such a thing, and . . . No!"

"Then what did he do to you?"

She worked her hand away from his and shook out her aching fingers. "Nothing!"

"Don't tell me 'nothing,' Mary. I know you better than that. You're upset, and I want to know the reason."

She realized her baby brother was grown up. She had to tell him all of the truth. "Do you remember much about that night?"

"That night? What—" Hadden stilled.

They'd never spoken of it, but Mary saw horror darken his eyes.

"Aye," he said. "I remember everything."

"Do you remember when we came back from burying the corpse?" Her hand crept back into Hadden's. "There was a man who stopped us in the stable yard."

He rubbed her fingers as if they had been touched by frost. "Aye."

"That man was Lord Whitfield."

"Dear God." It was a prayer. Hadden stared beyond her at the dark square of window where the candle still burned. "Did he accuse you to your face? I always thought it was my fault. I'll tell them when they come—"

"It wasn't your fault!" Now it was her turn to comfort him. "How can you say so?"

"It was me—"

"No. It was me." She said it with finality. "I was so stupid, and so miserable, and I dreamed that some prince would come and rescue me. I lived for dreams and wishes—oh, damn Papa for that!" It had been years since she'd cried, but tears dribbled down her cheeks now.

Hadden shot up from his chair and fumbled through his pockets until he found a handkerchief, then dumped the contents—some old rocks with strange carvings on them—on the table. Thrusting the handkerchief into her hands, he asked, "Why Papa?"

She swiped at the tears already released and sternly forced back the others. "He was nothing but a dreamer. He used to spin these tales. He called me Princess Guinevere, and said that after I had fought overwhelming battles, a prince would appear and lend his strength to mine, and together we'd win everything." She could scarcely bear to remember how eagerly she'd listened and believed. "Papa taught me to dream, and that was all I did. Even after he died, even after our grandfather rejected us, even after I had taken employment as a governess, I still dreamed."

"You were like a different person then."

"I *was* a different person then." That was the

truth. Mary Rottenson had eliminated Guinevere Fairchild from her being. Guinevere was gone. Truly and completely. Yet the consequences of her actions still ruled their lives. "Guinevere allowed the earl of Besseborough to visit the schoolroom. Guinevere thought he was the prince."

"When actually he was the slimy old toad." Hadden's face twisted in distaste. Then suddenly he placed both his hands flat on the table in front of her. "That's why you don't like me gathering the old tales and writing them down."

"No—"

"Aye. You think I'm like Papa."

She hated to admit it, for she loved him too much—but he was like Papa. He sought romance and drama, and what good could ever come of that?

Yet Hadden wanted to go to university. There he would be exposed to other influences, and this nonsense about preserving the old stories would fade. In that, she placed her faith. "Lord Whitfield didn't seem to recognize me."

"He *didn't* recognize you?"

"He knew I was the daughter of Sir Charles Fairchild. He already knew that when he arrived. Apparently Lady Valéry found out."

Sheepish, Hadden confessed, "She questioned me not long after we'd come here, and I told her—"

"Everything?" Mary cried.

"No, no. Just about Papa, and how you'd had to hire out because Grandfather hadn't let us live with them.'' Hadden showed the acrimony he still felt, that they both still felt, at that long-ago rejection.

''I don't even know why our grandfather wouldn't take us in when we needed help so desperately.''

''Didn't Papa ever say?''

''Not that I remember.'' She touched her forehead. An ache had formed there, the same ache that always formed when she thought of her father. ''We never went to Fairchild Manor to visit. I didn't think about it when Mama was alive.''

''I don't remember any of it.''

Hadden's lean features displayed his longing for memories. Their mother had died when he was two. Their father when he was nine. She'd done the best she could, but she'd been too young to know how to be a parent. She'd done so many stupid things. Looking at Hadden now, Mary worried, not for the first time, that Hadden had needed a man to look up to.

''No matter.'' Hadden shrugged as if he had come to terms with his loss long ago. ''You know what Lady Valéry is like, and I was young then.''

''I know.'' She touched his golden hair lightly. ''I just wish you had told me.''

''We agreed it would be better if you could do what you thought best.'' He smiled at her. ''In those days, Guinevere Mary, you were a very serious girl.''

''I was, wasn't I?'' As she remained.

''Tell me about Lord Whitfield.''

She dragged herself back from what had been done

to what must be done. "As I said, he didn't seem to recognize me."

"The night was dark," Hadden said.

"And I've changed. But he knew Papa."

"From where?" Hadden asked.

"He said they'd been neighbors. Lord Whitfield says I look like Papa, although not so attractive, of course."

Hadden leaned back, surprised, and studied her. "You're pretty, for a sister."

"Lord Whitfield is not my brother, and he wasn't impressed. Really, it's not surprising, is it?" She smoothed her plain dark skirt. "Nevertheless, he wants me to return to Fairchild Manor as his betrothed."

"What?" Hadden exploded out of his chair.

She grabbed for his wrist and hung on when he would have stormed out of the kitchen. "It's necessary. I swear it's necessary."

"Tell me, Mary." He stared down at her forbiddingly. "And this had better be good."

Swiftly she told him the tale of Lady Valéry's diary, and when she finished, he rose and paced across the kitchen, then came back and towered over her. "He must realize he's putting you in danger. The Fairchilds are totally disreputable. They threw us into the gutter to starve. They wouldn't cavil at killing you."

Weakly, she said, "I'm sure it's not so desperate as that."

"I'll go with you, Mary." He put his arm around

her shoulders. "It's clear this Lord Whitfield is more than you can manage, and anyway, it's time I started taking some of the burden."

"No!" She started up under his demand. "I can handle this."

"You can't. Guinevere Mary, you know you can't. Let me grow up. Treat me like a man." His eerie resemblance to their father disturbed her, but he sounded mature, reasonable. "I won't fail you, and maybe, just maybe, you could be happy once more."

Giving up a little of her burden sounded so tempting. But how could she? No. She had to retain control of this situation. Once she'd been to England and returned, unmarked by scandal, *then* Hadden could make his way as an adult. Protecting him for a little bit longer was the only sensible thing; she'd grown up in a swift and brutal manner, and she could save him from that.

Patting his shoulder, she said, "Please don't make this more difficult for me than it already is."

He straightened, obviously ready to argue once more.

"I can only do it if I believe you're safe here in Scotland. If I had to worry about you—" Her voice broke, and she let it. She hated to use guilt to control him, but right now she needed every weapon in her arsenal. "Just stay here this one last time. Please, Hadden. Please."

He walked to the table and stood looking down at those rocks he'd collected. The old people he'd interviewed had told him they were ancient stones,

carved with markings that could tell the future. He'd
tried to show her once, but she'd cut him off.

Now he idly arranged them in a line as he listened,
and when she'd finished, he looked up, expression-
less. "Of course, sister, you're right. It would be
better if you think that I'm safe in Scotland. Go in
peace, and I'll see you once more when the time is
right."

As she shut the door, she wondered what he had
seen in the stones that caused his sudden capitulation.

Chapter 5

"A *good housekeeper goes where she's* needed."

Sebastian heard the muttered phrase in the doorway behind him and turned. Mary was looking down at Lady Valéry's opulently decorated carriage with an expression so grim, she might have been looking down at her own hearse.

Good God, she talked to herself. Miss Perfection Fairchild talked to herself. What an entertaining eccentricity. An unscrupulous man would enjoy having a weapon to wield when dealing with Miss Guinevere Mary Fairchild.

Sebastian *was* an unscrupulous man. "Pardon me, Miss Fairchild, I'm afraid I didn't quite understand you."

He would have sworn she hadn't noticed him standing off to the side, but she didn't recoil. Her hands were clasped before her, fingers threaded together as if in prayer, and Sebastian thought he'd seen nuns who moved more restlessly. He'd seen nuns, too, who gave off more womanly warmth.

Mary looked him over without enthusiasm, and her breath puffed white into the cold air. "I wasn't speaking to you, Lord Whitfield."

He glanced around at the empty steps that stretched from the open door of the mansion and down to the line of carriages that waited to carry them to London, and then on to Fairchild Manor. "To yourself, then? All the Fairchilds have a reputation for eccentricity, but none of them, to my knowledge, are mad."

She turned her head away. "But then, you don't know as much about Fairchilds as you think you do."

"Ah, but I will." He relished reminding her, "After all, we *are* betrothed."

The heavy knot of blond hair at the base of her neck must have tilted her head back, for he knew Mary the housekeeper would never have looked down her nose at him as Miss Fairchild did now. "We are betrothed, yes, but only when we reach Fairchild Manor, and then only for the purposes of recovering my employer's diary."

He stepped close to her, crowding her back toward the door, and caught the hand she raised to ward him off. "Ah, but you're discounting the pleasure we could seek in each other's arms."

If she hadn't been wearing woolen gloves, her fingernails would have dug into his skin. As it was, her frigid tone and the gaze from her frosty blue eyes flayed him. "I find pleasure in no man's arms."

She objected to his handling, that was clear. He didn't care.

Readjusting his hold to ease the pressure of her grip, he said, "Perhaps you haven't been in the right man's arms."

"You misunderstand me, Lord Whitfield." She looked pointedly at their clasped hands. "I have been in *no* man's arms."

She had to be jesting.

"And I intend for that situation to continue."

She wasn't.

And he believed her. Believed a Fairchild, a liar by definition, because hunger writhed in his gut every time he looked at her. He'd told her she looked like a housekeeper, and that was true.

She wore a black dress and held herself rigidly erect with the help of an unfashionable corset. She eschewed the new, freer fashions and wore a whalebone petticoat, secure in the knowledge no man could discern her shape beneath the unbending hoops. She stuck her hair up in a bun, then used one of those netlike things to make sure her curls were sufficiently trapped, and sometimes she added a plain mobcap. No cosmetics brought color to her rounded cheeks, and no patches accented the disapproving, puckered mouth.

It was also true that those whalebones couldn't quite contain her generous breasts, and nothing kept those wisps of blond confined for long. Cosmetics might have hidden the betraying ebb and flow of color in Miss Fairchild's face, and he wondered—when he kissed her, would his lips leave a mark on her fair flesh? When he removed that dour headgear, would her hair taunt him with its ebullience? When he stripped her of that miserable corset and dress and touched her rosy parts, would she yield, become soft and generous, make him forget his enmity toward her entire intemperate clan?

He shuddered. No. No, he could never forget. That would be the betrayal he could never live with.

On the long trip up from his London town house, he'd made his plans. He would whip in and wheedle this Fairchild into doing his will. He hadn't thought it would take much effort—God knew the entire family responded well to flattery. Superficial emotions were all any of them understood. When he blasted her with his charm, she would melt like all the other Fairchilds.

Trouble was, when he was with her, he didn't use his charm. He felt compelled to incite her instead.

He shouldn't, he knew. He needed her cooperation. But something about her made him want to make the caged bird sing. Perhaps it was the way she spoke: softly, as if she feared being overheard, and slowly, as if she considered each word before she allowed it egress. Perhaps it was the way she moved: gracefully, as if she feared to cause an accident, and precisely, as if each motion should be measured and weighed.

He released her hand, then followed her as she glided down the stairs toward the carriage. She might not like it, but she was quite human, and beneath that shapeless black frock, very female.

He thought—he hoped—she would do him proud when dressed in silks and lace and presented as his betrothed to her family. They would know he had won a prize. That mattered to him. It mattered more than it should.

"Where's your brother?" he asked. "I thought he would be here to see you off."

Miss Fairchild smiled, a tight curve of the lips made up of half nerves, half defiance. "Hadden wished to speak to an old woman in the Highlands. He said she knew about the hauntings at the field of Culloden, and he's much interested in . . . the war."

She lied. Sebastian knew it as well as he knew the scar on his hand, but how could he prove it? His gaze scoured the landscape. Wisps of snow decorated those Highland peaks, and each night he'd been here, the ground had frozen hard. The road would be easier to travel because of the frost, but he also felt positive that Mary had deliberately kept her brother hidden away. Surely her actions bespoke a guilty conscience of some kind.

Her guilty conscience, rather than her integrity, had no doubt prodded her to pack efficiently. As promised, she had been ready to leave in two days. He hadn't had to wait on Guinevere Mary Fairchild.

Then he grinned. His godmother was another story.

"Sebastian, did you make sure every *bit* of my luggage was loaded into those carriages?" Wrapped in a fur cloak some long-forgotten Russian lover had given her, Lady Valéry stood high on the steps of her mansion and stared down her nose at him as if he were some peasant born to do her bidding.

And while he wasn't a peasant, he was born to do her bidding. She was the only woman in this world he respected—and feared. He was going into the jaws of hell—which some called Fairchild Manor—and he was doing it for his country, to save it from a political disaster. Yet he was doing this for Lady Valéry, too. He owed much to her, and he served her faithfully.

"Your luggage, my dear, rides within those extra vehicles." He waved at the two lumbering conveyances waiting behind her own well-sprung carriage. "Miss Fairchild's carpetbag rests on the knees of one of the lady's maids you brought, and my paltry trunks ride on the top, exposed to the weather."

"As it should be, my dear." She frowned as she descended the steps. "Except for Mary's carpetbag, of course. We'll have to spend some time in London, you realize, creating a persona for her."

"She has a persona," he retorted. "What she needs is some clothes."

"That, too," Lady Valéry replied tranquilly.

He heard a little snarl, and turned his head. Miss Fairchild was glaring at both Lady Valéry and him.

"Sensitive, isn't she?" he asked his godmother.

"She hasn't ever been before." Lady Valéry stopped on the bottom step and watched Miss Fairchild enter the carriage. "I wonder what brought that on."

Sebastian glanced at Lady Valéry's thin, upright figure. By God, she was the opponent of every man in England. A power-dealer, knowing more about the government and its works than most of Parliament and knowing, too, how to direct the course of legislation. He had to get that diary, not just to protect Lady Valéry's privacy, but to halt the spread of her sedition through all of the British Empire. If other women discovered it was possible to rule, and wisely, too, what use would they have for men?

He handed her into the carriage and stepped away, knowing the ladies would need time to arrange themselves and their belongings before he could join them. With a meticulous eye for detail, he studied the three vehicles. The wheel hubs shone from the labor of the wheelwright. Beside each coachman on his high seat sat a footman armed with pistols—highwaymen were always a problem. And each carriage carried an extra footman, his own or Lady Valéry's, in case of accident or in case the horses, excellent animals all, needed tending. The two lady's maids rode in the second carriage while his very efficient valet supervised the servants from the last.

Even now, a well-bundled Gerald strode along the length of the procession, doing his own last-minute check, and when he came abreast of Sebastian, Sebastian said, "We should reach London within the fortnight, God grant us good weather."

When the man turned his head toward him, Sebastian realized his mistake, and wondered why he'd made it. This fellow wore rough wool, not elegant broadcloth, and the muffler that covered his head and mouth had clearly been knitted by some granny in the hills. Gerald would never have been caught dead committing such a sartorial sin, yet this man—this footman?—had the same air of command that distinguished the upper servants from the lower.

But when he spoke, he used English well leavened with a Scottish accent. "God'll grant us good weather until we leave Scotland, m'lord," he said, "but after that we'll be in the Devil's hands."

"A proper Scottish sentiment." Sebastian couldn't help it; he grinned. Such a defiant spirit amused him. "Why are you going, if you find England so repugnant?"

"Someone has to go along to watch Miss Fairchild."

Normally, such impertinence would only amuse Sebastian more, but something about the way those blue eyes watched him wiped the smirk from his lips. The fellow was confronting Sebastian, man to man, and Sebastian didn't care for the challenge. "She'll be fine, I assure you."

"Nay, *I* assure *you*," the fellow said. "And that's why I should continue inspecting the procession."

"You're a footman?" Sebastian asked.

"The ostler."

And did this ostler imagine himself a suitor to Guinevere Mary Fairchild, descendent of a noble English line? "What's your name?"

"Haley, m'lord."

Sebastian hesitated. He should dismiss the man, tell him he'd lost the right to care for his beloved Miss Fairchild by his effrontery, but something about the way Haley stood—shoulders back, hands on hips— told Sebastian he would be wasting his breath.

"Very well," he said. "Watch over Miss Fairchild if you wish, and do that by making sure our journey is a smooth one."

"To that end, my lord." Striding to the back of Lady Valéry's carriage, Haley eased a large wash pan from beneath the ropes that held it. "Take this."

Sebastian gingerly took the banged-up old thing between two fingers. "What is it for?"

Now Haley was grinning. Sebastian could tell by the crinkles of merriment around his eyes.

"It's for Miss Fairchild," Haley said. "She is *not* a good traveler."

Chapter 6

Blearily Mary lifted her head from the pillow.
The carriage had stopped swaying, the wheels had stopped their eternal clamor, and the door opened to let in a draft of fresh air.

"Sit up, Miss Fairchild," Lord Whitfield said.

"Oh, now what?" Miserably aware that her appearance must be as wretched as her constitution, she groped on the floor for her bonnet.

"We have arrived."

The significant tone of his voice brought her erect as nothing else could do. She clutched the edge of the narrow padded seat that had been her bed for too many days. "At Fairchild Manor?"

"Come." His hand, marked by that forbidding scar, appeared beneath her nose. "I'll carry you."

"I don't want you to," she muttered as she tied the bonnet under her chin.

"You never want me to," he answered. "But I

doubt you wish to pitch forward onto your nose." He paused for a beat. "As you did before."

He wouldn't let her forget it, either. That first night on the road from Scotland had not been one of her brighter moments, true, but a gentleman would have simply offered his services without constantly harping on one wretched incident in that filthy inn.

Resentfully she put her hand in his and let him pull her off the seat. As she had every evening on the journey from Scotland to London, then again on this ride to Fairchild Manor, she balanced herself with her hands on his shoulders while he eased her through the door. Without ever letting her feet touch the ground, he picked her up with an arm beneath her back and one beneath her knees.

She hated this. She hated being touched, especially by him, especially now. On the way to London, she'd been protected by layers and layers of thick wool cloth. She hadn't liked being handled, but she'd been sick enough to be resigned.

Then they'd stopped in London for a whirlwind buying tour. Lord Whitfield had insisted, and Lady Valéry agreed, that Mary be outfitted with garments from the inside out. The new styles, the modiste had explained, eschewed whalebone corsets and petticoats. Instead, Mary wore a high-waisted satin and velvet gown over nothing more than a chemise and underpetticoat. Worse, as they'd traveled south into Sussex, the weather had grown warmer and she'd had to discard her pelisse.

Now Lord Whitfield's fingers pressed into her ribs, his palm rested on her thigh, and the contact she'd been scrupulous about avoiding, that of flesh against flesh, was sensuous reality. When the material slipped, he touched her in a new place. When he adjusted her in his arms, he violated another portion of her skin. With each breath, his chest moved against her and she clasped one hand over her stomach to ease the anguish. This wasn't traveling sickness, but the sickness of a woman so accustomed to loneliness, she'd forgotten the comforts of human touch.

Lord Whitfield reminded her of that too forcibly as he carelessly stripped the cushion of time and distance away, and she feared that when he finished with her, she would once more be needy, dependent Guinevere Fairchild.

Worse, he would know, and revel in it. She had no illusions about Lord Whitfield. He would use her, and if he hurt her in the process, he would consider that a bonus.

She'd met a man like him before. She'd killed a man like him before.

"I don't mind if you look sick," Lord Whitfield said in an undertone. "But do you have to look frightened, too?"

"I am frightened." Not of the Fairchilds, as he imagined, but of him.

"Do you want them to know?"

"Of course I don't want them to know." He made her so angry. "I don't want them to know anything about me. But you've taken care of that, haven't you?''

A small grin tugged at his mouth. "Now you look incensed. That's better, I suspect." He rejoiced, she knew, in his role of conqueror, returned from battle with his spoils. With *her*. If he'd planned it, he couldn't have created a better scene than this.

"Have you got her?" Lady Valéry leaned on the cane she seldom used, giving the impression—false, as Mary well knew—of fragility. "Poor dear," she said to Mary. "I'll wager this is not how you pictured your return."

"I never pictured my return at all," Mary answered, and it was true. Imagining Fairchild Manor and all its inhabitants crushed by her magnificence had been one of the many satisfying fantasies she'd not allowed herself.

"We're here now," Lady Valéry said. "The worst is over. You won't have to travel again."

"Until we leave." As miserable as Mary had been during travel, she still hoped they would leave soon. *Now* would be even better.

"Let us complete our mission." Lord Whitfield swept an austere glance about them. "Then we'll discuss escape."

What was it he saw that put that expression of disgust on his face?

Cautiously she lifted her gaze to the facade of her ancestral home.

She had hoped that her youthful fancy had created

a structure bigger and brighter than it really was, but no. The gleaming white marble edifice hadn't shrunk in the intervening years. The mansion still swallowed the sky with its height and spread like a bloated belly across the Sussex plain. Each finial, each cupola, each balcony, had been chosen with care to create an overall impression of wealth. Fabulous, overwhelming, consumptive wealth.

Emotions buffeted her. She wanted to shrivel with shame. She wanted to scream with rage. She wanted to own part of, *be* part of, the Fairchild legacy.

Yet she hated the house, the legacy, and the Fairchilds, and nothing could change that. Nothing, no matter how long she lived.

And Lord Whitfield, she saw, hated them, too. Hated all of them. Even her, the woman he brought as an offering, the woman he would pretend to love.

Perhaps the anguish he created when he touched her wasn't merely the collapse of isolation. Maybe it was hate, burning through his soul and touching hers.

She glanced longingly toward Lady Valéry's carriages and escape. The Scottish servants were already unloading the trunks, and the ostler was speaking to the horses, rubbing their noses, telling them they were almost done. Mary wondered why he still wore a roughly knit scarf tucked around his face and a cap pulled over his ears.

Then he turned and looked at her.

She blinked in astonishment, and looked again.

It wasn't Hadden. The man was old and stooped, and he limped as he turned his back and walked toward the next team of horses. She simply missed her brother, and saw what she wished to see.

"Pay attention." Lord Whitfield squeezed her. "The show is about to begin."

Servants lined the walk between the carriage and the door. Some of the younger maids and footmen poked each other and giggled. Female guests didn't arrive carried in a man's arms, as Mary well knew, and as well as she could, she tried to appear dignified. After all, she'd been a housekeeper, in charge of youngsters like this.

Then a burly footman stepped out of the crowd and bowed. "M'lord, would you like me to carry the lady?"

"No one is allowed to touch my precious Miss Fairchild," Lord Whitfield said. "She is mine, and mine alone."

Mary clenched her jaw to contain the words that wanted to boil forth. He mocked her and claimed her in one brilliant stroke, for this bold declaration had reached the nobleman who stood staring from the top of the broad stairway.

She strained to see. It wasn't Ian, her dark-haired rescuer of yore. She relaxed. Praise God it wasn't Ian. She wasn't ready to meet him yet. "Who is that?"

"Bubb Fairchild, the new marquess of Smithwick." Lord Whitfield smiled broadly and nodded up at Bubb. "The head of your family."

"My God!" Bubb started down the stairs. "Is that you, Whitfield?"

"Your eyes don't deceive you," Lord Whitfield

agreed. "I've come to attend your house party—should you wish to extend me an invitation."

As Bubb neared, she could see he looked like a Fairchild. Like her. Like Hadden. Only richer. He fairly reeked of money. A tailor had worked for days on the frock coat he wore so carelessly. A barber had styled his blond curly hair so it curved around his round cheeks. A valet had shaved his strong chin without a nick. He embodied the skill of a battalion of servants, and at the same time, he was flawless in himself. In his fifties, he was tall, well formed, and handsome enough to send women's hearts fluttering. If ever a man was built in the image of God, then God must look like Bubb.

He batted his brilliant blue eyes. Incongruously dark lashes lent him an innocent appeal, but his smile was different from Mary's. He smiled as if he meant it.

"Good God, man, of course you're welcome to my house party!" He extended an arm as if he would give Lord Whitfield a manly hug.

Mary felt Lord Whitfield stiffen.

Bubb must have seen, for smoothly he changed his gesture and clapped him on the back, instead. "If you hadn't ignored so many invitations before, I would have sent another one this time. And you brought . . . ?" He smiled at Lady Valéry, and she smiled back.

"My godmother, duchess of Valéry." Lord Whitfield introduced them, his gaze never leaving Bubb.

As unself-conscious as a babe in arms, Bubb beamed a welcome at the older woman. "It is an honor to have you in our home."

Lady Valéry inclined her head gracefully, accepting his words, and Mary heard Lord Whitfield suppress a sigh. He'd hoped for some indication of guilt, then, and failed to find it.

Then Bubb transferred his attention to Mary. His gaze inspected her from head to foot, and she gripped Lord Whitfield tightly as Bubb inventoried the same similarities she had noted.

He beamed and waggled his head in what surely must have been an imitation of delight. "Is this who I think it is? I know where all the rest of the relatives are—at least all the legitimate ones." He stepped closer and bent so he smirked right into her face. "Is this Guinevere Mary Fairchild?"

His singsong tone made Mary's already unsettled stomach even more rebellious, but she answered as civilly as she knew how. "Yes, I am."

"Guinevere Mary Fairchild." Bubb almost cooed. "Guinevere Mary Fairchild. We've been looking for you across the length and breadth of England."

She didn't believe that for a minute, and she let her skepticism show in her voice. "Why?"

Bubb clapped his hands together. "You're jesting."

She just stared at him.

Bubb stared back. "You're not?" He spoke to Lord Whitfield. "Didn't you tell her?"

Lord Whitfield smiled so pleasantly, Mary knew instinctively he was annoyed. "I left that privilege for you, Fairchild."

"Tell me what?" Mary was fed up with people talking about her as if she weren't there.

Bubb's sumptuous blue eyes grew wide, and he sucked in his breath. "Tell you . . . tell you that you, Guinevere Mary Fairchild, are an heiress. My father left the entire unentailed Fairchild fortune to you."

Chapter 7

"Send for my wife!" Bubb led the way to his massive study, shouting all the way. "We need Lady Smithwick. Nora will know what to do. Put my dear niece there on the couch." He jerked on the bell rope. "Has she been ill long?"

Lady Valéry walked at Sebastian's side and held Mary's limp hand in her own. "The poor dear, coming here is such a profound experience for her. She's simply overwhelmed." Overwhelmed by the news she was an heiress, Lady Valéry thought sourly. Why *had* Sebastian kept that a secret?

Seeing the scornful look he cast around Bubb's exquisitely appointed study, she answered the question herself.

Because he feared should Mary know of her good fortune, she would refuse to come to Fairchild Manor, and he needed her here. As a distraction, she was already proving her worth.

Sebastian laid her on the couch, then sat beside her. He was worried, Lady Valéry could tell. He hadn't supposed that Mary would faint. Lady Valéry had been a little surprised herself, but unlike Sebastian, she realized Mary's debility was more a result of traveling sickness combined with shock rather than any actual physical weakness. Besides, she suspected Mary was parlaying a mild swoon into the time she needed to collect her composure. A housekeeper didn't find out she was an heiress every day.

Bubb grabbed the footman who answered the ring of the bell. "Send for my wife. We need her *now*."

The footman was evidently used to Bubb's outbursts, for he spoke calmly. "Lady Smithwick is on her way, m'lord. Would you like me to pour some spirits?"

"Spirits? Spirits?" Bubb's voice got louder and louder. "Spirits for a poor crushed flower of womanhood?"

Lady Valéry settled into a chair and with her cane moved the ottoman close enough to put under her feet. "*I'll* take some spirits. A little brandy, if you please."

Bubb cast her a wild glance, but her stern aspect recalled him to his duty as host. "Of course, Lady Valéry. And Whitfield, would you care for—"

"Yes, brandy." Sebastian had unwrapped Mary's frivolous bit of a hat and was involved in removing her crespin. For some reason, he'd taken a dislike to that crespin and had spent their whole time in London trying to convince Mary to discard it.

His insistence surprised Lady Valéry. After all, the netting kept Mary's curly mass of hair under control, but then . . . maybe Sebastian didn't want it under control.

Lady Valéry watched as he spread her hair across the hard square pillow under Mary's head. No, Sebastian wanted Mary under control, but not her hair.

Mary's hand came up and grasped Sebastian's wrist, and she said something—"Stop," it looked like—but her voice was too soft to carry across the large chamber. Sebastian leaned close to Mary and spoke gently, and he had to be charmed by the picture Mary presented.

She wore clothes well. Even Lady Valéry, as discerning as she prided herself on being, had been surprised when Mary had clothed herself in the first of the new gowns. The pale blue velvet bodice accented Mary's lavish blue eyes, and the midnight blue satin skirt wrapped around Mary's legs when she walked, releasing hints of the charms beneath to the discerning watcher.

Sebastian had ever been a discerning watcher, and he knew, if Mary did not, that together they made a striking couple. In fact, Lady Valéry mused, if they'd only been nude, the two of them could have been models for a naughty miniature the Danish ambassador had given her during his last visit.

Bubb presented Lady Valéry with her brandy while the footman carried the other glass to Sebastian.

Sebastian took it and waved it beneath Mary's

nose, and this time she spoke so emphatically, everyone in the room heard her say, "No!"

Sebastian smiled, cajoling, and Lady Valéry bit back a sigh of happiness. How wonderful to be able to stir the pot, then sit back and watch the results. Age did have its rewards, after all.

Then Bubb bellowed, "Is she awake?" and everyone in the room jerked to attention.

"It would seem so." A small, neat woman appeared in the doorway, then made her way to Bubb's side. "Although your shouting is enough to give her a headache, Bubbie."

Lady Valéry's mellow thoughts of love, marriage, and great-godchildren evaporated under a rush of mirth. *Bubbie?* This woman called the marquess of Smithwick *Bubbie?*

"I'm Nora, Lady Smithwick." She introduced herself and smiled at Lady Valéry apologetically. "I'm sorry I wasn't here to welcome you, but we weren't expecting guests for another day."

"The apologies are ours. We came too soon, but Sebastian thought we should come early in case Lord Smithwick"—Lady Valéry badly wanted to call him *Bubbie,* but restrained herself—"decided to throw us from his property."

Nora looked astonished, then shot the fondest glance at her husband. "As if he would. Bubb is the kindest of noblemen."

And recalling the old rumors of scandal, Lady Valéry thought Nora must mean every word. She

studied the new marchioness with interest and noted
that though her smile was sweet, her demeanor was
self-effacing and . . . she was brown. Unfashionably
brown. Brown eyes, brown hair, which hung in
ringlets around her shoulders, brown skin that faded
to splotched freckles as it approached her paltry
bosom. The tale that Bubb Fairchild had married a
governess must be true.

Interesting. Lady Valéry glanced from Bubb to
Nora and back. She would have never thought the
big oaf would have worked up the nerve to defy his
father.

"I have recovered." Obviously Mary hadn't experienced the rush of charity toward Sebastian Lady
Valéry had, for she pushed at him until he moved
aside, then sat up. "I apologize for making such a
spectacular entrance to your home, Lady Smithwick."

"Nonsense." Nora moved forward with a rustle of
silk and laid a hand on Mary's brow. "Bubb is so
strong and vital, he doesn't realize a woman can be
overset by even the simplest of news." She cast a
censorious glance at her husband. "And that the news
of a massive inheritance should be broken inside in a
civilized manner, rather than on the steps like a
ramshackle boy."

Bubb's big head drooped. With his forlorn expression and his golden hair, he looked all the world like
one of Lady Valéry's golden retrievers when she'd
scolded it.

Lady Valéry examined him with a critical eye. He was a devastatingly handsome creature. But—she sighed—he was married, and Lady Valéry didn't poach on other women's property. At least . . . not often, and certainly not in what appeared to be a love match.

Besides, she liked Lady Smithwick immediately. That surprised her—she was old enough to know the unreliability of first impressions. But something about Nora's stalklike figure and resolute chin appealed to Lady Valéry. She sensed kinship here, the kind of kinship conveyed by similar intelligence and like goals.

"I was surprised to hear about the legacy," Mary acknowledged.

And for that, Lady Valéry thought, read "dumbfounded." And furious. She glanced at Sebastian, now standing off to the side. Mary had to be furious.

Mary swung her feet around and put them flat on the floor. Holding on to the seat on either side of her legs to balance herself, she hung her head down until she got her balance. She hadn't fainted, not really, but her ears had buzzed and her vision fogged, and it just seemed easier to collapse, at least until some kind of coherent thought was possible.

Now, she realized, coherent thought wasn't likely for hours, perhaps days. Bubb said she'd inherited the Fairchild fortune. If it was true, then she was no longer a supplicant to Lady Valéry or an anchor on Hadden. If it was true . . .

Slowly jubilation grew in her, and a heated triumph. If it was true, she could dictate the terms of her cooperation to Sebastian Durant, Viscount of Whitfield. She didn't know what he thought to accomplish by hiding the fact she was an heiress from her, but whatever he planned, it wouldn't work. She was independent now, and capable of giving Hadden whatever he wished. She was *rich*.

Shaking her tumbled hair back, she looked around and recognized this chamber. She remembered its sheen, the miracle of polished brass and expensive fabrics, the odor of beeswax and fresh flowers. She saw the massive desk, built of expensive dark wood with the express intention of intimidating whoever stood before it. The chair behind it was as tall as Mary herself, with gargoyles that dug their claws into the wooden finials and glared at any mere mortal who dared defy the master of Fairchild Manor.

She had dared, all those years ago, and she'd been ejected by her grandfather. Remnants of intimidation lingered, mingling with her sense of triumph. She was an heiress. *The* heiress. And ironically, because of her grandfather.

Fixing her gaze on Nora, Mary said, "Perhaps you could tell me more about this astounding legacy."

Nora stared back at Mary as she spoke to the footman. "You may retire, Henry, and shut the door behind you."

Silent, well trained, the footman bowed and did as he was told without indicating by a flicker of an eyelash his interest in the topic. And he had to be interested. The whole household must be fascinated by this turn of events. Mary wished she held the concession for the keyhole in the door.

The silence left by the footman's departure was broken by Sebastian, introducing himself to Nora, and by Bubb, offering more drinks. Apparently both men thought a liberal application of courtesy and liquor would ease the strain of the occasion.

Both, Mary was pleased to note, seemed subdued and on their best behavior. That was good; it meant they were unsure. As they ought to be—especially that twisted weasel who called himself Lord Whitfield.

"I remember seeing you when you came to speak to my father-in-law," Nora said to Mary. "You were little and brave, and he threw you out."

Sebastian glared at Bubb.

Bubb stared at his toes and rocked back and forth.

Heat climbed in Mary's cheeks as she realized her prayers had not been answered—the prayers that requested that episode be erased from everyone's recollection.

"He tried to do the same with me once." Nora pleated the silk of her skirt between her fingers and watched the motion steadily. "I had Bubb to stop him."

Mary felt an unwilling empathy with her aunt by marriage. "Better to be married to a Fairchild than to be one, then."

"Oh, I wouldn't say that." Nora frowned, then her brow cleared. "You're joking, of course. Excuse me, they say I haven't got a sense of humor."

Mary hadn't been joking, but neither did she want to disillusion Nora.

"When Lord Fairchild—Bubb's father—tried to throw me out, he'd already disinherited your father, so I suppose he had to tether one son at his side."

Not a flattering portrayal of Bubb's role all these years, Mary noted. But a fair one? "Then he left *me* the money. Why?"

"Guilt over the way he treated your father?" Nora spread her palms to indicate her ignorance. "Or you? I think most likely, spite against Bubb."

"If I might offer a supposition?" Lady Valéry said. "I knew the marquess for years, and I think he left the money to Mary simply because he knew it would cause an fracas among his progeny."

Nora's mouth puckered and her nostrils flared. She might have been consuming rotten meat, or smelling the sickly odor of decay. Mary suspected she was instead thinking of her father-in-law, although her voice remained polite enough. "You are probably right, Lady Valéry. One shouldn't speak ill of the dead, but such a scheme would appeal to him. Why else would he have left everything, the whole, immense fortune, to a granddaughter he easily dismissed before?"

Strange, how discussing Mary's newfound wealth vanquished the ill effects of road travel. "Just how much money are we talking about?" she asked.

"Bubb has the title, of course, and the lands are entailed to the eldest male heir." Nora stroked one curl that rested on her chest. "Aside from that, your grandfather amassed over one hundred twenty thousand pounds.''

A film of moisture suddenly formed all over on Mary's skin, and Sebastian murmured, ''You're flushed.''

Of course she was flushed. She'd never heard that much money even mentioned at one time.

Bubb clapped his hands, and the small explosion of noise made everyone in the room jump. ''This is a cause for celebration. Let's lift a toast to my newfound niece and her newfound fortune. It's good to be back in the fold, heh, Guinevere?''

Mary stared at him for a few moments, just long enough to make him squirm. Was he sincere? He couldn't be.

But a housekeeper always makes those around her comfortable.

Taking a careful breath, she told herself she no longer had to monitor the contentment of the people around her. Still, the habits of ten years died hard, and she kept her tone polite. ''I prefer to be called Mary now, Lord Fairchild.''

''Of course.'' It seemed Bubb was unaware of any undercurrents, for he beamed like a boy who'd been invited to share a confidence. ''Call me Uncle Bubb. After all, I'm your guardian now.''

In that instant, with that one sentence, Mary saw the genius in Sebastian's plan. Unmarried women had no rights over their money. If she kept quiet about the sham betrothal, she would be subject to Bubb's manipulations of her self and her fortune.

If she allowed Sebastian to lay claim to her, he could protect her wealth from Fairchild greed.

Whom did she want? Bubb, apparently good-natured, obviously a wastrel, and one of the many Fairchilds who couldn't be bothered to help her when her grandfather chased her away? Or Sebastian, who . . . She found herself staring at Sebastian, eyes glazed.

Sebastian.

Power hungry. Rude, impatient. A blackmailer.

But not weak. Although she'd never asked what Sebastian planned for her after this wretched masquerade was over, she didn't worry he would strip her of her fortune and, when that was done, throw her into the dung heap.

Into prison, perhaps, but not the dung heap.

Before she could change her mind, she said, "Uncle, I have good news. Lord Whitfield and I are betrothed."

Bubb didn't wilt or show signs of shock. He'd seen Lord Whitfield lifting her from the carriage, then, and seen the way they moved together with the ease of a couple accustomed to their ritual. He'd probably heard Lord Whitfield's carefully announced claim on her affections, too. Bubb seemed a simple, jolly man, but did he hide his financial schemes beneath that bluff facade? Mary's toes curled in her slippers as she remembered Hadden's prediction of trouble.

Of murder. Her murder.

Lord Whitfield moved to her side, placed his hand on her shoulder, and pressed firmly. "You'll have to remember to call me 'Sebastian,' my love, or your uncle will believe we are not fond.''

"I think my uncle understands a woman's need to maintain the proprieties,'' Mary said to the room at large.

"Possibly.'' Lord Whitfield sat beside her, and his hand slid along her arm in a leisurely, sensuous sweep.

Her fist clenched, and she called on those years of housekeeperly training to keep her from boxing his ears.

Turning her wrist over, Lord Whitfield unbuttoned her glove. One fingertip at a time, he loosened her glove from her hand. Slowly he stripped it from her. She watched, as fascinated as their audience, until he clasped their hands, palm to palm.

Then she understood his intent. The intimacy of his touch forced her to comprehend, and she struggled to free herself until he caught her wrist with his other hand and held it still.

He wasn't done with his show. Speaking loudly enough that his voice would reach across the study, he said, "Your uncle undoubtedly understands a lover's need to break down the barriers of propriety, also.'' He looked warmly into her eyes as he raised her hand to his mouth.

She would have been impressed, but she remembered a similar gesture made to his godmother not a fortnight ago in Scotland. So what? He would kiss her knuckles. Did the man have to depend on such a boring repertoire?

Then he took her forefinger in his mouth—and nipped it.

She jumped so high, everyone in the room no doubt observed, and she gasped when he soothed the ache by closing his lips around her finger and sucking on it.

Tangled in a web of embarrassment and fascination, she stared at him, at his mouth, the mouth she'd noticed the very first time she'd met him. Not even the horror of that bloodstained night had dimmed the memory of his lips, and now he used them to touch her flesh in a manner she could only describe as intimate. She didn't know what he meant by such a display, and at the same time her instincts informed her it was a gesture for lovers.

And he made it look so sincere. The way he watched her face, eyes glowing as he observed her struggle to deal with sensation as sharp as his teeth and as soft as his lips.

If he was going to simulate the part of her fiancé so sincerely, she would be hard-pressed to retain her good sense.

Good sense. Surely some resided somewhere in this madhouse. She looked at the others, appealing for help, but none abided within this chamber.

Not from Lady Valéry, who watched the proceedings with open fascination.

Not from Nora, who pressed her lips together in self-imposed discipline.

Certainly not from Bubb, who attacked the weakest point of their plan without hesitation. "Are the marriage contracts negotiated and signed?"

Sebastian relinquished Mary's finger so slowly, it looked as if he relished the taste of her. "Of course."

"It's unlawful to negotiate marriage contracts without a guardian's consent."

Resentment made Mary forget, for a moment, her indignation at Sebastian. "I didn't know I had a guardian. I've been on my own for so long . . ." She let the accusation linger in the air.

Bubb ignored her easily. "You knew, Whitfield."

"So I did."

"Then you ought to have told me, Lord Whitfield," Mary said. When she thought of the many things Lord Whitfield had kept from her, she could have screamed.

And she almost did when he slipped his arm around her waist. He could have made the motion a simple, proprietary gesture, but no. He had to turn everything into a production.

His open palm skimmed in circles across her back, and when his hand reached the far side of her, he used his strength to draw her along the slick, hard cushion and close to him. Too close to him. So close she felt the muscles of his thighs flex. Oh, for the return of her whalebone petticoat!

His breath brushed her cheek. "Sebastian," he said.

"What?" She didn't make the mistake of turning her head to look at him. He was much, much too close.

"Sebastian. My name is Sebastian." His voice

was only a trickle of sound, gauged to flow into her ears alone. "If we're to deceive your family, you're going to have to yield me at least that small familiarity."

She'd do anything to get him to release her. "I will."

He spoke again, and it was more of a sigh than a word. "Sebastian."

"Sebastian," she repeated.

He smoothed back her hair. His lips moved against her ear—her ear! What was he doing by her ear? She waited to hear something, then with a leap of intuition realized the motion she'd felt was a smile. He'd leaned close to the side of her head, put his lips to her ear, and smiled. A mechanical series of motions for him. A touching display of devotion as witnessed by the audience.

Nevertheless, she shivered because . . . why? Because he'd given her a chill? Or in anticipation of his next move?

He touched her, she reacted, and all the while she told herself he was despicable. He might masquerade as someone gifted with a rare kindness; he might have held her gently when he lifted her from the carriage and coaxed broth down her throat when she was so ill, but his actions hid an empty heart. He would have carried her all the way to London in his arms if that had been what it took to get her here. He wanted only to use her. She needed to remember that.

Grateful for the discipline she'd learned in the past

ten sterile years, she gathered her poise and smiled at her uncle. "As you might imagine, Lord Whitfield is very persuasive, especially to a woman so long on the shelf."

Sebastian pinched her when she called him by his title, but he replied sweetly, "Twenty-six is scarcely old, my darling."

"Still, he didn't tell you about your fortune, and he knew about it." Nora eyed Sebastian forbiddingly, possibly less impressed than Mary with his affectionate performance. "No doubt it slipped his mind the first time he—"

"Saw her unbound hair." Sebastian arranged a handful of the wild stuff over Mary's shoulder, and stared out at the audience with every evidence of sincerity. "I couldn't resist, Bubb. You know how it is with you Fairchilds, and you must know I *tried* to resist."

"Of course, old chap." Bubb consumed every one of Sebastian's words as if they were the golden truth and he were King Midas.

That gold will kill you, Mary wanted to say. That she even experienced the impulse to warn him surprised her.

Nora grasped Mary's still-gloved hand and pulled at her, as if attempting to remove her from Sebastian's influence. "Have you thought he wishes to wed you for your wealth?"

Mary might have considered it, if he were going to wed her, but she felt sure of only one thing in this farce—that Sebastian despised the Fairchilds. He wouldn't marry one if he were destitute and she controlled the Bank of England. Smoothly she lied. "If he wishes to wed me for my fortune, it is a fair exchange. I wish to wed him for other reasons, and it would not be easy for him to overturn the marriage contracts."

Nora gasped, and Bubb, after a moment of shock, laughed. Lady Valéry drank a large swallow of brandy, and Mary turned to Sebastian in bewilderment. "What . . . ?"

Softly he said, "You said you wished to wed me for 'other reasons.' They think you mean . . ."

"Mean?"

He maintained a solemn expression. "That you wish to wed me for my manly prowess."

Her every muscle clenched. He forced his touches on her, then forced her to enjoy them. Now he incited her with words, with images, such as she'd never conceived. Innocent phrases gained double meanings, and every movement, every word, became a snare to trip her. And where would she land?

In his bed. In his bed. Like the clapper of a bell, the guarantee slapped back and forth in her skull, and in a furious whisper, meant for his ears only, she said, "Not if you came wrapped in gold cloth. Not if you came with recommendations from every courtesan in Venice. Not if—"

"Not if I promised to make you the happiest woman on earth." He squeezed her hand and he gave her one of those smiles. The ones that made her think of a guard dog on a leash, waiting his chance. "I understand."

Mary turned and spoke to the room at large. "I wish to marry Lord Whitfield . . . Sebastian . . . for the power he wields. I know that as his betrothed, I will be safe."

"Safe?" Nora said. "From what?"

Bubb spread his arms wide. "Why, you're in the bosom of your family now!"

Nora spoke hastily, as if she didn't want Mary to think too closely on that. "Have you thought Lord Whitfield plays his own game? Perhaps you are in ignorance, but the Fairchilds and the Whitfields are old enemies."

Why didn't that surprise Mary? Why did she suspect that beneath Sebastian's suave exterior there lurked sinister secrets?

But she didn't care. She had her own purpose now, and that was wrestling control of her own fortune from the Fairchilds. "Then it's time the schism was healed."

"You're right." Bubb sounded heartily genuine. "It is time. Past time. And what a way to do it, heh? With a marriage. Why, you two will be the Romeo and Juliet of the Whitfields and the Fairchilds."

"An interesting concept," Sebastian murmured.

A repulsive concept, Mary thought with vehemence.

"Of course, Mary, you are a Fairchild woman," Bubb said. "And irresistible to men. And Sebastian is very much a man. Heh, Sebastian? Heh, heh?"

Bubb winked and jabbed his elbow at some invisible comrade.

Sebastian tried to hush him. "I don't want my future wife cognizant of my dissipation."

"Too late," Mary murmured.

He touched her, and just below her breast. She had never had a man touch her there, and she whipped around and glared.

"A lover airs her complaints about her betrothed in private."

He'd listened to the scoldings she regularly gave herself, she realized, and now he couched his words in the form she easily recognized.

The heat of his hand stirred currents in her bloodstream, but she whispered firmly, "I am not your lover."

"No, you're not," he whispered back.

His smile left her unsatisfied, and even disturbed. "I'll never be your lover."

"No . . ."

But he didn't sound convinced, and time ticked along, driving Mary toward sensation. Not the sensation of touching, painful though that was to her, but the sensation of emotion.

Quickly, defiantly, she stripped her remaining glove off her hand. She didn't want him removing it in the same ritualized manner he'd removed the first. He'd taken off her glove to impress on the Fairchilds the strength of his possession. Unfortunately, he'd impressed her, also.

She feared this man. Not because he could have her

arrested as a murderess, not because he was ruthless in achieving his aims, but because when he whispered in her ear with ardent intent and looked at her body with cold gray eyes, she felt something. Something inside. Pressure. Weakness. A surge of heat.

"You had the banns called?" Bubb said loudly, verbally trampling on Sebastian's turf.

The traveling sickness. Mary pressed her hand to her stomach. It had to be the traveling sickness affecting her.

"We did." Sebastian didn't seem to be having trouble talking. Of course, he never took his gaze off Mary, either.

"Where?" Bubb insisted, walking to the door.

Lady Valéry answered. "In Scotland. In the English chapel in my home there."

A neat answer. Not only was it difficult to verify, but to ask Lady Valéry to do so indicated doubt in her truthfulness. Mary appreciated that in some distant corner of her mind, while all the time she told herself lies about the passions that roiled deep in her belly.

She hated people who lied to themselves. She'd been an expert at it at one time, and only disaster had shaken her free from the debilitating habit.

But could she bear to put a name to the emotion Sebastian inspired in her?

For the first time in her life, a Fairchild came to her rescue. Bubb—big, unsubtle Bubb—announced, "Mary, it's time you were introduced to the rest of your family." He opened the door with a flourish.

The men and women who had been listening at the

keyhole tumbled into the room. Cursing, they rolled on the floor like the ramshackle bunch of scoundrels they were.

Mary's stomach nearly rebelled.

The Fairchilds had arrived.

Chapter 8

*Mary watched in astonishment as her rela-*tives adjusted their powdered wigs and recovered themselves.

Beside her on the sofa, Sebastian murmured in a fashionably bored tone, "Everyone who is anyone falls through an open door onto their faces. It's the newest way to enter a chamber."

Half-credulous, she turned to stare at him. Was this humorless man jesting?

With a great cracking of joints and creaking of corsets, the Fairchild men rose. They straightened their collection of crimson, canary, jade, and ame-thyst waistcoats, dusted off the knees of their trousers, and fought for space at the gold-framed mirror. It made no difference that four of the old gentlemen were as wrinkled as Christmas currants and had just as few teeth. Maintaining their cosmetics clearly held precedence over recovering their dignity, and they jostled and elbowed for position.

The girls took longer to come to their feet. First they admired their own ankles, set off by the ruffles of their petticoats, and one of them glanced up at Sebastian and winked.

The hussy.

Then they pushed down their skirts and whimpered, and their male relatives, recalled to their duty, came and offered their hands. One by one the women got up and struck a pose, each striving to outdo the next until the entire room seemed filled with exotic scents, waving fans, and so many colors, Mary fought the urge to shield her eyes.

"I was just going to have the servants call you." Bubb beamed, apparently unaware his family had been caught eavesdropping. "My uncles—your great-uncles, Mary—Uncle Leslie, Uncle Oswald, Uncle Burgess, Uncle Calvin."

The old men nodded in unison, leaving Mary to wonder which was which. These were her grandfather's brothers—the ones who'd so handily disappeared when she'd arrived long ago, begging for help.

The blackguards.

Bubb went on. "My daughters—Lilith, the dowager countess of Plaisted, Wilda, Daisy, and the twins, Radella and Drusilla."

One after the other, the girls curtsied. Emerald skirt down and up. Rose skirt. Dandelion. And two maroon moving in perfect synchronization. All comely, shapely, tall girls dressed in resplendent garb.

Mary found herself suddenly thankful for her new clothing. Her spirit might have lost its jaunty insolence years ago, she might not have that superior smirk, but none of *them* wore the very latest fashions from London.

"You have the best ankles," Sebastian said in her ear.

Again she turned to stare at him. Was her lack of confidence so obvious?

Bubb didn't seem to notice the undercurrents. He grinned ecstatically and waved an arm at Mary. "Uncles, daughters, this is our long-lost relative. We have finally found our heiress!"

"Such *good* news." The oldest of the old men couldn't have sounded more bored.

"And she is betrothed to Viscount Whitfield," Bubb said.

"But what is the reason for the *hurried* betrothal?" One of the girls—Lilith of the emerald gown—snapped her fan shut and let it droop from her wrist with a clear lack of enthusiasm.

"And to young Sebastian, too?" The youngest old man smirked toward the betrothed couple. "If she's expecting, Whitfield, I'd demand the child look *just like me.*"

Mary didn't, couldn't, immediately comprehend the viciousness of their comments. After all, they had no reason to savage her and her reputation.

Then she realized it didn't matter. They'd never

cared about her before; why should they start now?
She shouldn't mind . . . but when she tried to get her
breath, she found her lungs caught in a vise.

"Demons." Sebastian gathered himself, his muscles bunching, but Lady Valéry spoke before he could
make a move.

In a cool, amused voice, she said, "Unlike most
Fairchilds, Mary has managed to retain her maidenhead past the age of twelve."

Everyone in the room turned and stared at the
elegant older woman.

Sebastian relaxed against Mary, and Mary found
she could breathe again. She did, gratefully.

"She's lived in Scotland with me, and I've kept her
safe from"—Lady Valéry looked the uncles over—
"aging libertines. And from"—she stared at Lilith's
low-cut bodice—"unsavory influences."

"I say." The youngest old man sputtered. "I say!"

"Nasty old woman." Lilith snapped her fan open
and waved it vigorously over the vast expanse of her
chest.

"She's amazing," Sebastian murmured. "They're
aristocratic oafs until she takes them to task. Now
they're wounded." Acid with sarcasm, he said,
"Poor Fairchilds."

Lady Valéry pursed her lips. "I used to have
youngsters like you for breakfast, Miss Fairchild,
remember that." She pointed her cane at the uncles,
one by one. "And I won't say what I used to do with
men like you, but I'm sure if I thought about it long
enough, I'd remember."

Mary stifled her mirth as astonished expressions settled on each and every one of her relatives' faces. If only, she thought regretfully, she could give vent to her merriment.

But a housekeeper never calls attention to herself.

Then again, she wasn't a housekeeper now. She stirred uneasily at the novel concept. She was an heiress, and an heiress could be as rude as she chose. But did she choose to be so . . . so Fairchildish?

Nora rapped on the desk with her knuckles. "Your attention, please."

Her daughters turned to her at once. The uncles pretended not to hear.

"We have honored guests." Calmly she presented the family to Lady Valéry, behaving as if she routinely had to reintroduce them to refined behavior.

At the sound of Lady Valéry's name, the oldest old man shot a distraught, furious glance at Nora. She stared levelly back. He dusted specks of snuff from the front of his waistcoat, shook out the lace at his wrists, and changed from profligate to gentleman before Mary's eyes. "Lady Valéry? I think we've met. Weren't you the wife of the earl of Guldene?"

"Yes." The second oldest old man stepped forward. "I remember. After the earl died, every gentleman in London chased after you, and you cozened us all when you wed the duc de Valéry."

"That is true." Head cocked, Lady Valéry watched them.

The best-preserved old man sputtered in his excitement. "And all the time there were rumors that you—"

Two elbows, one from each side, struck him sharply in the ribs, and he bent forward in pain. His offending brothers oozed around him, cutting him from view.

"I'm Leslie Fairchild," the oldest man said.

"I'm Oswald." The next waggled his ink-stained fingers.

"Calvin." Calvin was quiet, thoughtful, watching his brothers for sudden moves as if they were domestic animals who had never quite been housebroken.

"Burgess," gasped the stricken man at the back. This one had been the handsomest once, before the good life had swelled his nose and broken veins in his cheeks.

Lady Valéry yawned.

Leslie moved to the chair closest to Lady Valéry and in the warmest of tones asked, "Is our dear niece your little protégé?"

"She's under my protection." Lady Valéry removed her riding hat and smoothed her waterfall of gray hair over her shoulder. "That's why I'm so pleased she is to wed Sebastian." She cast a general smirk over the assemblage. "Sebastian is my godson, as you know."

Heads turned toward Sebastian, who took Mary's hand in a gentle grip. "So surprising, to find myself enthralled by a Fairchild." He bestowed that now familiar razor smile.

Mary thought this time he'd turned it inside, and he almost bled from the sharpness of his delectation. He had finger-combed the windblown tangles from his dark hair, but it failed to civilize him. He pretended to conform; he would never conform. He lived on the fringes of society, collecting information and using it as a lever, never caring whom he hurt. Never caring if the law took her, tried her, and convicted her of a murder committed long ago and for good reason.

She needed to guard herself from any generous impulse while around this man. He took advantage.

"Whitfield, I heard great things about you," Oswald said. "I heard your shipping business last year made an immense profit."

"You're a"—Burgess paused delicately—"merchant?"

"Not just a merchant, Burgess," Calvin said impatiently. "A *highly successful* merchant."

Sebastian's hand tightened on Mary's, but his voice remained suave. "I'm glad you recognize the distinction."

Radella coiled herself around the tall post of her father's chair and moved sinuously against it. "I recognized you as a *distinctive* man."

Her husky tone made Mary's hand tense in Sebastian's. Unconsciously she caressed the scars that marked the back of his fingers, and he took that as a signal to renew his prowl across her body. He was obvious, dropping a kiss on her cheek, rubbing her bare knuckles with his thumb.

This time she was glad. Long ago Mary's father had taken his children to an exhibit of wild animals, and Mary had seen a large snake. Its colorful skin had been beautiful, its eyes slanted and intent. It had moved on its prey much as the Fairchilds moved now; standing, walking, pulsating, in a prearranged dance created to hypnotize its victims before the kill.

Mary shrank back toward Sebastian. She didn't discount the danger he exuded, but her relatives frightened her more.

"A nest of asps," he murmured.

Startled by his perception, she turned and looked at him again. His lips curved indulgently, deepening the creases around his mouth. England's southern sun had tanned him. In appearance he reminded her of the seamen of Scotland's coast—hardened by adversity, immune to insult, facing death and dishonor without flinching.

"I won't let them get you." He rubbed his cheek against her hair. "I swear I'll keep you safe."

"That is a vow you'd best honor," she answered.

"I can't reassure you, but events will tell."

The stillness in that cursed study attracted Mary's attention, and she noticed the dance of the Fairchilds had ended. For some reason they had turned toward the door and stared, and she tore her attention from Sebastian and did the same.

Ian. Even before he moved into the light, Mary recognized him. She came to her feet, not heeding the fleeting grip of Sebastian's hand.

Ian smiled as he walked forward, palms extended. "Is that you, little cousin?"

"Yes, it is I." So eloquent, Mary scolded herself. This was Ian, the man who had slipped her money on her last visit, the one relative who'd been kind and told her an innocent like her was better off living somewhere else. Anywhere else.

He was kind. And more, he was beautiful. Not like the rest of the Fairchilds, but darkly beautiful, like sable, like a starry night, like Mephistopheles himself. His brown eyes glowed as he lifted her hands away from her sides and surveyed her. "How you have blossomed, little cousin!"

She wanted to smile.

No, worse. She wanted to simper. She was living one of those dreams she'd forbidden herself to have, to have Ian look on her with favor.

Danger. Here was danger.

A *housekeeper*—she took a calming breath—*an heiress always maintains her dignity*.

"You're looking well, also," she said.

He chuckled so cozily, she could have warmed her hands in the sound. "I do what I can."

A sensation of cold struck her, and Sebastian stood beside her. She thought he'd been ruthless with her, but nothing could have prepared her for the chill he exuded now. Fixing his gaze on Ian, he asked, "Who are you?"

"This is my cousin." She took her hands back from Ian's grip, and found she was introducing him as if she were explaining herself. "Ian."

Ian smiled.

Sebastian didn't. "Cousin? I've never heard of a Fairchild born with dark hair."

"That's because Fairchilds breed with care," Ian said. "Usually. Usually we mate with our own kind, so our children will fit in with their other blond, blue-eyed cousins. Only sometimes, someone makes a mistake."

"Who made a mistake with you?" Sebastian asked.

"Leslie got careless back in his prime." Ian presented himself with a bow, and his beautiful moon-stone ring flashed in the light. "I was the result."

"Your mother was a Selkie." Leslie sat and watched his son with an air of distaste. "She enchanted me."

"He's a lovely man, isn't he?" Ian didn't look at his father as he spoke. "He would have denied me if he could, but apparently he feared my mother's family too much."

The Fairchild family proper shuffled and coughed, and Mary wondered that the influence of this one man could change them from predators into prey. "My father told me none of my great-uncles had ever wed," she said.

"Oh, they didn't," Ian answered.

Of course. Ian was illegitimate. Discomfiture

swept her that she'd reminded him, and the others. That explained his kindness to another outsider, and made her like him all the more. Even Sebastian, beside her, relaxed a little of his tension.

Ian looked behind Mary as if seeking something, then asked, "Wasn't there a brother or sister?"

"Mine, you mean?" Mary felt stupid when he nodded. "A brother." She touched her ear with her left hand, hoping he'd accept her falsehood. "He's no longer with us."

Ian watched her gesture as if it told him something, and she suspected it had. As housekeeper, she had learned to watch the nobles for unspoken signs of displeasure or discomfort. Ian's position at Fairchild Manor must be much the same as a servant's. He was unwanted, unsanctioned, and unlike them in appearance. Her sense of empathy grew stronger, and her lips trembled as she smiled.

"We Fairchilds do have a tendency to lose our relatives." Ian caught her hand again and brought it to his lips. "But we won't let you go now that we've found you, Cousin Guinevere."

"Her name is Mary." Sebastian swept her into his arms so abruptly, she squeaked like a mouse and grabbed at his neck. "And she's tired."

A complete and most unusual silence fell over the Fairchilds as they watched the Viscount Whitfield take their prize away from them.

Nothing escaped Ian's notice.

As the old lady, whoever she was, disappeared into the hallway, the uncles observed her with the avidity they might have shown a money bag in motion. Perhaps he should have arrived sooner, Ian thought, but then he would have missed his chance to make an entrance.

And what an entrance! His little cousin had remembered him, just as he'd hoped. She'd been dazzled by him, too, and too unworldly to hide her interest. He fought the urge to rub his hands together, pulling a handkerchief out of his pocket instead. Wiping the sweat from his palms, he moved to a chair in the corner and seated himself.

The rest of the Fairchilds scurried into position, placing themselves according to their standing in the family hierarchy. The oldest of Bubb's daughters, Lilith, claimed a seat. She had brought money into the family when she wed, and the death of her young husband had freed her to hunt again. The family had great hopes for Lilith.

The rest of the chairs were taken up by the uncles. Ian loathed them all—especially Leslie, his father.

Bubb placed his hands on the shiny desktop and slowly lowered himself into the purple overstuffed master's chair. He was imitating his father, but somehow ol' Bubbie just didn't have the ballocks to pull it off. The high-backed chair dwarfed him. The desk, richly carved with swirls and curlicues, dominated him.

As the second oldest brother, Leslie would have become marquess if Bubb hadn't been born, and he never forgot it. "Bubbie, you look like a puppet, not a king."

Bubb's beautiful Fairchild countenance fell.

Glaring furiously, Leslie said, "Oh, stop looking so morose. You'll never take your father's place."

"Thank God for that," Nora said.

Leslie ignored her. "What are they doing here now? What do they know?"

Ian straightened. What was Leslie babbling about?

Nora placed her hand on Bubb's when he would have answered. "We'll discuss it later."

Bubb nodded. "Later."

Nora had seated herself behind the desk, but off to the side like a properly submissive wife.

She wasn't. Oh, she played the part to perfection, but Ian would have sworn that in the privacy of the master bedchamber, Nora placed every reasonable thought Bubb espoused into his empty pate. Furthermore, nothing rattled Nora, not even the venial glare Leslie aimed at her.

Then he nodded, a swift up-and-down motion that set his chins jiggling. Taking an audible breath, Leslie said, "Our plan was to seek moneyed mates. Now three juicy mice have fallen into our trap. This Guinevere—"

"She wants to be called Mary," Nora said. She wasn't easy to read, but Ian thought that Leslie's constant strutting annoyed her.

"This *Guinevere*"—Leslie emphasized the name—"is the first Fairchild ever who is anything less than irresistible. If we can remove her from Whitfield's influence, we could control her and the money."

"Let me volunteer." Drusilla's little red tongue shot out, and she licked her lips. "I'll gladly detach Lord Whitfield from our cousin Guinevere."

"Her name is Mary," Bubb told her.

She ignored him until Nora pointed a finger at her, and she flounced in her chair. "Mary," she said, sulking.

"You can't be trusted to detach Lord Whitfield from our cousin." Daisy was eighteen, and in Ian's estimation, she alone of all the girls had received her mother's intelligence. Speaking to both the twins, she said, "Neither of you can. You've never had to perform such a delicate operation, and it's imperative we succeed."

Drusilla and Radella pouted.

Daisy smoothed her dandelion-bright skirt. "I'll do it."

"Unlikely!" Lilith burst forth. "You're still a virgin. Or . . . you're supposed to be."

"Lilith." Nora's tone was a rebuke.

"I *am* a virgin. Not used like she is." Daisy waved a hand at Wilda. "Or like you, either, Lilith. Apparently you haven't heard about Whitfield's reputation for fastidiousness."

"He *is* reputed to be fastidious, and Daisy has that ingenue look about her. So she'll have to do it." Lilith made the decision coldly.

"When do I get a turn?" Wilda demanded.

"You had a turn." If Lilith was cold, then Daisy was ruthless. "You yielded the baron everything, and for what? A measly settlement from his family."

"He loved me." Wilda's eyes filled with tears. She was the soft one, not ready to run with the pack of wolves she called her relatives.

"Of course he did, but his mother held the purse strings. The first rule is to investigate the source of their income. Even I know that." Radella looked smug. "Still, *I* say if Daisy doesn't bring him down within the week, then it's hunting season for all of us."

Daisy folded her hands in her lap. "I'll get him."

"You did at least one thing right in your life, Bubbie." Leslie snatched a pinch of snuff from Calvin's open container. "You bred up good daughters."

"They know their responsibility to the Fairchild family," Nora said. "I've taught them that."

Leslie laughed cruelly. "You'd do anything for the Fairchilds, wouldn't you? Why, I bet you'd sell your soul to the Devil to save us."

Bubb leaned forward in his chair, and for once, it didn't look too big for him. "We're grateful for Nora's dedication, Uncle Leslie, and we wouldn't have her any other way."

Leslie laughed again, but his gaze fell and he busied himself with inhaling the snuff.

Speaking over his sneezing, Daisy asked, "Once I've separated Whitfield from our dear cousin, what happens to her?"

Now was the time, and Ian made his move coolly. "It's not unknown for cousins to marry."

No one spoke, but eyes grew wide as this new idea

took hold. They'd seen the way Mary reacted to him, and they imagined he would work for the good of the family. Satisfaction settled on every countenance.

Every countenance, that is, except Leslie's. "Why shouldn't she marry an uncle?"

"Because it's against the law, Uncle Leslie," Bubb said.

"When has the law ever stopped us?" Leslie retorted.

Ian uncoiled himself from his chair and slipped to the liquor cabinet. "And because, Father, years ago when cousin Guinevere came for help, you fled in the opposite direction, and if you don't think she remembers, then you didn't see the way she looked at you."

"He was too busy ogling Lady Valéry and trying to decide if the rumors about her affairs were true." Radella giggled as her mother hushed her, and Drusilla laughed, too.

Leslie hesitated, then said, "Of course they're true. But unimportant. What I was trying to remember was the extent of her fortune."

Slowly Ian relaxed his grip on the glass. He had expected Leslie to denounce this plan just because anything his son did incited him. But the others had fallen easily for Ian's stratagem, and now Leslie succumbed, too. For the first time in Ian's life, the gods had smiled on him.

Of course, there was Whitfield and his claim on Mary, but Ian didn't respect that. He twisted his moonstone ring around and around on his finger. Living with the Fairchilds had taught Ian how to slither along, strike suddenly, and escape before vengeance could be wrought. Whitfield had best watch his back.

"I remember." Oswald, who was always good with numbers, smirked. "Fourteen thousand, four hundred pounds per annum from Guldene. Don't know for sure about Valéry—he was a Frenchie—but rumors place it at twice that amount, although it has probably ceased since those damned Frogs started beheading their betters."

The previously silent Calvin spoke up. "Such a shame about her French income, but as I understand it, you're saying Lady Valéry is wealthy." He took an audible breath. "Why am I sitting here? I need to dress for dinner!"

His brothers pushed him back to his seat.

"We'll not have a mêlée with all of us competing to get her bed and wed," Leslie said. "We have to do this fairly."

"What makes you think she'll be interested in any of you?" Lilith asked scornfully.

Three of the uncles stared at her in patent amazement while Burgess sputtered indignantly.

Oswald recovered himself first. "She's a woman, isn't she?"

"And a woman who in her youth freely sampled the fruits of love." Leslie displayed his Egyptian ivory false teeth in a crocodile grin.

"Everyone knows women who have enjoyed the pleasures of the flesh yearn for it long past the time when they can attract a man." Oswald pulled a long face. "Lady Valéry can't attract a man now. She's plump and wrinkled—"

"Just like you," Daisy said.

"It's different with men," Leslie said loftily.

Ian laughed out loud.

Leslie loathed him with a glance. "Men retain their potency and appeal long after women are dried up and disgusting. So I'll sacrifice and bed Lady Valéry."

Which explained why Leslie had surrendered Mary so easily to his son. Leslie was after bigger game.

"And get all the money for yourself?" Oswald sniggered. "Not likely."

Leslie adopted a wounded posture. "I would share with my brothers."

That brought universal laughter.

Disgruntled, Leslie said, "You don't trust me, but we can't all jump her. What say we draw straws to see who has to woo the witch?"

"Only if Bubbie holds the straws," Burgess said. "He's the only one we can trust not to cheat."

Bubb rang for the footman, called for broom straws, and when they arrived, summoned the uncles to his desk. But only three old men stood up.

Oswald stared at each of his brothers, then in every corner. "How long has Calvin been gone?"

"He's charged ahead." Leslie stomped his finely shod foot. "I won't have it!"

"I don't know how you'll stop him now." Burgess started toward the door. "Or me, either."

Oswald ran after Burgess and knocked him aside,

darting into the corridor first. Leslie followed, his hefty thighs pumping, and Bubb's daughters giggled.

Then the footman stepped into the open doorway. "The first of the houseguests are arriving, my lord."

The abruptly resolute girls rose en masse and fled, chattering like quarrelsome jaybirds, each determined to bag the biggest game from among the widgeons who dared attend the party.

Bubb and Nora ignored Ian as they stood and straightened their clothing. They had no mates to catch, but they had a role to play. They would welcome their visitors and divert any anxiety the single men might be experiencing at the thought of facing off with the famous Fairchild women.

Poor sots. The men didn't stand a chance.

Ian knew from experience that the Fairchilds were nothing but a tribe of cannibals who ate their own kind.

And he was about to prove himself a true Fairchild.

Chapter 9

Mary didn't like being carried. Sebastian could tell by the way she held herself, as if she were a queen and he a sedan chair.

He didn't care. He didn't care what she liked, and he didn't care what kind of games this Fairchild played to sweeten the ordeal of being handled by the man she'd better not betray.

He looked down at her. She trembled with the effort of holding herself rigid, but her off-putting attitude meant nothing when matched against the skin revealed by her off-the-shoulder gown. She had folded her arms across her chest, not realizing how her gesture pressed her breasts against the neckline and showed him a hint of cleavage.

She could damn well accept the fact that that view was his personal privilege, and that he had the right to carry her where and when he chose. And just because she was an heiress, and just because she had a handsome cousin who complimented her, didn't mean she could run away from her obligations to him.

And to his godmother, of course.

He glanced behind him. Lady Valéry walked behind them down the long passageway in the east wing, part of the procession of maids and footmen who labored under the weight of their baggage. The Fairchilds' housekeeper, Mrs. Baggy-face, led the way.

"Here we are, Miss Fairchild." Mrs. Baggy-face held the door wide to allow Sebastian to enter. "I hope this meets with your approval."

Sounding serene, Mary said, "It's lovely, Mrs. Baggott."

Baggott. That was it! Sebastian knew it was some *B* name.

Mary noticeably relaxed as he placed her on the bed, and Sebastian guessed she thought herself free of him. Amusing chit. She wouldn't be free of him until he chose.

At least the Fairchilds had been wise enough to place Mary in a luxurious bedchamber. The piles of blankets on the large bed would be pleasant to snuggle under of a night. The bed curtains would keep attendants from noticing if he chose to indulge in a morning romp. He pressed the mattress with his hand. It was firmly stuffed with feathers, so he and Mary could have their own sides or snuggle together, as they chose.

"I love the large wardrobe and the bed table," Mary said. "And what a huge mirror!"

He had paid no heed to those pieces of furniture, but he said, "The chamber is agreeable." It was also, he would wager, separated from his by miles of corridors and dozens of guards masquerading as servants.

Mrs. Baggott hurried to the bed and nudged him aside, then arranged the pillows so they formed a rest for Mary's shoulders. "I understand you've been ill, Miss Fairchild. I'll order a light meal for you to be served here, and tomorrow you can join the party."

Mary laid a hand over Mrs. Baggott's restless fingers. "I wouldn't want to put you to any trouble."

Mrs. Baggott stopped in the act of pulling a counterpane over Mary. She stared at Mary's hand on hers. "It's no trouble, miss. It's my duty."

"I'm sure you have many duties that must be attended to while hosting this party." Mary smiled at her. "How many guests are you expecting?"

Mrs. Baggott clearly didn't know how to handle this attention. Her hand remained in Mary's, and she shifted uneasily from foot to foot. "We've prepared for sixty guests."

"With servants, that's probably two hundred people to house and feed." Mary shook her head. "La, so much work!"

"I have never shirked my duties or complained about the hours," Mrs. Baggott protested.

Mary let go of her hand immediately. "And I

would never insinuate such a thing, either. The Fairchilds are lucky to have you.''

"Thank you, Miss Fairchild." Mrs. Baggott stared at Mary's earnest, friendly face with a caution Sebastian didn't understand. "I consider myself privileged to retain this post." Her smile curved her thin lips, just as it should, but the frown lines remained around her eyes. "Lord Whitfield, your room is in the west wing.''

So he *was* miles away.

"I can show you the way now." Mrs. Baggott moved toward the door and would have held it for him, except his godmother stood on the threshold.

"Where is my room?" Lady Valéry asked.

"I have put you just across the hall, my lady."

"That is delightful. Would you show me the chamber?''

"Well . . ." Mrs. Baggott glanced uneasily at Sebastian as he stood beside the bed.

"I'm not as young as I used to be," Lady Valéry said pitifully. "These extended journeys are rough on my old bones.''

Sebastian hid a smirk. The journey from Scotland had invigorated his godmother, and he'd worried she would tire her horse with her constant desire to go faster and farther.

But Mrs. Baggott didn't know that, and moved immediately to Lady Valéry's side. "Of course, my lady. This way.''

As the two women moved into the passageway,

accompanied by the servants, Sebastian wondered what scheme Lady Valéry hatched now. In Scotland she had insisted on coming with him, claiming that she had to protect Mary from his nefarious desires. Now she contrived to leave them alone where they could easily be compromised. His godmother's cavalier attitude was a signal to him to be cautious. Very, very cautious.

Mary snapped, "Did you have to frighten Mrs. Baggott like that?"

He looked at the flushed, indignant face of the woman on the bed. He looked at the loosened curtain of her hair, her dainty blue satin slipper and the white silk stocking with the slim ankle within, and tossed caution into the trash heap. Whatever Lady Valéry had planned, he would counter it, but first he would see if he could rumple the starched facade of his sham fiancée.

She said, "The poor housekeeper could be discharged for leaving us alone in my chamber."

"She worries too much." He gestured at the attendants who poured through the door. "As if *they* weren't chaperones enough."

Of course, they weren't. They were only servants, not proper chaperones. Not even Mary's Scottish maid, who directed the flow of hatboxes, shoe boxes, and trunks, was chaperone enough. He could order any and all of them out if he desired, and they would go. They had no choice.

Mary knew it, too. She watched him with the same

wariness she viewed Fairchilds. It wasn't nearly enough, for he was twice as dangerous, but by her caution she acknowledged that he alarmed her.

So he set himself to distract her. "That's not what I meant, anyway." He leaned against the tall bedpost at the foot of bed. "That housekeeper seems horribly anxious. She acts as if she's been abused."

Mary's eyes turned as cold as a Scottish lake in winter. "I assure you, a housekeeper is nothing but a thing that ensures every nobleman is comfortable and well fed. Normally she's invisible, and if that takes some getting used to, well, that's better than when the nobles are aware of"—she fumbled, not wanting to name herself—"the housekeeper. They only see her if they want to complain, or make trouble because they were bored, or because—"

She stopped short, but he finished the sentence with a snap. "Because they wanted a little romp with *you.*"

"We were speaking of Mrs. Baggott."

"No, we weren't." He stepped a little closer to her. "So they tried it often."

She ignored him and spoke to her maid. "Jill, is that the last of the trunks?"

Jill cast a worried glance toward the bed. "Aye, Miss Fairchild, so it is."

"All the clothing will have to be ironed. Don't ask Mrs. Baggott for help—the maids are too busy. Just do what you can as you find time."

But no one ignored Sebastian Durant. He stepped forward and caught Mary's puff sleeve between his fingers, then leaned down until his head was on the level of hers. She could look either at him or the wall.

She looked at him.

"The noblemen. They frequently tried to get you into their beds."

"Not frequently, and never more than once." Mary enunciated the words clearly, in warning. She had a haughtiness about her he'd seldom seen before. Her housekeeperly attitude had changed, not when she was revealed as a Fairchild, but when Bubb had conferred heiresshood on her.

Damn Bubb. Sebastian had hoped to publicly stake his claim on her before she heard the news. He had hoped to have her so thoroughly trapped, she couldn't try to wiggle out of her obligations. He was her betrothed. He could not allow her any doubts about that. Her, or anyone else. Such as . . .

"Who is Ian?" He pointed a finger at her. "And don't tell me he's your cousin. Tell me what he is to you."

"He's the one member of the family who was kind to me during my first visit." She answered stoically, but she blushed, damn her. She blushed.

"Visit?" Anger bubbled in him, blowing up from beneath the logical layers of his mind and exploding like noxious black tar. "Is that what you call it?"

"Would you lower your voice?" she whispered furiously. "You may believe the servants are deaf, but I assure you, they are listening to every word we speak, and I don't care to have my name linked with my cousin's in a romantic manner."

"I will lower my voice when you will tell me what Ian is to you."

"At my first visit, he spoke to me kindly." She glanced at the lingering servants.

They were distracting her from him. He swung around and commanded, "Out."

The men who carried the trunks dropped them without blinking, but the women who assisted Jill in stacking the lighter boxes milled around in confusion.

"Out!" He pointed to the door.

Jill rubbed her palms across her skirt. "Master . . ."

"I'll send you out, too," he warned.

Clearly unhappy, she nevertheless bobbed a curtsy at Sebastian while the last of the attendants fled.

"Smart girl," he said, then turned back to Mary. "Now, about Ian."

She humored him with her attitude. "He gave me money. That was what saved our lives. *He* saved our lives."

"So you're *grateful?*"

She didn't seem to recognize his sarcasm. "Yes. Grateful."

"As grateful as you are to me?"

She straightened so that her spine no longer rested against the pillows. "To you?"

"I brought you here. If not for me, you would still be an impoverished housekeeper in the outer reaches of Scotland."

She lowered her voice, but it whipped at him. "If

you hadn't kept me ignorant of my inheritance, I would have been able to stay in London and collect the money without coming here to this vipers' nest.''

"Ah, but then you would have never seen . . . Ian.'' He mocked the name by his tone.

Genuine anger flashed in her eyes, but she kept her tone civil. "Why should you care about Ian? He's no more spiteful than my other relatives. At least he didn't walk in and attack me.''

He waved a dismissive hand. "That was just their opening volley, and it was aimed at me.''

"Aimed at you?'' She bounded up, her infirmity forgotten in resentment. "Then why do *I* feel savaged?''

Looking down at the prim rosebud of a mouth, the rounded cheeks, the enormous eyes, all radiating fury and offended dignity, he wondered how this woman managed to project such an aura of power. Certainly her size had nothing to do with it. On the rare occasions he'd let her stand on her own two feet, the top of her head barely reached his shoulder. Her age, the age that she believed put her firmly on the shelf, was so much less than his, he could have laughed at her innocence. Yet her dignity gave the impression of maturity, so her indignation now seemed all the greater. "They were a herd of lousy swine,'' he admitted.

Indignation turned to outrage. "You *expected* them to treat me as if I were some kind of camp follower?''

"I didn't know for sure what their reaction would

be, but your uncles are renowned for their cruel tricks and practical jokes.'' Oh, yes, they were, as he could well attest.

Mary sank back onto the pillows, her brief flurry of exasperation undermined by hunger and exhaustion. ''What a hornet's nest you have brought me into, Lord Whitfield.''

He had, indeed. Seeing her right now, her eyes closed, her mouth turned down, flushed with a hectic color, he suffered the pangs of conscience. How could she fight the combined savagery of her relatives? He had to shield her against them.

''Excuse me, m'lord.''

He turned.

Jill stood behind him, holding a tray. ''I have a wee bit of supper for Miss Fairchild.'' She sounded patient, as if she'd been speaking for a long time and no one had been hearing her.

''Very good.'' This was just the kind of safeguarding he did best. He took the tray. ''I'll feed her.''

''I can do it myself,'' Mary said. ''And I'll keep Jill beside me.''

''Aye, I can help, m'lord.'' Jill bravely put her hand back on the tray.

He smiled, and as always happened when he smiled, the maid paled. ''I will stay to feed my betrothed.''

''I feel much restored from my traveling illness,'' Mary said resolutely.

''I will not rest comfortably unless I reassure myself.'' Sebastian placed the tray over her knees and shook the napkin out. He started to tuck it into Mary's neckline, but she snatched it from him and spread it in her lap in short, jerky motions.

She supervised her ire as ruthlessly as he supervised his business dealings. She had too much in common with that housekeeper, Mrs. Baggott. Not just the experiences with the noblemen, but the wariness and suspicion, too.

But illness had revealed a different side of her. On the trip down from Scotland, she'd been soft. Helpless. A child in need of care. And someone had had to care for her. Lady Valéry could charm a man right out of his breeches or guide a young man through the torturous maze of society, but children ran from her shrieking. So Sebastian knew if he wanted Mary to arrive at Fairchild Manor to perform on cue, he had to make sure she lived long enough to do it.

To his surprise, taking care of her had been a labor he enjoyed.

He frowned.

Perhaps he needed to acquire a pet. He obviously had some unfulfilled need to have a thing depend upon him.

Mary lifted the rounded silver cover off the tray. Neat as always, she placed the ornate cover on the table beside the bed and surveyed her repast. Baked bread pudding filled a small clay crock, and the aroma of sweetened cream and eggs, cinnamon and cloves, wafted into the air.

Sitting on the mattress beside her, he reached for the spoon.

Mary snatched it up and rapped his knuckles with it. "I'll feed myself."

Using the spoon, she broke the buttery bronze crust and a fresh rush of steam rose from the liberated filling. Smooth yet firm, the pudding enveloped the bread. Her lips opened and took the pudding in, and her eyes closed in ecstasy. His gaze followed the custard's progress as she savored the taste, then as she swallowed, it slipped down her pale silken throat. Her breasts, already so full and round, expanded as she sighed. Her rosy tongue flicked out and took a crumb from her lip.

He could almost imagine the bread feeding her strength, giving a glow to her skin and a gloss to her hair. He could imagine how she would taste after she had finished the pudding, how she would rest, replete and satiated, until he had removed her clothes and pleasured her in a new way. In a way that fed her soul.

In a kind of wondrous surprise, he realized he was going to have to take her. He'd always wanted her; Lady Valéry had pointed that out. But at some point, he'd lost his choice in the matter. She was his. Perhaps not forever, but at least while they resided at Fairchild Manor.

As Mary's appetite revived, she relished the mixed textures and the spicy flavors ever more. The divine flavor of the pudding almost masked her sense that she was being watched.

It was *him*, looming over her. He always loomed, and she planned to break him of the habit. He was only a man, after all. Lady Valéry swore they could be trained.

"That's a good offering for an invalid," he said huskily.

"Would you like a taste?" she found herself asking.

He looked startled. "You're the one in need of sustenance."

"Yes." She didn't really want to share. Yet for a single moment, that wretched man's face had softened and grown misty with some tender emotion. Benevolence, perhaps. Or perhaps, knowing Sebastian as she did, it had simply been intestinal gas.

But his gaze followed as the spoon cut into the golden crust, then neared her mouth. He might pretend to be above the simple joys of a bread pudding, but she knew a hungry man when she saw one. She'd fed enough of them in her housekeeping days. "You're drooling," she snapped.

He wasn't, of course, but when he looked into her face, his mouth was softly open and she could just see the tip of his tongue worrying the inside of his lower lip.

"I'll send for another spoon," she offered.

"Oh, no. I'll eat out of yours."

She tried to whip the spoon out of reach, but he caught her wrist and held it still. Opening his mouth, he took in the bread pudding. All expression smoothed from his face at the first taste. His nostrils flared and he greedily licked the bowl of the spoon.

Turning her wrist, he polished the back. Every remnant of pudding disappeared in his hedonistic relish.

Only a man could transform plain bread pudding into a passionate experience.

Hastily, to cover her reaction, she asked, "How did you get that scar on your hand?"

He glanced down. His four fingers had been slashed in a curve, and his index finger was slightly crooked. "As a boy, I worked with horses." Still clutching her wrist, he coerced her into digging another bite out of the crock. "It hurts when one steps on you."

She tried to release the spoon to him, but he didn't want it. He wanted to hold her wrist and force her to—she couldn't believe it—to feed herself. He put the spoon to her lips. She glared.

"Eat it," he whispered, and with his thumb he massaged the tender skin above her pulse. "You will need the vigor it brings."

True enough, although she wondered why he said it in that tone of voice. Deciding defiance was a foolish waste of energy, she accepted the bite.

Releasing the spoon into her control, he slid along the mattress so he rested at her feet, perpendicular to her body. He leaned on his elbow and smiled at her, using the grin she hated most. The one that said he knew something she didn't.

Jill noisily cleared her throat. "So many clothes to iron!" she fussed.

Sebastian just kept smiling, waiting for Mary to finish the bread pudding, and she ate and wondered what he had to tell her that he should assume such an intimate posture. Probably that he planned to ruin her reputation—as if she hadn't already figured that out.

Did she care? She didn't know. She'd committed murder once, and the weight of that great sin had changed her priorities. Then, too, the years as housekeeper had taught her to measure respectability with a new scale. The strictures of English society seemed foolish when viewed through the eyes of a woman, a servant . . . a criminal.

Other matters carried more weight, and if Sebastian chose to lounge on her bed and insinuate he was her lover, the only response she could work up—at least right now—was a weary shrug.

Jill marched to the side of the bed as soon as Mary had spooned the last of the pudding into her mouth, sipped her tea, and placed her napkin neatly on the tray. "Let me take that, Miss Fairchild." She peered at Sebastian. "And, Lord Whitfield, you should leave so she can rest."

She was a brave girl whose loyalty Mary had won, but she didn't stand a chance against Sebastian.

"Take it to the kitchen," he commanded.

"But, my lord—"

"To the kitchen. And shut the door behind you."

Mary looked at him as if insanity ran in Sebastian's family. "That is going too far, Lord Whitfield. The door must remain—"

He snapped his fingers at Jill.

"My lord, please, I can't leave you alone with my mistress."

He eased himself to his feet. "She's my betrothed."

"The proprieties!" Jill pleaded.

He ignored the maid and said to Mary as she struggled to sit erect, "Don't get off the bed. If you do, I will be obliged to chase you."

Mary paused. In the early days of her duties to Lady Valéry, she had been chased. It had been humiliating, and she had learned that by running, she marked herself as prey. Always better to calmly face the aggressor down.

Sebastian marched toward the retreating Jill.

Jill chattered about duty as Sebastian herded her toward the door, but he got her out in the corridor. "I'm going to get Lady Valéry," she threatened.

But he shut the door in her face with such an ominous thunk, Mary wondered—would her strategy for discouraging youths and aging libertines work with a mad nobleman called Sebastian Durant, Viscount Whitfield?

Chapter 10

No key had been placed in the lock. Sebastian cursed in frustration and disbelief. "Don't even try to tell me this is an oversight." He glared at Mary as if it were her fault. "What do the Fairchilds hope to gain by having access to your room at any time?"

"Rescue?" she suggested briskly. "From a lecher such as you?"

His eyes narrowed, and he pulled a chair to the door and shoved the back under the handle.

Mary glanced around. She didn't think a simple bowl of bread pudding had given her enough strength to climb out on the ledge outside the upstairs window.

"Lord Whitfield, I can scarcely believe a man with your wealth and power needs to resort to such childish tactics."

"I'm simply going to kiss you." He made it sound as innocuous as a hand of whist.

"Then why bar the door?"

He peeled off his frock coat and waistcoat, and loosened his cravat. "You have the most amazing air of innocence about you. Something must be done to cure it."

His linen shirt remained molded to his muscles, and she hurriedly dressed him in her imagination. "Innocence isn't a disease, my lord."

The cravat fluttered to the ground as he bent one knee on the mattress. "It is when other men consider it a challenge. There isn't a male alive who could look at you, Mary Fairchild, and not want to show you the wonders that can exist between a man and a woman."

"You don't need to come up here." She hoped she sounded brisk and knowledgeable. She wished she could keep her gaze away from his bare throat. "I am familiar with what men and women do between them."

He crouched over her like a wolf, and like a wolf he growled. "How do you know that, Mary?"

"Nobles are notorious for assuming a housekeeper is deaf and blind to their antics." She spoke briskly and without showing a sign of the nervousness his pose caused. "Some of them, I suspect, even enjoyed having me see them in flagrante delicto."

"We're going to have a talk someday." He pulled two of the pillows out from behind her shoulders. "About the things you have seen and the problems you have had. You're going to tell me who insulted you and who pursued you, and I will make them sorry."

She sat rigid, so he grasped her arms and eased her backward. The pillows fluffed up around her, cutting her vision like a nun's cowl. She could see only Sebastian, and the sight of an amiable Sebastian was enough to make her both fascinated and afraid.

"Relax." As always, he loomed over her. "Kissing is a pleasant exercise. Women like it, and I'm good at it."

"So modest."

He eased himself down, trapping her between him and the wall, and she struggled to control her acute discomfort. She hadn't thought it would be difficult to repel him; her sensible rebuffs had been a time-tested solution.

Only now, as he draped his leg over her thighs and his hands rubbed her sleeves, did she remember her prudence had never discouraged him before.

His habitual harshness had diminished, she didn't know why, and his lips seemed unusually full and soft as he formed the words, "I suppose you've been kissed before."

It seemed best to keep it brief. "Yes."

He stiffened. "Did you return the kiss?"

"No." But she'd learned that an umbrella stand, skillfully applied, would discourage a lustful nobleman.

He relaxed again. All lazy and sensual, he blinked. "Let me show you how, then." He brushed her lips with his.

She tensed at his touch, but it wasn't really a kiss. More of a fluttering, really, a hospitable invitation to explore should she chose to. She didn't, but she liked the warmth of his body sinking closer to hers. The experience seemed almost friendly, more comforting than threatening.

Then his rough-textured hands moved up past her sleeves, past the neckline of her dress, and settled onto the bare skin of her shoulders.

She shivered as panic flared.

Bare skin to bare skin.

Not friendly.

Excruciating intimacy.

She couldn't do this. She couldn't bear this. He'd lifted her, carried her, and she'd told herself the promised kiss could be no worse, but he took advantage. Each stroke of his fingertips reminded her of those moments in the study when he'd stripped away her glove in an elaborate charade to fool the Fairchilds.

Fool the Fairchilds. His goal was to fool the Fairchilds. He was merely rehearsing.

"Thank you," the new-made heiress said. "I've enjoyed quite enough."

His palms moved in slow circles. He lifted his head. "You have beautiful skin. When I press it"— he did—"the color seeps away, then rushes back in a rosy wave." He watched as if such a pastime could actually occupy his devious mind.

Righteous, sure she could end this torture now, she said, "You said we would only kiss."

"Thank you for reminding me."

He leaned toward her, but she brought up her arm and put it at his throat. "We already kissed."

Putting her palm to his mouth, he kissed again, and each nerve in her hand absorbed the heady sensation of him. As he trekked up her wrist and toward her inner elbow, the scent of him wafted toward her, and without volition, she relaxed.

At the end of each traveling day, he'd taken her from the carriage, and she'd laid her head on his shoulder and breathed in the scent of horses, fresh air, and soap. Right or wrong, that particular combination had come to mean solace and compassion to her, and she used it to reassure herself.

He was persistent, not dangerous. Not in this way. Not to her. She was a Fairchild.

She closed her eyes against the sight of him nuzzling her tender flesh. A Fairchild. Surely he could never forget that. God knew she couldn't.

"I watch you and watch you, and you guard your moods as if they were the rope that would hang you."

Her eyes flew open. What did he mean?

"I feel sometimes I could ensure your complete cooperation in everything I demanded, if only I knew your secrets."

He did know them, or at least the most important one. He knew about the murder.

Or perhaps he didn't. Perhaps she'd misinterpreted a simple phrase . . . but she didn't dare ask, did she?

As his mouth descended, she removed her arm's

barrier and did as he indirectly demanded. She kissed him.

Lips puckered, she tried to be as sophisticated as she had been years ago when she'd practiced nightly on her pillow.

Apparently she didn't succeed, for he chuckled, and his breath caressed her cheek. "Not like that. Let me show you."

She tensed, waiting for another umbrella-stand event, but it didn't materialize. What did was another one of those feather-wing touches, so tender as to be almost kind. No brutality marred the act; did he always cherish murderesses with such sensitivity?

His fingers crept along her collarbone, feeling his way to her neck and throat, and he stroked the hollows. His hand was cool against her warm skin. He traced the length of her collarbone, and when he touched her so delicately, she had to struggle to remember he was blackmailing her.

His tongue soothed her lips, and she recognized his desire. He wanted to shove his way inside until she choked from his attentions. She tensed.

Massaging the cords of her neck, he said, "It's just a kiss."

And William the Conqueror was just a bastard.

He touched his lips to hers again, deepening the pressure so her nerve endings sang—or at least hummed. Mary didn't recognize the tune, but if she wasn't careful, she would be learning the lyrics.

He touched her with his tongue again, probing to the depth of her teeth, and she tasted him. Tasted the spices of the bread pudding and an indescribable flavor that must be him alone. Cautiously she eased her tongue toward his, enough to get the savor of him, and he met her halfway.

If he hadn't been lying on top of her, she would have flown from the mattress. As it was, only his mouth muffled the little chirp she gave, and her hands came up of their own volition to grab his arms and push him away.

He sat back obligingly. "What's wrong?"

"You did something to me. When our . . ." Trying to talk about it made her feel stupid. Why should she explain this to the very man who'd been there?

"When our . . . ?"

"When our . . . tongues"—was she supposed to talk about tongues with a man?—"touched, it almost hurt."

"Like . . . I bit you?"

"No! Like . . ." She tried to subdue her thought, but irrevocably it formed. *As if I caught a shooting star and put it in my mouth.*

The two of them had created a spark.

No, wait. That wasn't right. The spark had always been there, but they had given it fuel to make a fire.

Looking into his dark, knowing eyes, she realized he had fathomed the attraction from the beginning.

"Let us test this." He kissed her. The spark and light flared between them at once.

He drew away, but his hands still cupped her face. "Any pain? Or pleasure?"

What could she say? That she had now identified
the source of her discomfort? He would be amused.
Worse, he'd be pleased. So she stared into his heavily
lashed eyes and nodded.

"A virgin mouth, too." He smiled, all white teeth
and rough, tanned skin, and she noted that his broad
nose had been broken. That one feature had escaped
his dominion. He couldn't control it as he did his
smile and the expression in his eyes. His nose told
plainly of his past, of the fights he'd been in, but his
jaw said that he'd won every one. He was a fighter,
was Sebastian Durant, and she resisted him at her
peril.

He brought his mouth back to hers. His hands
explored her chin, her cheeks, her ears, then delved
into her hair, and he massaged her scalp with his
fingertips. At the same time her hands tightened on
his arms and her fingernails kneaded the muscles in
sentient demand.

She had observed those muscles when he had
lounged in his godmother's library. Now she experienced the ripple of their movement beneath her
palms, and that stirring heightened the notion that
this man was created for her, and her alone.

Then he moaned as if he experienced the painlike
symptoms, also.

She shivered as he shared his breath, pouring
himself into her in a primitive symbol of possession.

Where was her housekeeper's discipline? She
willingly—no, eagerly—explored his mouth with her
tongue and let his hands roam her ribs. Then his

fingers passed the high waist of her frock and nudged the underside of her breasts.

She should be shocked. She *was* shocked. She tried to get away, but not too hard, because she wanted . . . more.

"Shall I touch you?" he murmured. "Would you like that?"

He knew! How embarrassing that he knew that she wanted him to touch her bosom. All of her bosom. Most especially her nipples. They had clenched tightly. They ached. They needed to be soothed, and illogically she thought only he could soothe them.

"Like this," he said, and engulfed each breast in his fingers.

Tears of forbidden craving rose in her eyes as he rubbed her, paying special attention the peaks. The lace of her chemise rasped her skin, but it didn't irritate, it aroused—not only her, but him.

His compulsive delicacy seemed driven, wild, insurgent, and a faint anxiety nudged her mind.

Was *he* in control? Yes, of course. He had to be. He was the mighty Lord Whitfield.

But his body spoke of urgency—his? hers? He shifted; she paid only passing heed. The delights of his hands on her breasts, his breath on her skin, masked her anxiety.

Then his knee moved her legs apart.

She shoved his head aside. "Wait!"

He waited until she eased the pressure, then impatient, imperious, he nuzzled her neck.

"My lord, you must stop." She grabbed his hair, pulled his head back—and saw his face.

There would be no stopping. Passion had pulled the muscles taut. His gaze blazed so intensely, he shielded her from it by half shutting his eyes. Worst of all, he was smiling. Not his cutting smile. Not his too knowledgeable smile. But a smile that told her he was addicted to this pleasure.

He wasn't in control. His kiss had become a rampant creature. A dangerous creature.

But a housekeeper never panicks or shows anxiety. "Lord Whitfield!" she said clearly.

He heard her, for he focused on her, and she saw clear to the seething depths of his soul.

"Sebastian." His lips barely moved.

She shook him. "We've got to . . . You must halt immediately!"

Intently he watched her speak as if he could see the words. Could he hear her scent, and taste the feel of him on her hands?

"Sebastian," he repeated.

"If I call you Sebastian, will you stop?"

"I'm not a fool. What kind of merchant would I be if I agreed to that pact?"

Did he know she trembled on the edge of succumbing? He touched her ear tenderly, then followed with his tongue.

She tried to scramble back, but he was heavy. She didn't have a chance, unless an umbrella stand stood nearby. Or unless the domed silver tray cover remained on the end table where she'd placed it.

But how could she hit him with that? She could hurt him.

He kissed her chest, and the sensation tickled. Tickled and made her want to press against him. She shuddered and clutched him, whimpering. Perspiration glowed on her skin as the heat of the shooting stars rained down on her.

Then he stopped, and she realized he'd used her neck as a distraction to accomplish his real objective. He'd worked her skirt up, and now his hand slid over her knee toward the edge of her stocking. Toward the place that had grown damp. The rough skin of his palm snagged at the silk. She tried to press her legs together, to hide her vulnerability, but he was there. Everywhere, he was there. If she didn't do something now, he would touch her bare skin again, and this time the shooting stars might turn to ashes. This time Mary Rottenson might totally lose her battle, and Guinevere Fairchild would take her place.

And once Sebastian had experienced the irresponsible Guinevere, he would mock Mary until all of her maturity and authority shriveled and died.

His head thrown back, his eyes closed, he looked like a man on the verge of ecstasy.

She stretched her arm toward the silver cover.

Now.

His hand found her garter and released it.

Now.

Her fingers slipped on the slick silver. She tried again, and caught the handle.

"Now." His eyes opened, blazing with triumph.

His finger stroked her between the legs, unerringly finding that place.

She arched up, stars exploding in a tumult of fire and sparks, of passion and pleasure.

And frantic, she brought the cover around with a full swing of her arm. It clanged loudly against the back of his skull.

"What the . . . ?" He clambered back, freeing her for another swing.

This one cracked against his cheek. With a roar of pain, he grabbed his face and rolled off onto the floor.

She leaned forward to swing again.

He backed away.

Furious, humiliated, aroused, she held the cover like a shield before her. "Get out!" she whispered, afraid that if she spoke aloud, she would shout. "Get out and don't come back."

He took his hand away from his face and looked at the blood on the palm. Then he looked up at her.

Civilization? Control? What had possessed her to think he comprehended even the concepts? In the force of his dark gaze, she saw the savagery of an animal deprived of its right to mate. She saw the promise of future encounters. Fighting a mix of fear and excitement, she tried to duck behind the safe facade of Mary Fairchild—and failed.

He came back toward the bed.

She raised the cover.

"Put it down," he said in his normal cold tones. His mastery had returned. "If I wanted to, I could take it, and take you. But this isn't the time."

A knock sounded at the door. How long had someone been trying to get their attention? Stupidly she said, "There's someone outside."

A particularly frantic pounding sounded through the room, and Lady Valéry's clear tones called, "Sebastian!"

He simply glanced at the door, indifferent to the concerns of propriety and society, and Mary clutched the cover tighter. She didn't care what he said. She didn't believe that he would care if the king himself knocked on the door, and she wasn't putting down that cover.

"You know now what's between us." The skin on his cheek was bruising as he spoke, swelling, purpling, and blood trickled out of a cut. "I want you to remember, Mary, what happened on this bed. Tonight when you slip between the sheets, think of me. Think of what we almost did. Imagine how good it would have been." He went to the door and pulled the chair away, then turned back and looked at her. "It'll be that good again. That good, and better." He sketched a bow. "Until next time, Mary."

Chapter 11

Jill squealed. "Miss Rotten— I mean, Miss Fairchild, you look fairy-bright."

Mary forgave her maid the unflattering exhibition of amazement. Jill had viewed Mary as Lady Valéry's drab housekeeper for so many years, she couldn't contain her wonder now, when that same housekeeper was . . . Mary stared into the mirror. When she was dazzling.

She reined in her own incredulity.

Vanity. All this staring into the mirror fostered pride in her remaining beauty, and she knew well enough how fleeting youth had proved. Turning away from the reflection of a maiden dressed in white satin, diamonds, and gold glimmering at her ears, wrists, and neck, she said, "Beauty is as beauty does. And do remember, without your skill with the hairbrush, I would still be plain Miss Rottenson."

Jill wrapped the now cool iron curler in the quilted

pad she used to protect her hands. "Nay, Miss Fairchild, 'tisn't true. We ladies' maids used to talk about it in the servants' quarters, saying as how we'd like to get our hands on you. We knew you'd dress out fine. I can't wait until I get back home and tell them we were right." She shut the dampers on the brazier she'd used to heat the round steel bar. "And that one of *us* is a rich heiress!"

Silenced, Mary took the lacy handkerchief and put it in the purse that hung off her arm, then let Jill help her draw on the long, diamond-seeded gloves. She picked up her ivory fan. Jill pretended to busy herself, but Mary cleared her throat and held out her hand. Silently Jill handed over the shoulder scarf, disapproval implicit in her stance.

"I am not going out in public with a neckline as low as this," Mary said.

"As you say, Miss Fairchild."

Mary did say, and Jill would not have her way on this, at least.

Jill had refused to allow Mary to wear formal hoops, insisting instead on a cambric petticoat, for the newest mode demanded a tubular skirt. Jill had refused to allow Mary to wear a wig, for only those who clung to the old ways wore wigs. Jill had dabbed her lightly with the subtle fragrance of damask rose, for fashion emphasized cleanliness with only a subtle fragrance.

When Mary had inquired with irritation why she must ignore custom, Jill had smiled wisely. Mary needed to establish herself as a style leader from her first appearance.

And who was Mary to disagree? She had paid fashion little heed in the last ten years, and besides . . . she liked the lighter perfume. Her hair gleamed like polished gold, and she hated to cover it with a wig. And if she found the lack of hoops disconcerting, well, she could hide her blushes behind her fan, and her bosom beneath her lacy scarf.

Once more she tugged her neckline up, then tied the scarf in a loose knot over her chest. "I'm ready."

"Aye." Jill picked up the discarded hoops and stacked them in the bottom of the wardrobe. "Just remember—don't let Lord Whitfield take you into the garden. Grass stains are monstrously hard to remove."

Mary drew herself up to her full height, which was only a little greater than Jill's. "Are you being insolent?"

Jill looked surprised. "No, Miss Fairchild."

Deflated, Mary reflected Jill probably was being truthful. It was Mary's fault she'd tamely allowed Sebastian to remain in her bedchamber with no chaperone. She had foolishly thought she could handle him, that his discipline never slipped, that he despised the Fairchilds too much to wish to couple with one.

She knew better now. She knew, too, he would be at the party tonight and she would have to face him for the first time since that magnificent—no, that *humiliating* scene yesterday. She never would have guessed his revenge would take this form.

What would he say? What would he do? And how would she respond? Never had she dreamed she would allow a man to be so familiar.

Allow? She mocked herself. *Encourage* would be a better word. She'd let him kiss her, fondle her, and she'd kissed and fondled him in return, searing the tang and taste of him deep into her very being. Just as he'd instructed, she'd awakened last night and thought of what they'd almost done, imagined how good it would have been.

And she, of all people, knew the results of such heedless dreaming. She knew the trouble imagination could create. She'd taken that pillow, the one with his scent, and thrown it as far as she could from the bed.

Such precipitous behavior hadn't helped, but she felt better for it nonetheless.

"Miss Fairchild, it's time to go to the ballroom." Jill held the door for her. "But you haven't been out of your chamber since you arrived, and I fear you will get lost. Would you like me to walk you down?"

Jill tactfully hinted that she'd noticed Mary's anxiety. Jill thought it was shyness; Mary knew it was the lingering fear of being identified.

Ten years ago she'd been a governess, protected by the cloak of anonymity that covered all servants. Unfortunately, silly Guinevere Fairchild had been young, beautiful, impetuous, and by her behavior had called attention to herself. If one person recognized her as the governess who had fled after the earl of Besseborough's murder . . . She shook herself. Such imaginings were futile. If someone recognized her, then she would deny it. Or better still, laugh it off. Or dare her accuser to prove it. Or crumple . . . No.

Housekeepers do not crumple in the face of adversity.

Nor did heiresses. "I'll go myself. If I lose my way, I will certainly ask one of the servants or the other guests for directions."

"Aye, Miss Fairchild." Jill smiled at her, her eyes agleam. "I'll be waiting up for you when you come back, and you can tell me how you're the belle of the ball."

"I'm sure I will be," Mary said austerely. "After all, how many other heiresses will be attending?"

She sailed into the corridor, but she heard Jill's protestation anyway.

" 'Twill not be the money that'll first turn their heads, Miss Fairchild, but the sight of those bosoms—if you'd be wise enough to let the gentlemen see!"

Mary walked slowly in the direction of the formal chambers, not knowing whether to hope she met someone or hope she didn't, and when a door opened beside her, she wished she could blend into the woodwork.

Uncle Calvin stepped out into the passageway. He held his wig in his hand, and uneven fluffs of hair stuck out in all directions on his head. His waistcoat was buttoned crookedly, his cosmetics were smeared, and Mary guessed by his girth he'd lost his corset.

He didn't seem aware of her. From the dazed expression on his face, she wasn't sure he was aware of anything. He stared into the darkened chamber behind him and in a trembling voice said, "My dear, that was a transfiguring experience. Might I assume we will repeat it soon?"

Mary pressed herself against the wall.

A woman's voice called from within. "You are assuming we were both transfigured, Calvin."

"B-but . . ." Calvin stammered.

"If you're good and make yourself pleasant to my godson, then perhaps I'll dance with you tonight."

Mary recognized the voice, but she could scarcely credit it, and she didn't know whether to be shocked or amused.

"Do you promise?" Calvin begged.

A plump, bejeweled hand came out of the darkness and pushed him by his shoulder. "I make no *promises*. I told you that last night. Now, be a good boy and go back where you came from. I must get ready for the ball."

The door snapped shut, leaving Calvin staring helplessly at the painted panels, and Mary staring in amazement at Calvin. With the air of a man who had wrestled with fate and lost, he trudged down the hallway.

Mary followed at a discreet distance, pondering what devious plan Lady Valéry had hatched. The news that Lady Valéry had virtually controlled the English government for years had come both as a surprise and a confirmation. Seeing Calvin in his turmoil only gave credence to Mary's suspicion. Lady Valéry would try to recover the diary on her own. Working without Sebastian's consent, she had begun to test the suspects.

Mary wanted to help; no one desired the return of that diary more urgently than she. Every day she remained here on display was a day she might be identified. But Lady Valéry's involvement filled her with unease. Obviously Lady Valéry felt no compunction in bedding the enemy, and she'd watched Mary and Sebastian react to each other with something that looked like delight. So would she think twice about manipulating Mary and Sebastian into a similar situation? Mary didn't think so, and swore to watch not only her enemies, but her patroness.

With grim determination Mary walked toward the ballroom, and the farther she walked, the more people she met, until she felt like a raindrop that had merged with the stream. A rather unimportant raindrop, at that.

Slipping into the ballroom, she almost trod on the train of a lady wearing hoops. Had she created a social disaster for herself by listening to Jill's fashion advice?

Then she looked around her, and fashion no longer mattered.

The chamber had been transformed into a fairyland. The entire room was draped in midnight blue silk. The delicate material fluttered in the breeze from the open doorways, moving sinuously and catching the light. Golden ornaments hung from the ceiling like stars in the night sky, and the brilliance of a thousand candles created magic. Behind the polished expanse of dance floor, an orchestra played a romantic piece by Thomas Linley.

Smiling, lost in luxury, Mary stared. She hadn't allowed herself dreams of this, her unofficial debut, but if she had, she couldn't have imagined anything so grand.

The brilliantly clad nobles didn't speak to her. Instead, they looked at her. They observed her unpowdered hair and her informal petticoats and they leaned close to sniff her perfume. The men smiled insolently, and the powder-wigged women commented on her innovative dressing in tones that revealed their conviction that if they didn't know her, she must be a nobody.

And she wasn't, of course. She was only a governess-turned-housekeeper, with a brief stint as murderess in between.

But as she went forward, she took the time to examine the faces that examined her. She recognized none of them, and none appeared to recognize her.

"Here's our new heiress." Bubb's voice boomed over the buzz of many voices. "Mary! Come and stand with us as we greet our guests. You are our honored Fairchild, you know."

The Fairchilds stood in a row. As the marquess of Smithwick, Bubb was at the head, his blond handsomeness drawing the eye. Beside him, Nora appeared slight and insignificant, although she was clothed in a shimmery pink silk. The uncles were next in line—except the drained Calvin—and the daughters. Each man and woman was dressed in the finest of materials. None of the Fairchilds, nor their servants nor their home, showed the least sign of poverty. Mary wondered if they were truly on the brink of ruin, and even more whether any of them even understood the concept encapsulated in the word *economy*.

"Gracious, didn't anyone tell you, you must wear formal court wear for evening occasions?" Daisy snapped. "You look silly with your natural hair hanging loose."

"I think she looks magnificent." Drusilla shut her eyes and screwed up her mouth like a child about to throw a tantrum. "It's not fair."

"You must have spied out our design, you naughty girl." Lilith smiled with sickly enthusiasm.

And Mary understood at last why Jill had insisted she wear white and gold.

Lilith wore azure. Wilda wore glimmering silver. The twins, who were too young to be there at all, wore matching gowns of saffron, and Daisy was splendid in cloth of gold. Each gown glittered like one of the ornamental stars, but no one shone more brightly against the cobalt setting than Mary.

"You really should discard that scarf." Radella

pulled her skirt aside as Mary passed her. "Modesty is for peasants."

If Radella thought that, Mary knew she was right to conceal herself, and she pulled the tie tighter.

"I think you look pretty," Wilda said timidly.

Mary gave her a grateful glance.

"Stand next to me." Nora held out her hand. "We'll introduce you to the ton in a manner appropriate to the Fairchild heiress."

Mary moved to the place between Nora and Uncle Leslie, wondering all the time if Lilith and Daisy and Drusilla and Radella hid daggers somewhere on their tight-laced, ruffled persons. She saw the venomous gaze Leslie cast toward her, and she knew herself surrounded. With the possible exception of Bubb and Nora, none of the Fairchilds wanted her here.

If only they realized how little she wished to be here.

Bubb introduced her to the guests already in line, and Nora expressed her joy at having recovered their dear niece and heiress. As each guest moved on and another took his place, Mary smiled until her jaw ached. The noise in the ballroom rose as the tale was repeated time and again.

Nora lifted her fan and spoke to Mary from behind it. "Look, at the back of the line, it's the earl of Shaw and his son. The son is unmarried and in hopes of making a good match."

Mary looked at the pimple-faced boy. "I must be ten years older than he is."

"No more than eight." Nora sounded matter-of-fact. "But you're an heiress, and a beauty at that. That's a rarity which can't be ignored."

With a mounting sense of relief, Mary said, "I'm betrothed."

Bubb had apparently been listening, for he ignored the viscount whose hand he shook and leaned behind Nora. "Your fiancé hasn't arrived yet, Mary. Perhaps he's feeling a little embarrassed about exhibiting that black eye you gave him."

Mary groaned softly. "I gave him a black eye?"

"It's not the eye so much as his cheek." Nora's smile was more than a little implacable. "Are you less fond of him than you'd led us to believe?"

This interrogation was exactly the sort of conversation Mary had feared. She hadn't told falsehoods for the last ten years. She didn't think quickly when challenged. She'd been dreading the confrontation with Sebastian tonight; now she wanted him. "Not at all. I simply believe it is necessary to teach a man respect early." She smiled at the snubbed viscount with extra charm to make up for her relatives' rudeness.

The viscount smiled back, delighted, and asked, "May I be so bold as to beg a dance later, Miss Fairchild?"

Nora interceded before Mary could answer. "She's not accepting invitations yet, Lord Thistlethwaite. Give the other gentlemen a chance."

Leslie forcibly moved him with a hand on his arm. As the Fairchild daughters closed around the precipitous suitor, Leslie snapped at Mary, "Lord Thistle-thwaite is unsuitable and a fortune hunter. Try to remember you are a Fairchild, and save your smiles for more appropriate mates."

Vicious bully. She turned on Leslie fully, looked up into his gorgeous Fairchild eyes, and said, "I behave decorously for my station at all times."

"Your station? Your station?" Leslie sputtered. "How would you know the correct way for an heiress to behave?"

"Lady Valéry taught me well. Perhaps *you* could go to *her* for guidance."

"Go to . . . go to . . . a woman for guidance?" Like a capon waiting to be butchered and dressed, Leslie gobbled and shook his head until the flaps of skin beneath his ample chin jiggled. "I'll have you know I have never asked guidance of a woman."

"Ah, that's why you are wearing such old-fashioned breeches." Mary delivered the insult coolly, depending on her sharp tongue and her poise to give it the proper bite.

While Leslie squinted self-consciously down at his clothing, she greeted the earl of Shaw with his son. When the son begged a dance, she said, "This is my debut, and Lady Fairchild won't let me accept invitations yet. She says we must let the other gentlemen have a chance."

And what could Nora say? She smiled and murmured agreement, and Mary experienced the beginnings of triumph. Maybe she *could* be more than just prey in this den of Fairchild wolves.

If only Sebastian were here to share the moment with her.

She allowed her gaze to search the ballroom, but she saw no Sebastian among the crowd. How could he abandon her at this crucial moment? Unless . . . while everyone was dancing, he planned to search for the diary.

Mary wondered at her own inconsistency. She wanted to leave this place, yet wanted the dark, brooding, bruised man who would make leaving possible to remain at her side. Perhaps the upsets of her trip and her arrival had unsettled her mind. She preferred that explanation to the other—that she craved Sebastian and his kisses.

"Look, dear." Nora sounded poised and pleased. "Here's someone you must reward with a dance. Here's Ian."

Mary brought her attention back to the business at hand. Ian was dark and brooding, and undoubtedly bruised within, but he wasn't the man she sought.

"Little cousin, every time I see you, you are yet more beautiful."

The giddy excitement of her debut returned full force under Ian's appreciative gaze. Mary knew he was safe; she knew he wouldn't laugh at her enthusiasm. She twirled around. "It is a lovely dress, isn't it?"

"I would say it was the woman within the dress."

"The woman within the dress was always there," Mary said tartly. Giddy excitement could not destroy the sensible housekeeper within her. "Nobody noticed before."

"That's because I wasn't with you," Ian returned.

She focused on him fully. "You are so nice!" she said, and she meant it genuinely. He understood her discomfort in this unfamiliar situation, and he sought to put her at ease.

He stared at her as if her compliment took him aback, then his customary cynical mask fell into place. "Men do not wish to be known as *nice*. Dashing, handsome, witty, attractive—but never *nice*."

"I will remember," she said, then leaned forward and whispered, "But I'll still think you're nice."

"Mary has met almost everyone," Bubb interposed. "Ian, escort her onto the dance floor."

She hadn't met almost everyone, of course, but she understood what Bubb meant. She'd met everyone who mattered, and if someone of consequence came in late, Bubb or Nora would make sure she was introduced.

As Ian slipped his arm around her waist and led her into the throng, she confided, "It feels good to be away from our relatives, does it not? I very seldom think of myself as extraordinarily kind or virtuous, but here, you and I are veritable saints!"

Ian was silent for so long, embarrassment crept up on her.

"I didn't mean to offend you," she said. "You probably find it difficult to live with them without

experiencing some affection for them. I won't speak
ill of them again.''

"Affection?" Ian said. "I assure you, it is quite
possible to live with them without experiencing affection. I'm just surprised you don't group me in
with . . . them.''

"You?" She laughed up at him. "You gave me
money, remember? You told me to get away from
Fairchild Manor, that I was lucky to be rejected. I've
lived to appreciate your advice.''

He seemed to be struggling within himself, but
before he could reply, a man's hearty voice interrupted. "Ian, old man, you've brought us the beaute-
ous Miss Fairchild. Thank you, and begone!''

She stared at the laughing intruder and placed him
at once. She'd met him while in the receiving line; he
was the Viscount Dyne, a single man of probably
forty years who had done his best to ingratiate himself
with her.

"Begone, begone, Miss Fairchild wishes to dance
with me,'' he said emphatically.

"I think not.'' Ian kept his arm around her. "She
is my cousin. I have first right.''

"First right?'' Another male voice spoke from
behind. "A cousin has no right at all. Nor do you,
Dyne—now, get you gone. Miss Fairchild already
adores *me*.''

She turned and saw the earl of Aggass, younger
than Dyne. His frock coat sported the longest tails,
his waistcoat the most extravagant embroidery, but
his face was heavily pocked and he attempted to

disguise it with an excess of white powder and a variety of patches. More irritating was his air of supreme confidence that Mary called conceit.

"Miss Fairchild wishes to spend time with none of you." Mr. Mouatt appeared and straightened the ruffles on his shirt. "It is me she loves."

"Actually, gentlemen, I love none of you." Mary spoke with the authority of a housekeeper quelling an incipient quarrel among her underlings. The men's faces reflected astonishment, so she followed her initial advantage with a word of warning. "I love not the quarrels of babes or popinjays, either, so should you wish to please me, you must behave in a courteous manner."

The men fell back and glanced among themselves while Ian smothered a grin.

Then another voice, smooth, amused, and pleasant, said, "Have you been making fools of yourselves, lads? Let Mr. Brindley show you how it's done."

A tall, well-made gentleman of perhaps fifty moved forward and bowed to Mary. "Miss Fairchild, I have adored you from afar this past hour. Would you do me the honor of granting me the first dance?"

She didn't recognize this man or his name; he was probably one of the many gentlemen her aunt and uncle considered unsuitable. That made him all the more attractive to her.

"I would love to dance with you, sir," she replied. "But I have not danced for years, and I fear I would step on your feet."

Taking her hand, he stroked it between his own large palms. "To have such a lovely young woman facing me across a dance floor, it would be worth any amount of crushed toes."

She couldn't help it; she smiled up at him. His aging skin crinkled with each passing expression. He seemed strong as a coal shoveler, and his broad shoulders had not yet begun to stoop. He dressed in clothes that had been in style twenty years ago, and his powdered wig was horsehair at best, but his charm easily overcame all disadvantages. As she walked onto the dance floor, her erstwhile suitors watched glumly.

"I'm Mr. Everett Brindley, my dear, and I was reckoned quite a dancer in my youth. There is none better to guide you through this first minuet." He placed her in the line with the other ladies, then as the music began, moved to take his place among the men. "I'm also a merchant, and not a proper suitor for one so noble and enchanting, so I will promise not to woo you if you promise not to fall in love with me."

What a flirt he was, this unsuitable merchant! "That might be difficult, sir, as it is obvious a man of your grace is not easily discounted."

"I recognized you as a true lady from across the ballroom." He nodded brusquely toward the aristocratic suitors she had left behind. "Those worthless leeches aren't worthy to lick your slippers."

She was startled by his vehemence. "You are too harsh, sir."

"And you are too kind." Abruptly he seemed

recalled to his role as gentleman-merchant, and he smiled whimsically. "In truth, you remind me of my dear, departed Mrs. Brindley." He pressed his veined hand just above his heart. "I have heard that you are betrothed to Viscount Whitfield."

She nodded acknowledgment and concentrated on imitating the slow, graceful movements of the other dancers.

"What a sad state of affairs for the men who even now watch you hungrily."

"I doubt that more than their pockets will suffer from the loss." Mary pointed her toe, turned her head at the proper time, and realized with triumph that she remembered her father's instruction on the fine art of the dance.

Nostalgia assailed her. How her father would have loved this evening of celebration! How proud he would have been of her! Usually she tried to crush the memories of her father, but tonight invoked only the golden glimpses of his long-lost kindness and his never-ending joy.

And briefly she wished she had allowed Hadden to come. She'd feared danger, but how could danger exist in such a setting?

"So Viscount Whitfield is already firmly ensconced in your heart," Mr. Brindley said as they wove in the intricate steps of the dance. "And you in his, I suppose?"

Startled by the familiarity of his inquiry, she missed a step and had to hurry to catch the beat.

"Ah, I've embarrassed you." In a low tone he

instructed her on the next few steps, then resumed their conversation. "Forgive me the liberty of old age."

She couldn't let him think that. He moved gracefully, like a man who kept active, and he displayed a veiled strength. "You're not old."

"I thank you, but my youth has slipped away, leaving me to think I have little time to set the world to rights." He chuckled, disparaging himself. "Little time to see Whitfield set to rights. I've known him for years, you understand. We've occasionally been partners in some venture or another, and I've grown to respect the lad. He reminds me of myself when I was younger." He clenched his fist to punctuate his words with it. "Dynamic. Unstoppable. Determined."

"Yes." Mary scrutinized the other dancers to keep Mr. Brindley from noticing the color in her cheeks, and to see if anyone was eavesdropping on their unorthodox conversation. "He's all those things," she almost whispered.

"No one can hear us," Mr. Brindley said kindly. "A man of my background knows well how loud to project his voice." He cleared his throat. "Business deals, you know."

Mary surreptitiously glanced around again. Although the dancing couples appeared to be straining to hear their conversation, they also wore the deeply disgusted expressions of those thwarted.

"But we were speaking of young Whitfield, and I wish for him a deep and abiding love." He squeezed her hand, and his firm chin wobbled. "A love such as Mrs. Brindley and I had for each other."

Mary's chin wobbled, too. How sweet he was!

"I see by your blush, Whitfield is lucky in this, too." Mr. Brindley couldn't have sounded more fond. "And the dance is finished. You must have been jesting."

"What do you mean, sir?"

His hazel eyes twinkled. "You dance very well."

"Only with the proper instructor." She curtsied when Mr. Brindley returned her to the sidelines.

"Oh, stop scowling, all you young men," Mr. Brindley said to the enlarged cluster of suitors. "She's not yours, anyway. She's Viscount Whitfield's, and don't you forget it."

As he walked away, his step firm, the earl of Aggass said in a low voice, "Dockworker."

"He is." Mr. Mouatt sneered. "Or used to be. He brags about it."

"They say he's an anarchist, or worse." Again Aggass spoke almost in a whisper.

"Why is he here?" Mr. Mouatt asked. "I didn't know the Fairchilds allowed merchants in to mingle with the upper ten thousand."

"The upper ten thousand have borrowed enough money from Mr. Brindley to get him invitations wherever he chooses to go," Viscount Dyne replied, but without the discretion of his younger rival. "As the Fairchilds have undoubtedly discovered."

"Inviting him to a party is better than finding

yourself facing three of his thugs on a dark night in London.'' Aggass looked ill, and he flipped his lace handkerchief in Mary's direction. ''It's a frightening experience.''

Mary didn't believe Aggass for a moment. The despicable earl wanted sympathy, nothing more. ''Mr. Brindley is an agreeable man,'' she said. ''You should be thankful he will lend his money.''

Ian gave a bark of laughter as the other men shuffled uncomfortably. ''You're supposed to pretend you can't hear them when they talk about usury. Young, unmarried women are required to be ignorant of such matters.''

''I'll try to remember,'' Mary promised, thinking that being a woman in any walk of life was much the same as being a housekeeper; one had to play dumb to please the men.

''Personally, I find Miss Fairchild's frankness enchanting.'' A man in his thirties with a hard air of dissipation bowed before her. ''Baron Harlow, at your service.''

''Almost as enchanting as her beauty.'' The pimple-faced son of the earl of Shaw captured her hand and pressed a kiss on it.

''She is truly the loveliest in the land.'' Lord Thistlethwaite tried to elbow his way to a position directly in front of her, but the other men pressed close and he had to be satisfied to call his compliment over their heads.

Wistfully Mary yearned for her old gullibility. If the sixteen-year-old Guinevere Fairchild had been standing here, splendor all around, compliments inundating her, she would have believed herself blessed. She would have been so happy, for in this moment the dreams of her young life would have been fulfilled. Instead, Mary Rottenson looked at the decorations and wondered how much they had cost and how long the servants would have to work to remove them. She heard the flattery and wondered how these noblemen who had been previously blind to her charms could suppose that she would believe them now.

A housekeeper, she thought wistfully, never indulged in self-deception.

Ian grasped her hand. "The orchestra is playing. Would you do me the honor?"

They took their places on the floor. Ian waited until the music had started, then asked, "Where did you go when you left here so many years ago?"

She was silent, unable to lie to the cousin who had been so good to her. Yet she couldn't confess, either. Even Ian, with his kindness and empathy, would condemn a murderess.

"You don't have to tell me." He patted her hand. "You don't owe me anything."

"But I do! If not for you, Hadden and I would have . . . starved." And been tortured and hanged.

"Were you . . . You're so comely."

She curtsied as part of the dance, and when she rose he touched a lock of hair that rested on her chest.

"Was it a man? Were you . . . compromised?"

There was a man, of course, but not as Ian feared.

"I wasn't compromised," she answered steadily. "After much searching, I found a position as Lady Valéry's housekeeper."

"Housekeeper?" Ian's mouth drooped. "You couldn't have been her housekeeper."

"Yes, I could, and a good one, too." She could have laughed out loud at his expression. "What did you think would happen to me?"

"I thought you'd become some rich man's mistress. I pictured you comfortable and safe, and whenever I went to London I looked for you." His soft brown eyes were pools of outrage. "It would have been more appropriate if you had been compromised, I think."

"Is that what everyone thinks? That I'm Sebastian's mistress, and he'll take me to wife now that I'm an heiress?"

"More or less. He *is* marrying you for your money, you know."

"That's stupid," she said without even having to think it through. "If he were marrying me for my money, he would have done so in Scotland before I learned the truth. Then he would have had control of my fortune before I knew I had one."

Ian squeezed her hand a little too hard, and when she winced, he apologized swiftly. "Don't tell anyone the truth. It's better if they think you were a mistress."

"Nobles are so odd, don't you think? That they would prefer to think I had spread my legs for a man than to think I put myself into honest service."

"What I think doesn't matter." Ian spoke urgently, as if he had limited time in which to convey his message. "Just don't let anyone lure you into a secluded spot."

The nape of her neck began to tingle, and she barely refrained from putting her hand there. What was wrong with her?

"Any man here would consider it a triumph to toss your skirts over your head and compromise you for the money." Ian glanced behind her.

She would have sworn he was nervous. Was it the whispers she heard sweeping the ballroom? Or the sudden chill in the overheated atmosphere? "I'll keep your warning in mind," she said.

"Your betrothal wouldn't save you."

Sebastian. Sebastian was in the ballroom.

"If Whitfield is not marrying you for the money, then he's marrying you because he's just like every other man. He can't resist a Fairchild."

Sebastian was watching her. That explained the heat that rose from within her, her impulse to flee, her stronger impulse to stay.

"Everyone also knows he would strangle you rather than marry a woman carrying another man's babe."

Even now, Sebastian threaded his way through the dancers to claim her on the dance floor. She knew it without looking. She knew, also, that he wasn't pleased to see her talking to Ian.

Ian looked defiantly over her shoulder as he finished. "He'll not be made a buffoon by a Fairchild again."

Sebastian slid his hand along her bare arm, disengaging her from Ian's grasp. She wasn't startled. She expected his touch, almost craved it. When she faced him, his cheek was high and swollen, dark with bruising, but his eyes still glittered, and with the passion stoked by his soul's forge.

"We're dancing, old man," Ian protested.

"Not anymore," Sebastian answered, leading Mary away.

She followed without a protest.

Chapter 12

Sebastian marched Mary across the ballroom, but when they reached the terrace she dug in her heels. "I am not to go with you out into the garden," she said.

He whipped around so fast, he obviously had anticipated a protest. "And why is that?"

"Jill forbids it."

He examined her face intently. Then slowly his gaze traveled her body, down toward the satin slippers that peeked from beneath her skirt. "I can see why," he said, acknowledging the whiteness and delicacy of the material. Or was he insinuating he couldn't be trusted with her? "Then let us step into this alcove and talk."

She hung back, and he turned on her again.

"What's wrong?"

"We can't be alone, either. Ian forbids it."

"And when has *our* cousin become arbiter of

proper conduct?'' Sebastian glared and touched his face. ''If you're displeased with my behavior, you can always strike me with a silver tray cover.''

The bruising reached from his cut cheekbone to under his eye, giving him the look of a street fighter. An apt image, she thought, but probably humiliating in view of his conqueror's identity.

Worse, she was glad to see she'd marked him, and her pride hinted at a possessiveness that horrified her. Falling back on safety, on the education she'd gained as a housekeeper, she folded her hands before her. ''I take satisfaction in teaching a lesson the first time.''

His mouth tightened. His nostrils flared. ''You are so damned prim.'' He gestured. ''Would you rather we spoke in public?''

She glanced around. Hundreds of eyes peered at them without any attempt at circumspection. They registered Sebastian's bruise and had undoubtedly heard tales from their servants about the scene in Mary's bedchamber. And since no one had witnessed the most familiar of the moments, she could imagine the tales that were flying about the staircases and corridors. Not turning her back on him, she inched toward the alcove. ''I promise not to hit you again, if you promise not to . . .''

He followed her into the retreat formed by two columns on either side of a curving wall, and his mouth curled with the unprincipled smile of a fallen angel. ''Promise not to . . . what? Kiss you? Desire you? It's a little late for that, *Miss* Fairchild.'' He mocked her with a formality made false by their recently shared intimacy.

The columnar enclosure should have given her a sense of security. Instead she felt cornered, at bay. "There are other Fairchilds here, more beautiful than I. Why don't you go talk to them?"

"I'm not betrothed to them."

"With very little effort, you could be, I suspect." Oh, why had she put the idea into his mind?

Yet while he heard, he didn't seem to care. "I don't want them. You serve my purpose."

Well. That put her in her place, and cured any propensity she might have for conceit. "The others are prettier."

"Who?" He sounded annoyed.

"The Fairchild daughters. Look." With her fan, she pointed to the dance floor, and he turned. How could he not be impressed? All her erstwhile suitors were watching, practically salivating, as her cousins swirled in the graceful motions of the country dances. When she looked at those women, she knew herself to be a plain dab. Sebastian would no doubt see the obvious, and, she told herself grimly, better sooner than later. "They dance gracefully, they're well spoken, they compel the eye to follow them by their very loveliness."

"Yes, yes, they're very nice, but I suppose you're fishing for a compliment." He slapped a hand against the wall on either side of her head and leaned toward her. "It's not any of them who have put coals in my trousers."

Not a *pretty* compliment, she thought, and glanced down, expecting to see smoke rising from the dark material. Of course, no such oddity occurred. Instead, when she looked back into his eyes, she could have sworn the fire existed in his soul.

"You are the most beautiful woman here." He couldn't have sounded more impatient. "I can't keep my eyes off you, nor my hands off you, and unless you want a demonstration of my needs right here in Bubb Fairchild's bloody damned ballroom, you'll stop flaunting yourself."

She went from surprised to pleased to astonished during one coarse speech. "What flaunting?"

"You're . . . looking at me." He shifted from foot to foot as if he truly did have coals in his breeches. "And why did you buy that dress? It shows all your . . . bosom."

"*You* insisted on this dress!"

"I'm a stupid sot."

"I won't argue with that."

He relaxed a little. "You wouldn't, you little harpy."

Shocked and infuriated, she said, "You dare . . . you . . . you hardheaded ass."

"My dear Miss Fairchild." He pressed his hand to his heart. "I am shocked! I am horrified! I am dismayed!"

She was, too. Sebastian must think she had changed personalities before his very eyes.

Worse, she had. She had become Guinevere Fairchild, imagining that the world was a blancmange and petulantly demanding a serving of it. Dismay flung her back against one of the columns, and he caught her waist as if he feared for her.

"What's wrong?" he asked.

"I can't believe I called you a . . . an appellation."

"An ass." He rubbed his hand across the small of her back and smiled that hard-edged smile. "You called me an ass. No doubt I deserved it."

"No, you didn't."

"Have you forgotten I called you a harpy?"

"That's no excuse for me to lower myself, too!"

"So I am allowed to lose my temper. You are not." He pulled a thoughtful face. "What an interesting woman you are."

He watched her too closely, but she thought he understood her.

Why did that make her uneasy?

"I humbly beg your pardon for calling you a name," he said, "and forgive you for calling me an ass, which is a mild term for what I really am. Think nothing of it."

Think nothing of it? She could think of nothing else. She had tumbled to the depths once more. And he realized it, for his hands rubbed her back in a manner reminiscent of their familiarity the day before. He must think her an unprincipled slut who couldn't even restrain a flare of temper.

With what she hoped was dignity, and not simply desperation, she said, "I have been poor, and a housekeeper, but I have always been able to call myself a lady. Don't take that title from me.''

His mouth opened slightly. She could see his white teeth, and the minute movement of his lips as he breathed. The warmth of him crept through the layers of material at her bodice, and each one of his fingers pressed into the flesh of her back as if he wanted to restrain her regardless of her desires.

She was far too intent on him, noting his every action, analyzing him for pleasure, for anger, for pain and for passion.

"You'll always be a lady." He sounded sincere, and rather surprised. "Not like the rest of the Fairchild women. Not like so many of the women here who own the title but lack the deportment."

She heard the buzzing of those ladies behind him, but her view of them was blocked, some by his chest and shoulders, but mostly by the fact that when he stood so close, she noticed no one else.

"Sooner or later, you and I will mate."

His certainty frustrated her. "I am not an animal. I do not *mate*."

"Aren't you?" His scarred, long-fingered hands reached out to her and caught the scarf tied to conceal her bosom. The lace gave easily under his coaxing, and he lifted the ends away from her skin. He looked at what he'd uncovered, then looked up at her. "Won't you?"

He was crazed, and he'd infected her with his madness; that was the only possible explanation. After years of self-imposed isolation, with only Hadden to relieve the loneliness, she had placed herself beyond such physical response. Even this evening when she walked into the ballroom, she had been nervous, but outwardly placid. Now she betrayed herself.

Her toes curled; her lips throbbed. She wanted to tear the shawl away from him, but her hands trembled too much. Beneath her skin lived a different person than she'd ever met before. Not Guinevere or Mary, innocents both, but a woman who anticipated and wanted, all because of one man and his devastating scowl.

She thought thankfully of the party proceeding just over his shoulder. Others were gathered about, else she couldn't vouch for Sebastian's actions, or even her own.

There was danger here, and if not for her loyalty to Lady Valéry, she would shove this man aside, go to London, demand her inheritance, and with Hadden at her side, she would tour the world. Instead she had to remain here, and she *had* to make him understand her circumstances. "I have to remain untarnished, with a character as cold, hard, and polished as platinum."

"Platinum can be melted if the flame is high enough." His fingers brushed her skin as he retied the scarf. "You'll see. When you have melted, you'll still be a lady. A very . . . well-pleasured . . . lady."

He spaced the words deliberately, and an improper thrill shook her. He was doing this on purpose. He wanted her pliant, and she wanted to be whatever he wished.

How distasteful to find one subjugating oneself to a man.

He might have been reading her mind. "You were a housekeeper, but that was merely your role to play. You were not born to be a lump of platinum, nor could you force that precious metal into your soul. You are simply Guinevere Mary."

"Fairchild." She added her surname. "You say I was not born to be a lump of platinum, but I was born a Fairchild, and I tell you it's better to seek the precious metal than to become one of those wretches."

He frowned and tried to speak.

"No, don't interrupt. Now that I've started, I might as well be frank, also. You told me in Scotland this betrothal would be a sham. Now you tell me we must 'mate,' give in to the . . . the base emotions. For what purpose? When we finish, I will still be a Fairchild and you will still hate me and everyone in my clan. And I'll be ruined."

He didn't deny it. "So you've heard the tale of the feud."

She was tempted to lie, to say that she had, but like an insurmountable wall, there existed her damnable propensity for truthfulness.

He read her too easily, for he said, "You haven't heard. I would have thought the Fairchilds would use that as a weapon to separate us. But perhaps they can't think of a way to make their own part sound anything less than despicable."

With an emotion that felt like despair, she said,

"You see? You hate Fairchilds, and I don't know why, but I do know if we . . . mate . . . you will have sullied yourself with one of the family you despise."

"Sometimes a little sullying is good for a man."

He jested, but if he ever recalled what Guinevere Fairchild had done, he would know she was worse than any Fairchild yet born.

"Living away from your cursed clan strengthened you."

Sebastian remained before her, a big block that stood between her and the ballroom, between her and freedom . . . between her and the safe, sterile world Mary Rottenson had inhabited. As arrogant as any man, he thought he could change her. He didn't know how she had changed herself. "I've already been through the flames, Sebastian. I was a weakling once—I'll never be one again."

He watched her, craving her with an inexplicable madness. Her eyes were so big and the same blue the ocean turns during a storm. Outrageous lashes fluttered as she spoke, and her lips formed a kiss with each word. Her skin flushed with earnest eloquence, and her elaborate coiffure slid from formality into sociability. She was twenty-six, yet she acted with both the resolution of a much older woman and the innocence of a girl. She defied him so consistently, he was convinced of her virtue, her morality, and her integrity. Unfortunately, what he wanted of her pertained to none of those merits.

She frustrated him. He wanted her so badly, he

dared not unbutton his coat lest everyone see his condition. Yet he unwillingly admired her, and even more unwillingly had begun to wonder if his godmother was right when she'd said Guinevere Mary Fairchild could be his salvation.

"So you don't care that I have destroyed your reputation, you only care that I want you and am determined to have you," he said. "It's not the appearance that affects you. It's the reality."

"I do care about my reputation. It is very difficult for a woman not to care." She fingered the fringe of her shawl to avoid looking at him. "Yet I don't have to live, night and day, with the effects of a ruined reputation. I have to live with myself, and if I allowed myself to become your mistress—"

"No. It's not the 'mistress' part of it that frightens you." He clasped her hand and brought it forward so that it lay flat on his chest. Pressing it where she could feel the thump of his heart, he said, "It's that you would lie in my arms, and I would find all the ways to make you give yourself completely. You know, Guinevere Mary, the kind of woman you could be, and I know it, too. And I won't be satisfied until you are."

Her fingers curled and she tried to pull her hand away. "I don't understand you at all. Who would you have me be?"

He still held her close. "Part Mary Rottenson, and part Guinevere Fairchild."

She jerked back so forcefully, he lost his grip. "Why would you want her? That silly, vain thing."

"You're talking about *Guinevere*." He didn't quite

understand why she had divided herself in half, but he was getting close. "You're talking about her as if she were separate from you, but she's—"

"And why would *you* want a Fairchild at all? Are you using me for revenge?"

He should be, but when he was with her, he forgot the need to make the Fairchilds pay. "This is sweeter than any revenge."

"Don't talk that way to me!" She was so perturbed her voice rose, and she seemed unaware of the listeners who hovered behind him.

Not that he cared about the nobles who strolled past, hoping to hear a tidbit of gossip. But he did care if she embarrassed herself. In a low tone he said, "Most women would be insulted if a man *didn't* want them."

She turned her head away as if she were afraid to have him read her expression. "I'm not like other women. I have done things other women would scorn."

"Yes, you've worked. Perhaps it's just that I'm no different than any other man." Reaching up to one of the gold ropes that secured the billows of midnight blue silk to the wall, he jerked it free. The shimmering cloth, still connected to the ceiling, fell around them. Not quite as good as a curtain, for the drafts in the chamber waved it back and forth, but it gave them a partial privacy, and he hoped that music from beyond the curtain would mask their voices. "Perhaps I can't resist a Fairchild woman." A frightening thought, if true. "Lucky for me I have found the one

Fairchild with a platinum streak of honor. A rare jewel in a sterling setting.''

He stroked her round, soft cheek, but she jerked her head back. ''I just want to finish our purpose here and go.'' She sounded frantic, pleading. Then she lowered her voice and glanced around. ''Have you looked for the diary? Have you found any clues?''

''I've looked, but without success.'' He stroked her cheek again, insisting she take the comfort he offered while reveling in the sensation of living velvet beneath his fingertips. ''We've been here only a full day. You surely knew finding the diary would take longer than that.''

''Yes, but I didn't know how much I would hate this farce.''

Hate him? Ah, but she didn't. He never claimed to know a woman's mind, but he knew this woman's body, and she wanted him. She didn't want to, but she did.

''I can distract Bubb's daughters while you search their rooms,'' she said. ''I can befriend the servants and question them. Let me help.''

She allowed his hand to cradle her face, but more in resignation than enjoyment, he thought.

''You have helped. I've avoided our hosts this last day, pleading embarrassment because of the bruises.'' He smiled as pleasantly as he knew how, trying to coax a small one from her. ''See? Already you've created a marvelous distraction.''

She looked at the floor, sulking like a child who

was too young to play the game but wanted to imitate her siblings. In truth, the woman never smiled. At least . . . not at him. "I wandered the halls," he said, "and reacquainted myself with the layout of the manor."

She looked up, rancor forgotten. "You've been here before?"

Damn! He hadn't meant to say that. "Years ago." She started to question him, but he said quickly, "Tonight before I arrived in the ballroom, I searched Bubb's study."

As he had hoped, curiosity distracted her. "What did you find?"

"Plenty. Your grandfather's will, a pile of unpaid accounts, another pile of unpaid accounts, a safe . . ."

Her mouth turned down. "Locked, of course."

He grinned. "Yes, and none of the keys I brought worked."

"You brought keys?"

"I brought everything I thought I would need to search this house inside and out." He grimaced. "But evidently I didn't bring the proper key."

"I could break into it." She rubbed her fingertips together as if she remembered the sensation of a file scraping the skin.

"How would you have such a talent?" he asked forbiddingly.

"My father insisted I learn." She looked him in the face. "He said the knowledge might be useful."

Her father, Charles Fairchild.

Sometimes Sebastian saw the image of Charlie in her features, and he confessed, "I visited Fairchild Manor when Charlie was still a favored son."

"You remember when my father lived at home?"

"Of course." He found himself wanting to please her, so he revealed yet more. "In those days Charlie was older and dashing, and I wanted to be just like him."

A subtle glow lit her features. "Everybody liked my father."

"Except for *his* father."

The glow was extinguished. "Papa said he was disinherited because he wasn't foul enough."

"I believe that." Charlie had disappeared and Sebastian had lost everything at about the same time, and it had been years before they'd seen each other again. By then, Charlie had been married, widowed, and much reduced in circumstance. Sebastian had been bitter, orphaned, and also much reduced in circumstance.

Charlie had expressed penitence for the Fairchilds' brutal prank and its deadly results. Sebastian had accepted the apology, because Charlie had not a mean bone in his body.

But Charlie had lived for gambling, adventure, excitement. The last time Sebastian had seen him, he'd borrowed money . . . money Sebastian had given. Money he'd known would never come back, because even the best Fairchild had a touch of larceny in him. Sebastian mused, "I can't imagine him raising two children—especially not a girl."

"He did the best he could after my mother died," Mary said.

He hastened to assure her, "I liked Charlie, I really did."

A mixture of fondness and pain shifted across her face artlessly. Then the display faded, and she slid back into that persona he'd first seen in Scotland— that of an upper servant, cleansed of all sentiment. "Every man my father ever met liked him."

They'd gone beyond her pretending to be a housekeeper and hiding her emotions from him. Women were supposed to comprehend these sentimental intricacies; why didn't she?

He wanted to shake her, make her be Guinevere and Mary and open to him, but he knew already she wouldn't respond. Instead he paid tribute to the only decent Fairchild he'd ever known—until now. "If your father taught you to open a safe, then your father was a wise man."

Mary relaxed. The edges of her eyes tilted up, a dimple quivered in her sweet-cream cheek, and he realized he'd done it! He'd made her smile.

A very nice smile, with teeth and lips . . . those pouty, kiss-shaped lips . . .

He was kissing her before he realized it. She didn't even struggle, although a less-skilled man might attribute that to surprise. He preferred to think that she'd acquired a fondness for his kisses yesterday.

He recognized her hesitation now as she remembered, and he loosened his grip on her waist, rubbed her back with gentle hands, disguising the greed that drove him to claim her regardless of the consequences.

''Sebastian.''

She whispered his name, and he heard the quaver of uncertainty. No matter how hard he tried, he still swamped her with desire. Too much desire for this little virgin to welcome.

Hell, he wasn't even sure of his restraint, and they were in the middle of a ballroom with only a thin sheet of silk separating them from avaricious eyes.

But he couldn't stop just yet. Not yet. Not until she responded.

He pressed his parted lips on hers gently, allowing his breath to warm her, depending on her curiosity to let him in. She took longer than he liked, but when she leaned against the wall and allowed her stiff muscles to go lax, he knew he'd won.

His sense of triumph far exceeded the accomplishment.

Her mouth opened; her soothing breath swept into him. Gently his tongue touched hers; slowly she accepted him. Her hands gripped his shoulders, then slipped around his neck.

He wanted more. He wanted to feel her slide her fingers into his hair. He wanted to discover the type of sounds she would make as he touched her bared breasts for the first time.

Blood thundered in his head. Images blossomed in

his mind. He could almost feel the globes of her bottom in his hands as he lifted her against the wall, stepped between her legs, and–

"God!" He pulled away and stared at her as she stood all sleepy-eyed and pliant.

When Guinevere Mary Fairchild was stiff and formal, he desired her. But when she yielded even the tiniest bit . . . oh, then he would give anything to have her.

Breathlessly the miniature siren asked, "When and where do you want me to meet you?"

His heart beat so fast, he thought he would collapse. Triumph! Here was triumph! He would go to her bedchamber, to that huge bed. He would find her waiting in her nightclothes, a little wary. He would be gentle, strip her slowly, kiss her body.

"You need me to open the safe." She straightened. "When do you want me to meet you?"

He could lay her down, or stand her up, or kneel behind her, but however he did it, he would enjoy it.

And he'd make sure she did, too.

"No safe," he choked. "Not you." He'd been mad to even think he could expose her to danger. "Not ever. Don't you understand? That diary is dangerous."

"I do understand." She lifted her chin, and her eyes sparked. "But there are more important things to be afraid of."

She didn't know what she was talking about. Closing his hands on her arms, he rubbed the muscles beneath the silk. She was strong, sturdy from her years of manual labor, yet she was slight, delicate, and in need of protection. "I'm here to *steal* the diary."

"I know that, and I'm here to help you," she said earnestly.

"Someone else has to be here to *buy* the diary, and I assure you, he is desperate to lay hands on it. In addition, the Fairchilds need the profit from the sale, and only a fool doesn't think the Fairchilds would kill for a shilling." Damn the woman, she could just get that mulish expression off her face. He was perfectly willing to use logic, but if she didn't see sense, he would tie her to her bed. He would *like* to tie her to the bed. "You receive all the attention because of the mystery surrounding you, your background, and most important, your inheritance. Just be a good girl and distract the curiosity from me." He lifted her chin in his hand and looked deep into her eyes. "And I promise you a reward you'll remember always."

Chapter 13

Sebastian strode away from the alcove where he'd hidden Mary, and he was smiling so delightfully, at least three of the Fairchild daughters almost swooned.

Lady Valéry wasn't impressed. In her opinion, the Fairchild daughters would never swoon for a smile worth less than a hundred thousand pounds. But when he brushed past them as if they were nothing more than pesky midges, she had to concede the boy had some taste, although she'd had to personally refine it more times than she liked to remember.

Lady Valéry watched as he stopped and spoke to that merchant, that Mr. Brindley, a pretty bit of manners considering how out of place a merchant was in this august gathering.

An august gathering that stared fixedly toward behind the blue silk curtain, riveted by Sebastian's possessiveness and anticipating Mary's appearance.

Curiosity was a vulgar emotion, and if Lady Valéry didn't make a move to protect Mary, she would be exposed in a perhaps less than perfect moment.

Tucking her cane under her arm, she walked regally toward the alcove where Mary remained hidden. In the act of pulling the curtain back, she heard Mary mutter, "A housekeeper never drives a knife though the heart of the man who is claiming to be her betrothed."

Lady Valéry paused.

Then in a frustrated tone—"So it is a good thing I don't have a blade in my hand."

Lady Valéry chuckled and stepped inside. "You've already marked the boy—think of the extent of your fame should you succeed in murdering him."

Mary paled. "I wouldn't really murder him," she said quickly. "I couldn't commit murder lightly."

"Of course not. I never thought you could," Lady Valéry hastened to reassure her, wondering all the while why Mary had reacted so to a simple jest.

Mary pressed her lips together and looked down at the floor, struggling to subdue what appeared to be guilt, unbridled anger, and leftover passion— emotions Lady Valéry had never seen Mary expose in all the years of their acquaintance.

Conversing casually to give Mary time to pull herself together, Lady Valéry said, "Everyone is panting to know what's going on back here, but I'll stand guard if you would like."

"Y-yes," Mary said jerkily. "Thank you." She

paced toward one of the columns, rested her hand on the white fluting, and made a pronouncement. "Your godson is a boor." She spoke with the assurance of ten years of boor-watching experience.

Lady Valéry chuckled warmly. "I would be the last woman to argue with you. What has he done now?"

"He wants to protect me from danger."

"How rude!"

"He told me to be a good girl and act as a distraction for him."

"I can see how that would upset you . . ." Lady Valéry rapped her fan on her own wrist to subdue her amusement. "Isn't that what he said he required of you when you originally spoke in Scotland?"

Mary ignored that. "He promised me a reward if I was successful."

"How promising." Lady Valéry was baiting Mary now. "Do you think it will be jewels?"

Mary swung around and glared. "I believe your godson plans to present himself as the reward."

"A typical man." Lady Valéry tucked her arm in Mary's and leaned on it, then drew her out from behind the drape. "Although you could do worse than to take Sebastian." She nodded at the horde that swam toward them like a school of sharks. "For instance, you could wed one of them."

"True," Mary said fiercely, "but I don't believe Sebastian is talking about marriage."

The girl saw all too clearly, but she remained in ignorance of Lady Valéry's plans. And to keep her in ignorance, Lady Valéry would have to let other men have their chance. But oh, how it went against the grain to see the earl of Aggass, that putrid little pimple, descending on them.

He bowed, his coattails flapping. "Lady Valéry, I wish to dance with the estimable Miss Fairchild. Do I need to ask your permission?"

He made it clear by his tone that he only humored an old lady.

Well, this old lady could teach him respect with the business end of her cane. But she didn't. Instead she said, "Indeed you do, and you are required to bring her back to me as soon as the set is over. Miss Fairchild is not to be trifled with, Aggass, and I'm here to make sure you behave yourself."

"I'm quaking," Aggass answered as he took Mary's hand.

"You should be," Lady Valéry shot back as he led her onto the floor.

He was scowling as he placed Mary opposite him in the dance, and Lady Valéry smirked. He would be surly and rude when he talked about her, and Mary would take exception, and he would have ruined himself in the eyes of the very heiress he sought to court.

Men were so easy to manipulate.

Lady Valéry turned to Mary's other suitors as they gathered around. "Which of you gentlemen wishes to dance with Miss Fairchild next?"

She decided the order of Mary's partners, and succeeded in subtly undermining the ones who might have appeared attractive to Mary. She failed with only one—that Fairchild cousin, Ian. He stood off to the side and watched as if he were highly entertained, and more than once it occurred to Lady Valéry that the service she performed for Sebastian, that of guileful obstruction, could easily be utilized by Ian, also.

She would have to keep an eye on that young man. Besides being darkly handsome, he was intelligent and ambitious, and therefore a challenge.

Lady Valéry relished a challenge.

In fact, she delighted in the whole evening, and would have kept Mary dancing well into the wee hours, but just as the midnight dinner was served, Calvin walked into the ballroom.

She thought she had exhausted the absurd man, but there he stood, dressed in the most vibrant shade of purple she had ever seen, looking through the crowd—for her. Because he now sincerely adored her. And how was she to know that he had never been entertained in that particular fashion? Obviously he had never visited France.

Patting Mary's arm, Lady Valéry said, "Dear, I find myself fatigued. Would you mind escorting me to my chambers?"

Still bound by her duty, Mary never hesitated. She walked away from the compliments and the smiling faces without a pause. A howl of protest followed them, but she only tucked Lady Valéry's arm closer to hers.

As they walked the long corridors lit only by the occasional candelabra, Lady Valéry asked, "Are you enjoying yourself?"

"It's odd to be the center of so much attention." Mary nodded at the servants who waited outside the bedchambers. "The men flatter me so excessively, I doubt them even when they give me their names."

Lady Valéry laughed. "Wise woman. They would do anything to get their hands on you . . . and your inheritance."

"So Ian said."

"Did he?" Lady Valéry still smiled, although her mirth had disappeared. "So good of him to warn you."

"He's very kind."

"Not a word you would use to describe Sebastian."

Mary slanted a look at her. She obviously knew Lady Valéry was fishing, although her words proved she didn't know for what. In a lowered tone she said, "No, but such ruthlessness makes him the perfect candidate to find your diary."

"I have no doubt he'll be successful, and I hope"—how to handle this delicate inquiry?— "you're not hurt in the process."

A brief tremor swept Mary, but she gained control immediately. "I will endeavor to keep my person secure."

"When I called for him, I had no idea he would be so attracted to you." That much was true, Lady Valéry comforted herself.

"I acquit you of that," Mary, the innocent, said. "No one could have foreseen any of this."

"I also had no idea you would be equally attracted to him."

Mary blushed swiftly and thoroughly. "I have no designs on your godson, my lady."

"Of course not. Why would you want him? He's a savage with a taste for revenge against the Fairchild clan. And for good reason. Have you ever heard the tale of the Fairchilds and how they destroyed Sebastian's family?"

"No, I haven't."

Mary's polite little voice didn't fool Lady Valéry. The girl wanted to know, but she had practice—too much, in Lady Valéry's opinion—in disguising her emotions.

No wonder Sebastian both attracted and repelled her. Being with him had torn the veil of her composure and she was revealed to him.

"The Durants are one of our oldest noble families. They claim there was a Baron Whitfield on the field of Hastings, although what noble family doesn't?"

"Not the Fairchilds," Mary said, her tone heavy with sarcasm.

"No, the Fairchilds are newly come to the court. But when Sebastian was a boy, they had one thing the Durants did not. They had money."

"My father claimed that money ruined his father."

"Probably," Lady Valéry agreed. "He made enough to buy a title, and after that he thought he could force the world to dance to his tune."

Mary halted and glanced up and down the corridor.

Her discomfort increased visibly, as it always did when darkness threatened. "Have we taken a wrong turn?"

"I believe you are right."

They walked to the next pool of light, a square caused by the combination of candles and firelight from an open bedchamber, and Lady Valéry snapped her fingers at the valet who lurked there. "You! Young man! Tell us where we are."

The valet straightened. "M'lady, you're in the west wing."

Lady Valéry saw Mary glance around. Sebastian's room was in the west wing.

"Could you direct us to the east wing?" Mary sounded pleasant enough, but when the valet stepped forward and the light fell on his face, she shrank back, jerking Lady Valéry's arm.

An older man, suave and well turned out, he stared boldly back at Lady Valéry's protégée. "Are you lost, m'ladies?"

"No!" Mary tried to step back into the shadows.

"I think you are." He spoke well, a servant who had reached the top of his profession. "I think you're very lost."

He spoke with a kind of baneful relish.

"No, we're not lost," Mary repeated.

Lady Valéry had had enough of this nonsense. "I wish to go to the east wing. Direct me now."

The valet responded to her authoritative voice, bowing his head respectfully and saying, "Go forward, take a left. Proceed to the next left, take that. You'll be on the far end of the east wing."

His words followed as they walked away, with Mary huddled close to Lady Valéry's side.

"Do you know him?" Lady Valéry asked.

"What?" Mary seemed oblivious.

"Did he visit us in Scotland? Does he recognize you as my housekeeper?" Lady Valéry sought to alleviate Mary's palpable horror. "I knew it could happen, but I hoped your appearance had changed so greatly no one would recognize you."

"He recognizes me," Mary whispered.

Lady Valéry patted her arm. "Don't worry, dear. I'll send Sebastian to warn him off and offer him money, and if he knows what's good for him, he'll take it. Sebastian's enemies have a nasty way of disappearing. It's those ships of his, you know. They travel all over the world, and the captains aren't particular about whether their passengers really want to come aboard."

Mary turned her head and looked at Lady Valéry. Gradually she seemed to comprehend Lady Valéry's words. She turned even whiter. "No! Don't send Sebastian!"

"Why not, dear? Sebastian wouldn't really hurt him."

"No. Really. I don't want Viscount Whitfield involved." Mary's teeth were even chattering. "Anyway, I don't know that man. I thought I did, but I don't."

Lady Valéry glanced back. The valet watched them, grinning in a most insolent manner.

Oh, she believed Mary. Certainly she did.

Mary's past was a mystery, but Lady Valéry had already planned her future, and nothing, certainly not an upstart valet, could contest her scheme.

In a coaxing voice Mary said, "My lady, you were telling me about Sebastian's feud with the Fairchilds."

So the gel thought she could distract this old woman, did she? Well, Lady Valéry would allow it to seem so for the moment. "Yes, where were we? Ah. The Fairchilds had money, the Durants did not. And the Durants sought to recover a fortune by sinking everything into breeding horses. It is a marginally respectable way to earn money, and Sebastian's father had always had a way with horses."

They turned a corner, and Mary took a deep breath, as if merely being out of that valet's gaze gave her relief. "Did they do well?"

"Very." Lady Valéry rubbed Mary's hand through her glove. "So well that the Fairchilds decided to give horse breeding a try, also. You can imagine the tangle that was! Neighbors, with their fences right together, trying to breed the best horses in England. The old viscount was furious, and Lord Smithwick had the bit in his teeth, so to speak." She chuckled. "Bit in his teeth. Do you comprehend?"

Mary smiled dutifully, but she couldn't fool Lady Valéry. She was still shaken, and the tale that had interested her earlier now held no appeal. "Look," she said. "There are our maids. Our rooms must be down this corridor."

"So they are." Lady Valéry allowed Mary to lead her to her door, then she brushed a kiss on Mary's cheek. "Sleep well, dear. I won't allow anything or anyone to harm you."

Mary touched the place where the kiss had been and stared at her fingers as if she could see visible proof of Lady Valéry's affectionate gesture. Lady Valéry saw the glimmer of tears in her eyes. "Thank you, my lady, but there's no need to disturb yourself about me."

"I'm not disturbed," Lady Valéry answered. *But regardless of what you say, I am going to discover what that valet has to do with you.*

Thankful for the moonless night, Sebastian crept around the outside of Fairchild Manor toward the master chamber windows. He had already tried to walk the halls and simply enter the room, but a maid stood outside the door, and when he'd tried to go in, she'd explained that these were her mistress's chambers. Kindly she'd offered to call a footman to escort him wherever he needed to go. She'd imagined him lost and probably drunk; he let her think so and wandered off.

But he had to get inside. He stared at the stone wall before him and the windows one story over his head, then took the coil of rope off his shoulder. He swung the grappling hook above his head. The rope slithered out, the hook caught on the jutting windowsill with a satisfying thunk, and he thanked God for his early experiences on the docks. He hadn't thought so at the time, but the physical labor he'd done to establish his empire had more than once proved useful.

The rope was just long enough, reaching within four feet of the ground. Yanking on it, he tested the hook's hold, and when he was satisfied, he hoisted himself up. Using hands on the rope and feet against the wall, he climbed until he reached the window. With one hand clutching the rope, he shoved at the window until he had an opening large enough to fit his body through, and crawled inside.

Two maids spoke outside the door. Inside, a fire burned on the hearth, the master bed looked too impressive for Bubb, and the light of the candles showed Sebastian a myriad of hiding places. He moved silently, searching the shelves and drawers for a black leather book.

He found several, his breath catching each time. Was this it? Would he be able to take it and leave with Mary . . . and never see her again?

Funny how that concept gave him no gratification. Indeed, each time he opened one of the books and saw the typeset pages and the name of a London publisher, he was almost pleased.

Then, as he searched the bed table, he found another, filled with handwritten scrawls, and for one moment his hands tightened in anticipation.

But this wasn't his godmother's handwriting, and turning to the fly page, he saw Nora's name penned in blue ink. Disgusted, he tossed it back and finished searching the chamber.

Nothing. Just like the study, only the study held that safe, the likely repository of the diary. Unfortunately, without Mary's safecracking abilities, he could not examine the contents. That perturbed him; he had suddenly developed qualms about using Guinevere Mary Fairchild's skills to their fullest extent. When had he grown so squeamish?

After taking care to leave no trace of his presence within the chamber, he inched out of the window and pulled it shut behind him. With the rope in his hands, he began to lower himself. His feet walked down the wall, taking part of his weight and balancing him, but still his arms ached from the unaccustomed exercise. A man in his late thirties had no business climbing around the outside of a country manor. He should be home in front of a fire, looking at the face of a woman . . .

Mary. Why did his mind call up Mary? Why wouldn't he use her to open that safe? His scruples surely couldn't be caused by an inappropriate attachment. Damn her, she confused him with that facade of sterling propriety which so overlaid the passions of a decade.

He grunted as he descended.

For years she'd done a fine imitation of a woman dedicated to nothing but respectability. Well, he could understand that. Mary undoubtedly felt she had plenty to hide, and no one knew better than he the

lengths one would go to right the wrongs of yester-
year.

There! That was the problem. He felt empathy for
her. He felt he understood her—as if any man could
ever understand a woman. He certainly desired her,
but her blow to his face had caused him to take stock.
If he did as his desires demanded, he would take her
virginity, ruin her reputation—even more than he
already had—and possibly impregnate her, all without any intention to do the honorable thing and wed
her.

Yet when he'd seen her in the ballroom tonight
talking to her too-bloody-handsome cousin, all he
could think of was holding her against all comers, as
if she were a merchant ship and he still a youth
desperate to forge his fortune. Seen as a Fairchild, she
didn't deserve that much regard, but seen as Guinevere Mary, she deserved . . . everything.

His hands tightened and slipped at the frayed end
of the rope, and he realized with surprise he had
reached the ground. He hadn't thought he'd climbed
down far enough, and that was something else he
could blame on Mary. He wasn't paying attention,
and all because she had confused him. Lowering his
feet, he expected to find solid earth.

It wasn't there.

As he registered the fact he was still much too high
on the house, two hands grabbed him from below and
jerked. He lost his grip and hit the ground flat on his
back. Before he could do more than gasp for air, a
meaty fist hauled him up by the shirt. He swung out

instinctively and felt a solid crack as his fist made contact with bone.

His assailant grunted, loosened his grip, and while Sebastian hung unbalanced, the attacker struck him in the nose.

This wasn't like the blow from Mary. This man was a fighter; he knew exactly what he was doing. As Sebastian struggled to stand, the assailant punched him in the chin. Sebastian's head snapped back. He collided with the wall as the attacker swung him up against it. A well-muscled arm leaned against Sebastian's windpipe. A face, hidden by a scarf and by darkness, leaned close to his.

Slowly, in a hoarse voice, the man said, "If you hurt her again, I'll kill you."

Sebastian could scarcely speak for the blood that flowed from his nose. "What . . . ?"

The attacker drew back his fist and rammed it into Sebastian's stomach.

"Don't play stupid with me. Everyone in Sussex has heard how you treated her."

The arm across his throat tightened until Sebastian gagged.

"Mary Fairchild is not for you. Leave her alone."

Chapter 14

A housekeeper moves silently about her duties.

Mary straightened her dark gown, adjusted the mobcap covering her springy curls, then pushed open the kitchen door. Most of the Fairchild servants sat huddled around the fire or catching a hasty bite at the long-scrubbed table. Nostalgia struck her when she heard the low buzz of conversation; just so had her own dear attendants sounded in Scotland. The scents of toast and fried rashers wafted toward her as she made her way to the empty chair. As she hoped, no one paid the slightest attention to her.

No one except Mrs. Baggott.

Mary expected no less. The meals were exquisite, the party last night had run smoothly, the manor shone from top to bottom. Mrs. Baggott was a premier housekeeper, and a premier housekeeper knew every person who walked through her domain. She stood close to the stove where pots of oatmeal bubbled and watched Mary now with narrowed eyes. Obviously she couldn't quite place her, but Mary knew that state of blessed anonymity wouldn't last long, so she smiled.

Mrs. Baggott lurched as recognition struck, then she bustled forward. "Miss Fairchild! What's wrong that you're awake so early?"

"Nothing is wrong." Mary laid a hand on Mrs. Baggott's arm. "I'm hungry, so I came to breakfast."

Never had Mary seen appalled suspicion so hastily disguised. Mrs. Baggott didn't believe her, but she wouldn't insult her by saying so. Instead she smiled, the wrinkles on her craggy face splitting into thin snips of courtesy, and said, "Please, take a seat in the dining room, Miss Fairchild, and I'll attend to your needs personally."

"No, no." Mary walked to the table and pulled up a chair. "I don't want to put you out. I'll just sit here."

The servants backed away as if she were a vampire in search of blood, but Mary didn't care. She'd escaped into her chamber last night staggering from the shock of seeing that valet in the corridor. She'd tried to convince herself he wasn't really who she thought he was, and when that failed, she'd curled herself around the pillow that carried Sebastian's scent and prayed.

But the habit of rising with the dawn stood her in good stead. She woke before the first rays of the sun and knew what she had to do. She had to use the skills she'd learned as a housekeeper to find that diary and steal it back. It was the only way to escape this purgatory before it became her prison.

Mary smiled around at her unwilling audience briefly, until Mrs. Baggott dismissed the servants with a snap of her fingers. "The dining room is so much more comfortable, Miss Fairchild, but if you insist, you can, of course, eat here."

"Thank you, Mrs. Baggott. I always ate breakfast in the kitchen of Lady Valéry's home in Scotland."

The servants glanced among each other, clearly wondering if she'd run mad.

Determinedly cheerful, Mary continued, "It's a bit of a backwater there, you understand, but this is a pleasant habit I would be loath to abandon."

Silent, Mrs. Baggott placed a heaping plate of golden eggs, deviled kidneys, and crumpets with marmalade in front of her. Mary took a bite of the kippers. "The housekeeper in Scotland always kept me company, too."

"Well." Mrs. Baggott carried two teacups to the table and sat down, her chair creaking. "I'm glad we can make you feel at home."

Mary left the kitchen that morning alight with a sense of triumph. Mrs. Baggott had sat with her for the whole breakfast, and they'd much in common. Not that Mary told her she had been a housekeeper. Oh, no. On that subject, she took Ian's advice and kept silent. But Mrs. Baggott assumed that Mary had been the mistress of a large household, and Mary let her assume what she wished.

After asking for directions from a servant only once, she slipped back into her bedchamber. Looking worried and tapping her foot, Jill swung around as Mary shut the door behind herself.

"Miss Fairchild! What are you doing out at such an hour?" Jill ran her astonished gaze over Mary's outfit. "And dressed in such a garb!"

"I just went for a walk," Mary said soothingly.

"Without me? Unchaperoned?" Jill bustled toward Mary. "Miss Fairchild, you know better. What would the gentry say?"

"Nothing, if you don't tell them." Mary looked at the handful of papers Jill held. "What are those?"

"Love letters, I suppose, from your suitors. The servants have been slipping them under the door. That's what woke me." Jill handed over the stiff, sealed sheets. "'Tis the only reason I knew you were gone."

"Yes, I had hoped you'd sleep. You were up late waiting for me last night." Mary seated herself in a comfortable chair and looked through the notes. All the sealing wax had impressions on them. All except one. She put it aside for last.

"Sleep through your absence? Why would I want to? Miss Fairchild, don't you realize your position here? You're the heiress. One of these men could come along, bop you on the head, and carry you off ere anyone knew it."

Aggass, Mary thought, noting the design pressed in the wax on the first note. "I think we can acquit all of these gentlemen of being early risers," she said to Jill.

"For a fortune, any one of them would get up early of a morning. They'd kidnap you, and where would I be, I ask you? Where would I be?"

"With a new mistress?" Mary guessed.

"Not likely." Jill snorted. "After Lady Valéry had taken my guts for garters, your Viscount Whitfield would take his turn. There wouldn't be enough of me left to serve another."

Dear Miss Fairchild,

I toss and turn, unable to sleep for want of a smile from your sweet lips . . .

Indigestion, Mary diagnosed, and opened the one from Mr. Mouatt. "Lady Valéry would be unpleasant, but I doubt that she'd kill you."

"You didn't mention Viscount Whitfield," Jill said shrewdly. "And, mistress, don't you see? All any of the men need to do is catch you and drag you away to have his way with you, and you'll have to marry him."

The generous spirit who lives in you, Miss Fairchild, must surely see that I languish for your love . . .

"Dear, that's just not likely." These notes were all nonsense, and Mary began to suspect they had been written, not by the suitors themselves, but by their secretaries. "Who would even realize I was away from my bedchamber?"

"Promise me you won't go again."

"I can't make that promise."

"Then I'll go with you."

"No! Jill, I was a housekeeper, and have walked the corridors alone all those many years. More than once some gentleman saw an opportunity for fun, and believe me, I know how to scream loudly and use whatever is available in way of a weapon." She opened the last note, the one without a seal in the wax. Looking up, she smiled at Jill, then saw the girl was wringing her hands in distress, and felt contrition. Her maid was really worried. "Truly, Jill, all will be well. I feel it."

Raising the paper, she read the words before her, and realized that never had she been so wrong.

It held only one word.

Murderess.

There she went again.

Dressed in coarse, dark clothing, Mary had crept downstairs early every morning for the past three days. She had glanced behind her occasionally, as if she were guilty, or as if she feared something, but always she disappeared into the kitchen. Ian would have never noticed, except that he'd been getting nowhere in his seduction of her.

He hated that. A sense of failure nagged at him, one made more troublesome by the fact he liked the woman. He would have thought he was immune to any Fairchild lady, regardless of her looks or charm.

Mary was different. She admired him. She didn't seem to see the darkness that plagued his soul, and paid no attention to the sniggering caused by his illegitimacy. She was just what she had accused him of being—nice—and he almost hated himself for plotting her downfall.

That guilt had caused him to drink so much the first night of the house party that he'd fallen asleep on one of the sofas in the great hall. He didn't know why he'd woken when she tiptoed past; he liked to imagine it was the bond between their souls.

He used to think that, until he saw her with that wretch Whitfield.

She loved Whitfield. Ian didn't think she knew it, but her emotions, unrealized and unacknowledged, made Ian's scheme to wed her all the more nefarious. Still, he had to follow through.

So he followed Mary every morning and watched her disappear into the kitchen, and he plotted. Should he kidnap her? Should he entice her? Should he ''inadvertently'' ruin her reputation?

Ah, but Whitfield had already done that, and that irked him. Ian was no different from any other man. He would like to have a woman who adored him, but Mary adored Whitfield. He would like to have a woman untouched by a man, but Mary had been touched, and more, by Whitfield. He would like to have a woman with money . . . ah, money.

Moving away from the kitchen door, Ian waited for that delightful little serving maid to come out. Sally had been easily seduced into doing his bidding, and this morning she would give her first report on Mary's conversation with the housekeeper.

Whitfield might have won her favor, but he wouldn't get the money. Not if Ian had anything to say about it.

Daisy's bedchamber.

Sebastian put his hand on the knob and stared down at it grimly. Another room. Another search. And, he feared, another failure to find Lady Valéry's diary.

Hell, he already knew where it was. It had to be in that safe in Bubb's study. So he'd tried opening the safe again. After all, Mary had thought she might be able to do it, and surely he was as accomplished as any woman. Instead, the lock had held fast, and here he was, getting ready to search another bedchamber in the west wing.

Turning the knob, he strolled in as if he owned the place. His experience—and he'd had a lot of it lately—proved that walking boldly was more effective than sneaking. Certainly a lordly attitude made explaining himself to the chambermaids less imperative.

Fortunately for him, the sun's fading rays showed him that this room seemed uninhabited. He called, "Excuse me? Are you here?" in a falsely impatient tone, but nothing stirred. The bed's pink ruffled curtains were drawn and petticoats were scattered about the floor. It appeared Daisy's maid had sneaked off rather than pick up.

Good luck for a change, and about time.

He normally investigated the bookcase first, but there wasn't one. Moving to the bedside table, he fumbled with the half-opened drawer instead. Brushes laden with long blond hair lay scattered, and he shoved them aside with distaste as he rummaged for the diary.

Nothing.

Rubbing his aching jaw, he glanced toward the dresser. Fringed shawls and lace handkerchiefs spilled out of it in such disarray, the drawers seemed to have burped.

God, he was sick of this endless pawing through others' belongings. Not that some of his finds hadn't been interesting. Uncle Burgess kept a large store of laudanum hidden in the back of his closet. Bubb's twins stole freely from the guests and sequestered their ill-gotten gains in an attic room. The eldest daughter smoked opium. Wilda kept a young man's lock of hair pressed between the pages of her journal. Ian . . . He'd discovered nothing about Ian. Ian lived in a room furnished so starkly, Sebastian thought he'd entered the wrong chamber. But no, the man had either been refused the luxuries so esteemed by the rest of the family, or he deliberately lived like an illegitimate son to remind himself of his place.

If only Sebastian could believe he had been re-fused. But seeing Ian, his restraint, the way he watched the others so hungrily, Sebastian knew the man was dangerous.

And Sebastian wondered if Ian had been the fiend who'd beaten him so severely. He didn't think so. He'd made contact with his attacker's face, he knew he had, but Ian showed no signs of bruising.

No one at the party showed any signs of bruising—except him.

He normally healed quickly, but the swelling from Mary's blows had just gone down when he'd been jerked off that rope and been thrashed again. In the space of three days, accomplished street fighter Sebastian Durant had been battered by a woman and a . . . a stranger.

A stranger who had warned him away from Mary. And except for brief, respectful contacts, Sebastian had obeyed.

But it irked him. God, how it irked him.

With a sigh, he turned away from the bedside—and felt something crawl up his shoulder. He grabbed at it, whatever it was, and found himself in possession of wiggling fingers.

He looked at them in horror. He held a female's hand.

Its partner caressed the other side of his neck. "Lord Whitfield, you surprise me. I'm afraid I'm not . . . dressed."

Aghast, he turned toward the bed. Daisy peeked out from the pink curtains, and she was right. She wasn't dressed. That filmy, silky thing she had draped over her could scarcely be considered clothing.

"Excuse me!" He tried to vault away, but somehow her arms had become entwined around him. "I didn't realize . . ."

"That I was here? But what were you doing?" Her eyes widened and her lips parted, and she smelled of tobacco.

He hated tobacco.

"Were you looking for a memento of me?" she cooed.

Of course not, you stupid cow, he wanted to snap.

But he didn't. He was in trouble here, more trouble than when he'd dangled from the rope, and he had to extricate himself as quickly as possible. "You have attracted my attention." It was only a partial lie. She had been *trying* to attract his attention.

She lowered her eyelids. "I didn't know that you'd noticed."

"Noticed? I noticed." He tried to edge away. Her nails bit into his neck. "A man would be hard-pressed not to notice you." *And run as if the hounds of hell were after him.*

"Oh, Lord Whitfield." Her red mouth puckered, her eyes slid shut, and she gave the impression of a woman on the verge of rapture. "You've made me so happy."

"Good. Well. I'd best leave now." He jerked away, sure that she'd marked him with those talons of hers. Not that he needed more marks.

"Shall I tell my father?"

"Tell him what?"

"That you've expressed an . . . interest." Seemingly on its own, one of her breasts popped free of its confinement.

"I'm betrothed to your cousin." Sprinting toward the door, he jerked it open. "Mustn't betray her."

"But, darling . . ."

Daisy's reproachful voice echoed in his mind as he hustled down the corridor. He knew damn well what that woman wanted from him, and it wasn't his manly form or his nonexistent repartee. It was his fortune. A Fairchild woman could easily impersonate a shattered innocent to get her hands on so much money.

So he needed an alibi. He needed one now.

He could go to the boxing room where the young bucks practiced knocking each other senseless. Unfortunately, there he would be forced to endure teasing about the beatings he had endured at Mary's hands.

Of course, the last beating hadn't been administered by *her* fists, but the guests thought otherwise. They had loudly speculated that he'd trifled with Mary again and come out the worse for it.

He didn't deny it, mostly because the ton wouldn't have believed him, but also because the constantly circling flock of buzzardlike suitors maintained a respectful distance from Mary's fists. No other man wished to be taunted that a woman had beaten him up.

Hell, Sebastian didn't want to be taunted. He didn't even want to care, but he did. These people who thought so much of themselves should be inconsequential to him. But in the years before he'd made his fortune, he'd been mocked often, and found himself unable to take their sniggering lightly.

So he couldn't go to the boxing room, and he refused to run the gauntlet of laughter in the dining room where the meal was set up.

That left the game room. The gamblers were always so deep in their cards—and their cups—they wouldn't note the time of his arrival, and they would provide a plausible alibi in case . . . well, in case that Daisy sought to bag him tonight.

Satisfied with his destination, he strode along the corridor. All the unmarried women were housed in the west wing, he'd discovered. Yet Mary's bedchamber was the only one he wanted to enter. He wanted to enter it so badly, he had consciously avoided it— partly because of his fear of ambush, but mostly because she made him insane. She had him by the curly hairs, and she acted as if she didn't know it. Worse, she acted as if she didn't care.

He walked to her door and placed his hand on it. He felt the vibrations of her presence, and he knew she was inside. He'd seen her shudder as she walked into a gathering. He'd seen her glancing over her shoulder as if she expected to be stabbed in the back. He'd seen her grow more and more uneasy as the days wore on.

She *didn't* know that he hated to see her flirting with other men, or that he found comfort in the fact she did it poorly. Yet no one seemed to be immune to her charms. Even the merchant, Mr. Everett Brindley, seemed captivated by her, and from previous business dealings, Sebastian could have sworn he was a cold fish, interested only in money and politics.

Bringing Mary should have simplified the task Sebastian had set himself. He thought that using her as a distraction would grant him the time he needed to find his godmother's diary, secure it, and save the country—and his business—from revolution.

Instead, her presence had complicated every aspect of his life, and now his encounter with Daisy forced him to reach a reluctant conclusion. He would have to let Mary open the safe.

Well, why not? Every day they stayed, he trusted her more. Every day he liked her more. Every day he marveled at her intelligence, at her beauty . . . at her allure.

And he wouldn't find her alluring if he didn't trust her.

His breath quickened and his heart beat faster.

He was almost dizzy at such a revelation. Then reality struck him like a glove. He snickered at himself. He was a shipping baron. He'd earned his fortune through a combination of guts and sharp intelligence, and he knew better than any man there was no correlation between allure and trust. It was Old Horning that found Mary alluring. But his mind, his heart, found her trustworthy.

He stroked the painted panel as he might stroke her skin.

After they were away from this tomb of festering corruption, he might call on her, and then they might—

But he didn't want to see Mary occasionally. He wanted her with him all the time, and he wanted to take her to bed. Only to bed. And she was a Fairchild, he was a Durant, and he'd be betraying his parents with every fond caress.

Funny, that he could have easily fornicated with Mary when he believed her to be without conscience, but when she proved to be so much more, he faced a moral dilemma. He almost wished she would show her Fairchild traits so he could take her as he longed to.

But the only place he would take her was down to Bubb's study, early tomorrow morning, to open the safe. And after they'd returned the diary to Lady Valéry, he'd take Mary back to her chamber and he'd tell her . . . he'd tell her . . .

The door across the hall snapped open and Uncle Leslie stumbled out under the impetus of a slippered foot.

"You are a disgusting creature," Lady Valéry's voice said from the inside of her chamber. "You have neither the dubious charm nor the physical attributes of your brothers, and I do not know why you would think me desperate enough to welcome you into my bed. Don't come back."

The door shut with a slam, and Leslie glanced up and down the hall. When he spotted Sebastian, his rouged cheeks reddened more, and he blustered, "She's a woman of passion, your godmother."

Sebastian allowed his mouth to curl in one of his

most effective sneers. "It seems she has conceived a heated one for you."

Leslie moved his plate of ivory teeth within his mouth. Without a doubt, he hated Sebastian, and hated more that his humiliation had been witnessed. But he wasn't a bright man, and in lieu of a brilliant retort, he fell back on the old scandal. "My niece is a woman of a passionate nature, too. You'd best guard her stable carefully, or the newest Whitfield mare will throw a piebald colt."

Mary wouldn't betray Sebastian. Sebastian trusted her.

Still he removed his hand from her door. "Thank you for your advice, old man. I find treachery remarkably easy to detect now. The Fairchilds taught me that lesson."

Sebastian followed as Leslie limped down the hall, bruised from Lady Valéry's well-aimed kick. "What my brothers and I taught you was nothing compared to the treachery of a Fairchild woman. Why, our mother was the most heartless fiend ever born. My brothers and I suckled perfidy from her breast, and with each succeeding generation the Fairchild women built on her reputation." He grinned evilly at Sebastian. "There's no use thinking your little Guinevere is any different. It's bred in the bone, man. Even as she betrays you in my son's bed, she's laughing at you."

Sebastian's gut cramped. He knew what Leslie was doing. Lady Valéry had made him a laughingstock, and like a little boy, he jeered at Sebastian to make himself feel better. But Sebastian *had* been a little boy when the Fairchilds had ruined his family.

Leslie grinned. "Left you without a word for your glib little tongue to say? Poor boy. Poor little Sebastian."

A tableau from that time remained frozen in Sebastian's brain. His youthful bewilderment as the creditors threw his family from their home. His mother dabbing at her reddened eyes, and the hiccup of her suppressed sob. His father, standing away from them, remote as he had never been before and as he would remain until his death.

This man, this Leslie Fairchild, sitting on a finely bred horse and smirking as he witnessed their humiliation.

Now, coldly, Sebastian used the information he'd gleaned in his futile search through Leslie's bedchamber. "No one laughs at me like they laugh at an old man who dreams of inhabiting a woman's body."

"That?" Leslie waved an airy hand back at Lady Valéry's door. "No one would believe I really wanted her."

"I wasn't talking about your futile attempt to seduce my godmother." Sebastian stopped and let Leslie hobble a little farther along the corridor. "I mean that you actually want to *be* a woman. The guests at your party would be quite entertained by your habit of wearing bosom extenders in the privacy of your chamber."

Leslie staggered to a halt.

"And think how the *ton* would laugh if they were

informed of your cherished habit of dressing in skirts and forcing the maids to dance with you.''

''Quiet!'' Leslie quivered, but he didn't turn around. ''It's not true, but I suppose you will slander me unless I . . . pay your price.''

''I don't have a price,'' Sebastian answered. ''I'm too rich to have a price. And there's your predicament, Leslie.''

Not waiting to see the results of his intimidation, he walked the other direction.

''She knows about the diary,'' Leslie called softly.

Sebastian's feet suddenly tangled, and he stumbled to a halt.

''She's always known where it is.''

Sebastian turned and started toward Leslie, but at the sight of his face, Leslie seemed to have discovered an elixer of youth, for he turned and fled down the corridor. Sebastian skidded to a stop and tried to calm his racing heart.

The diary. Someone had admitted to knowing about the diary. He'd begun to worry that he had made a fatal mistake, that the diary was not here. But Leslie knew about it, and Leslie claimed that Mary . . .

Turning once more, Sebastian walked past Mary's door without a glance. Leslie claimed that Mary knew. He said she and Ian were lovers, laughing at Sebastian as he fruitlessly searched the manor, risking life and limb, getting himself beaten by unknown assailants. And all for a diary that Mary . . . had stolen? That was what he'd first suspected in Scotland, but her innocent manner and her seeming sincerity, coupled with Lady Valéry's assurances, had convinced him otherwise. Now Leslie said . . . But Sebastian knew better than to believe a Fairchild.

But if two Fairchilds told two tales, which Fairchild should he believe?

He scolded himself. This was stupid. Of course he trusted Mary. Nothing, *nothing* Leslie said could change that.

Sebastian found he had clenched his teeth, and made a conscious effort to relax.

He *did* trust Mary. He *would* enlist her help in opening the safe.

And God help her if she betrayed him.

Chapter 15

"Ah, you're a beauty, too good for the likes of this place." Ian leaned forward earnestly and spoke with all the conviction of a lover.

The young filly to whom he spoke lowered her eyes flirtatiously.

"Let me take you away. We'll run through the moonlight together, and we'll never come back." Lifting the bottle of brandy he held in one hand, he drank until his stomach burned. When he lowered the bottle, he found she was watching him reproachfully. "Yes, yes, I know. We would have to come back. Me, to ruin a good woman's reputation, and you"—he sneered, a truly nasty full-bodied sneer that made him feel comfortably superior—"you for your feed. You females are all alike. Only interested in what money can buy. A good saddle, a comfortable stall." He gestured around at the Fairchilds' horse stable, then glared at the mare before him. "And a handful of

213

oats when you want them. That's all any of you care about.''

The mare tilted her head as if to ask what was wrong with that.

''You jade. Well, to hell with you, then.'' He picked up the lantern off the post and staggered away. Then he backed up and leaned over the gate into the stall, and made his final pronouncement. ''To hell with all women. They're more trouble than they're worth.''

The mare made her opinion of that clear with one moist exhalation, and he jumped backward and wiped at his face with his sleeve. Brandy sloshed onto his elegant velvet waistcoat, and he stared, dumbstruck, at the dark stain.

''Now see what you've done,'' he said. ''You've made me spill my gargle. But there's more.'' He leaned down and searched the packed-earth floor until he saw the second, still-corked bottle sitting where he'd left it. ''I suppose you're wondering how I will pick it up, with a lantern in one hand and a bottle in the other. But you see, that is the marvel of having fingers.'' Carefully he retrieved the bottle by its neck, then showed the disinterested horse. ''Don't you wish you had some?''

She didn't reply, and he nodded triumphantly. ''Ha! Got you there.''

The two bottles clinked together as he continued down the aisle between the stalls, and the lantern cast flecks of light around the stable. He passed through the entrance into the area where the stallions were kept, and the great, muscled creatures whispered to him as he walked, acknowledging his superiority in the quiet way of well-trained animals. The lead stallion, the one who had established domination over all the other males, dipped his head, and Ian returned the salute. "It's a full moon tonight," he said to Quick. "Don't you feel the pull? Don't you want to run and run until you find the end of the earth?"

Quick nodded in full, graceful motions.

"Me, too." Ian lifted one bottle. "But I drink instead. There's no such comfort as that for you."

"And best not be, either," a crisp voice said from inside the stall.

Ian stared hard at the stallion, then relaxed when a blond head slowly rose from the dimness. "I thought it was Quick speaking," he confessed with a laugh. Then laughter died as he lifted the lantern and the blond man stepped into the light. "B'God, it's another Fairchild bastard!"

The young man took a hasty step forward and made to grab Ian's coat, but Quick moved smoothly and knocked him into the wall. Not meanly, so Ian knew the young man was favored among the animals, but inexorably, so that Ian would not be hurt.

"I meant no harm," Ian protested while the young man shoved at the horse. "I'm one of the Fairchild bastards, too. I just thought we knew of them all."

"Come on, old man, let me by. I'll not beat him." The young man spoke to the stallion as an equal, and

Quick stepped away. Moving toward the front of the stall, he leaned his arms over the door and asked, "What makes you think I'm a Fairchild?"

Ian laughed again. "Your face. Your hair. Your size, your charm . . . At least, I assume you have charm. I've never met a Fairchild who doesn't."

The young man stared solemnly, then a slow grin transformed his dour countenance. "Aye, I'm at least as charming as you."

A touch of Scottish, Ian thought. But well spoken and obviously educated. Interesting. Where had dear Leslie been wandering now? Or was it Burgess? Or . . . "Do you know who your father is?"

The young man looked surprised. "Of course."

"So do I." Ian lifted the bottles. "Let's have another drink."

The young man opened the gate, then latched it behind him. "I haven't had one yet."

Ian handed him the untouched bottle and waited while the young man uncorked it and took a long pull. He didn't cough, but his eyes watered a bit, and he said, "Fine stuff."

"The best. Fairchilds only drink the best."

"Why don't you give me that?" The young man took the lantern from Ian's unresisting hand. "A fire in the stable is an ugly thing."

"And where should we drink our fine gargle?" Ian asked.

The young man considered Ian carefully. He seemed unsure of how to respond to his new relative, but finally he said, "I have a place that's private where we can . . . talk."

Ian followed him toward the back of the stable. "I'm Ian. And you are . . . ?"

"Had . . . Haley."

"Good to meet you . . . Hadd Haley." Ian grinned at him, and Hadd stared stoically back. "Keeping yourself a secret, are you? That's all very well, but your face'll betray you soon enough. Looks like it must have betrayed you to the stable hands."

"Why do you say that?"

"You've got bruises." Ian pointed at the black eyes Hadd sported. "Been fighting to quiet the whispering, have you? It'll never work." He touched his chest with his thumb. "*I* know."

"I'll remember," Hadd said.

"So I have a new brother. Or is it cousin?"

"Cousin, I would think. We could go up to the loft, but I don't know if you could negotiate the stairs."

Ian shook his head in rueful acknowledgement of his own incapacity.

"So we'll stay here." Hadd gestured to the bay where clean straw was stacked and waiting to be distributed after the stalls were mucked out in the morning.

"Very good." Ian flung himself onto a particularly thick layer, then writhed as the straw stuck him through his trousers. "How do the horses sleep on this stuff?"

"They don't lie down, usually." Hadd hung the

lantern on a hook and settled more sedately. He studied Ian with his blue Fairchild eyes until Ian wanted to squirm.

Instead, he said, "Drink. It'll ease my shock at finding a cousin working in the stable."

"Ease your shock, will it?" Hadd's solemn face crinkled in a little smile, and he tilted the bottle as instructed.

"I take it you haven't gone up to the manor and announced yourself?"

"No, and I'll thank you not to, either."

Hadd took the situation too seriously, much more seriously than any of the uncles would. But he would find that out on his own soon enough, so Ian lifted his hand, palm out. "I have enough problems with the cousins already living in the manor. I'll leave you to find your own way."

Hadd watched Ian steadily. "What are you doing in the stable?"

"It's a fine place to get bosky." Ian felt the need to clarify. "More bosky. Really, really, stinking bosky. The company is good." Ian waved toward the line of stalls, then dipped his bottle toward Hadd. "I've got relatives here. And I don't have to see my lovely object of desire. I don't have to hear her chirpy little voice whispering how much she admires me, and I sure as hell don't have to pretend I have only her best interests at heart."

"Don't you?"

Ian laughed a little too long. "Don't be stupid. Not

her best interests. I don't love her. Not *love*." He gave
the word its most lascivious intonation. "I just want
her money." He glared at Hadd as if the young man
had chided him. "And what's wrong with that?"

"Nothing, I suppose." Hadd sounded mild. "I
understand that's the way society chooses their
mates."

"That's right. I am just as evil as the rest of the
Fairchilds, damn it!" Ian tried to maintain his bellig-
erence, but it slipped when he mumbled, "I just don't
revel in it like the others do."

"I suppose that makes you admirable."

"Oh, *please*. As if suffering agonies at the thought
of seducing a woman makes me better than the rest of
that leprous family." Too late, Ian noted the dry note
Hadd had injected into his voice. "You're laughing at
me."

"Perhaps." Hadd stretched out his long legs and
crossed them at the ankles.

"You haven't lived with them like I have. Lucky,
lucky . . ." Ian forgot his train of thought as he
noticed the bits of hay that clung to his waistcoat,
particularly in one oval spot. He brushed at it and
realized it was wet, and wondered who had drenched
him. Unbuttoning his waistcoat, he lifted the wet
place away from his chest. "What was I saying?"

"That you're courting a young lady for her
money."

The situation with Mary came rushing back so
swiftly, Ian wondered how he could have ever forgot-

ten. "Every time she smiles at me, every time she dances with me, every time she laughs with me, I almost confess and beg forgiveness."

Hadd took another drink. "You could."

"Don't be ridiculous. I can't turn back now! This was all my idea. The first time anyone in the family admired me." *Where had that thought come from?* "But if I don't follow through, I'll be ostracized. Not that I care what Fairchilds think—with their brains, I'm not even sure you could call it thinking—but I've been with them too long. They've corrupted me." They had. It had taken years for him to seek inside himself and find the depths of immorality the other Fairchilds sported so easily, but he understood the appeal of such wickedness now. "One gentlewoman who believes me good isn't enough to change me back."

"If courting this one bothers you so much, couldn't you find another heiress?" Hadd asked curiously.

"There weren't but four heiresses invited to the house party," Ian informed him. "And the others have been kept well away from me—Fairchild reputation, y'know, coupled with that pesky illegitimacy. No, there's only the one heiress for me."

"Too bad." Hadd seemed amused rather than perturbed.

Ian steadied his shaking hand and tilted the bottle, grimacing as the glass clinked against his teeth. Lowering it, he wiped the edges of his mouth with his ruffled cuff, and said, "I know now to take what I want when I want it, or suffer the consequences. Why are you looking at me like that?"

"Like what?"

"Like you know something I don't. I assure you, I'll go through with this." As he contemplated his situation at Fairchild Manor, his resolve strengthened. "I want no more deprivation. I'm tired of the humiliation. And I am never, never going to depend on Fairchilds again."

"This young lady you're courting." Hadd ran his finger around the rim of the bottle he held. "Are you going to neglect her?"

"No."

"Beat her?"

"No!"

"Move your mistress in the house with her?"

"Certainly not."

"Very well, what's the problem? These society girls, as I understand it, are raised to be bred for their fortune. You say you're just as corrupt as the rest of the Fairchilds, and I'm not a man who views other men with a feminine eye, but I suspect you could make this woman happy with very little effort."

"Of course. I'm a hell of a lover. She should adore me."

"Then what is the problem?"

Ian knew all the circumstances, and he was too drunk not to confess them. "She's in love with another man."

Hadd smiled at the disclosure that so pained Ian. "How do you know that?"

Ian stared. Hadd didn't think her love important. Or else he didn't believe Ian knew what he was talking about. So Ian told the truth. "Didn't you know? I'm the son of a Selkie."

"A Selkie." Hadd sat forward. "Your mother is a seal-lady?"

Surprised, Ian looked at this newest Fairchild. He was younger, cleaner, more honorable than Ian, better in every way, and now . . . more knowledgeable? "How did you know that?" Ian asked.

"I've studied the old legends in Scotland." Hadd's burr strengthened. "But I've never met anyone who claimed to be the descendent of a Selkie."

"I don't claim anything," Ian said flatly. "I am."

Hadd took a long pull from the bottle, acting for the first time like he needed the drink. Pulling a leather bag from his vest pocket, he tossed it to Ian.

Ian caught it, held it, looked inside it. "Rocks?"

"Throw it back." Hadd caught Ian's wild toss. "Where's your mother now?"

"She went back to the sea." And abandoned her son with his father. "They always go back to the sea."

"Transformed into a seal." Hadd scraped a spot on the floor clean, then poured the rocks out. He stared at them, then stared at Ian, then stared at the stones again. "Fascinating. And what effect has that had on you?"

"I miss her." Ian spoke faintly, for the pain had subsided through the years and he barely noticed it anymore.

Hadd didn't notice it at all. Gathering up his rocks, he put them in the bag and slid them back into his vest. "I mean, why has being the son of a Selkie made you know that this girl loves someone else?"

"Oh, that." Ian shrugged with an elaborate lack of concern. "I can see . . . feelings."

"Feelings? Like what?"

The young man gave every evidence of excitement and none of disbelief, so Ian told him. "I see auras. Colors and light around people." He rubbed a hand over his suddenly weary face. "I'm a difficult man to lie to."

"And this young lady—what kind of light do you see around her?"

"There's a halo of golden light that rings her, and it grows and pulsates when the man she loves comes near her." Ian was aware he sounded morose, but he didn't care. He stared at the smooth surface of his ring, and half wondered if Hadden could see how the moonstone lit from within as Ian rubbed it. "I don't see *that* very often. Usually only with couples who have been married a long time. *Happily* married for a long time." Ian watched Hadd, waiting for the first sign of disbelief or amusement. "This gold is a little brighter than that—that's the unrequited passion, I suppose."

"I see." Hadd seemed to think he did. At least he didn't taunt Ian, or laugh at his expense. "But why is she bothering with you if she loves another man?"

"She doesn't realize I'm courting her." Humiliating to admit. "And she doesn't know she loves him."

Chapter 16

Mary woke with a start. Her eyes flew open, and as she had each morning for the last four days, she stared into the gray predawn air and tried to calm the thumping of her heart.

Murderess.

She heard the echo of the word. It followed her from a nightmare, a nightmare filled with valets who pointed and accused, with corpses who rose and stalked, from long walks to a gibbet swinging with nooses.

Murderess.

Rising from the bed, she dressed herself in her dark clothing and tiptoed to the pile of notes that had been slipped under her door during the night. Taking them to the window, she sorted through them until she found the one she sought. The one with the plain blob of sealing wax closing the flap. She already knew what it said.

Murderess.

That was all the rest of them had said. The single word unnerved her more than lengthy accusations.

Oh, she knew who had written those notes. She hadn't seen him again, but she didn't have to. All the valets in her nightmares wore the same smirk and exuded the same menace as the man she'd seen in the corridor that night. He was after her.

With a glance at the cot that held Jill's unmoving form, she unlocked the door. She had asked Mrs. Baggot for the key after she received that first note; she had hoped it would make her sleep more securely, but in vain.

As she prepared to slip out, Jill whispered loudly, "Be careful, Miss Fairchild."

"I will."

Jill showed a marked lack of respect for Mary's good sense. She continually insisted that her mistress was both foolish and foolhardy to wander the halls by herself, and since the first note had arrived, Mary had wondered whether she might not be right.

She walked quietly and quickly to an alcove by a window, broke the seal, and spread open the sheet.

Murderess.

Besseborough's family still offers a reward.

One hundred quid will buy my silence. I'll let you know when and where.

The paper rattled in Mary's shaking hand. A hundred pounds? He might as well have asked for a thousand. She might be an heiress, but she had no money, and no way to get it.

She had to get away from here—*now*.

She rose in a panic and started to race to her room, but the mere act of running jarred her to her senses. She was behaving impetuously, and no good would come of it. If she tried to leave Fairchild Manor, Jill would got straight to Lady Valéry and tell. Lady Valéry would send for Sebastian. Sebastian would stop her and demand an explanation.

Mary leaned against the wall and closed her eyes. She was trapped. She knew it. But the threat of the note made finding Lady Valéry's diary more imperative than ever before. She had to get that diary. She had to get away.

Her resolve strengthened, she calmed herself. Placing the note in her capacious pockets, she walked to the kitchen once more.

The servants glanced up as she walked in, but in the last four days she'd proved herself. Every morning, while they finished their own breakfasts and began the long preparations for the day ahead, she'd been friendly, courteous, and undemanding. They still watched her cautiously, but no longer acted as if she were a cannonball that had landed in their midst. It was time to proceed. It was time to find out who among her relatives had the diary.

Mrs. Baggott poured boiling water into the teapot and came to the table. They both seated themselves, and while Mary poured two cups, she said, "I'm looking for someone to explain my family to me, and I hope you can help. How long have you worked for the Fairchilds?"

Of course, Mary told less than the truth, and Mrs. Baggott was too astute not to have her suspicions. But neither could she comprehend the real reasons for Mary's interest, so she accepted the cup and saucer and said, "Started out here as a scullery maid, Miss Fairchild, when I was eight."

"Oh, my." Mary could scarcely believe her luck. Mrs. Baggott must know every family secret. "It's a rare thing to find a woman who has risen so far."

"Better the head of an ass than the tail of a horse." Mrs. Baggott imparted common servant wisdom. "I'll tell you, it's been nothing but hard work, but when a woman's been given a face like mine, what option does she have but work?"

Mary began to make disbelieving noises, and stopped. Mrs. Baggott didn't want disbelieving noises. She wanted to be taken for what she was—a sharp woman dedicated to her own security. She wouldn't put her post at jeopardy for Mary; she'd made that clear, but she'd relaxed enough to gossip.

"I suppose no one knows my family like you do."

"I'm not bragging, Miss Fairchild, when I say that's the truth."

"Then perhaps you could help me."

Mrs. Baggott made a production out of measuring sugar into her tea. "Perhaps."

"Why are my great-uncles so cruel to me? That Leslie never misses a chance to mock me or correct me or—"

"Mr. Leslie treats you no different than he treats anyone else." The spoon clinked and clinked again against the china cup as Mrs. Baggott vigorously stirred her tea. Lifting her spoon out of her tea, she pointed it at a serving maid who hovered near. "What do you need, Sally?"

The tall, gangly girl mumbled, "Nothing, ma'am."

"Then find something to do or I'll find something for you." Mrs. Baggott watched as Sally slunk away, then wiped the drops of tea off the table. Turning back to Mary, she said, "Your uncle Leslie is a mean old man, he is, and never so happy as when he makes others miserable."

"He's been making you miserable for years?" Mary guessed.

Clink. Clink. "Yes. Him and his brothers." Mrs. Baggott folded her lips tightly, as if she regretted her confidences.

"I thought it was just me! I didn't want to sound peevish, but all of the uncles seem—"

"Cruel? Indifferent? Given to nasty jokes against those unable to hit back?" *Clink. Clink.* The sound had grown louder, but Mrs. Baggott's voice lowered. "You see Emma over there by the stove?"

Mary did, and marveled at the young woman's abilities. She stirred, cut, and ground, and all with one hand. The other had been removed at the wrist. "She does very well."

"She did better when she had them both." *Clink. Clink.* Breakage threatened. "Mr. Leslie got it into his head it would be funny to put a fox trap into his closet, then call one of the chambermaids to do some cleaning for him.''

Mary stared at Emma, then turned her horrified gaze on Mrs. Baggott. "You don't mean . . .''

"He had his laugh, did Mr. Leslie, and that was the result.'' Mrs. Baggott stopped stirring at last and waved her spoon in Emma's direction. "He would have had her turned away—said she complained past the time it was amusing—but I wouldn't have it. I know his secrets, I do, and I had only to tell him so to put him in his place. But he's dangerous when he's thwarted, so I've kept Emma in the kitchen and out of his sight ever since.''

"All my great-uncles are so . . . evil?'' A mixture of shame and loathing drove Mary to ask. Was this the reason she had committed murder so many years ago? Because of her relationship to the abominable Fairchilds?

"None so bad as Mr. Leslie, but about *him*, I could tell you stories . . . which is what makes Lord Whitfield's presence here all the more astonishing to me.'' Mrs. Baggott sipped the well-stirred tea at last. "He must truly adore you, Miss Fairchild, to take you as his betrothed after what those wretches did to him. But that's old news to you.'' Mrs. Baggott smiled, and the bristles of her slight mustache smoothed down.

"Is Bubb like that?'' Mary asked.

"Mr. Bubb?'' Mrs. Baggott released a sharp, breaking laugh. If Mary had been less charitable, she would have called it a cackle. "I beg your pardon, miss, it's Lord Smithwick now, but I forget that with his silly ways. Although isn't he the handsomest thing you ever saw?"

"All the Fairchilds are handsome," Mary said dryly.

"Well, of course they are, miss. *You* are." Mrs. Baggott seemed surprised, as if she'd almost forgotten Mary's background. "But I've had to dismiss maids who fell so deeply in love with him they made themselves a nuisance."

"Does he encourage them?"

"Keeps to Lady Smithwick, he does. And he's a likable sort, kind to the servants even if he can't pay wages half the time."

"The family is in financial straits, then?"

"Ever since old Lord Smithwick left the money to you." Mrs. Baggott obviously relished the notion. "But the new Lord Smithwick is always boasting he has a scheme to keep the family afloat."

"Now?" Mary wrapped her hands around the bowl of the cup and let the warmth seep into her fingers. "I mean, have you heard him say anything lately?"

"Nothing important. Not a fortnight since, he was telling Lady Smithwick he would save the family, but he's nothing but a bag of wind. Lady Smithwick knows that. She just rocked and did her needlework and agreed."

Since the house party began, Mary had seen Nora

acting as hostess, matching up her daughters with the most eligible men, all the while graciously guiding Mary, the newfound Fairchild, through the intricacies of proper behavior. "Lady Smithwick is no fool."

"No, not ever. She used to be one of us, you know." Mrs. Baggott gestured around at the servants, and saw the serving maid standing off to the side, head cocked as if she were listening. "Sally! What do you mean by this?"

Bright spots of color rose in Sally's cheeks. "Ma'am?"

"Go and stir the oatmeal," Mrs. Baggott said sharply. "After I'm done here, I'll start you peeling the onions. Maybe that'll remind you how to work."

Sally curtsied and fled toward the stove.

"I don't understand what's wrong with that girl," Mrs. Baggott confided. "She's usually so responsible. It must be a man."

"It usually is," Mary agreed.

"Look at the sun." Mrs. Baggott started to rise. "I have so much to do!"

"But you were telling me about Lady Smithwick," Mary protested.

"Oh, yes." Mrs. Baggott glanced again at the window, then settled herself in the chair and leaned closer. In a low tone she said, "Lady Smithwick used to be one of *us*. One of the servants."

"Fascinating." Mrs. Baggott couldn't know how fascinating.

"She was a governess at Bramber Court, not far

from here, and Mr. Bubb—excuse me—Lord Smith-wick was a charmer. Well, you can imagine the ending of that tale.''

"No." Mary was fascinated. "Tell me."

Mrs. Baggott glanced behind her. "It's just the same old tale, Miss Fairchild. You know."

"No," Mary insisted. "Really."

Mrs. Baggott shifted uncomfortably. "I can't gossip about Lady Smithwick. I just can't." A restraint that obviously caused her considerable torment. "But I can tell you this. She's been fanatically loyal to Lord Smithwick ever since the wedding." She nodded wisely. "In my opinion, not that anyone ever asks it, if there's one who will save the Fairchilds from themselves, it will be Lady Smithwick."

"But the details . . ." Mary pressed for information.

Mrs. Baggott glanced at the window where the morning sun now beamed brightly. "Look at the light! Here I've been loitering, talking to you, when there's to be a meal set up outdoors in the gazebo." Standing, she curtsied.

"But—but—" Mary sputtered. She wasn't done yet! She hadn't heard everything. Catching Mrs. Baggott's fingers, she pleaded, "Just one more thing. Tell me about my cousins."

Mrs. Baggott looked down at Mary's hand. Lifting it, she examined the back, then turned it over and looked at the palm. "There's not many noble folk who have calluses like this, Miss Fairchild. It occurs to me to wonder where you got them."

Mary wanted to snatch her traitorous hand away. No one else had noticed the marks ten years of housekeeping had worn into her skin, but Mrs. Baggott had experienced eyes.

"Don't fret, Miss Fairchild." Mrs. Baggott patted the well-worked palm. "I had wondered why you woke so early and why you fit in down here so well, and if this gives me an answer, well, I'm good at keeping secrets."

Was she? Courted by a little courtesy on Mary's part, Mrs. Baggott had told most of Lady Smithwick's story readily enough, and tattled on Uncle Leslie with relish. Yes, Mrs. Baggott's indiscretion gave Mary another thing to worry about.

"Your cousins?" Mrs. Baggott swept the two cups off the table and stood with them in her hand. "They'd sell their father's liver for a price. Does that tell you what you wish to know?"

"Yes." Mary stood also. "Unfortunately, it does." It told her that she'd wasted her time. Any one of her family could have stolen that diary.

As she left the kitchen, she could hear Mrs. Baggott giving the dawdling Sally yet another scolding. Stifling a yawn, Mary walked toward her bedchamber. She'd been doing her duty as Sebastian saw it every night, and doing her duty as she saw it every morning. She was worried sick about the threatening notes, and she couldn't begin to imagine how she would get her hands on a hundred pounds. And, she realized as she glanced around her, she was lost. Again.

Funny that she was so good at deceiving and manipulating, but so bad at directions. She'd used Mrs. Baggott, as all Fairchilds used people, and she'd done it effortlessly. It reminded her of the days when she had thought intrigue was exciting, and lying a justifiable method of getting her way.

The specter of Guinevere Fairchild drifted ever closer. When Mary thought about the unrestrained pleasure she'd found in Sebastian's arms—and she thought about it too frequently—she wanted to get as far away from him as she could. At the same time Guinevere whispered, "What's the harm in a little fun after so many years of discipline?"

Mary couldn't run far enough to get away from that voice. It rose inside her every time Sebastian respectfully bowed before her. He hadn't shown one sign of interest in her since the night of the first ball, but inside her Guinevere whispered, "I could make him want me. I could trap him and keep him happy forever."

Guinevere, God rot her, was apparently indestructible.

Perhaps worse was Mary's desire to explain the circumstances of the murder. Sebastian was a sensible man. He'd understand. Then she could tell him about the extortion that terrorized her, and he would take care of everything.

Closing her eyes, she shook her head. How selfish of her to want not only Sebastian's compassion, but his protection.

"Mary." A male voice spoke behind her. "You came to see me."

She jumped and swung around. In the protection of an open doorway, a menacing form stood silhouetted. Alarm shuddered through her for one brief moment. Was it one of the aristocrats who would use this opportunity to discredit her? Worse, was it the treacherous valet?

Then the man moved toward her, and she recognized him. Relief flowed through her. Stepping forward, she took his hands. "Ian! I have been blessed in my cousin once more. Won't you direct me to the west wing? I'm abashed to say I'm lost."

She smiled up at him, this nice cousin of hers, but for once, he didn't smile back. He just stood, head cocked, and watched her with all the astringency of seawater.

"Ian?"

"I thought I told you not to let anyone know about your housekeeping."

"I haven't told anyone," she protested.

Freeing his hand, he jerked the mobcap from her head and held it in front of her face. "This is as good as a confessional. And your hair!" He started snatching pins out of the bun at the back. "What a monstrous coiffure for one of the devastating Fairchilds."

For a moment she didn't understand why he was acting so brusquely. Then she realized—he was teasing her. Just so had Hadden behaved when they were younger and more carefree. With a light laugh, she grabbed his wrist. "Stop! You'll make me look like a serving maid coming back from an assignation in the stables."

"Yes." He stared at her with those big brown eyes and dropped the pins on the floor. "Better. But there's still this."

Putting his hands on her waist, he pulled her toward him. She didn't struggle immediately, because she didn't comprehend immediately. When he put his lips on hers, she yanked her head away. "Ian, what do you think you're doing?" In her tone, she heard the echo of her housekeeping authority.

"Shh." He wrapped one arm around her. "I'm debauching you."

He kissed her again. It should have been a nice kiss, she supposed, coming from a nice man, but he didn't know what he was doing. He fumbled with the buttons at the front of her gown, and she heard the pops as thread broke. He made stupid little noises in the back of his throat—they reminded her of a whimpering puppy—and he ground his lips on hers too roughly.

She bit his tongue to get his attention.

He jerked back, hand over his own mouth this time, and his outraged expression made her sputter with condescending laughter. "Well, really, Ian, what did you expect? I'm your cousin!"

He brought his hand down and stared at it. "Blood. You drew blood."

"And likely to do it again if you don't release me."

This time she didn't use her housekeeperly tone. This time she used her sharpest big-sister tone, and he dropped his hands away so quickly, she might have announced she had the galloping clap.

Exasperated, she put her hands on her hips. "What is wrong with you?"

"Nothing." His face turned a dull red, and he mumbled just like Hadden when he was hiding something.

"Your sanity seemed intact last night, so I can't believe you've run mad. Are you ill?"

"No."

He tried to wiggle away from her, but she placed her palm flat on his forehead. "You *are* a little warm."

"I'm well." He was still mumbling, and he wouldn't meet her eyes.

"You go to bed right now. I'll send Jill down to the kitchen to order you a posset. You drink it and sleep, and see if you don't feel better when you wake." She shook her head. "You young men are always trying to push your endurance to the limits."

Ian straightened. "I'm older than you are!"

"Then act like it!" She seized her mobcap off the floor. "Now, how do I get to the west wing?"

He couldn't wait to tell her, and she couldn't wait to go. As she strode toward her room, she vacillated between wanting to box Ian's ears and demanding just what he thought he was doing.

Every man who'd stuck his nose into her business lately—and barring this brief event, that man had been Sebastian—every man had been demanding something. Something like loyalty. Honor. Integrity.

Or else he'd been intent on teaching her something. Desire. Passion. Emotion. Any kind of emotion.

Well, Mary had taught herself loyalty, honor, and integrity in the past ten years, and no one had had to teach her emotion. She was Guinevere Fairchild, too, and Guinevere understood emotion in a way that cold, imperious Sebastian could never comprehend.

Right now, emotion roiled through her. Frustration at not discovering the diary thief. Disdain for Ian's audacity in thinking he could use her as a substitute because he'd failed in some romantic tryst. And fury at Sebastian because . . . because he was Sebastian.

"Miss Fairchild." Jill waved frantically at her from an open door.

Mary marched toward her. "Is this my chamber?"

"Yes, but I have to tell you—" Jill pointed inside, but when she got a good look at Mary, her eyes bulged. "Miss Fairchild, what happened to you?"

"What do you mean?"

"Your hair's all down. Your dress is all jumbly." Jill flicked a button and it fell off and rolled away. Now *she* sounded like the big sister. "Your lips . . . they're swollen!" She put her hands on her hips. "Some man tried to force his attentions on you, didn't he? I *told* you not to wander the halls by yourself. It's not safe for an attractive heiress."

Irritation bubbled in Mary. She shouldn't be upset with Jill, the girl meant it all for the best, but right now she wasn't in the mood to have her shortcomings cataloged. "It was just a mistake. Now, listen, Jill, I need you to go down to the kitchen and get a posset sent to Mr. Ian."

Jill's voice squeaked high and loud with indignation. "Mr. Ian did this?"

"Sh." Mary glanced up and down the corridors. No one was in sight, but she'd rather this incident remain a secret. No good could come if Sebas—Mary stopped herself short.

Why should she care what Sebastian thought? She didn't, but still . . . no good could come if word of Ian's attempt became common knowledge. Some men, especially men who openly admitted to despising Fairchilds, might find this a suspicious incident.

"Mr. Ian's ill," Mary said quietly. "He'll be better soon and we'll be good friends again, but not until he—" She took a deep, exasperated breath. "Mr. Ian is a lovely man, just rather confused right now. And ill. I'm sure he's ill. He needs that posset."

Jill didn't move off. Instead she stood, mouth working, until Mary made shooing gestures. "Go on. Do as you're told."

Mary pushed open the door of her bedchamber, and she heard the click of Jill's teeth as her mouth snapped shut.

"But, Miss Fairchild, I have to tell you—"

Mary stepped inside the room, and the door slammed behind her. She whirled around, but she didn't need to hear that deep voice or see his stolid form to know Sebastian stood there, arms folded.

''She wanted to tell you that I waited for you. And I want to tell you''—he stepped forward and picked up a lock of her loosened hair—''that you are, without a doubt, the most treacherous Fairchild ever born.''

Chapter 17

Mary had had a very difficult morning. She had been called a murderess and threatened with extortion. She had seen her plan to foil the diary's thief ruined by the prospect of too many suspects. She had been roughly handled by the one cousin she held in great esteem. Now a seething, accusatory Sebastian leaned against the door in her bedchamber, glaring at her as if she were the lowest of vermin.

But she, who had so vigilantly maintained her calm against insolent servants and brazen noblemen, would remain in control.

"What are you doing in my chamber?" Her voice came out louder than she intended it to, and she took several deep breaths to calm herself.

"I *came* to tell you I trusted you enough to let you open the safe." Sebastian laughed briefly, bitterly. "Instead, I discovered your uncle Leslie was right about you."

She didn't ask what Sebastian meant by that. She didn't have to. Whatever Uncle Leslie had said, it had been slander. "You *fool*."

He staggered as if she had put a bullet in him, and recovered immediately. "I *am* a fool. I've watched the men circle you and comforted myself when you didn't encourage them. I've brooded over your affection for your cousin and assured myself it was pure." She'd left the key in the lock this morning, and he turned it with all the ceremony of a magician who had made the world disappear. "But even fools know how to find revenge."

He paced toward her, and she discovered she had brought her fists up to her waist.

She tried to unclench them.

She couldn't.

How long had this man stalked her? From the moment he'd seen her with the blood on her hands, he'd haunted her dreams. And on that evening in Lady Valéry's study, she'd discovered her imagined dreads were not half as formidable as the reality of him.

Now he had the nerve to insinuate she was to blame for the men's attentions, for Ian's attack. And she, who had readily accepted blame for so much, knew herself innocent.

He reached out for her and she knocked his hands away with her knuckles. "Don't you touch me!"

Swift as a striking asp, he grabbed her wrists. "I'll touch you as I please."

She saw nothing more than an impression of tan

skin, bared teeth, and flaming eyes. With the ugly
bruises still marring his cheek, he looked like the
Devil himself, but she'd feared this Devil for too
long. Now she found herself responding with a blast
of her own flame. "You have no right to judge me,
either."

"There is no one better to judge you." He pulled
her toward him. "And find you guilty and execute
your sentence."

Did he refer to Besseborough's murder?

Did she care?

Shreds of self-control peeled away from her. She
sensed them go; it almost felt like liberation. "Another injustice done to an English working woman."

"You're not a working woman." He moved her
arms behind her back, then stepped in close to her
body.

Too much intimacy. Too much pure, physical
awareness.

"Or at least—not at an honorable profession."

But if she stood very still, perhaps she could retain
her dignity. She knew what he thought. She also
knew the truth. If she were angry enough to be stupid,
she might fling his accusations back at him. She
might defy him out of sheer stubbornness, but heat
radiated off of him. Danger lurked in the thrust of his
chin and the power of his muscles. She had to tell him
what she'd been doing, and she had to make him
listen, because if she didn't, he'd be his usual
ironheaded self and try to . . . to . . .

"I've been doing what you commanded me to

do.'' She didn't sound conciliatory, but then, she didn't feel conciliatory.

"I *asked* you to keep attention away from me while I searched for the diary.''

"You *commanded* me to help you find the diary.''

He snickered, quick and cruel. "I had heard you already knew where it was.''

"What are you talking about? In Scotland you demanded I help find the diary.'' She twisted against his grip, ignoring the pain of wrenched joints in favor of bravado. "I've been doing that. I've been down in the kitchen questioning the servants.''

"Why? You already know where the diary resides.''

"You are insane.'' She was sure of it now. "Every morning I've been rising before dawn and—''

"Meeting your cousin Ian for a quick romp.''

Incandescent with rage, she said, "You ass!''

"You called me an ass.'' He mocked her. "Aren't you going to pretend a spasm of guilt?''

At the ball, she hadn't *pretended* guilt when she'd called him an ass. She'd *experienced* guilt. But now she exulted in her new freedom.

The event she had feared for so many years had just happened. Guinevere Fairchild had rejoined Mary Rottenson.

And she—Mary or Guinevere or whoever she was—didn't care. "Two truths exist here in this chamber—the truth I speak, and the truth about what you are.''

He laughed.

The ass laughed. He didn't act insulted. He even had the nerve to relax, as if she'd pleased him with her inappropriate, rude remark.

"You are everything I thought you could be." Fiercely elated, he walked her backward, directing her with his body, his clasp on her arms. "Except honorable, of course, but right now your duplicity frees me to do as I please."

"And when you find out you're wrong?"

"I'm never wrong." He sounded as if he believed it. "You just proved that with your wantonness."

Her skin felt hot, like the time she'd thoughtlessly remained in the sun and it had blistered her, and she knew how red she must be. "Let go of my hands."

"So you can hit me with another silver cover? If I were you, I wouldn't hope for that."

They reached the wall, and he pressed her against it, leaning on her as if he needed support. This intimacy brought a low burn in her belly, and she recognized it as wrath. "You're hurting my arms," she said craftily, and when he released her, she boxed his ears.

He staggered back, clutching his head.

She used a precious moment to taunt him. "I don't need a silver cover." She darted around him.

He grabbed her skirt and swung her in a circle, aiming her at the corner. Momentum propelled her. She caught herself against the wall before she could slam into it. He dove at her from behind and pushed. She found herself trapped in the corner. Her cheek and palms rested on the cool wall. Her breasts and stomach were pressed flat by the pressure of his body behind. She tried to wiggle away. He just leaned harder. She tried to collapse to the ground. He shoved his knee between hers. She tried to turn her head. It only moved so far.

Out of the corner of her eye, she could see him.

He wasn't smiling. She thought he would be. One of his cruel smiles, perhaps. Or a triumphant one. Certainly a mocking smile. Instead he looked serious, intent, as if he'd just been given a project and resolved to give it all his attention.

She would have preferred one of his smiles. *Any* of his smiles.

"You can't do this." *Fatuous,* she railed at herself. *Inadequate.*

He leaned very close. "I can. And I'll do it well." His breath warmed one of her cheeks. The paneled wall remained cool against the other. She could see the long, flat surface stretching beyond and the grain of the dark wood. She could see another corner, another wall, and somewhere along that wall she knew the door existed.

That exit might as well have been on the continent for all the good it did her.

"Let me go!" She tried to use her elbows on him, but they wouldn't reach. Using all her weight, she dropped, trying to land on his intruding leg hard enough to break his constraint, but her petticoats protected both him and her from injury.

Instead, he said, "Do that again. You might come to like it."

"Oh!" She slapped her palms against the wall in frustration.

"Really." He tugged at her skirt. "I insist."

Her petticoats slid upward along her stockings until they reached the garter tied at her knee. The ruffles tickled her skin as they slid up her thigh. She hoped, she prayed, that he would stop short of uncovering her to the light of day, for she wore nothing to cover her bareness. She'd heard some immodest females of the haut ton enticed men by hiding their privates under newfangled drawers, but Mary was a decent woman—and in a moment she was going to be indecently uncovered.

As the fresh air fanned her, she realized her hopes had come to naught. She was naked as a babe, and he sighed as he caressed her nether cheeks. "Lovely," he whispered close to her ear.

She snapped her head back, hoping to smack his face, but he swayed sideways in time. She tried to skitter away while he was off-balance, but he thwarted her before she'd taken a step.

"You've taught me to respect your fighting skills." He tugged at her waist as if he could rip the clothes off through her flesh. "I'm not a man who easily forgets such a lesson."

She had a flash of wondering if madness had truly overtaken him, but she should have known he would never be so irrational. Instead, her petticoats dropped to the floor, and she realized he'd worked to untie the tapes.

She burned with humiliation to have him see her in

such a position. The back of her wool skirt frothed around her waist, spilling over to the front, and Mary tried to thrust it back into place, to take control of this out-of-control situation. He just ignored her, his hands molding her.

Infuriated, Guinevere cursed in outrage, using words Mary was sure she didn't know.

"Such language." Warm breath rushed across the nape of her neck. "You shock me, Guinevere Mary."

So he recognized the foolish girl had returned. Mary feared he would use that advantage just as ruthlessly as he used the advantages of position and strength.

He moved his leg up, spreading her until she rode his thigh. "Lean forward." He coaxed her with his voice and his hands. "Move with me."

He seemed to understand her reflexes well, for he tilted her until the pressure of his leg created tremors in her nerves. In *her* nerves, in the nerves of Lady Valéry's hitherto imperturbable housekeeper. She set her teeth. He rocked her, carefully, gently, handling her as if she were precious to him. Well, she wouldn't beg him to stop, no matter how he annoyed her.

Nor would she give vent to the little snippets of sound that wanted to escape. She stood on her toes, trying to evade the inescapable responses, but tension began to build in the base of her belly.

"That feels good to you." The man had the audacity to report her reactions. His fingers traveled beneath her skirt until they reached the front where the triangle of hair grew. "Do you like it if I do this, too?"

He pressed firmly.

She yelped.

"Too much?" He eased the pressure.

That didn't help. She leaned her forehead against the wall to hide her incipit tears. He forced her to move until her knees shook; she glided fully onto his leg. He forced her to feel too much. He didn't allow her to retreat, and now, now . . . Her hands curled against the wall, trying to grab something when there was nothing to grab. She shuddered, passion breaking from her in waves.

He chuckled, triumphant at having wrenched such an ungoverned response from her, and dropped his leg. Then he plunged at her bareness as if she were a cat in heat and he the stray who had tracked her. He held her much as a tomcat would, too; his teeth nipped her neck when she squirmed and he leaned on her heavily, pressing her into the wall. Inside his breeches he carried a rod, and like every man, he would use it to hurt her if she let him.

She sucked in a breath, trying to convince herself all this impetuous emotion was only anger. "*Would* you let me go?" It wasn't really a question, it was a demand, but he chose to pretend the former.

"I'll let you go when I'm done." He slid his palms down her hips to her thighs. "I'm not nearly done yet."

What did that mean? Did he mean to humiliate her more? Or was he going to try and take her as if she were some sixteen-year-old dunce?

She *was* trapped. That rod of his pressed into the cleft of her buttocks. He wasn't thrusting now, but nestling, as if he'd found a place on her that gave him a little pleasure.

And no man who had ever found a little pleasure thought it enough. Every nerve under her skin still jumped, and she took a deep breath to calm her burgeoning panic.

Then he lifted his body off hers, easing the pressure, and she raised her head off the cool wall.

He moved back far enough to alleviate her sense of oppression, and she would have celebrated except the air still struck her bare skin with the sharpness of a lash. She tried to twist around, to glance over her shoulder, to *see* what he was doing, but he seemed to have disappeared. Except for those hands. Except for . . . the bite of his teeth.

She screamed. There was no other word for the way she vented her outrage, and that scream was just one more casualty of control.

"Hush." His voice came from below her waist. "I didn't really hurt you."

He hadn't, of course. Unable to think what to say for the shock, she stammered, "You . . . you can see me."

"And a lovely view it is." This time he used his lips to soothe the sting of his bite.

She shivered from the contrast. Pain and pleasure. Mortification and desire. Fury and compliance. God, how could he incite these contradictory emotions in her? Where was good sense and self-respect? How she hated him! Hoping to knock him socks over nightcap, she kicked back at the kneeling man with all her might.

But her position was awkward, and her foot glanced off his thigh. He caught the offending ankle in a firm grip. "That's not polite."

"*You* speak of politeness?" she sputtered. The fire of her frenzy rose while his fingers pressed the bottom of her foot. It tickled, and more, it combined with every other sensation as stimulation.

She didn't want stimulation.

She jerked her foot away and stomped it on the floor to remove the trace of his touch.

His fingers moved up the cleft of her buttocks until they touched the base of her spine, an intimacy that made her forget her foot and try to swat him with her hand. She struck only the wad of her skirt bunched around her waist, and she realized he could easily pull the full bell over his head and hide beneath like a boy playing tent. The impotence of her position played havoc on her remaining composure. "You like humiliating me, don't you?" she asked, accusation making her voice tremble.

"Is it humiliation you're feeling?" His open lips left a trail of dampness as he explored the skin no one had seen since she had been a babe. "It doesn't taste like humiliation.'' His tongue swabbed her on the crease where her leg met her behind. ''It tastes like excitement. Am I exciting you, Guinevere Mary?''

''I hate you,'' she said, and she meant it.

''But am I exciting you?'' he insisted. ''I'm kneeling behind you, begging for a crumb of compliance. You can feel me. Don't you want to feel me?''

Until he said it, she had refused to think of it. He *was* kneeling behind her like a supplicant. And why? Why would a man like him behave so oddly? What was he gaining from this game he played?

What was she losing?

Nothing, except her innocence. And worse, every last shred of her remaining detachment.

''Guinevere Mary,'' he crooned. ''Answer me. Tell me how you crave my touch.''

''I don't.''

''You lie.''

Of course she lied. How could she remain insulated from experience, from life, when his hands kept stroking her? Something inside her was melting. It expanded within her and flowed between her legs, slow and damp and warm, and if she didn't do something soon, he was going to discover the harvest. She didn't think she could stand that. It embarrassed her that her body rebelled against her mind's dominion. And although she'd never heard anything about this phenomenon of moisture, she suspected he would view it favorably, even jubilantly, and damn him, he'd already had too many victories this morning.

Slowly he slid behind her, moving from the outside

of her thighs to the inside. He alternated his touch
with those distracting openmouthed kisses, but still
she knew enough to fight the way he spread her wide
with his skillful fingers. Her legs trembled from the
constant pressure to keep them close together, and she
closed her eyes to concentrate on her effort.

Then she opened them, because when she cut off
her sense of sight, she experienced the melting all the
more acutely.

His fingers stroked the thin fair hair on her legs. He
was getting close, too close, so close. He fondled just
the ends of the curly blond hair over her privates, but
the sensation reached her skin, then deep inside her.
He was going to touch her soon, and she was a tangle
of terror and a craving so strong she trembled with it.

Touch. His touch. A feast of touch to a starving
woman. And when he gave her the ultimate touch,
she would surely burn to a cinder.

Mary had to regain control to save her life.

And even as she thought it, Guinevere mocked her
with the chant *It's too late. You'll never get control
back as long as you live.*

"Please." Pride crumbled. Mary's voice cracked.
The length of the wall wavered before her gaze.
"Don't. Don't do this. You hurt me more than I can
possibly express."

His thumb paused. "Hurt you?" He sounded
shocked. His fingers flexed, kneading the muscles of
her inner thighs.

She held her breath. Had she saved herself with her
appeal?

"No, I don't hurt you." Now he sounded positive and angry again. "Don't try guilt with me, Guinevere Mary."

She had enough intelligence left to be afraid— right before his finger swept inside her.

This time she put her fists to her mouth to muffle her scream, because this wasn't a scream of outrage, but of pleasure. She didn't want him to hear that; it would confirm his suspicion she was a wanton. Or worse, it would puff him with vanity. Make him laugh at how easily he'd manipulated her . . .

His finger slid out, then in again. He'd found the moisture, and he used it ruthlessly to ease the shock of his caress. Or else he used it ruthlessly to give her even more sensation. She didn't know which. She didn't know anything.

She whimpered. Her eyes closed, her head fell forward. The cool wall supported her cheek again, and she wished she were lying down. It would be better than trying to stand while he created such turbulence that her knees almost gave way.

With the thumb of his other hand, he opened her folds.

She was open now, completely open. He could touch wherever he wished. And he would, too. That was why his thumb hovered over the nub normally protected from exploration. "Please." Her breath wavered so much, she could scarcely speak. "Don't."

"*Don't* is a challenge."

She couldn't see him. She hadn't seen him through

this whole ordeal, but she didn't need her sight to know what he looked like. This was Sebastian. Sebastian, with his hard-bitten features and darkened bruises. With his broad shoulders that concealed such strength. Sebastian who tormented her, Sebastian who pleasured her, Sebastian who *dared* . . .

But when he stood and swung her around, his face provided a shock. Her head struck the wall as she tried to jerk back from the taut emotion that pulled his muscles tight. His midnight eyes glittered, and he handled her relentlessly, crowding her deeper into the corner. As if he had the right to, he pushed her thighs open and slid his hand under each one. The muscles in his neck strained as he lifted her. Her knees touched the walls as he stepped between her legs.

Had she thought herself open before? No, now she *was* open.

Reaching up, she grabbed his hair and yanked, and he grunted. Grunted, and took the chance to kiss her. He used his tongue to give her a message, and she heard it as clearly as if he had spoken. She could batter him as she wished; he'd be inside her regardless.

She punched at his arms until something touched her below. Touched her in the place where he'd slid his finger. Aghast, she stared at him.

Solemnly he stared back—and he pushed.

When had he opened his breeches?

Then—how did he think he could put that thing inside her? He'd just begun, and already she burned from his entry.

"Don't!" She tried to wiggle, and he let her. He let her, because as she wiggled and he loosened his grip on her legs, she was inexorably forced down on him. The pain grew stronger. Pressure grew as irresistible force met immovable object.

Then the immovable object snapped.

Abruptly he was inside her, all the way inside her.

"Don't!" she cried again. Tears brought a husky edge to her voice and she brushed at her face with her shoulder. She didn't want him to see her crying, but there was no place to run, no place to hide. This act was the most intrusive she'd ever endured in her life.

And that was at least part of the reason he'd forced her. She knew from the way he watched her, as if every wince gave him power. Damn him, damn him, how did he know that she hated the loss of privacy almost as much as she hated the turbulent emotions?

Leaning over, he licked the moisture from her cheek. "They're worth more than your maidenhead," he said. "Your tears are gold to me."

"How can you be so cruel?" she demanded. "Why does it give you pleasure to make me suffer?"

"Suffering. Joy. Passion. I don't care what emotion you show, as long as you show it to *me*." He braced his legs and held himself still. "Are you still in pain?"

She was. Of course she was. If he moved, she thought she would die. But her thoughts darted about, trying to figure an escape, knowing none existed. "And I *was* a virgin," she blurted.

"I wasn't . . . right," he acknowledged.

"That isn't the same as saying you were wrong."

"No."

He stood between her legs, chest heaving, holding her by her nether cheeks, and as deeply inside her as he could go. He didn't look regretful, and he certainly didn't apologize, and irrationally, she found herself glad of that.

Rather, his eyes glistened as if he were under intense strain.

He said, "You can punch me *now* if you want."

His lips were full, and he wet them as if he wanted to admit his fault. Then he leaned forward and kissed her, and she realized he didn't want to admit his fault at all. That was too difficult. He just wanted to have her hit him until his guilt and her resentment had been satisfied. Then they would go on and finish what they'd started.

The discomfort was easing. The sense of fullness gave her an odd sort of satisfaction. And God help her, she wanted to finish, too.

Lust. She was in lust.

"Go on," he urged, "punch me."

She put her hand up to his face. He flinched back, but she just laid her palm flat against his cheek. "Later."

Chapter 18

It burned. The sensation was too intimate.

Mary burned. This entanglement was calamity.

Yet the faint moan that broke from her wasn't caused by pain or embarrassment, but by the shimmer of sensation as Sebastian shifted her. He lifted his knee and braced it against the wall, then with his free hand he opened her as he had before. She whimpered even before he touched her, anticipating the shock.

"Don't close your eyes," he warned. "Don't you dare try and hide from me."

The strain on his face told the truth. He might have started this out of fury, but he was involved now. He'd laid claim on her, but she'd returned the favor, and now they were so tangled she didn't know how to escape.

"I hope you know what you're doing," she whispered.

"I do." His mouth curled in the most beautiful

258

smile she'd ever seen. "I just hope I have the stamina to do it right."

Gently his finger dabbed at her, and she arched back as if lightning had struck.

"God in heaven." He sounded worshipful.

"What?" Grabbing at his shoulders, she took bunches of his coat in her fists.

"I can feel your muscles clench on me when I . . ." He touched her again.

She could feel it, too. This wasn't the massive assault she'd envisioned, but a thing of delicacy, of perception in each individual nerve.

"A little more, Guinevere Mary." His husky voice fought a battle between satisfaction and frustration. "Let's do this a little more."

Her inner muscles rippled.

He flexed.

She shuddered.

He lifted her.

It hurt.

"Don't," she said urgently.

He laughed, his tone a little off. "Too late for that. You should have been saying 'don't' before."

"I was!"

"Let's see." He pretended to think. "You boxed my ears. You tried to run away. You objected. Hm. So nothing could have stopped me, and nothing will stop me now."

Furious once more, she snapped, "You are abominable."

He looked down where they were joined. His hair fell around his face in strands. Then he looked up into her eyes. "Yes," he admitted. "But only with you."

He shifted, planting his feet firmly on the floor and holding her with his hands, then he lifted her again. His eyes half closed in ecstasy.

"You look like you did when you ate the bread pudding." She gurgled with laughter, and she realized hysteria threatened.

He opened his eyes all the way, observing her. "You're a tasty morsel," he whispered. He moved in close to her, so his pubic bone touched where his finger had been before. "And I'm better than all the dreams you never allowed yourself."

Then he kissed her, a full-bodied, passionate kiss. The touch of his lips and the puff of his breath in her mouth stilled the laughter. Her blood leaped and lust came billowing back. He *was* better.

His kiss had broken rules, but why should that surprise her? Sebastian broke rules. Sebastian did whatever he needed to get his way.

He milked passion from her mouth, and her muscles clamped down on him as if her flesh sought to return the favor.

He bit back a groan, then started moving her. With each stroke, he roused more of that rapidly expanding bundle of nerves. Steadily he probed, backed away, probed. Now she was grateful for the dampness that had embarrassed her. It eased the way, made this ordeal almost pleasurable . . .

Another whimper crept from her. Pleasurable? Her

lungs, her heart, every organ in her body, flared with excitement. The walls slid against her back. The room wavered before her vision. Each action led him a little deeper, when she'd thought there was no deeper left to go.

"So good. Better than I'd dreamed."

He was murmuring, and she thought vaguely he was trying to comfort her, to keep her from killing him now when he was vulnerable. But her body had taken over from her mind. The only violence she considered was squeezing him between her legs. She flexed her knees, adjusting herself as he moved, trying to pull him inside when he wasn't really trying to escape.

He didn't seem to mind, or even notice. He just kept talking. "That's it, sweetheart. A little more. A little tighter." A gasping laugh. "Couldn't be tighter."

She was shivering continuously. She had goose bumps, but she wasn't cold.

He agreed. "But hot. You're hot. Can't you feel it? Feel it, honey? Can you—"

"Yes!" Grabbing him by the shirtfront, she shook him. "I can feel it. Now, shut up and hurry!"

He didn't need to be told twice.

The cords of his neck pulled taut with strain as he lifted. Her legs and arms trembled as she worked, trying to help, to get this *right*.

"I can hold you." His voice quivered from the motion of their two bodies dancing to this primitive rhythm. "Just feel it, damn it. Relax and feel it!"

She couldn't relax. She couldn't stop moving. She heard cries: her own. She saw her lover's face: intent, exultant. Need built. She felt constriction where they matched. Again, then again. Suddenly sound, sight, *everything*, blacked out, and only sensation remained. Rapture overwhelmed her. She twisted, writhed, trying to get away, to get more.

"That's it, sweetheart. That's it." He pounded at her, talking, gasping, giving. "Hot. God!"

She heard Sebastian, but she didn't really. She processed only the fire, the bliss. She screamed.

All inhibition, all discipline, all Sebastian, disappeared under the massive upsurge of pleasure. She beat on him with her fists, struggled with him to reach satisfaction, and he just grinned with savage enjoyment.

Grinned until he stiffened, thrust on her harder, and gave a shout that matched the fervor of hers.

His head pounded in the aftermath of exertion. Exertion, and the most fabulous sensuality he'd ever experienced. And it was with her. Guinevere Mary Fairchild, of the house of his greatest enemies.

And he didn't care. He'd claimed her now. Let no one step between them.

The pounding in his head grew louder. He glanced at the door. It wasn't in his head at all. Someone wanted in. Damn that maid, she'd called in assistance.

Gently he withdrew from Mary's body, not wanting to leave but needing to set the situation to rights.

He wouldn't put it past those idiots to break down the door.

"I'm going to let your legs down, sweetheart."

Mary barely blinked, and he wanted to chuckle. Not with scorn, but with celebration. He'd done this. He'd changed the prim housekeeper into a creature of fire and light. What a triumph to take her so far . . . on her first time.

"Can you stand?" he asked gently.

She nodded, and he lowered her legs and propped her in the corner. With his hands on her waist, he supported her while she gained her balance.

He'd known Mary was a virgin from the moment he'd put his finger in her, but from what he'd overheard of her conversation with her maid, Ian had tried to change that, and Sebastian had been furious.

Yes, he had known immediately Mary had been too tight to have ever been with a man, but like the bastard he was, he'd continued to assault her. Creating those unfettered reactions in her despite her resistance had fed his sense of power.

Not pretty sentiments, but he didn't lie to himself about his less attractive traits. Those traits had helped him survive when everything else in his life had died. He got what he wanted any way he could, and he had wanted Mary Fairchild.

"Come, Mary." He slid his arm around her. "Let me put you to bed."

"Not likely."

Startled, he studied her. *She* was alive, and the

spark had begun to return. Even as he watched, she was throwing off the lassitude of sexual satisfaction and returning to her starchy self.

So now he knew. Guinevere Mary was never pliant, except for approximately five minutes after sex. If he wanted to extract promises or demand obedience, he'd have to do it then.

"You should lie down," he said.

"You would think so."

Yes, she was recovering almost too quickly. She pulled back from him, but he wouldn't let her. She was trying to reassert her independence, was Mary, and he would have none of that. He controlled her with his hands as firmly as he would a defiant two-year-old.

"What makes you think I'm so weak I have to lie down after that?"

He kept moving her toward the bed, and he allowed an edge of exasperation to creep into his voice. "Even *I* had to lie down after my first time. In fact, my first time occurred while I *was* lying down."

She jutted her chin. "Women are hardier than men."

Obviously. "I had hoped to have this discussion in a more relaxed milieu."

"Relaxed?" She jerked her head toward the door, which now shook beneath the persistent pounding. "What is it they want?"

He had manipulated her so they stood beside the bed, but she took no notice. She was ignoring him.

Ignoring his touch, ignoring his gaze. Pretending to be elsewhere? Annoyed, he swung her into his arms, tossed her lightly on the bed, and imprisoned her between his arms—just as he had done before. "I imagine they'll want to know that what just happened didn't happen."

She blushed. Really red, from the edge of her collar to the top of her forehead. And he was glad to see it. He didn't like to think he'd gone through an earth-shattering experience that had left his partner only briefly incapacitated.

"And failing that, they'll want to know when the wedding will occur."

Now the color drained from her face.

"Didn't you think of that?"

She looked up at the ceiling.

He cupped her chin in his palm and turned it toward him. "Didn't you?"

"I wasn't thinking," she snapped.

Good.

"But neither were you, I would guess, or we'd not be in this situation." She tried to sit up. "If you'll let me off the bed, we will do what we can to remedy our plight."

"I am anxiously awaiting your suggestions."

"I'll smooth my gown, you'll comb your hair, we'll let them in and deny any wrongdoing—"

"What will we say about those bloodstains on your thighs?"

She flinched, but he was abruptly as furious as he had been before.

"They match the ones on my—"

"No!" She clapped her hand over his mouth. "Don't say it."

Grasping her wrist, he pulled it away. "Don't say it? Not saying it won't change the truth. What's done is done, and I'm *not* a Fairchild. I pay my creditors. Lying is not a way of life for me. I don't destroy my neighbors."

"What did my relatives do to you to make you so bitter?" she demanded. "I should know. After all, I *am* a Fairchild."

He cursed himself for mentioning their family's differences, but the rancor had burned in him for so long, it was a part of his very soul. "It doesn't matter. I'm a Durant, and I'll do the honorable thing. I'll wed you."

"No."

She was trying to be her usual firm and housekeeperly self, but he saw the tremor of her chin. "We will mend the feud with our union."

"No."

The pounders on the door had become shouters. They were making enough racket to wake a corpse— or to thoroughly announce Sebastian's presence in Mary's chamber. "Where will you run with your ruined reputation?"

She pushed her hair out of her face and held it in a tail at the base of her neck. "Where will you run when you're wed to a Fairchild?" she asked, revealing a streak of ruthlessness to match his.

"To bed."

She let her hair drop back again. "That won't change who I am!"

"I will make you a Durant by infusion."

She stared at him, unsure what he meant or perhaps skeptical about his ability to jest.

But it *was* a joke, although he didn't blame her for her uncertainty. He wasn't like the men who danced attendance on her. He cared nothing for the social arts and had found little to amuse him in life. But he would be a better husband for her than the others. He knew the truth about her; no one else did.

"Why don't you want to marry me?" he asked more gently. "I'm not an easy man, I know that, but I'm rich—"

"So am I," she answered quickly.

"Not nearly as rich as I." A fact for which he was ecstatic.

Still, he didn't fool himself that their disagreements were over. He knew very well that lust was a poor reason to succumb to marriage. But he didn't have a choice; he had to have Mary.

"I can't marry you. There'd never be respect between us, or love"—her lip curled with as much scorn as ever he'd seen in an expression—"or even truth." She faltered on the last word.

So she wouldn't tell him the truth? Her distrust stung him, and he levered himself off of her. With an expression of acquiescence, he said, "As you wish." He stalked toward the door. "Let us face our audience."

* * *

"She wasn't truly compromised." Bubb held a glass of straight rum in his trembling hand and glared at the assemblage in his study. "They both had their clothes on."

"Sebastian was in Mary's chamber—alone." Lady Valéry held just as large a glass as Bubb, filled with brandy, and she held it without a quiver. "You know how improper that is."

Mary sat in a chair, stared fixedly at the dreadful gargoyle carved into the huge desk, and wished she were anywhere but here where the ghost of her grandfather hung like a choking miasma.

"Apparently my uncle Oswald was in your bedchamber alone, and he's barely been able to stand since." Bubb seemed uncertain whether to laugh or scold.

"That is not to the point. I have not been a maiden for . . . never mind how many years," Lady Valéry said. "My reputation cannot be stained."

"No, no." Bubb waved a dismissive hand. "Of course not. Forgive me. It is just I have never seen my uncles behaving with such—"

"Infatuation?" Lady Valéry relaxed and smiled. "Lovely gentlemen, both of them. But not well traveled, I assume."

"What does that mean?" Bubb covered his eyes with his hand. "No, I don't want to know. The point of this conversation is my dear, dear cousin Mary, and if she says what passed between her and this base lord was innocent, who am I to disbelieve her? I would be the last man to force nuptials on my unwilling cousin after her previous lamentable experience with the Fairchilds.'' Bubb tried to sound pious.

''You were forced to wed,'' Lady Valéry said. ''Aren't you happy?''

''Eh, eh . . .'' Bubb recognized his dilemma, but knew not how to escape unscathed. ''Of course I'm happy. But like your virginity, my marriage is not germane to this discussion.''

Laughter cracked from Lady Valéry. ''Good one, Lord Smithwick.''

Bubb wiped his sweaty palms against his breeches and smiled modestly.

''But Sebastian was unbuttoned,'' Lady Valéry said relentlessly. ''Good God, what more proof do you need?''

The debate had been going on for what seemed like hours as Lady Valéry argued for marriage, and Bubb glanced around helplessly. Alone, he hadn't a chance against Lady Valéry's brisk resolve.

If Nora were here, he might have succeeded, but she had come to the study and listened to the opening volleys of argument. She had examined first Mary, then Sebastian, from head to toe. She had smiled, with a rather sad and desperate expression, and she had walked from the chamber and not returned. Very odd, Mary thought, and in her absence Bubb had lost more and more ground to Lady Valéry.

Yet he struggled valiantly on. ''Another solution exists which is preferable to this hurried and embarrassing union. Our cousin Ian has expressed a willingness to—''

Mary swung her gaze to Bubb. "Don't even say it," she pronounced coldly.

Bubb didn't argue for her sake. No, he argued because he was desperately trying to keep a hand, however feeble, in the honey pot of her money. His attitude and words explained that incident in the hallway with Ian more clearly than Mary could have wished, and it hurt to think the handsome, affable Bubb had schemed to ruin her with her own cousin. It hurt more to discover Ian was a false idol.

Oh, yes, her grandfather lurked in his study, mocking her. She could scarcely draw breath as she remembered him saying, "I told you, you were like your father—allowing your lesser emotions rein and thus losing to a ruthless opponent."

Mary glanced up at Sebastian. There was her ruthless opponent. He lolled against a bookshelf, looking relaxed and disgustingly satisfied. And why not? He'd gotten what he wanted from her, and he was well on his way to getting his way in this matter. In the matter of her marriage.

"Sebastian," Lady Valéry called. "Do you desire to do the right thing by Mary?"

Mary had argued for the first hour after Sebastian had opened the door. Now that she had given up, they spoke in front of her as if she were unable to comprehend, and from Lady Valéry's tone, Mary might have been in the same predicament as a rapidly increasing, desperate belowstairs maid.

Worse, that was how everyone viewed the situation. Everyone except Sebastian, that nasty devil who stood smirking at her while he mouthed generous offers to rescue her stained reputation. "I will, of course, do the right thing by Miss Fairchild."

When he'd opened her bedchamber door, hell had spilled in. It seemed every servant and guest had entered, led by Lady Valéry and the perfidious maid, Jill. The old lady had had a spring to her step and a gleam of triumph in her eyes; she could not have been more indiscreet in her "discovery."

Sebastian himself had lent fuel to the fire that consumed Mary's good name. He hadn't even had the good taste to claim he'd forgotten to button his breeches.

But Mary was not a belowstairs maid. She was a Fairchild, and a Fairchild who had not only killed when she had to, but had given up her youth to support herself and her brother. She might have yielded her virginity, but this housekeeper did not easily yield her hard-won control over her life.

She had to try again. "I do not wish—"

Lady Valéry pointed a crooked finger at her. "You keep quiet, gel. We're arranging your future here."

"My lady, I don't need anyone to arrange my future." Mary kept her voice polite, her demeanor reasonable. "I have done an exemplary job of taking care of myself these last ten years."

"Tut, child," Bubb said. "A woman can scarcely be expected to know what's best for her. Witness your lack of discretion."

Lady Valéry cackled at Bubb's inadvertent admission.

He added hastily, "Innocent though those actions may have been. You just sit and be quiet like a good girl, and let your elders settle your future."

"Say what you will, I won't marry him."

They weren't listening. Bubb and Lady Valéry had their noses in each other's faces again, arguing her future.

Mary stared at Sebastian. This was all *his* fault. Everyone at the house party now deemed her giddy and reckless, when really she was calm and stable. At least, that's what she had been until she'd met him for the first time in ten years.

Moving closer to her, he said softly, "Don't glare so evilly." He dropped a hand on her shoulder and rubbed the knot of tension that had gathered there. "Rebelling will do you no good, you know. You're going to marry me. You're too sensible not to."

Sensible. Yes, she was sensible—until he touched her, as he was doing now. Until his palm massaged the muscles beneath and her treacherous body forgot the pain he'd caused her. She forgot that someone lurked within the corridors of Fairchild Manor who knew the truth of her past and demanded money for his silence. When Sebastian's fingers grazed her skin, this detestable room blurred before her eyes, the other voices faded, and moisture gathered low in her belly again. Then Mary lost her domination and Guinevere, that imp of emotion, emerged triumphant.

Sebastian always brought Guinevere out of hiding. *That* was why Mary couldn't marry him.

"Think of it," he urged. "You'll be secure."

"I'm secure now," she muttered, and wished he would move his hand to her other shoulder.

He did. "Be logical, Mary. You're an heiress. Even in our enlightened age, it's not uncommon for men to take heiresses to wife any way they can, and now that you're ruined, the men would not even bother with the niceties of courtship. If you married me, you'd be safe from all that."

He was right, Mary thought.

I don't want to, Guinevere wailed.

Mary was startled. Guinevere didn't want to wed him? Not even to experience once more those shattering elevations of passion and satiation?

Both hands enclosed the back of her neck now, and he tilted her head forward to work the tightly clenched cords. "I can do much for Hadden, too. I can get him into Oxford if he desires, or send him on a grand tour."

"I have money—money I would have no control over if I married you."

"I don't want control of your money. It is your grandfather's money, and I want no truck with him or his wealth."

Money easily scorned, she thought, when more is available.

"When we wed," he continued, "it will be yours to do with as you will."

She snorted. "Readily said." But she was speaking into her chest, her eyes half-closed as he used his thumbs to knead each side of her spine.

"As of this moment, I swear to relinquish all

control of your fortune. You may do as you wish with your moneys.'' He seemed to think that promise enough, for he continued, ''But you have no connections that would help Hadden, and you're not likely to get them.''

She stiffened and tried to raise her head. ''Because of my reputation, do you mean?''

''That's a handicap, too.'' He slipped his fingers under the mobcap she'd hastily slapped on and rubbed her scalp right behind her ears. ''But I was speaking of your femininity. The deacons of the colleges have no respect for a woman's opinion. But if I should use my influence to have Hadden recommended by . . . say . . . William Pitt, I'm sure they'd listen.''

''Bribing me with my own brother's welfare.'' She meant to ridicule him. She feared she sounded wistful.

And she must have, for he stopped massaging and came to kneel at her feet. She didn't want to look at him; he was temptation incarnate.

But he spoke softly, not demanding or commanding as he usually did, but coaxing like a suitor. ''*Why* don't you want to marry me? I can't apologize for what I did, at least with any measure of sincerity. It was too magnificent an experience for that.''

His voice might sound contrite, but his words proved him to be his usual self. ''You are such an ass.''

''You have told me so often, I now fear it is true.

But I was wrong to do what I did. I was wrong about your character.''

He smoothed her cheek with his palm and lifted her face until she had to look at him. At his sharp features. The hair she'd rumpled with her hands. The broad shoulders and strong body. God, she ached from the strength of his body. But she'd been sitting here, thinking about the scene in her bedchamber, and now she asked, ''Did you think I knew where the diary was?''

He flinched. Visibly flinched. ''I am an ass, a guilty, judgmental ass.''

He did look guilty. That didn't assuage her distress. ''Have you thought that ever since we left Scotland?''

''No.'' He shook his head. ''No. It was just a momentary madness, brought on by the memory of the old feud.''

By the knowledge she had killed a man, too? Surely not. Surely he would scorn to marry a murderess. Briefly she shivered as she remembered the note and despaired of what to do.

''Are you cold?'' He rubbed her arms.

''No, I was just wondering . . . if we married, and if you heard something about me that was so dreadful—''

''I wouldn't believe it!'' Still he rubbed her arms, as if he wished to warm her. ''You are a Fairchild, but mostly you are Guinevere Mary, and I've learned much about you. You could be accused of any crime, and I would know you justified in your actions.'' He looked at her steadily. ''Is there something else about you I should know?''

She almost told him. She opened her mouth. The words were there. *I murdered a man.*

But she couldn't. She should, but she couldn't. And her hesitation wasn't even because of Hadden's future or Lady Valéry's shock. She hesitated because she couldn't bear to see the indulgence on his face turn to shock and disdain. She couldn't bear to have Sebastian despise her.

She shut her mouth. She shook her head.

''No?''

She shook her head again, and thought that his fleeting expression of disappointment must have been in her imagination.

''No matter. Even if you had broken every commandment, I would still wish very much to wed you.''

''You don't know what you're saying. No.''

''Why not?''

She closed her eyes. ''You're a Durant.''

He chuckled. ''You don't care about the feud. You don't even know what caused it.''

She opened her eyes again. ''Then tell me.''

''It has nothing to do with us. You're hiding. You're stalling. And that doesn't sound like the Mary I know.'' He peered at her. ''Is this the Guinevere you fear? For I can see that she *is* illogical.''

Mary looked up and saw Bubb and Lady Valéry watching the scene play out before them with open fascination. She glanced around the study and noted how firmly her grandfather's presence remained entrenched. But neither Bubb nor Lady Valéry nor her grandfather had ever comprehended her, or even cared enough to try.

Sebastian had cared enough, and it was too mortifying to realize how well he succeeded.

Mary *was* firmly in control again, thinking clearly and doing what had to be done, and that, she supposed, included marriage. He didn't ever have to know about the murder. She'd get the money and pay off that valet somehow. And she was ruined, and she would be a good wife to Sebastian.

Yet that other part of her, that *Guinevere*, was whining, *I don't want to, I don't want to. Guinevere* cast around desperately for rescue, and why? Why? Mary knew very well why, although she could scarcely bear to admit the truth.

Guinevere Mary Fairchild had been hanging on to the dream of giving herself to a man who loved and respected her.

And hadn't she seen often enough that dreams were for simpletons?

Realizing that she had been such a simpleton made up Mary's mind. She nodded once, firmly, in assent. "Lord Whitfield, I will marry you."

Chapter 19

Ian lurched through the stable. "Hadd, my old friend, where are you?" Straw dust coated the fine polish of his boots. He didn't care. He didn't care about anything. "Hadd . . . Oh, there you are." He leaned into one of the stalls and spoke to a young, broad-shouldered blond man who curried one of the geldings. "Didn't you hear me calling you?"

The stableboy stood up, and light from the afternoon sun struck his face.

"You're not Hadd," Ian said accusingly. "Stop pretending to be and tell me where he is."

The stableboy pulled his forelock and, like all good English servants, didn't protest Ian's injustice. " 'E's workin' with that stallion. Ye'll find him behind in the pen."

Ian groaned. He didn't want to face the sunlight, but he badly wanted to speak to Hadd. He felt a kinship with the other Fairchild bastard, and they'd drunk with each other more than once in the past week. Hadd never made judgmental remarks about Ian's background, and Ian, after a few delicate attempts, never tried to find out about Hadd's.

They talked about horses, which they both revered. They talked about English society, which they decided neither of them could ever comprehend. Infrequently Ian answered Hadd's questions about being half-Selkie, and what he remembered of his mother's stories. Hadd's interest in the old ways never faltered. Ian knew he wasn't just a curiosity for Hadd, but a friend.

The blue glow around Hadd betrayed his regard. As Ian had said, he was a difficult man to lie to.

As he feared, the sunlight blinded him as he tramped out to the fenced enclosure, but he grinned when he saw Hadd coaxing Quick to accept a ride. Ian thought Hadd focused on the triumph of the moment, until he heard Hadd ask, "Isn't he a beauty?"

"He is indeed," Ian said.

One of the Fairchilds' finest, a remnant of the days when the uncles had dreamed of making money by breeding horses. They could have, too. They'd had the stock. But breeding horses took concentration over a long period of time, and none of the uncles could sustain such interest. The chance to renew the Fairchild fortune had faded away.

Now Ian's chance to grab the Fairchild fortune had faded away, too, and it was his own fault. His own damn fault.

Hadd rode toward the fence and made to dismount. "Help me," he invited.

Ian hesitated not at all. He was foxed, true, but with animals he never made a wrong step. So he climbed through the rails and came to the stallion's head. Gently he held out his hands and allowed Quick to sniff them. He took hold of the bridle while Hadd slid out of the saddle.

Hadd patted the stallion and praised him, then said to Ian, "It's early to be drunk as a piper."

Ian squinted up at the westering sun. "No, it's not. It's a good time to be drunk. Join me. I'm going to the tavern in the village. We can remain there all night."

Hadd looked him over. "I have work to do."

Reckless, determined to have company, Ian said, "I can get you out of it." And immediately knew he'd made a mistake.

Hadd stiffened, and his lips thinned. Sarcastically he said, "No, I thank you, my lord. Most men have to work occasionally. Most men even enjoy it."

Maybe it was the excessive amount of brandy Ian had consumed. Maybe it was his own self-disgust. But the wrong thing to say came out of him without his even thinking. "B'God, you're a Fairchild! You have no need to work."

Hadd swung toward Ian, his fist up, and Ian thought the only thing that saved him from a thrashing was Quick's restless protest. Hadd glanced at the stallion, then turned back to Ian. "You didn't hear me, then. I enjoy working, not chasing young women for their fortunes.''

Ian snorted. ''That's not my employment.'' He flung out his arms, and the stallion stumbled back, snorting, too. ''That part of my life is over.''

''You're engaged?'' Hadd made the word a mockery.

A mockery that meant nothing beside the mockery Ian had just suffered from Leslie. ''Worse. I'm a failure. A failure, I tell you!''

''So the young lady decided to marry the man she loved.''

''Yes. Yes, damn it, she did. And it was my fault.''

Hadd seemed a little less piqued with Ian. ''I can't see you as a matchmaker.''

''An inadvertent one, I assure you.'' Ian fell into step as Hadd led the stallion toward the stable. He didn't know why he insisted on telling Hadd these things. It wasn't making him feel any better. Nor was he finding sympathy in the bottom of his bottle, and he certainly wasn't going to get it in the manor. ''I tried to compromise her, but she got angry.''

''Angry?''

''She didn't like my kisses.'' That still stung. ''She treated me as if I were her little brother who needed a good slap.''

''Oo.'' Hadd seemed a little more sympathetic now. ''I'm familiar with that feeling.''

''Then she went back to her bedchamber, and who should be waiting for her but Sebastian Durant, Viscount Whitfield.''

Hadd stopped so abruptly, Ian had to shove him aside or Quick would have stepped on him.

"Careful, cousin." Ian staggered and almost stumbled into Quick's path in his turn. "Hurts when a horse crushes your foot, you know."

"Viscount Whitfield?" Hadd said.

Ian grabbed a fence rail and steadied himself. Only a little farther to the barn, where at least he'd be out of this blasted sun. He was beginning to feel rather ill, as if all the bottles he'd consumed in the past week were taking this moment to make their stand.

"Answer me, damn you!"

"Wha . . . oh, yes. Viscount Whitfield." Ian's sense of ill usage took dominance again. "Yes, that cretin, that *barbarian,* decided to compromise her, too. And he did it where I couldn't. He actually did the deed." He kept saying it, hoping the repetition would bring the reality home. Unfortunately, it did, and he barely realized how ominous his companion's silence seemed. "They'll be wed before the sun sets if Lady Valéry has anything to say about it." He wiped a trickle of sweat off his forehead. "And she does. She knows the archbishop of Canterbury."

"Before the sun sets?" Hadd glanced at the clouds turning orange and red in the sun's last rays.

"Or sooner. B'God, they're probably already wed. Yesterday Lady Valéry sent a messenger to her friend the archbishop to request special permission to marry, and she received the license this morning." He sneered as he thought of having such influence—a small defiance of the envy he felt. "How fortuitous that Canterbury is so near."

Hadd took Quick's reins and looped them around one of the fence rails. Then he reached over, grabbed Ian's neckcloth, and dragged him forward. "Tell me the name of the woman who is going to marry Viscount Whitfield."

"Old man, be careful." Ian tried to shove Hadd away. "You'll crumple my—"

"Tell me!"

Hadd directed his question in the manner of a man demanding his rights, and for the first time an inkling of the truth niggled at Ian's mind. Slowly he said, "My cousin Mary Fairchild." He watched Hadd's face, and saw the flare of raw fury that lit the young man's eyes.

Hadd tightened his grip on the cravat until Ian could scarcely breathe. "And she was who you tried to compromise?"

"You said you knew who your father was," Ian whispered. "Who was he?"

Hadd showed his strong white teeth in a snarl. "Guess."

"Could it be Charles Fairchild?" Ian gulped when Hadd nodded. "And Mary is . . . ?"

"My sister." Hadd pulled his big fist back. "You're not the first man I've thrashed for trying to seduce my sister—and you won't be the last."

* * *

Cane in hand, Lady Valéry moved through the
gloriously decorated ballroom, eavesdropping on the
wedding guests with so much wicked delight, she
thought she must go straight to hell when she died.

Stopping behind a column, she heard one of
Bubb's daughters wail, "But, Daddy, he was in *my*
bedchamber."

"Well, your cousin had him in her bedchamber
with his breeches unbuttoned," Bubb said tersely.
"Now they've wed, and we're happy. Happy, I tell
you, so smile."

Lady Valéry strolled past and turned to see which
one of the girls had thought to trap Sebastian. That
jade, Daisy, dabbed her handkerchief to the corners
of her eyes while she smiled, as instructed—until she
caught sight of Lady Valéry. Then she tossed her head
and walked away.

Everyone was smiling, Lady Valéry noted, although some smiles were more genuine than others.
Bubb's daughters smiled dutifully. Mary's suitors
smiled with gritted teeth, especially Mr. Mouatt,
who, rumor had it, needed a quick infusion of cash or
he would find himself without a feather to fly with.

Mr. Everett Brindley smiled at the newlyweds with
a sharp gleam in his eye. He might have been the
matchmaker, rather than Lady Valéry, for all the
pride he showed in their union, and Lady Valéry
wondered if he wasn't a bit dotty.

But there were a lot of dotty old men smiling here
tonight.

Leslie smiled as if his rear hurt, which it certainly

should. She had, after all, been wearing a particularly sharp set of heels when she'd kicked him. Calvin smiled at her, trying to look suave and alluring, and not succeeding. Oswald smiled with weepy-eyed infatuation—well, really, how was she to know he'd never been to the Orient? And Burgess . . . ah, Burgess was untried. Burgess showed potential. Burgess smiled hopefully, and Lady Valéry thought perhaps she would fulfill his dreams tonight.

Had he ever, she wondered, been to Italy?

Bubb smiled dutifully, and Nora . . . wasn't there.

She hadn't been there since Sebastian had been discovered in Mary's bedchamber, and Lady Valéry would desperately like to know why. The Fairchild fortune had been removed forever from their jurisdiction today, and the woman who clearly directed the Fairchilds' every move had disappeared. Inquiries as to her health produced smiles and shrugs from Bubb, and when he thought himself unseen, looks of consternation.

He was lost without his wife, and he hadn't been able to do more than babble when Mary had stood up and announced her intention to wed Sebastian. Nora would at least have had something intelligent to say, but not even the wedding had flushed her out of hiding. Where would the Fairchild hostess be in the middle of an important house party?

Of course, Lady Valéry had admitted to a good deal of relief that Nora hadn't appeared to lend her support to the beleaguered Mary. Better than anyone, she knew Mary's strength of mind, and Lady Valéry applauded whatever Sebastian had said—or done—to convince her to wed him.

Now the newlyweds stood together, formally posed beneath an arch where they could be congratulated by the assemblage. No bride had ever looked lovelier than Mary in her light green gown with the wreath of broom in her hair. No groom had ever looked more handsome than Sebastian, dressed in his usual severe black, but wearing such a triumphant smile, Lady Valéry thought Mary must want to slap him.

Certainly his expression made Lady Valéry's hand itch. Didn't he know *she* had planned this? *She* had trapped him? He had no business looking so pleased, and she made up her mind to tell him so the first chance she had.

But Bubb was standing beside the musicians, calling for everyone's attention, and the laughing guests quieted. "Once again," he said in a hearty voice, "the Fairchilds have taken into the family a prize of a bridegroom. Lord Whitfield brings not only a title and a fortune—"

Lady Valéry winced.

"—our cousin's marriage to him has also brought an end to a long-lasting and infamous feud. Speaking as the head of the Fairchild family, I sincerely welcome Lord Whitfield."

A polite round of applause accompanied the speech, although Lady Valéry knew most of the guests preferred the entertainment of open rancor to artificial harmony. Sebastian bowed to Bubb. As

Bubb bowed back, Mary looked happier than she had all evening.

Then Leslie spoke up. "Well said, nephew. Too much has been made of a youthful prank done many years ago."

Sebastian's smile disappeared.

"But my brothers and I wish to show we hold no grudge against the Whitfields—"

"Grudge!" Sebastian exclaimed.

"—and so we offer our wedding bequest to the newlywed couple." Leslie smiled sweetly at the indignant Durant, and gestured to someone outside of the ballroom.

Lady Valéry was reminded of an evil elf presenting a gift to ruin the festive occasion.

Four men carried the large, heavy object concealed with a blanket. They set it on the floor and stepped away, and Leslie jerked off the covering.

A fine bronze of a rearing stallion stood almost waist-high. The workmanship was exquisite. Lady Valéry could see each muscle and vein on its body. The lifted hooves shone from polish, and rising from its belly was its organ, proudly rendered.

A moment of stunned silence gripped the ballroom.

Then someone tittered.

And Lady Valéry, whose hearing had not failed with age, heard Bubb whisper, "God help us."

Sebastian might have been a statue himself, he stood so still, his face empty of any emotion. Mary, poor girl, understood nothing of what happened, nor did she seem to care. Instead, she stared at one of the accompanying servants with concentrated horror.

Lady Valéry looked, too.

It was that damned, slippery valet who had spoken to Mary in the corridor. Without knowing his name or who he served, Lady Valéry hadn't been able to find him. Now as she would have nabbed that buffoon, Leslie turned his evil, false-toothed grin on Mary.

He waved at the bronze with expansive theatrics. "Let the statue remind you what a real stallion should be."

Mary paid him no heed, but Sebastian stared at the old man as if he contemplated murder, and Leslie had the good sense to step behind the bronze for protection.

Then a commotion at the doorway turned heads. Voices trumpeted in indignation or anger, loud in the unnatural quiet of the ruined celebration. A struggling group of footmen tumbled into the room. They looked like bees swarming around a queen, and the queen—or was it a king?—bore them inexorably onward.

Someone broke free, and Lady Valéry recognized him at once. *Disaster,* her mind buzzed. *Danger.* She had to do something, and do it immediately, or Sebastian would find himself sprawled on the floor with new bruises to nurse. She moved toward the young man who bore down on the newlyweds. She caught his arm, but he tried to knock her hand away. Then he realized who held him, and stopped—and glared. He knew her well enough to know who to hold accountable for these nuptials.

"Hadden!" Mary's glad cry arrested his silent reproach, and she flung herself at her brother.

He wrapped her in his embrace. "Mary." Holding her away from him, he searched her face. He seemed to find some kind of evidence there, for he said, "Then it's true. You are wed."

"Not an hour since. Did you come from Scotland?" She clung to him. "You could have been here!"

"He's been here all along." Sebastian's heart still raced from the challenge Leslie had sent him, and now a new challenge presented itself. He saw the black eyes Hadden sported, and he knew he'd solved one puzzle. "I would say he is responsible for my second set of bruises."

"And your third." Bunching his fists, Hadden stepped around Mary toward Sebastian, but Mary caught his arm.

"Not here," she begged. "Please don't make a scene here. There have already been enough scenes to last me for the rest of my life."

Hadden glanced around at the rapidly gathering crowd. Whispers of "Fairchild" and "ostler" and "bastard?" were racing through the ballroom. Sebastian heard them, and he knew Hadden must have, too, for he took his sister's arm and marched her toward the door. She desperately glanced once behind her, not at Sebastian, as he expected, but at one of the men who had brought in the bronze.

The man smirked at her most unpleasantly, and Sebastian stopped. Who dared to leer at his bride? He began to walk back to the servant.

Lady Valéry seized him. "Never mind the stallion now. We face a grander crisis."

Sebastian looked again for the insolent man, but he had melted into the crowd. And Sebastian had to let him go. As his godmother had pointed out, they had Hadden to deal with. He led her through the throng and saw Bubb standing on the sidelines, indecision written on his face.

Lady Valéry shook her head at him firmly, then when with an expression of relief he stepped back, she murmured, "Bubb misses Lady Smithwick. He doesn't know what to do without her."

"Shoot his uncle comes to mind," Sebastian said.

Leslie stood sullenly, his rouged mouth pouty as Hadden's arrival overshadowed his cruel act.

Sebastian spoke to the three remaining footmen. "Bring that damnable bronze. I don't want it to encourage more jests at my expense."

The impassive footmen obeyed, grunting as they lugged the heavy statue into the corridor.

"Here." Sebastian indicated a convenient chamber, and the butler rushed in ahead of them with branches of candles.

Mary hesitated, then with a tiny shiver walked in.

The footmen brought that dreadful statue and set it on the floor in the center of Bubb's study. Sebastian could scarcely wait until the last one had been ushered out before indicating the rearing stallion. "I'll have to have it melted down into pennies. A lot of pennies."

Lady Valéry studied the offending sculpture from all angles. "It's really rather good. You could keep it and put it in the entry by the—"

He glared.

"But pennies *would* be a better idea," Lady Valéry acceded. Going to the decanters standing in a row on the cabinet, she poured drinks for everyone.

Mary paid them no attention. She had eyes only for Hadden. "Why did you come? I told you I didn't need help."

"No. You just got yourself compromised by her ladyship's godson." A blond god, Hadden towered over Mary.

But his sister goddess didn't acknowledge his superiority. "I don't know how your presence could have changed that."

Hadden looked at Sebastian. "I would have openly beaten the—"

"Fighting!" Mary clasped her hands at her bosom. "And with Lord Whitfield. Hadden, you might have been hurt."

Hadden closed his eyes for a brief moment of exasperation, and Sebastian came to his rescue. "You're his sister. What did you think he would do when he found out a man had been in your bed-chamber?"

"He's too young for fisticuffs," Mary said primly.

Sebastian subdued a laugh, but he couldn't completely contain his amusement. "Some"—*every-one*—"might say he has reason for his animosity toward me, and I would like to point out he got the best of me."

"Don't interrupt, Sebastian. This is between my brother and me."

Sebastian lifted his eyebrows at Lady Valéry as she handed him the liquor, and she murmured, "This should be entertaining."

Hadden looked both frustrated and tolerant. "Mary, you're wed and I have a right to question the circumstances."

"You sound like Uncle Bubb." Mary waved Lady Valéry and the glass of spirits away.

"I already know how this man forced your hand." Hadden swallowed his brandy in a gulp. "It will be the talk of England for years to come." He scowled at Lady Valéry.

She smiled serenely back.

"I have the right to know everything else," Hadden said.

"Certainly not!" Mary ruffled like an offended peahen.

"I don't think he meant *that*." Lady Valéry sank into a chair.

Hadden walked to the statue and smacked it. "I want to know why a Whitfield would wish to marry a Fairchild with the memory of *this* standing between them."

"A statue? What of it?" Mary turned to Sebastian. "What is so special about a horse?"

The study grew quiet, and everyone looked to Sebastian. Should he explain? Now, today, with his wedding night yet to come? "It isn't important," he said.

Again Hadden considered the statue. Eyes narrowed, he leaned over and plucked a sheet of paper from beneath the prancing hooves. He studied it intently.

"Leslie's calling card?" Sebastian asked bitterly. Then he held up his hands. "Truly, the statue and what it represents is not important. The important thing is that I realize now all Fairchilds are not cut from the same cloth."

"I wish someone would tell me—" Mary began.

"What of the contracts?" Hadden placed the sheet of paper in his pocket. "I assume, Mary, you did sign a marriage contract."

Sebastian relaxed a little. Hadden didn't want the old feud retold, either. "We signed contracts," Sebastian admitted.

"I negotiated on Mary's behalf." Lady Valéry sipped her ratafia. "She has a substantial allowance and complete control of her fortune. Should anything happen to Sebastian, she acts as his business manager until she desires otherwise."

"Most generous." Hadden seemed taken aback.

"To wed your sister was my dearest desire," Sebastian told him.

"You see, Hadden." Mary put her hand on his arm. "Nothing dreadful has happened that required your interference."

"I don't believe I would call a young man's concern for his sister interference." Sebastian strolled to her and brushed a lock of her hair off her shoulder. "I would call it familial responsibility."

"You don't understand." Mary appealed to Lady Valéry. "Shouldn't I be worried about my brother's safety?"

"Of course." Lady Valéry smiled at her. "As he should be worried about you."

"He's barely more than a boy!"

Lady Valéry cackled, and Sebastian placed the flat of his hands on either side of Mary's face. He turned her toward Hadden. "Look at him. He's not a boy, he's a man. He can take care of himself now."

"And he can take care of you," Hadden said.

"*I'll* take care of my wife." Sebastian softly put in his claim. "She's mine now, and I swear to you you'll never have reason to come at me with your fists again."

Hadden looked into Sebastian's eyes, judged him, found him worthy, and held out his hand. "As long as you know that if you hurt her, I'll find you and make you sorry."

"You're talking in front of me as if I don't exist." Mary sounded exasperated and disbelieving as the two men shook hands.

Sebastian moved close to her and put his palm on the base of her waist, letting her feel the strength and warmth of him. "Let us go to our bedchamber, and I will talk to you in a manner guaranteed to please."

She stiffened when he tried to guide her away, and turned quickly when Hadden spoke.

"I would like to ask my sister one question, if I could."

"Of course you can." Mary pulled away from Sebastian. "What is it?"

"Has there been any mention of the . . . problem which we formerly encountered in England?"

Hadden phrased his inquiry carefully. So carefully. Sebastian exchanged a look with Lady Valéry, who shrugged, and they both gazed at Mary.

She stood with her hands folded at her waist, eyes down, a faint flush on her cheeks. "I have scarcely thought of it," she said.

Hadden stroked his chin and considered her. "Really?" Skepticism colored his tone. "There's been no trouble at all?"

Mary developed a convenient deafness. Resting her fingertips on Sebastian's arm, she said, "You wished to go, Sebastian. I await your pleasure."

That phrase! *I await your pleasure.* It wasn't true, of course. She wanted only to escape Hadden's questioning, but Sebastian wasn't about to sabotage his own good fortune.

Nor was he likely to forget the slight twitch he saw in the corner of Mary's eye or the tremble of her lip. Some kind of trouble had found her, and he would discover the source of it soon.

Perhaps tomorrow morning. After their wedding night.

Only after Hadden had watched his sister and her new husband leave, and Lady Valéry had gone off to ensure him accommodations in Fairchild Manor, did Hadden remove the sheet of paper from his pocket. *Lady Whitfield*, it said on the outside. A dab of wax closed it, but no seal marred the wax.

He broke it open. He read the message. He cursed. Then he strode out of the study and back toward the stables.

Chapter 20

"*Is this bedchamber to your liking?*" Sebastian smiled at her as he gestured around the room located in the wing for the married couples. He was, she thought, trying to be charming. "The servants moved us this afternoon . . . as we were being wed."

"This bedchamber is fine." *It's you I don't like.* But she didn't say that, because he would consider it a challenge, and because it was not strictly true. He'd been quite amiable since she'd consented to be his wife . . . just yesterday.

And why not? He'd gotten his way.

She looked at him as he leaned against the door, blocking any chance of exit. And he would get his way again, if the look in his eyes was anything to go by. He was watching her with all the possessive pride of a new horse owner.

"You look quite panicked." His voice was soft; her master approaching with bridle and saddle.

"Panicked?" Studiously avoiding his eyes, she went to the dressing table and rearranged the hairbrushes. "I'm not panicked."

"Really?"

She heard him walk up behind her, his leather soles hushed against the hardwood. She felt his eyes watching her, and when he touched a lock of her hair—she jumped.

Quickly she said, "Everything's fine." A stupid reassurance when so obviously everything was *not* fine.

"That's not anticipation in your eyes when you look at me—if you look at me." He touched her hair again, and this time she twirled away and turned to face him. "I'd call it caution, or even fear."

"I'm not . . ." But she was. She was torn between watching his every move so she could counter it and just shutting her eyes and steeling herself to accept his touch.

"Virgins are meant to be tenderly initiated, not thrust against a wall and forced to respond. I hurt you." He stood with his fists on his hips. He looked impatient, but he sounded thoughtful. "The guests will celebrate until the wee hours. The Fairchilds are busy tending their guests." He tapped his foot. "Would you like to go open the safe?"

The floor beneath her seemed to have dropped away. "Your pardon, sir?"

"I was in your chamber yesterday morning to ask if you would go with me to open the safe. You distracted me." He stripped off his cravat and his simple, well-made frock coat. "But there's no reason we can't do it now."

"Do what now?" she parroted stupidly.

"Open the safe." Obviously he had mastered his desires. "I had forgotten our mission. But dear Uncle Leslie and that damnable statue reminded me—if we can recover that diary, we can leave here."

She floundered. How to respond?

He proceeded as if she had agreed. "You should change into that old-fashioned gown you were wearing when you came back from the kitchen."

Head whirling, she looked down at the green silk gown she wore. "Take off my gown?"

"Behind the screen." In a wry tone he added, "I promise not to help." Removing his waistcoat and his snowy white shirt, he strode to the standing closet to rummage inside. Mary had one moment to stare at the corded shoulders and muscular back before he turned around, clutching a simple black shirt and coat. When he saw her standing, hands limp at her sides, he allowed a brief flare of passion to light his eyes. "Hurry, before I change my mind."

After that threat, Sebastian thought, she moved briskly. The green gown flew over the top of the screen, then the filmy silk petticoat. She stood clad only in her shift, he realized, and if he walked around that screen . . . But he wanted to give her some time. He wanted to show her he could curb his desires, and he couldn't allow himself to have second thoughts.

Pacing across the floor, he did his best to wrench his mind away from the activity behind the screen,

and when she stepped out, he took her hand and
surveyed her dark-clad figure. "A housekeeper to the
unobservant only." With his finger he flicked the
mobcap that covered the telltale blond of her hair.
"But this makes a good disguise for a Fairchild."

"I always thought so."

She even sounded like a housekeeper when she
donned that garb. How he would like to help her
discard it!

The turned-down bed seemed to grow larger,
swallowing the available space in the chamber and his
willpower. Sweat broke out on his brow and a circus
began performing in his trousers.

"Let's get out of here."

They passed only an occasional servant and gave
the ballroom a wide berth, reaching the study without
incident. He glanced around and pushed open the
door. As he had hoped, it was dark inside and they
slipped in quietly.

"I don't like the dark, and I hate this place," Mary
said. "It gives me chills."

Her voice quavered a little, and he subdued the
urge to wrap her in his arms. If he did that, he would
do more.

"Chill? The study gives you chills?" He locked the
door behind them. "Why is that?"

"I remember my grandfather in here, dispensing
his cruelty with such relish."

Mary, he realized, still stood by the doorway as if
she were afraid to come farther into the chamber. She
was only a dark shadow among lesser shadows, and

he wished he could see her expression. Tinder and a candle resided in his coat pocket, but he wouldn't strike a light unless he had to.

"He was nothing but a gut-vexer." Sebastian's gaze was drawn to the statue, shrouded in dark. "Too bad the old man died in his bed. He deserved much worse." Striding to the drapes, he opened them and allowed the cool moonlight into the room. "That's better."

"Yes, I thank you," she said, but despite the light, the huge room swallowed her.

They needed to get the job done, and at once. At the cupboard where the safe resided, he jiggled the lock. It opened easily, as it always had, and he looked in disgust at the intact safe. To broach it, he had to depend on his new wife, when he would just as soon be slowly stripping her clothing from her, caressing each part as it was revealed, admiring each slim line and delicate curve . . .

He tried the safe one last time.

He'd never seen her undressed.

His fingers slipped. "Devil take it." Standing, he gestured to the gray iron box that so perplexed him. But Mary wasn't paying attention. Instead she stood hugging herself and rubbing her hands over her arms.

"Here," he said. "Do you need light?"

Recalled to her duty, she knelt at his feet. An exciting position—some other time. She ran her fingers along the lock. "No. I should be able to do it with my eyes closed." She slipped her hand into her apron pocket. "Charlie made me practice until I was that skilled."

Sebastian heard the tinkle of something hitting the floor, and Mary's swiftly muffled exclamation. Kneeling next to her, he said, "What have you lost?"

"A small, thin file, much like a needle." She sighed in relief. "Here it is." She held it up, then hastily pulled her hand back out of sight.

She was trembling.

"What's wrong?" He caught her hand in his and found it ice-cold. "Don't be afraid. We have the right to open this safe and retrieve the diary."

"I know."

She tried to withdraw, but he wouldn't allow that. Instead he slipped the needlelike tool back into her pocket and chafed her fingers. "Tell me what's wrong, then."

She glanced about her and hunched her shoulders. "I feel like he's still here."

He glanced around, too. "Your grandfather?"

"He haunts this room. I can see him sitting in that chair and rejecting me and Hadden." Her mouth, which could be so wonderfully generous and giving, was pinched into a thin line. "He destroyed my life and he never cared."

Sebastian agreed with her wholeheartedly. The old earl had helped destroy his life, too. He was like a blight on Mary, and on Sebastian, also, and Sebastian wouldn't allow anyone, living or dead, to retain such power. "He sat in the chair behind that desk to reject you?"

"Yes. It's a dreadful chair, anyway, with its high back and its gargoyles." She looked down at their still-clasped hands. "I still dream of that gargoyle coming at my throat, and I take a fireplace poker and hear the crack of its skull. I see its brains spill out and I see . . ." She stopped, shivering, apparently horrified by her own recitation.

He understood why she was haunted. "Then come." He stood and pulled her with him. He towered over her, but she'd never let that stop her from defying him. She'd never let her size stop her from doing what she thought was right. Only now, when she recalled her demon of a grandfather, did she seem in need of a champion.

He would be that champion. He had made a pledge this day, and this Durant always kept his pledges. But right now her fears couldn't be fought with his fists or even with logic. Only exorcism would work. "Let's vanquish this ghost who haunts you."

She dragged her feet as he conveyed her to the desk. "I don't like this."

"You will." They circled the desk until they stood behind it. With his arm around her waist, he turned her to face the room. "Look. The chamber seems different from this angle."

She seemed uncertain of his intention. "Not really."

"Of course it does. The power is wielded from here. You're exercising the power now."

She leaned away from him as if he'd lost his mind.

"Truly," he said. "Bubb is the holder of the title,

of course, but in the Fairchild family right now, you hold all the power because you have control of the fortune.''

"So you said."

"I meant it. Your fortune is your own to dispose of in any manner you wish. You have the power." Then he muttered, "You could make *me* do anything you desired."

"What?"

He didn't clarify his statement. How could he, when it had taken him by surprise, too? But it was the truth. For whatever reason, the claiming of her body had claimed him, as well. His insistence on marriage had little to do with his reputation or hers, and everything to do with the sight of her blood on him and the knowledge he would never allow another man to get even half so close to her.

Even the comfort she found in her brother's embrace had shaken him, and he wanted her now with a gnawing hunger that stirred him to madness. The man who all his adult life had been cold and unfeeling had just been vanquished by a woman—but she didn't need to know it.

If he could only keep from telling her.

He pushed the chair back, then urged, "Sit."

She was watching him guardedly, and did as he told her. The chair's tall arms reached almost to her armpits, and its high back dwarfed her. The desk before her was elevated, so she looked like a child sitting at the dinner table.

"That won't do," he said decidedly, and picked

her up by her waist. Her legs, she kept at a right angle, not knowing what he intended, so he commanded, "Stand."

She did. Right on the seat of the chair.

"There." He kept his hand lightly on her. "That's better."

She didn't seem to think so. She stood unsteadily, her shoes sinking into the purple cushion her grandfather had used to ease his noble ass, and Sebastian half expected her to topple off in a faint. But Mary was made of sterner stuff, and he held her firmly until she gained her balance.

"What do you see?" he prompted.

She looked out over the desk. "The study."

"And out the window?"

"The estate."

"You control it all." He knew this, and he informed her so with pitiless enjoyment. "Make your wishes clear, and the Fairchilds would cower before you."

She looked down at him in astonishment. "I don't want to do that!"

"But you could. That's power—power your grandfather no longer has. He was a tyrant, easily replaced by another tyrant, should you choose to be one. He's truly dead." And she looked beautiful in the moonlight, like a fairy who had discovered her wings for the first time. His loins ached with need, and his voice thickened as he said, "But you are alive."

Now she looked around her with poise and a heightened interest. "That's true. No one mourns my grandfather. For all the fear he inspired in life, he's left nothing behind but bad memories.'' She gave a little bounce on the cushion. ''It would be agreeable to be in authority here. I'm good at it, you know.''

''Yes, I know.''

''When I was the housekeeper, my servants were well trained and efficient, and I kept a firm hand on the helm.''

She was gaining confidence, was his wife, and he liked that.

Then she frowned. ''But there's the taint in the blood. I would find power addictive, and abuse it to the others' detriment.''

''Did you find power addictive in your stint as housekeeper?''

''I found,'' she said gently, ''it preferable to being powerless. But there is no pleasure in hurting those less fortunate.''

He didn't say anything. She was intelligent enough to comprehend her own words.

He saw when she did, for she looked down at him with a half smile. ''But it seems such a shame to discard this power without using it on some sniveling beast who needs correction.''

She offered him an opportunity to redress his injustices to her, and he would be a fool not to take advantage of it. Slowly he lowered himself to one knee and touched his chest with one hand. ''Not a sniveling beast, but a beast nonetheless. Do your worst, madam. I deserve your punishments, and more.''

She frowned and clutched the chair as if his gallantry alarmed her. ''I don't know what you mean.''

''I abused you most dreadfully when last I visited your bedchamber.''

She blanched at his plain speaking.

''I unfairly accused you of dishonor,'' he continued, ''and took you roughly even though I knew the truth of your purity. You can take your revenge now. I vow to allow any liberty.''

She stared at him strangely, and he supposed he must appear silly—a sinister figure, dressed all in dark colors, kneeling before his wife. But he didn't care how he appeared, he only cared that Mary, his new wife, knew herself safe from harm at his hands.

''A housekeeper doesn't take revenge.'' She sounded prim, all Mary, no Guinevere.

''You are not a housekeeper anymore. You are an heiress and my wife.''

She slid down on the chair, her spine against the back, her feet on the cushion, and her knees akimbo. She examined him curiously. ''Why do I have the distinct feeling you have something in mind?''

The hem of her skirt fluttered as she settled more comfortably, and her ankle peeked out. He looked at it, and at her lap, then into her face. ''It would pleasure me to pleasure you.''

''We can't have that,'' she said decisively. ''I

would like to make you suffer, Sebastian Durant. I would like to torment you heartlessly.''

Visions of an imperious Mary struggled to life in his mind, and he mocked himself for his own magnanimity.

"Take off your shirt,'' she said. *"I* will pleasure *you."*

He almost overbalanced. He couldn't have heard right.

"Well? What are you waiting for? Stand up and take off your shirt.'' She paused. "Slowly.''

He stood, numb with delight, and stripped off the studs that held his shirtfront over his chest.

She watched intently. "I've never seen a barechested man before.''

Of course she hadn't. He'd been in too much of a hurry last time to undress her, and the brief glimpse he'd allowed her in their bedchamber could scarcely have whetted her appetite.

Now he didn't make the mistake of thinking she was excited by his appearance. She watched him clinically, comparing him to that horse statue, perhaps, or a favorite dog. But he thought perhaps he *could* excite her. Certainly he wanted to try. "I'll light a candle.''

She frowned as he fumbled for his coat and the flint that resided therein. "No, that would attract attention.''

He didn't care. He'd locked them in her bedchamber twice and ignored those who sought to interrupt. Did she think he couldn't ignore them again?

Looking at her, he saw the way her chin jutted. He remembered his vow to do as she wished, and he cursed himself for a fool. A completely aroused, slightly desperate fool. He dropped his coat.

She rewarded him with a smile. "What do you normally take off next?"

It depends on how desperate I am to free myself from restraint. But no, such a reply might frighten her. "My shoes and stockings." He tried to sound meek, and not at all as if he were swelling so big, the trousers would soon remove themselves.

She nodded regally. "Do so."

He didn't care to hop around, nor did he relish sitting on the floor like a child. Her grandfather's big desk was almost clear of clutter, so Sebastian patted the surface. "Do you mind?"

She waved a hand in invitation. "Please."

He eased himself onto the smooth wood and removed his shoes. He jerked his stockings free of his garters and dropped them on the floor, and all the while he wondered if she knew he was almost naked. One more item, only one more item—

"What are you waiting for?" she asked. "Remove them."

"Them?"

"Don't be coy." God, she sounded like him. "Take off your trousers."

He hadn't envisioned this, nor imagined she would turn the tables on him and satisfy her curiosity in so blatant a manner, or even that her gaze on him would create such turmoil.

He slid off the desk and slowly unbuttoned his trousers, and when his privy member sprang free, she gasped.

Very flattering.

Then she slowly reached out a hand.

Touch it, touch it, touch it . . . She touched it. Tentatively, brushing it with her fingertips as delicately as an artist would use a paintbrush. Heat rushed through him, making him so hot, his skin surely blistered, and he reached down and enfolded her hand in his own. "Like that." His voice was guttural, broken.

"Firmly." She stroked him. "Like that?"

He couldn't even nod. If he moved, he would break into big chunks.

"Yes." She sounded pleased. "Like that." Abruptly she withdrew her hand. "What else can you show me?"

Closing his eyes, he regained control. Her pleasure. He had offered her pleasure.

He stroked his breeches down his hips and stepped out of them. Again she reached out, this time to cup his ballocks, rolling them in her fingers.

"Fascinating," she said.

He heartily agreed. "Mary." He'd be on his knees if she didn't stop. "Don't stop."

She sat back and gripped the arms of the chair.

He sucked in air, trying to regain his balance, trying to retain poise. Trying to keep his promise. "To show you more," he said craftily, "I would have to remove *your* clothing."

"Not yet."

Spreading his arms, he turned in a half circle. "There's nothing else to see on me."

Then he stopped. Her hands followed a muscular cord from his back down over his buttocks.

"You are constructed very differently from me." She caressed his other cheek. "I like it."

"Good." It was nothing more than a grunt.

"Am I tormenting you?"

"Yes."

"How gratifying," she purred. "Would removing my clothing also torment you?"

He gripped the edge of the desk so hard, the imprint of the carving dug into his palm. "Yes." He saw no need to inform her that the torment would be unbearably exquisite.

"Then you may do so."

He turned quickly, and her hand fell away. Taking her arm, he helped her to stand, and he saw the quick flare of alarm in her eyes when she realized how close she stood to a naked man. He wondered briefly if she would change her mind, but she didn't.

He unlaced her gown as quickly as he could and pulled it over her head. He untied the tapes of her petticoats and helped her step out of them, and while he was bent down performing that service, he stared at her silk-clad calves. The chemise she wore, unlike the gown, was fine linen, light and soft, long enough to cover her knees, but short enough to tease.

"I don't want to remove any more clothing," Mary said abruptly. "This is enough."

Her courage had evaporated. For some reason—perhaps his intent stare or the heat of his hands on her waist—she wanted to stop now.

"There is more pleasure you can give me," he said craftily.

She was startled into laughter. "Oh, yes, I know that." Taking him by the shoulders, she urged him around until the seat was behind him, and the desk behind her. "Now you sit."

With prudent care, he did as instructed, and waited.

She seemed unsure, and he said, "I would like to see you."

"I think you've seen enough."

"All of you. You could take it off as slowly as you wished. I wouldn't complain."

She leaned against the desk, then with her hands on the edge, she lifted herself onto the surface. She swung her feet back and forth and considered.

He considered, too. He considered that heaven hovered not two feet from him, and with the proper urging, heaven would sit with him.

"I have an idea." He scooted the chair closer between her knees. "I would like to taste you again."

She tried to close her legs. She couldn't. "I don't know what you mean."

With a hand on each ankle, he opened her wider and slid her closer on the wood surface. "I'll show you."

She started to struggle as he pushed back the hem of the chemise and bent his head.

The flavor of her burst onto his tongue. Ah, yes. Mary-flavored cream, indeed. Vaguely he heard a whimper. She struggled to move away, but he wrapped his hands around her. She arched backward, but the action thrust her toward him. He could taste shock and reluctant pleasure, and when he heard a groan, he knew the pleasure was winning.

Then she grabbed a handful of his hair and jerked his head back. Glaring into his eyes, she said, *"I* was going to pleasure *you."*

She slid into his lap, her legs over the arm of the chair, and somehow his inexperienced almost-virgin lifted herself, positioned him, and slid down on his shaft.

The word he used described the act precisely.

"Sebastian!"

"You're shocked?" He held her in place, trying desperately to retain enough mastery to make her happy. "When we're like this?"

"I've never heard the word used"—she struggled to explain—"in the correct context."

He didn't laugh. He couldn't. Not now. But later . . . With her hands still on the desk behind her and her legs over the chair arms, she lifted herself.

He groaned.

"Pleasure?" she asked.

"Yes. Mary . . ."

She lifted herself again, and again, setting the rhythm she wished, finding her own delight while seeking his. It was like nothing he'd ever experienced, totally out of his power, magnificent and savage and the first time he'd ever been made love to in his life.

He trembled and panted, watched her face and exulted. She wasn't afraid. She liked this. She looked at him, at his bare chest, at his arms, at the shadowy place where they were joined. She gazed as if the sight gratified her. She made him feel like a king, like a god, like the best lover in the world.

Mary's lover.

Her soft buttocks pressed against him with each stroke. Her breasts bobbed beneath the chemise, and he brushed them repeatedly with his fingertips.

She closed her eyes and opened them, moaned softly and bit her lip, and moved ever faster.

Inside she was warm, tight, slick. Inside her, he was growing, straining, almost ready to burst.

Soon, please, soon . . .

He touched her knees, caressed her inner thighs, felt each muscle flex as she worked to rise and fall. She was strong, his Mary, strong and tender. His palms followed the path to the place where they were joined, and carefully he explored her. Found the place that would give her the most pleasure.

An expression of mingled elation and amazement swept her face. She tightened around him yet further. She would climax now, now!

Her spasms brought on his own orgasm, and her inner contractions milked him until he thought he would expire from joy.

She came to rest in his lap, and he took her head

and pressed it to his chest. "Relax. You've worked hard."

She gasped softly for air as her roughly used muscles relaxed.

He let his own head fall against the back of the chair. "If that's the result I get for letting you abuse this sniveling beast, then I shall be a beast more often."

"Can't happen." Her breath touched his bare chest, her voice was muffled. "You're a beast all the time."

He smoothed the hair off her neck. "Your beast, my dear beauty."

She chuckled and groaned.

"Have we vanquished your grandfather?"

"Grand . . . ? Oh, him." She flexed her shoulders. "Yes, I would say his ghost is defeated."

"I hope he's spinning in his grave." Stroking her spine, he realized he still hadn't removed her chemise. As stealthily as the Bond Street Burglar, he slid the soft material up, but she caught at his hands.

"I still haven't seen you." He tugged at the gown. "Perhaps you have an anomaly, such as too many bubbies or a misplaced navel."

"Well, you're stuck with me now, aren't you?" she snipped.

But she sat up to let him remove the chemise.

She was as beautiful as he had imagined. Polished skin, a taut body. Breasts the exact size to fit in his hands. Long legs and between them, a golden nest.

"Perfect," he said hoarsely, and smoothed his palms over her belly.

"No anomalies?"

"Perfect," he repeated, and with a tug untied her garter.

She said, "Sebastian, we have a duty to perform."

He rolled her stocking down and kissed her bare thigh. "Soon."

"The ton is still celebrating our marriage." A particularly raucous burst of laughter punctuated her admonishment.

He faltered, then sighed and rolled her stocking back up.

"Are all men like you?"

"No." He put his forehead on hers. "I'm better than every other man."

"I mean, do all men want to . . . to mate to the exclusion of all else?"

Sitting back, he shook his head. "*I'm* not even like that. Only with you, my dear Mary."

She smiled and squirmed in his lap.

He groaned at the sensation. "If you wiggle again, we're never getting the safe opened." Moving the chair back, he gently helped her to rise. "If we hurry, we can go upstairs and investigate my interest in mating."

"As you wish." She sounded prim, Miss Mary Housekeeper, but her nudity revealed the lie.

With the proper tutoring, his wife could easily be a wanton. He'd never bothered to be a good tutor before, but with this incentive he could easily learn.

He helped her into her clothing first, caressing her only when he couldn't bear not to. Then while he dressed she went to the safe. By the time he knelt at her side, fully clothed and holding a lit candle, she gave an exclamation of triumph. "The lock is undone," she said. "Would you do the honors?"

"I thank you." She was a generous woman. "I would." He reached out and swung open the sturdy iron door.

The safe was empty.

Chapter 21

He was drowning. Son of a Selkie, and he was drowning with his feet on dry land. Ian thrashed his arms and kicked, but his attacker was relentless. He held his head down in the water, lifted it, thrust it back. At last, as Ian gulped in fresh air in one of his brief returns to the surface, he gave in and roared, "I'm better! B'God, I'm better! Now, let me up."

"Truly?" Hadden paused in his dousing.

"Truly," Ian said sullenly. Hadden let him go, and Ian stumbled back from the horse trough. "That was disgusting." He coughed and spit in the muddy, hoof-marked stable yard. "Horses drink in there, you know."

"I know." Hadden stood with his fists on his hips, watching his still badly hungover and bruised cousin. "Led them here myself on occasion."

"Well, you won't have to do that anymore." Ian wrung water from his hair, stripped off his soiled shirt, and twisted it until water splattered from it. "You're the brother of the heiress."

"You're not going to hold that against me, are you?"

Hadden sounded polite, but Ian recognized sarcasm when he heard it, and he glared. "Why not? You've lied to me about your identity, got your hands on the money I coveted, punched me in the face—"

"You deserved it all," Hadden said.

Ian couldn't disagree.

"Besides, who do you think carried you to that comfortable, straw-lined stall last night? Furthermore, I left you to sleep it off until I couldn't wait anymore." Hadden gestured toward the sun. "It's nigh onto high noon, and the guests are starting to leave."

"Good riddance," Ian said.

"Aye, they've got such a tale to tell, they're vying to see who can get to London first to tell it."

"Nosey parkers."

"But I have business with one of them, so we've got to move now."

Ian leered. "A woman?"

"I've scarcely had time for that, have I, with my stable duties."

Ian still had trouble comprehending that this breaker of horses, this drinking partner, this *Fairchild*, held the accolade of legitimacy and the advantage of wealth. It wasn't fair, but then, nothing in Ian's life had ever been fair. He wished he could despise Hadden as he did the other legitimate Fairchilds. But he was Mary's brother, and Ian didn't despise her. Furthermore, he and Hadden had been companions. And finally, Ian was just too weary this morning to work up a rage. "What's so important you have to drag me out of my stall—no doubt my permanent home now that I've lost your sister—and subject me to torture?"

"This." Hadden thrust a paper covered with scrawls toward Ian. Ian wiped his hands on his pants and took it. He read, then looked up at Hadden. "Who is a murderess?"

Hadden just stared back, arms crossed over his chest, feet planted firmly on the earth.

"You?" Ian guessed. "Or Mary?"

Hadden didn't respond by word or nod, but who else could it be? None too steady on his feet, Ian staggered as he tried to comprehend. He didn't; this was beyond him now. But the Devil knew he wouldn't allow a blackmailing serpent to destroy either of his cousins. "We're going to take care of this."

Hadden's mouth kicked up into a smile. "I thought you might want to."

Eager now, Ian asked, "Do you have a plan?"

Hadden flung his arm around Ian's shoulders. "I do."

Carriages lined the drive. Coachmen struggled to control the high-spirited horses. In the entry, society matrons waved their handkerchiefs to each other and lamented the time they would spend apart. On the terrace, gentlemen shifted their feet restlessly and compared horseflesh. And the crowd constantly thinned as more and more of the guests left to spread an exciting and inaccurate tale of the infamous Fairchild house party.

The Fairchild family did their duty, standing in the entry and on the terrace to bid their visitors good-bye. But the strain of being pleasant for so long was telling on them. Their smiles were forced, their voices sharp.

Sebastian stood protectively beside Mary as if to make sure the repeated congratulations were courteous, and as the crowd of guests thinned, he cocked his head, then nudged her closer to Leslie. "Listen," he urged.

Mary tried not to be obvious as she eavesdropped, but no such restriction occurred to her uncles.

"You seem to have lost weight, Calvin," Leslie snipped at his brother. "Are you pining for your lover?"

Calvin's woeful face crumpled, and in a tone of worshipful desire, he proclaimed, "Lady Valéry is wonderful."

With a curl of his lip, Leslie turned on Oswald. "A grown man, and sickening for want of a woman's love. He has no pride."

"Pride?" Oswald left off glancing at the upper windows where Lady Valéry lodged. "What is pride when a man has been to heaven?"

Leslie harrumphed indignantly. "Nonsense. That ugly old hag couldn't take a man to heaven."

Oswald chortled. "You wouldn't know. She won't have *you*."

Leslie shot a hostile glance at Sebastian. "I don't want her. She's old. She's ugly. She's—"

"My true love, and if you say another word, I shall kill you." Oswald advanced on Leslie, fist clenched.

Leslie clamped his mouth shut until Oswald had turned away. Then he asked sharply, "Where's Burgess? He should be here."

Calvin sighed deeply.

Oswald kicked at the marble steps.

Leslie swore and strode inside.

"It's always the same," Sebastian said in Mary's ear. "She enslaves them."

An irreverent smile touched Mary's lips. "Good for her."

"You would say so." Sebastian nodded at Bubb, who scrutinized the drive with forlorn care. "He's looking for Nora."

"Yes." Mary watched Bubb trudge back inside to do his duty by the guests who were still too foxed to yet leave. The rest of the Fairchilds followed. "I don't understand where she could have disappeared."

"Most peculiar," Sebastian agreed. "I do not know what it portends."

Inevitably Mary's mind went to the empty safe. Had Nora's disappearance anything to do with the diary?

"I wish I knew where that diary was." Sebastian echoed her thought. "It's the only thing keeping us here."

They hadn't spoken of the diary since their shock in the study in the night before. They had almost not spoken at all. Not that they were angry with each other—no, Sebastian had held her tightly all through the night—but there was a constraint. Had this entire journey been a fool's quest? "I think Daisy has it," Mary said.

"Why?"

Because she still watches you hungrily. "Because she's willing to do anything to get what she wants."

"That assessment fits every one of the Fairchilds. I think it's Leslie." His mouth puckered, as if his bread pudding had soured.

"Why?"

"Because Leslie knows about the diary," he said.

Mary stared. "He does? And how do you know that?"

"He mentioned it to me." His grim mouth twitched. "When he was mocking me."

"When he told you I had it," she guessed.

"I believe in you now."

She wished she could give credence to that without any doubt.

"Now, if you will excuse me, I have to seek that life-altering, damned, and still elusive diary." He cupped Mary's cheek in an affectionate gesture and left.

And Mary understood more of Sebastian's deceptive fury that day in her bedchamber. She had her uncle Leslie to thank for this marriage, and she wondered—should she thank him indeed, or should she call on the gods to curse him?

Regardless, she was still wed, and nothing could change that.

A housekeeper always faced reality. *Mary* always faced reality. And Mary needed one hundred pounds to pay her extortionist. She thought briefly of going to Lady Valéry, but that would involve explanations she didn't want to give. And what had happened to her blackmailer? He had promised to get in contact with her, yet no more anonymous notes had been slipped to her. Had he perhaps left with his master?

A fine carriage rocked up the drive. A returnee, she supposed, someone who had forgotten his or her best gloves or yappy dog. She started to turn away, for she wanted to speak no more about her rise to fortune and her abrupt marriage, when she saw the crest on the side.

This was the Fairchild carriage.

She watched curiously as the coachman pulled up to the manor, as the footman set the steps and opened the door, and she stared openly as Nora popped out. "Mary," Nora called. "Mary Fairchild. Or is it Mary Durant now?"

"Durant." Mary faltered over the name. "Lady Whitfield."

"So I suspected after that scene in your bedchamber." Nora looked bone-weary as she climbed the stairs. The feather on her hat drooped, and her shawl hung limply. A small bag dangled from her arm, and it bumped her leg with each step. When she stood beside Mary, she said, "That is why I left so abruptly. Come, my dear." She put her hand on Mary's arm and together they entered the manor. "I went to London to get your wedding gift."

"You went to London for a gift? All the way to London?" Incredulous, Mary could scarcely keep from calling Nora a liar. "You missed my wedding to collect a gift?"

"It's a very important gift."

Seeing Mrs. Baggott hurrying toward them, Mary ordered, "Tea for Lady Fairchild at once."

"That would be pleasant." Nora led the way into the study. She discarded her hat and shawl, sank into a chair beside the fire, and placed her bag at her feet. "It's a wretched road to London. If I never had to travel it again, that would be too soon for me."

Mary's curiosity intensified. Something very odd was transpiring.

"That's something else we have in common," Nora continued. "We don't travel well, we have both worked as servants—"

Mary made a muffled protest.

Nora raised her brows. "Mrs. Baggott told me. Did you think she wouldn't?"

So much for Mary's clever investigation. "If she told you, I suppose everyone knows," Mary said bitterly.

"Not at all. She is loyal to me, although inclined to gossip when the right kind of flattery is applied. But I told her if word of your tenure as housekeeper got out, she would be turned out without a reference, and I would make it a personal vendetta to make sure she never found another position. I think she believed me, don't you?'' Nora was revealing herself, or perhaps Mary was simply looking more closely. This woman before her wielded power deliberately. The authority was there in her level gaze, in the cool, overly civil expression, in the unsmiling mouth.

A knock sounded on the door, and Mrs. Baggott brought in the tea tray. Silence reigned as she fixed them both cups of the steaming liquid and set out a variety of cakes, and Mary barely kept the scalding words of reproach from her lips.

But a *lady* doesn't scold her hostess's servants.

As the door closed behind the housekeeper, Mary said, ''I don't understand. Why are you telling me you know of my past? Why did you go to London when you believed Sebastian and I would marry? What is happening?''

''It's very easy, my dear. I never meant you should suffer in any way. You are one of the chosen few. You are a Fairchild.''

Indignant, Mary said, ''I am my own woman.''

''As all Fairchilds are their own person,'' Nora agreed.

Mary wanted to protest this obvious untruth, but courtesy kept her silent.

''I have few passions, but the ones I have are strong.'' Nora picked up her tea, then put it down untouched. As she took off her gloves, she said, ''You have no doubt heard I was a governess when Bubb and

I were wed. But have you ever heard the details of our nuptials?''

Mary was glad she could honestly deny any knowledge.

''I was just fifteen when I became a governess at a neighboring manor, quite ignorant of the ways of the world, although I assure you, I don't consider that an excuse.''

Mary winced and shook her head.

''Bubb discovered me crying one day because I missed my mother, and the children had been difficult, and—oh, I don't remember the details. I cried a lot in those days. He was kind . . . Well, you know. He's always kind, and when he came to visit again, he sneaked away from the girl he was supposed to be courting to give me some sweets.'' A smile hovered on Nora's lips as she straightened the gloves in her lap, then straightened them again. ''It was the beginning of a lovely time for me. I looked forward to his visits. They were the only light in a very dreary existence, and before long . . . the governess Nora was increasing.''

Mary murmured, ''A common tale.'' Too common. Too much like her own for comfort, and she hung on Nora's next words like a carp on a hook.

''I didn't even realize . . . Well, I didn't know anything about it. But my mistress recognized the symptoms and threw me out. Bubb found me''— Nora had her hand over her heart now—''and we went to Gretna Green, and he married me.''

Mary released her pent-up breath. This story didn't

end like hers. There was no hidden murder here, only misplaced passion and unexpected integrity. "Good for Bubb!"

"He is more of a lord than any man I ever met." Nora's eyes shone with the soft glints of a woman in love. "With his prospects and his good looks, he could have had any woman. But he picked me. La! He could still have any woman, but he cleaves to me. He's a good man, Mary. A good man. But to hear his father tell it, he was nothing but an idiot who had ruined the family. What was his heir doing, marrying a governess, a nobody? Until I heard his father shouting, I hadn't comprehended the magnitude of Bubb's sacrifice, and at that moment I swore to be worthy of the honor done to me."

With an effort, Mary remained civil. "Quite an honor." *Quite the opposite.*

"Yes, and I must tell you, everything I've done, I've done to advance the Fairchild circumstances."

A chill ran up Mary's spine at the fervor in Nora's tone. She sounded like a zealot, too intense and almost frightening. "I should have you speak to Sebastian," she tried to joke. "He seems unaware of the honor *I've* done *him.*"

"But with what I have to give you, he will comprehend." Leaning down, Nora dug around in the bag at her feet and brought forth a black, leather-bound book. Calmly she handed it to Mary. "There you have it."

Stupidly Mary stared at it. "Have what?"

"Lady Valéry's diary, child." Nora chuckled.

"You look dumbfounded. Who did you think had the diary?"

"I had begun to think it was a myth," Mary blurted, "conjectured to lure me here."

"Not at all. Instead, it was, so I hoped, the salvation of the family."

"My lady?" Mary shouldn't have been bewildered.

"Since the Fairchild fortune passed to you, I don't need to tell you we have been in dire straits, so I have been taking some of the . . . valuables . . . to sell. That fool of a pawnbroker wanted to peddle Lady Valéry's jewelry case with the contents intact, but I realized the value of the diary far exceeded the case. I got the diary for a pittance."

Nora had appeared to be an unimaginative, dutiful wife. Now Mary discovered Nora was the driving force behind the Fairchilds' survival.

"Many careers could be ruined by this little book. I sent word to Lady Valéry first, suggesting she pay for its return. I got a haughty response, so I contacted the men I thought would be interested in publishing it for profit, and arranged this house party to hold the bidding . . ." Nora looked mildly interested. "Has Aggass left?"

"Yes," Mary said faintly.

"I had Bubb tell him—tell them all—I'd be turning the diary over to you."

Mary took a hard breath. "But why? Why now?"

"Certainly I cared nothing about Lady Valéry and her reputation. But now she's family by extension."

Nora smiled faintly. "Through Sebastian, and a family friend through both Calvin and Oswald, I suspect."

Mary lifted her hand.

"Burgess, too?" Nora asked.

"I suspect." An unexpected compassion touched Mary. "Without the diary . . . what will the Fairchilds do?"

The teacup quivered in Nora's hand. "I will visit the pawnshops with more regularity."

Mary stroked the diary. "Perhaps Sebastian—"

Mouth puckered, Nora shook her head. "I don't expect the sense of family which moves me to return the diary will also move Lord Whitfield to forgive the unforgivable."

Such implacability offended Mary's sense of order, and besides . . . Sebastian had sworn the mysterious feud didn't matter. "I still don't know what happened."

"If your husband wishes to tell you, well and good. Otherwise"—Nora shrugged—"let it go."

Perhaps the uncles deserved poverty. Perhaps the daughters deserved sorrow. But Bubb seemed almost innocent, a victim of his upbringing. Ian, whatever his crimes toward her, deserved more than scorn. And Nora shouldn't have to bear the burden of the Fairchilds' survival. "I have a thought," Mary said. "Would you perhaps accept a portion of the Fairchild fortune as a gift?"

Nora sat forward eagerly. Then wariness stopped her. "Why?"

"I would like to express my gratitude for returning the diary."

Nora's mouth thinned. "It is a gift."

"Yes, of course. But at least let me express my gratitude for . . . handling my debut." Mary could see Nora was still offended, so she said, "Let us speak plainly. I don't scorn money. More than anyone in the Fairchild family, I understand the power and the despair a lack thereof creates. But my grandfather's money is tainted. It was given to me, not as reparation for past wrongs, but with the intent I would make the Fairchilds suffer."

"How do you know that?" Nora asked.

"*I* know." Mary pushed a tendril of hair off her forehead and sighed. "I know, because I have been tempted to use it for just that reason."

Nora's eyes widened.

"On that afternoon over ten years ago when I came to beg for help, only Ian offered assistance. Nothing else was forthcoming, and I hated the Fairchilds. I hated all of you." This confession bared the evil place where the heart of a Fairchild flourished, but Mary spoke steadily, for she had won out over the demon revenge. "So I would now release two thirds of this fortune to you. The remaining third I will settle on Hadden."

Nora stared incredulously. "You mean you'd do that . . . allow even my daughters access to the fortune? And the uncles?"

With the release of the money, Mary had released a sense of ill usage that had shadowed her for ten years.

Lightly she said, "Yes. Dole out the money as you see fit."

Nora's eyes gleamed, then dulled as she slowly shook her head. "My child, Lord Whitfield has no love for the Fairchilds, and he is your husband."

"He has control of my fortune, you mean. But he has sworn to let me manage it as I choose, and this is what I choose."

"When did he promise this?" Nora sounded more than doubtful. She sounded cynical and a little amused. "Was it before the wedding?"

"Yes, but Sebastian—"

"Is just like every other man and will promise anything to ensure he's trapped his quarry." She must have seen Mary would protest, for she lifted her hand. "I'm not saying he's not better than most men. Only that he'll say anything to get his way. You'll get used to the disappointments as time wears on."

"No!" Denial sprang from Mary. "He wouldn't lie to me. He was most emphatic. My fortune is my own."

"Hm." Nora put the teacup on the tray and pushed it away from her. "I see your reason to hope, and I would, of course, take the money with appreciation. But if it doesn't happen, I assure you, you still have my deepest regards. In my opinion, you are the best of the Fairchilds."

Mary didn't know whether she was joking or not. "I think much the same about you."

Chapter 22

Sebastian stood on the low-pitched roof, leaned on the wall that rose to waist level, and stared across Fairchild lands toward the adjoining estate. Toward the estate that should have been his.

Another family owned it now, upstart merchants who made more money than they knew what to do with. Upstart merchants—much like himself. He'd tried to buy the estate back once, but he hadn't been surprised when they refused. Now he could admit he was glad. He didn't really want to live among the painful memories haunting that house. He'd rather make a fresh start . . . with Mary.

Only since he had married did the issue of a country property again arise. He would have children with Mary, and those children deserved to have an upbringing such as he had had in the early years. They would have the freedom to climb a tree, to run through the fields, to fish in a stream. More than that, they would have parents who supported them their whole lives.

He only wished he could take Mary away from this place and start on those children.

Instead, he still searched for Lady Valéry's diary. An elusive diary, surely an illusion—except that Leslie had taunted him with it.

"Sebastian?"

He turned away from the view as Mary emerged from the stairwell. She moved toward him through the chimneys, appearing to be clothed in a mist of smoke. Then the wind puffed up and blew the smoke aside, and the sun fell full on her uncovered head and turned her hair to gold. The fringe of her shawl tickled her skin as if the breeze itself wished to caress her. Sebastian felt an odd tug at the sight of her, not just the heat of lust—although that certainly swelled within him—but something beyond that. Pride, he told himself. She carried herself well, despite her heritage. Or admiration. She had overcome much misfortune to become a dignified, collected woman.

Yet whatever name he put on this new emotion, reticence kept him from declaring it.

He had spent the last fortnight in Mary's presence, learning to trust her. He had spent thirty years of his life despising everything about her family.

Although he thought he had conquered his distaste, still he held a small part of himself in reserve.

Mary smiled at him, an open, joyous smile that rocked him back on his heels. Was this the first time she'd genuinely smiled at him? He thought it must be, for his heart took its first beat. His lungs opened and he took his first breath. His vision cleared, and for the first time he could see into eternity.

He was mad. Mad for her. Yet he didn't want her to know of his insanity, for such it must be, so he fumbled for dignity. "What are you doing up here?"

Apparently he had chosen haughtiness, for her smile faded.

"How did you find me, I mean?" He tried to smile pleasantly. "I thought the roof would be solitary."

She didn't seem reassured, for she took a step back. "I asked where you were. One of the servants saw you come up."

He tried heartiness. "Well, I'm glad you came. It's almost like old times."

"What old times?"

"The last time I was up here, I was with your father."

"My father?" She shaded her eyes against the sun and looked him over as if he were acting oddly.

Like a host seeking to put a guest at ease, he made conversation. "Your father liked the roof. He said it was a good place to dream."

"He would." Her hand dropped from her forehead, and in a solicitous, elderly-sister tone, she asked, "Sebastian, are you ill?"

Determined not to alarm her further, he bowed. "I am in excellent health, I thank you."

She bobbed a curtsy back. "Because I think there may be a sickness preying on the guests. I saw Mr.

Brindley in the corridor outside the study. His complexion was almost green, and he hurried away without speaking to me."

Sebastian enunciated the words through his teeth. "I am well."

Her brow cleared. "Then I have good news."

He noted she clasped a book to her bosom, hugging it as if it were a treasure. "Yes?"

She extended the book toward him. "This is it."

He looked at the plain black cover. "It?"

"The diary. I have it!"

With one stride he was beside her. He snatched it out of her fingers and opened randomly to a page. Beautiful, well-rounded penmanship sprang out at him. Lady Valéry's handwriting.

I caressed him in the Russian manner until he promised to do as I instructed and "influence" enough of the lords to get the bill passed through Parliament. Then I gave him satisfaction such as he never had before, and he almost begged to do another favor for me. So I let him pleasure me.

Abruptly embarrassed, Sebastian snapped the book shut. "You're right. This is the diary. Where did you get it?" He'd searched for it so long, so hard, and now his wife just handed it to him, as if finding it were a snap.

"Lady Smithwick." Mary was smiling again, a quietly amused smile. "We could have searched forever for it here and never found it. It was in London. That's where she's been the last two days."

"Fetching the diary to give to you?" He couldn't keep the incredulity out of his tone.

Mary recognized his ill humor this time, for her smile dimmed. "No, actually she brought it to give to *you*."

"No Fairchild ever gave anything but trouble to a Durant."

"It was her wedding gift to us, and a precious gift it is, too. She was going to sell it to the highest bidder and keep the family from debtors' prison with the proceeds. Instead, because of our marriage, and because she is incredibly loyal to the Fairchilds, she gave it to us."

"Wait. Wait a minute." He held the diary out at arm's length. "You're telling me she stole this diary, was going to ruin an old lady, my fortune, and possibly the entire country in the name of profit, and now she's giving it back to us as a *gift?*"

Mary sighed with what sounded, impossibly, like exasperation. "She didn't steal it, she found it in a shop where the thief pawned it."

"Whew." He pretended to wipe sweat from his brow. "I was afraid she might be involved with dishonest dealing." He projected sarcasm, enhanced with a prowling, low-grade fury. "Tell me—how much do we have to pay for this *gift?*"

Mary's gaze left his face to inspect the vista.

"I thought so." He started to slip the diary into his jacket. "How much?"

She plucked the diary out of his hand, then stuck it in her pocket and looked at him. "Nothing. She asked for nothing in return.'' She nodded firmly. ''So I gave her my fortune.''

''What?'' It wasn't a question so much as a roar, a protest that rose from the depths of his sin-ridden soul. He grabbed her shoulders and lifted her until she rose onto her toes. ''Tell me you're joking.''

''Sebastian, you're hurting me.''

He dropped his hands away and waited, and she rewarded him by admitting—no, just telling—she had bestowed two thirds of her fortune on her dastardly, cruel, traitorous, and evil family. On the Fairchilds.

He couldn't believe it. Her prosaic revelations struck like a frost on his tender new emotions. He withered as she spoke. He squirmed, he writhed, he died. His hands clenched. He wanted to strangle her for what she had done. Instead, when she finished, he simply said, ''No.''

The hussy had the nerve to look amazed. Confused even. ''What do you mean?''

''I mean *no*. No, you cannot give your fortune into Fairchild keeping.''

''But it's not going into Bubb's hands,'' she explained, as if that made a difference. ''Nora will handle it.''

''As if I cared about that. Before me I see a great future. A future in which every Fairchild is desperate for money, reduced to penury, begging . . .'' Mary was staring at him, so he reined himself in. ''No. Let them all rot in hell.''

''I find you lacking in compassion.'' She judged

him calmly. "However, that is not important. What is important is your promise to let me do as I wish with my money. Was that a lie?"

"No, it wasn't a lie. No. You can do anything you wish with your wealth—except this."

As she gazed at him, her bright countenance dimmed. She looked as grieved as if he were at fault, rather than Nora and all her wretched family.

"Why do you want to do this? I thought you hated them as much as I do," he said harshly.

"I look at the family, and I see one whole generation which is rotten to the core. I don't know why, I only know it's true."

Sebastian remembered Leslie's comment that they had suckled perfidy from their mother's breast. But that was only an excuse. He didn't care.

"But I am a Fairchild," she said proudly. "My father was a Fairchild. My brother is a Fairchild. We're not wicked. Neither is Bubb, although he is . . . misguided. Bubb's daughter Wilda is rather sweet. With another generation, perhaps the taint will be gone. In the meantime, I can't sentence them to certain disgrace when I have the means to save them."

With the backing of years of experience, he projected implacability. "You will not rescue the Fairchilds from the result of their follies."

She could project implacability, also. "It is not their follies which has resulted in their penury, but my grandfather's will."

She was stubborn. God, she was stubborn. And she

was judging him unfairly, without knowing all the facts.

He didn't like having her judge him harshly. He didn't like it at all. So perhaps it was time to tell her. "Have you heard how the feud between our families came into being?"

Her eyes flickered. "Lady Valéry told me both families used to breed horses."

"The Fairchilds, as a lark. The Durants, because we desperately needed the money."

He waited to see if she was repulsed by the realization that even though his father had been a lord, his family had been involved in business.

She only nodded.

"A particularly fine stud came on the market, and after careful study my father decided that stallion would breed champions. He told old Fairchild about it—we were neighbors and didn't bid against each other—but when the auction arrived, the Fairchild foreman bid against Father." Sebastian smiled, one of his razor-sharp smiles. "We won the bid."

"But if the Fairchilds had more money—"

"The foreman only had permission to go so high, and old Fairchild didn't realize my father was willing to gamble everything, *everything,* on that stallion."

"I see."

No doubt she did. The tale he told had all the elements of disaster marked on it. "The Fairchilds were furious, and as revenge, your uncles introduced their most feeble, piebald stallion into our mare stable."

He had accepted the facts years ago, but telling Mary did something to him. Embarrassment rose in him, dying him a ruddy tint, carrying the old bitterness to the surface as he exposed himself and braced himself—for laughter. "That stallion bred all the mares, ruining them for one season and rendering the prized stud useless."

She wasn't laughing yet. "Then the stallion Leslie gave us as a wedding gift—"

"A taunt." Fury mixed with the old pain.

"Were you . . . was your father ruined?"

Still no laughter, but she had a rather soft, compassionate expression in her eyes. Pity? That was worse than laughter, so he straightened his shoulders and hardened his tone to show he no longer cared. "We had invested all our capital in one venture, and as the result of the malicious jest, we lost our horses. We lost our home."

"Would no one extend a loan?"

This time he laughed. Not with merriment, but he laughed. "The trick the Fairchilds played made of us a joke. No one . . ." For one moment, humiliatingly, emotion closed his throat and he couldn't speak. He shut his eyes and struggled for his usual impassivity. Something touched his arm; he grabbed for it and found himself holding a hand. Mary's hand. Her fingers curled around his, their palms met, and she offered comfort with her touch. He opened his eyes and looked at her, and miraculously he could speak again. "It was actually a rather funny trick, the stuff farces are made of."

She murmured, a low, throaty disagreement.

"So no one would loan money to us for fear of the scorn they would get."

The memory of that laughter still haunted him. That was why Leslie had taunted him with Mary's infidelity. That was why he had reacted so violently when he thought Mary might have betrayed him.

But she hadn't, and surely she wouldn't, not even in this matter of her fortune. When she had heard the whole story, then she'd do as he wished. "The Fairchild uncles made sure they came to witness our eviction from our home. My mother cried. My father just stood apart and watched as though his heart had broken. And I suppose it had, for he committed suicide less than a week later."

He was rather proud of himself. He had never said the words out loud—*my father committed suicide*—but he had this time, and he fancied he'd sounded normal.

Mary squeezed his hand ever more tightly. And she wrapped her arm around his waist. And she pressed herself against him. And hugged him. Just as if he needed comfort.

Which, he discovered, he did.

"Poor little boy." Mary's voice shook. "How did you live? Did you go to relatives? Did your mother seek employment?"

"No relatives."

"Lady Valéry, then."

"Lady Valéry is a friend from my father's side of the family. Mother refused to go to her." He embraced Mary fervently, not knowing how he could draw strength from a slip of a woman but finding he savored it more than . . . more than bread pudding. "And Mother couldn't work. She . . . cried." Until she was sick. Then she cried some more. An endless, relentless stream of tears. Whimpering, sighing, with never a word of solace for her bewildered son.

Remembered agony tried to well up through the cracks of his composure, but he tamped it down with the ease of long practice.

As if she didn't realize how well composed he was, Mary rubbed her hand across his back and made shushing noises.

He both disdained the comfort and relished it. Beneath her stroking hand he was melting like butter on a hot cross bun. "I worked. On the docks. When Mother died, I went to Lady Valéry. She smoothed the rough edges I had acquired and loaned me money to start my shipping business. I have since repaid the loan and she has made a tidy profit."

"Of course," Mary murmured.

Being in her arms had a narcotic effect, but he injected his lax muscles with resolution. "So you see why you can't give your fortune to the Fairchilds."

She released him so quickly, he swayed. She turned her back to him, walked away, stood looking out over the lands as he had earlier.

Did she see wealth ill tended? Did she see ill-gotten gains? Or did she simply see the hint of lush summer green? He wanted to tell her to look below the surface, but somehow he feared to do so. Somehow he feared if he suggested she look closely at her own family, she would look closely at him, too. She would see the lad who had walked London's streets looking for a job, and had found only other children, tougher children, who'd fought him, stripped him of his fancy clothes, and rolled him in the mud. She would see that lad hardening as he grew. She would see the times he'd stooped to theft, the times he'd been almost caught, the tears he'd wept when he'd come home to find nothing he'd done had been enough, and his mother had died of grief . . .

Her words came to him on the breeze. "So you did marry me for my fortune."

That jerked him from his melancholy. "No!" He strode to her. "I tell you, you can take that money and fling it out the window, for all I care."

"But you did," she said stubbornly. "You married me so the Fairchild fortune would never return to the Fairchilds."

"I never thought of such a thing." He turned her to face him. "Good God, woman, why would I? I couldn't have imagined you would come up with such a witless idea."

She didn't answer, ignoring the story he'd just told. The story that so clearly explained why she couldn't give her fortune to her family.

He'd plastered over the hurts of the past. His parents' betrayals no longer affected him. He'd been strong, stoic, enduring—until Mary had come into his life. Now he needed something, something he didn't comprehend but something he knew she could give him, and instead of showing any kind of compassion, she whined about her family. In an unrehearsed and thoughtless phrase—all right, a stupid phrase—he gave an ultimatum. "Choose. Them or me."

In some wild part of his soul, he must have hoped she would enfold him in one of those gratifying embraces. When she just stared at him blankly, his stomach sank. His emotions seesawed from anguish to denunciation, from resentment to rage. Deep, bubbling rage. *That,* he knew how to release. "Fine." He almost spat the word. "You don't want me. You can have your precious Fairchilds, although I'll be interested to see how they'll react when you're hanged as a murderess."

The color leached from her skin, and her eyes grew round and wild.

"What's the matter?" he taunted her in a low tone. "I told you my secrets. Didn't you want me to know yours?"

"It's not only my secret," she blurted. Then she shuddered, and clasping her hands, she raised them in entreaty. "I beg you."

He wasn't enjoying this as he should. He actually felt a little sickened by his own cruelty.

She fumbled in her pocket and produced the little book. "Here. Take it. Only don't turn me in."

"You'd do anything to save yourself." *Not just her secret.* Of course, it wasn't just her secret. He knew that.

She took his hand. She was trembling so hard, she could scarcely close his fingers around the diary. "If that's what you think, then think it. But please—"

He looked down at the diary. The damn, stupid little diary that had caused all the problems. That and the damn, stupid Fairchild fortune. He didn't give a damn about either one.

"Take it." She dropped to her knees before him. "But promise me—"

"Hell." He shoved the diary back at her. "Keep it. Give your money to the Fairchilds. Do whatever you want. I don't care." When he stepped back, he knew he was running away. Running away . . . from what? He glanced at the woman groveling just for him.

Was he running from her? Ridiculous.

He pointed his index finger at her. "Just stay away from me."

And he fled.

Chapter 23

Murderess.

Meet me alone at the fountain in the garden with one hundred pounds, or I'll tell all and collect the reward.

Murder. Ian flinched. Hadden hadn't given out any details, and Ian hadn't asked, for really, it didn't matter. He was going to help his cousins.

He knocked on Wilda's door and smiled flirtatiously at the maid when she opened it. "I would like to speak with your mistress."

The maid bobbed a curtsy. "She's resting, sir, and will see nobody."

"She'll see me." Over the maid's protests, he pushed his way into the bedchamber.

Wilda lay on the bed with the pillow over her eyes.

Leaning against the mattress, he crooned, "Wilda, I need you," and lifted the pillow.

He found himself staring at a face marred by tears.

Her nose was blotchy, her eyes were rimmed in pink, and she looked thoroughly miserable. Ian sighed. She still mourned the young man who had ruined, then jilted her. Someone needed to take her in hand.

"What do you want, Ian?" Her voice sounded scratchy and her chin quivered.

He sprang back. She was going to cry again. Oh, God, she was going to cry again.

But he needed one of the Fairchild cousins. He needed that distinctive hair, that body, and that height. The other sisters would simply laugh if he requested a favor. In fact, they would delight in thwarting him. But Wilda was soft, so Wilda, it would have to be. "Dry your tears, dear," he whispered. "I need your help."

Sebastian knew.

Deficient in sight and hearing, keeping one hand on the wall, Mary shuffled like an old woman as she traversed the halls of Fairchild Manor.

He'd always known.

Shock held her in its grip. Sebastian remembered the bloodstained girl who had killed Besseborough, and he'd been waiting, withholding that information until such time when he could use it against her.

She shouldn't feel so crushed. She'd always known he might remember. She'd always known of Sebastian's ruthless character. But somehow the past week had changed her opinion of him. She thought she saw glimpses of vulnerability, portions of caring. She'd begun to cherish thoughts of having more than a sham betrothal, more than a forced marriage. She'd begun to dream . . .

Ah. She'd begun to dream.

She laughed aloud, then silenced herself when she heard the shrill note in her voice. "Papa," she whispered. "Why do I still dream when everything I ever dreamed of or hoped for is a chimera?"

Stupid, stupid. She swiped a trickle of tears off her cheek. Stupid to cry about something so obviously ordained. Stupid to dream about a life spent learning to smile, to trust, in a slow, sweet communion called marriage.

Dreams. Dreams were the cause of all her tears.

A sob escaped her and she glanced around in embarrassment. A maid lugging a bucket looked at her curiously, but kept walking, and no wonder. A thorough cleaning would be necessary to return the manor to pristine order after the house party. *A housekeeper knows these things.*

She stopped by a table and with head bowed she squeezed the bridge of her nose as if that would force back the tears. *A housekeeper keeps control.* But she wasn't a housekeeper anymore. She was . . . She didn't know what she was. She had to hold off this bout of crying, at least until she could reach her bedchamber. And dear God, where was that?

"My dear?" The kindly voice was only too familiar. "Is there anything wrong?"

She kept her head down. "Nothing, thank you, Mr. Brindley."

He stepped in front of her and bent to peer into her face. "Tut, tut. Those look like tears. Why is the blushing bride crying?"

"I'm not." Her voice wobbled.

"Of course not." He offered a clean handkerchief, and she wiped her face with it thankfully. "There. You're better now."

"Yes. Thank you." She glanced at him. His wig was askew, making his head appear crooked. And the color in his face had not improved. Remembering that earlier he had appeared pale and distressed, she said, "You don't look well. You should go lie down."

He didn't seem to hear her. "We will go somewhere and talk."

"I thank you, but no." She had no intention of talking about the day's events to anyone, no matter how well intentioned.

"You don't want someone else to see you in such a state," he insisted.

"Then direct me to my bedchamber."

Taking her arm, he led her down the corridor, and she went gratefully until they reached the small stairway that led up to the servants' quarters and attic. She'd traversed these stairs today on her way to the roof to tell Sebastian the good news, and she'd come down them broken by Sebastian's contempt. "This isn't the way." She tried to tug back.

He didn't allow it. "We'll go on the roof. I believe you were there before."

"Does everyone know my business?" she asked petulantly.

"I hope not," he muttered, and yanked her by the arm.

She stumbled after him up the steps. For an older man, an ill man, he was surprisingly strong. She didn't want to go with him, but neither did she want to make a fuss. "Really, Mr. Brindley, I don't think . . ."

"Don't think, dear. Let kindly old Mr. Brindley take care of everything." They went up the even narrower stairway to the roof, and she gave up and just let him drag her along. Somehow it seemed easier than struggling.

They stepped out into an afternoon of changing weather. Smoke hung low against the roof, and long, gray clouds slithered across the sky. Mary's mood slipped lower. Even the sky would weep with her.

"Tell me what's wrong." Mr. Brindley didn't sound sympathetic at all. In fact, he sounded rather brisk.

She pulled away from him. The myriad of chimneys and vents raised themselves like some doomed volcanic landscape. She zigzagged among them to the wall that encircled the roof, to the place where she had looked out over the Fairchild lands and realized Sebastian would never relent of his hatred. She should have known then it was hopeless. She shouldn't have been so surprised at his accusation of murder.

Mr. Brindley spoke again, his voice rough, surprising her with a lower-class pronunciation. "Tell me what happened between ye and yer husband, madam, to make him storm from here so furiously."

Threading her fingers together, she sought the right words. "Really, Mr. Brindley, as much as I treasure your kindness, what happened between my husband and me is not any of your concern."

Coldly Mr. Brindley said, "I think he was raging because ye didn't give him the diary."

"You've made a fool of yourself now, Sebastian."

Sebastian stood before Lady Valéry in her bed-chamber, his toes lined up on one of the floorboards, his hands behind his back. He fought the sensation of being a young boy again, of having disappointed Lady Valéry. He was a man grown now, and she shouldn't be able to intimidate him like this.

If only someone would tell her.

"Your wife came to me and told me the most incredible story about how she recovered my diary without a bit of trouble to anyone. And you accused her of murder."

"She wanted to give her fortune to the Fairchilds."

"Her fortune, Sebastian." Lady Valéry sat in her chair and pointed her cane at him. "*Her* fortune. *And you accused her of murder.*"

"Well, I saw her," he muttered.

"Saw her what?"

"Saw her after the murder." In the low light of the stable yard, the bloodstains and dirt had mixed together, and he'd thought nothing about it except that the girl—a Fairchild—had been romping in the dark with her lover. He'd reprimanded her and gone on his way. "I realized she'd done it when they discovered the body in a shallow grave."

Lady Valéry didn't care, that was obvious. "Does that give you the right to use her guilt as a weapon? She almost destroyed every last bit of joy in her own life as penance for that killing, and whom did she kill? I ask you, whom did she kill?"

He tried to wait her out, but her flaming gaze demanded he answer. "Besseborough."

"Besseborough." The name was a profanity on her lips. "The most notorious child buggerer in England. Why, I know noblemen he caught and defiled who would today reward Mary for having killed Besseborough."

"I realize that!" Of course he had known about Besseborough.

"And why did she kill him?"

"Don't know." Sebastian tried not to visibly sulk, but he suspected his lip was drooping.

"She's got a brother who was nine years old at the time. You guess."

Sebastian had guessed correctly ten years ago, and once again he winced at the thought of the earl of Besseborough and Hadden. In his secret heart, he wanted to applaud Mary. It was just that she—

"She frightened you, didn't she?" Lady Valéry demanded. "You wanted to give up your stupid vengeance for her, and that scared you."

"I wasn't 'fraid." Damn, he sounded just like a child. "I was not afraid." He enunciated clearly this time. "I simply thought she should choose between—"

"She told me. What a jackass you are, Sebastian. You want your wife to be charitable, loyal, kind, and honorable, and when she displays those qualities, you reproach her for them. If she had willingly disowned her family, you would have spent the next fifty years waiting for her to disown you, too."

Lady Valéry was right. He hated it, but she was right. "Maybe."

"Were you just chagrined because after all your skulking around, she got the diary without even searching for it?"

"No!"

Lady Valéry stared at him.

"Certainly not."

She still stared.

"I wasn't chagrined because she got the diary." Not too much. "I was chagrined because I wanted her to want me. I wanted her to—" He hesitated. What was the word he searched for?

"To love you." Lady Valéry shook her head. "Sebastian. Sebastian. What am I to do with you? Of course she loves you. If she didn't, do you think a woman of impeccable integrity and unshakable virtue would have a man like *you*?"

A little twinkle of hope blinked in his soul. "Really?"

"Really. And I suspect she would like to know you love her back."

"Do I?"

Lady Valéry cackled. "Don't you?"

He rubbed his mouth with his hand. "I don't know, I've never . . . But then, I've never felt so . . . It's as if she . . . But I didn't, either."

"There you have it, then." Reprimand over, Lady Valéry smiled at him kindly. "Come and give me a kiss on the cheek, then off you go! Find Mary and tell her you love her."

Mary swung around and stared as Mr. Brindley strode toward her. "The diary? What do you know about that?"

"I know I came here to buy it. Lord Smithwick told me Lady Smithwick would give it to ye when he was trying to chase me off." Smoke clung to Mr. Brindley. Demonlike, he waved it away, and the smoke obeyed. "And I'm not leaving without it."

"You want the diary?" she asked stupidly. He was one of the people Sebastian spoke of so disparagingly. She stared at Mr. Brindley. Did she recognize him? This wasn't the kindly countenance she'd come to associate with him. This man had a hard glint in his eye. His fists were large and meaty, and he held them as if he would strike her.

She glanced around her. There was nothing with which to protect herself. No umbrella stands, no domed silver serving covers. She backed up, skirting the wall, trying to avoid the corners created by juts in the outer wall. "I don't have the diary."

"Let me see."

"What?"

"Turn out that purse ye're clutching."

She shook her head. "I don't have the diary anymore."

He took a giant step forward and loomed over her. He reached for her, and she hastily turned out her purse. "See? I haven't—"

A black leather-bound book tumbled to the ground.

She gasped. "But that's not the diary!"

Snatching it up, he chortled. "I'll bet it's not."

"You don't understand!"

"No, madam, ye don't understand." He shook the book in front of her face. "This is mine now, and there's nothing—"

A blur streaked out of the smoke and mist. Mary yelped. Mr. Brindley half turned. And the blur materialized into Sebastian.

Mary heard the thud as the two men slammed into the wall. As they rolled onto the rooftop, Mr. Brindley lost his wig. It rolled like a gruesome head from a French guillotine. Then someone landed a punch.

Sebastian. Sebastian had landed the first blow. The book flew from Mr. Brindley's hand. Mary grabbed it before it could tumble three stories to the ground.

The men, grappling wildly, rocked toward her. She scrambled out of the way.

Sebastian was younger. Mr. Brindley was larger, and he had obviously been raised on the streets. But Sebastian, too, had learned from his time in London's slums. Together they created a brutal dance, kicking, punching, grunting with each powerful blow.

Mr. Brindley used his longer arms to catch Sebastian, then wrestled him into a hold with his arm around Sebastian's neck. Sebastian stabbed his elbow into Brindley's ribs, and as Brindley wheezed, Sebastian rolled free. Brindley staggered to his feet and kicked at Sebastian's stomach. Sebastian caught his foot and jerked it out from under him. Mr. Brindley went down like a large rotten elm, smacking his head on one of the chimneys, and the fight stopped as suddenly as it had started.

Sebastian stood, bleeding, gasping for air. "Yield, traitor."

Leaning against the brick, Mr. Brindley dragged himself to his feet. He fumbled in his coat—for his handkerchief, Mary thought.

Sebastian shouted, "No!" and launched himself at Mr. Brindley.

Too late. Brindley held a pistol in his hand, and the black eye pointed right at Sebastian.

Sebastian skidded to a halt. "You don't want to do this."

Out of his other pocket, Brindley brought another pistol. "Don't tell me what I want, lad. I came up the hard way, and I've always known what I wanted." With his wig gone and his face scratched and bleeding, Mr. Brindley looked like an escaped inmate from Bedlam. "The whole government's corrupt, nothing but a bunch of aristocrats in need of a revolution.

We'll do to ye what the French did to their nobles. Then we'll see who comes out on top."

Mary remembered Aggass's comment about Mr. Brindley. *Inviting him to a party is better than finding yourself facing three of his thugs on a dark night in London.* She hadn't believed it at the time. Now as she watched him, saw him holding the pistols steady, heard him praise the terror of the French Revolution, she knew it to be true. The man was completely ruthless.

"I have such plans for that diary, and I won't hesitate to kill." He gestured to Mary with the other pistol. "Ye've got it. Ye love him. Give it to me."

"Brindley, *think*. You're on the roof," Sebastian said. "You can't escape without being apprehended."

Mr. Brindley grinned. His lip was split, and blood bathed his teeth crimson. "I'll lock ye two up here. Ye can pound on the door. Ye can yell all ye want. The servants won't be in their quarters until tonight. No one'll hear ye from the ground. I'll be long gone before ye're released."

The first raindrop fell, and Mary stared as it splashed on the roof. She didn't believe Mr. Brindley. A revolution wasn't started in a day; he needed time to publish that diary and to foment unrest. Just leaving them up here wouldn't keep him safe from the law. He must kill them.

Mary glanced at Sebastian. He knew it, too. He was gathering himself to spring. Preparing to die from a bullet.

Acting on instinct, Mary held up the book. "Look!"

Brindley almost went for it. Sebastian almost went for him. Steadying the pistol on Sebastian once more, Brindley extended his hand. "Bring it to me."

"Mary, no," Sebastian said.

"Don't tell her what to do," Brindley said. "She's a smart lass. She'll make the right choice."

"Yes, I will." Mary extended the book over the wall. "And if you shoot Sebastian, I'm going to throw it over the edge."

Distracted, Brindley jumped toward her. "Don't!"

Sebastian started toward him.

Brindley steadied his aim toward Sebastian. "Nor you, either, lad."

"It's starting to rain." Mary backed down the wall, careful to stay out of reach. "If I drop it now, it could be soaked by the time you get it. Useless. The ink running together."

A fanatical expression hardened Brindley's face. "Be a good lass and give that to me."

"I won't let you shoot Sebastian."

"Very well." He turned the pistol on her, and she saw his intention in the tensing of his face. "I'll shoot you."

Chapter 24

Wilda stood in the middle of the garden circle by the fountain. A thin veil covered her head. It blurred her features but allowed the Fairchild golden hair to shine through. From where Ian hid in the shrubs, he thought she looked like a sacrificial goat staked out to lure the predators. The blackmailing Johnny Bum had better show up soon, or Wilda would break and run.

"Ian." Her voice quivered when she called him. "How much longer do I have to stand out here?"

"Not much longer." He hoped. "He's late already."

From among the branches of the willow that overhung the fountain, Hadden said, "Be patient, Wilda."

"But it's starting to rain." Wilda might have been dying of a lung infection, she sounded so pathetic.

"You won't melt," Ian said. "Now, would you please be quiet? You're supposed to be alone here."

"I'll buy you a new pair of gloves if you'll just be patient," Hadden promised.

She threaded her fingers together. "I want a pair of silk stockings, too," she announced finally.

"B'God, Wilda, you are—" Ian began.

"You'll get them," Hadden said in the voice he used to soothe a fractious horse.

She made a face in Ian's direction, and unseen, he made a face back.

The waiting was getting to them.

Then a thin, tuneless whistling floated in on the breeze, and Wilda stiffened. "Try to be calm," Ian whispered. "Remember, keep your head down and don't let him see your face until he's under the tree."

She nodded.

As he came around the bend toward the fountain, Ian thought he recognized the man. A visiting servant—a valet, by his clothes and bearing. He walked casually, glancing from side to side, but as he neared Wilda his gaze fastened on her with ever-increasing intensity. She kept her shoulder half-turned, but she was visibly shaking, and Ian hoped the villain expected his victim to be nervous.

"Lady Whitfield. I knew you'd come." The man was gloating, the halo around him dark and sinister. "Did you bring the money?"

He reached out and turned her toward him, and she threw back her veil at the same time. He recoiled in shock. "Damn your eyes!"

As he turned to run, Hadden dropped out of the tree onto him, throwing him into the gravel. He tried to fight, but Hadden knocked him witless with a fist to the chin.

Ian strolled out of the hedge with the ropes. Wilda jumped up and down and squealed. As Hadden tied his hands and feet, the valet began to struggle, first weakly, then with increasing vigor.

"Let me go," the valet murmured. Then more loudly. "What are you doing? Let me go!"

"You're going to pay for your sins now." Hadden tightened the knots. "This is justice, be assured."

"I don't know what you're talking about. I've done no wrong."

The valet sounded so earnest, Wilda stopped squealing and started listening. "Should you let him go?" she asked timidly.

Hadden looked up, and Ian was shocked by his cousin's transformation. Every bit of kindness had been wiped clean of Hadden's countenance, and only fury and disgust remained. "I promise you, Wilda, he's a bad man."

"I don't know what you're talking about!" the valet repeated.

Hadden looked down at him. "Yes, you do. You see, I recognize you."

The valet stilled, and stared.

"But you don't recognize me, do you?" Hadden smiled such a terrible smile, even Ian flinched at the sight. "The last time you saw me, I was nine years old, and you had let your master into my bed-chamber.''

The color drained from the valet's face.

''I see you remember.'' Hadden nodded. ''I'm glad. I would hate to think I was only one in a long line of evil deeds you have done.'' He hauled the valet up by the ropes around his wrists. ''Now you'll get a taste of your own treatment. My new brother-in-law has many merchant ships, you see, and you have a reservation on one as a crewman.''

''No.'' The valet tried to drop to his knees, but Hadden jerked him erect. ''I beg you.''

''It'll be a new start for you.'' Hadden signaled to Ian, and he picked up the valet's feet. Hadden took his shoulders, and together they started toward the waiting carriage. ''Who knows? Maybe after thirty years or so, you'll find you like a seaman's life.''

The pistol roared. Mary jumped aside, but not fast enough. Pain exploded into her side. As she fell, another, more human roar sounded. Sebastian brought Brindley down as a wolf would bring down a rat, and Mary knew this time Brindley had no chance. She'd seen the look on Sebastian's face when Brindley fired. She thought Brindley had seen it, too. It was the end of hope for Brindley, for his cause.

Wincing, she touched her side. It burned like fire, and when she brought her hand back, she saw blood. Blood on her fingers. Just like the last time. Just like when she'd killed Besseborough.

Black dots swam before her eyes.

When she revived, she saw Sebastian standing above the fallen Mr. Brindley. He clutched the unfired pistol in his hand.

He was going to kill Brindley. And Mary couldn't allow that. "No." She tried to shout, but the word came out in a whimper.

Sebastian turned to her at once. "Mary? Are you . . . ?"

"I'm fine." An exaggeration, but surely a forgivable one.

Brindley stirred. "See? She's not dead. I didn't aim for her heart."

Mary knew that to be a lie. She'd saved herself by jumping aside.

"Brindley, you shot my wife." Sebastian's voice was cold, his intention plain. "And I'm going to kill you."

"No." This time, Mary knew, the word came out stronger. "For the love of God, Sebastian, don't shoot him. Don't kill him."

Sebastian ignored her. She might have thought he hadn't heard her, except for the tightening of his jaw.

Mary wanted to sob with frustration. Slowly, working around the pain, she pulled herself up. "You don't want this on your conscience. Sebastian, please, for my sake. I beg you."

"Listen to her." Brindley scooted backward on his rear. "She's right. You don't want me on yer conscience."

"To hell with my conscience!" Sebastian said.

"He's not worth it." Mary leaned against the wall. "He'll have to leave England anyway, or be imprisoned. Isn't that punishment enough?"

"I thought he had killed you." Sebastian's voice cracked.

"I'm fine." Mary thought she truly must be. It hurt to draw a breath; the bullet must have struck a rib. Her flesh burned, and she didn't look forward to letting someone clean the injury. She didn't look forward to letting someone bind her ribs or bandage the lacerations. But she would survive. "Please, Sebastian, trust me. Killing a man, even a man who deserves to die . . ." She shook her head as her eyes filled with tears.

Sebastian glanced at her. "If I let him go, Mary—"

"Aye, lad!"

"You have to do something for me."

"A pox on me!" Brindley exclaimed.

"I hope so," Sebastian answered.

Mary's head felt slightly fuzzy. "A favor?"

"You have to forgive me."

Mary might have suspected Sebastian of trying to torment Brindley, but he sounded so earnest. She blinked, trying to change the scene, but it remained the same. Sebastian still stood over the cowering Brindley. He still held a pistol. He still gave the appearance of a man determined to exact his revenge. "Forgive you? For what?"

His mouth crooked in one of those mocking smiles. "For everything. For bringing you here, for exploiting your relationship with the Fairchilds, for doubting you, for forcing you to wed me, for promising to allow you freedom to use your fortune as you wish and then rescinding on that promise." He looked at her out of the corners of his eyes. "For trying to make you choose between your family and me, and when you rightly refused, for using what I know of your past to hurt you."

As apologies went, it seemed somehow lacking. "You're going to shoot him if I don't forgive you?"

"With greatest pleasure."

"Miss Fairchild, I was nice to ye. I taught ye to dance." Brindley was babbling.

Mary ignored him. "But if I don't want you to shoot him, then I have no choice."

"Hurry up, woman," Brindley injected. "Before he changes his bloody mind."

"You shut your maw," Sebastian commanded him. "The lady can have as long as she likes."

Mary wanted to laugh, but her side hurt too badly. From the first moment she'd met Sebastian, he'd been demanding, rude, uncaring of the niceties of life. He wanted his own way, any way he could get it, and if it wasn't fair—well, the end justified the means in his opinion. Marriage to him might be occasionally painful, and often infuriating, but always a challenge for a lady-turned-housekeeper. Primly she recited one of her rules. "A housekeeper never allows a shooting. It makes a mess to clean up."

"You're not a housekeeper," Sebastian said firmly. "You're my wife."

"Wives don't like messes, either."

"Does that mean you forgive me?" Sebastian pressed.

"Yes. I forgive you."

Sebastian waved the pistol at Brindley. "What are you waiting for? Get out of here."

Brindley crawled the first few yards, his gaze fixed on Sebastian as if he expected to be shot in the back. When Sebastian pocketed the pistol, Brindley clambered to his feet and ran to the door.

"Do you think he'll lock it?" Mary asked.

"Doesn't matter." Sebastian knelt in front of her. "You can pick the lock. Tell me truly—how badly are you hurt?" Without waiting for her answer, he lifted her arm and looked, then probed the wound carefully.

She winced and looked away as he wiped his bloody fingers on his handkerchief. She still had blood on her fingers, too. It had grown sticky. "It's difficult to wash blood away once it stains."

Deliberately he misunderstood her. "To hell with the handkerchief," he said, and wiped her hand. "You have a flesh wound. The blood has clotted already. Come on, I'll carry you downstairs."

She caught his arm before he could move. "Not yet. I wanted to say . . . I wanted to ask you . . ."

He took her hand, pressed it between his two palms, and answered the question she was too humiliated to ask. "I recognized you as soon as I saw you at Lady Valéry's."

She moaned. The blush that ignited her skin was almost as painful as the wound.

"I didn't ever intend to hurt you with my knowledge." He sat next to her, back against the wall, on her good side. Moving with exaggerated caution, he put his arm around her. "I knew what Besseborough was. When I heard about his murder, when I heard the governess who ran away had a little brother, I knew why you killed him."

"I thought he was coming to the nursery to see me." She could scarcely speak, she was so numb with remembered misery. "I was so miserable, caring for those horrible children, I wanted any escape, and I thought Besseborough was the prince Papa promised would come. I flirted and he played along."

"You don't have to tell me." He hugged her tighter. "I really do understand."

She scarcely heard. "One night after I put the children to sleep, I came back to our chamber and found him . . . His pants were down and he was trying to get Hadden to . . . I was so angry. I was so angry. I thought . . . I don't even know what I thought. I just picked up a fireplace poker and smashed Besseborough's skull." She could see the scene again, hear Hadden's screams, smell the death. "Blood spurted into the air. He twitched, so I hit him again."

"That's it." Sebastian scooted one arm under her knees, one around her back, and lifted her onto his lap.

Pain shot through her, but whether from her wound

or her recollections, she couldn't say. He settled her against his chest, arched over her as if he could protect her with his body.

The march of memories was relentless. "I had to touch Besseborough, pull him off of my little brother, comfort Hadden. I couldn't drag that weight alone, so I had to use Hadden. I had no choice. I swear I had no choice."

"I believe you," he said softly.

"We wrapped the body in a rug, got it down the stairs and outside to bury it. It took us hours, looking over our shoulders all the while. We had separated to sneak into the house when you saw me." She shuddered repeatedly. "I've always known I deserved to hang."

"You arrived in time," he said matter-of-factly. "You saved Hadden."

He sounded sincere. She stared at him. He didn't seem repulsed. With a catch in her voice, she said, "Someone's blackmailing me."

He stroked her hair off her face. "I'll take care of it. Mary, I'll take care of *you*."

Overwhelmed with a sense of relief and absolution, she turned her head in to his chest, dug her fingers into his waistcoat, and cried softly into his shirt. He didn't say anything, he just held her, stroked her, cradled her.

Finally, when the worst of the weeping had diminished, he said, "When I heard the authorities were looking for the governess because they thought her guilty of the crime, I told them I had seen someone in the stable yard.''

She stiffened in his arms.

''I told them I'd seen a strong, young man with a scar on his face dragging a heavy sack behind him. I said I'd spoken to him, and he'd seemed defiant and angry, and he had a foreign accent. I said I now realized the marks on him weren't dirt, but blood. I laughed when they said they were looking for you. Shamed them for thinking a small woman could kill and bury a man the size of Besseborough. So you see, even then I didn't think you deserved to hang.''

''I . . . Really? You did that?'' She stared up at him, her eyes wide, and it was like looking on the slightly battered and still bruised face of love. This harsh man, this believer in vengeance, wasn't judging her. They were speaking of the murder she committed, and he seemed more concerned with her comfort than her guilt. ''I was stupid. Impulsive.''

''You were Guinevere Fairchild.''

''Yes!'' He did understand. ''Where Guinevere reigns, chaos results.''

''Sometimes chaos is good. It creates change. Guinevere has certainly changed me. Where's your handkerchief?''

''My . . . ?''

''Your handkerchief.''

Moving with care, she dug out the handkerchief.

He tilted her face up, wiping it tenderly. Her skin was blotchy from crying, her eyes red-rimmed, and her hair slid around her face as the rain dampened it. He thought he'd never seen anyone so beautiful. "That side of you called Guinevere took over that morning in your bedchamber, and I loved the result."

She took the handkerchief away from him and blew her nose. "Loved being forced to marry me?"

"I might have been smart enough to do it on my own, but it would have taken much longer before I admitted how much . . . how very much . . ." He almost couldn't say it, but he took a breath and brought the long-lost words to his lips. "I love you, Guinevere Mary Fairchild Durant."

He'd seen that expression on someone else's face not long ago. He tried to remember who, and then it struck him. When he held the pistol on Brindley and offered to spare his life only if Mary forgave him, Brindley had looked like that. Frightened, appalled, affronted . . . hopeful.

Mary seemed hopeful. She hoped his declaration of love was truthful, and he relaxed just a little. Perhaps Lady Valéry had spoken the truth.

But the frightened part of Mary spoke. "You don't love Guinevere. No one could love Guinevere. She's wild, undisciplined, foolish beyond belief."

"She, *you,* were just young. The young are all those things." She made him so impatient! Why couldn't she see . . . ? "Guinevere Mary Fairchild is who you are. All the parts of you. All of your past formed you. That's the person I love—and respect."

She sniffed.

"Really, Guinevere Mary, think about this. Have you been moved to murder since that long-ago night?"

She seemed to be thinking as she studied the chimneys and the smoke that curled out of them. Finally she looked back at him. "Only yours."

He laughed. God, how he loved her! She answered him back without fear. She put him in his place smartly. She brought him to life after too many years in the shadows. He owed it to her to return the boon. "Today you saved my life. Brindley would have shot me if not for you waving that damned diary over the wall."

She shivered. "I know."

He wrapped the edges of his coat around her. "You took a life once, but today you saved one."

She contemplated that silently. Finally she tilted her head back. "That's true."

"So you'll forgive yourself." He didn't ask her, he told her. "You'll decide saving the life of your beloved is apt compensation for taking the life of a monster."

"Yes." She stroked his cheek. "Are you my beloved?"

"Lady Valéry says I am."

"Did she say anything else?"

He flinched at the memory of Lady Valéry's tongue-lashing. "Nothing of importance. Only that you loved me and I loved you, and you know we dare not think her wrong."

"No." She stretched up and kissed him softly,

savoring his lips as if they were dusted with cinnamon and flavored with honey. "She's not wrong. The reality of you is better than any prince I ever dared to dream."

His body stirred at her sweet salute, and his heart stirred at her tender avowal. He wanted to convey her to their bedchamber and . . . and call a physician to tend her wound. Shifting her, he stood and carried her toward the door. "You will never, ever put yourself in danger for me again."

"He was going to kill you." She seemed to think that explanation enough.

He clutched her tighter. "I thought he *had* killed you, and over that damned stupid—" Stopping, he turned and scanned the area. "What happened to the diary?"

"The . . . Oh, you mean the book. I think it went over the edge to the ground."

Disgusted by the trouble Brindley had caused, Sebastian said, "He'll get it. After I've put you in bed, I'll have to go after him."

She laughed weakly. "He can have it. I gave Lady Valéry the diary hours ago."

If she hadn't been injured, he would have shaken her. Instead, he turned sideways to get her through the door and demanded, "Explain."

"As soon as you left me up there"—she pointed back up the stairs—"I went to Lady Valéry and told her what had transpired."

"Of course." Sebastian hadn't thought it through. "That's how she knew."

"She kept the diary, and gave me a book she got from a lover who had been to India."

"What kind of book?" He had his suspicions.

"Um." Mary kept her face averted, but he thought he could see her cheeks flaming. "It had illustrations. Lady Valéry suggested I look through them, and should the time arrive when we might reconcile, we could use the book as a reference."

They entered the main corridor. "The *Kama Sutra.*"

"I believe that was the title."

"That woman is incorrigible," Sebastian muttered.

"Yes, well, it doesn't matter." Mary began to shake with suppressed laughter. "Mr. Brindley has got it now."

When Lady Valéry heard their voices, she snapped open her bedchamber door and stepped into the corridor. As she expected, Sebastian held Mary as if she were fragile and might melt like a confection in his mouth. Mary hugged his neck as if he were an angel who might at any moment spread his wings and fly away.

Two more unlikely events, Lady Valéry couldn't imagine. But that was love. She'd seen it enough times to know. And that meant she'd succeeded once more. Briskly she tied on her bonnet. "Are you two reconciled at last? Because I need to leave."

Mary turned a dazed expression toward her. Slowly she absorbed Lady Valéry's impatience, then just as she had trained herself to do, she put Lady Valéry's needs before her own. "What's wrong, my lady? Can I assist you in any way?"

"Not likely." Sebastian frowned thunderously at Lady Valéry. "Mary has been shot. She's not going anywhere."

"The devil you say!" Horrified, Lady Valéry went to Mary at once. "What happened, child?"

"Nothing to trouble you about, my lady." Mary tried to soothe her.

Sebastian had no such concern. "One of the buyers for the diary tried to kill us."

Lady Valéry touched Mary's side. She had experience with gunshot wounds, and this one was minor. Then she looked up at Sebastian. New contusions, she noted, but he seemed strong enough. She sighed in relief. "A little blood, but you don't appear to be suffering."

"I'm better. If you must leave, we can go," Mary said firmly.

"I'll tell you when you're better." Sebastian gripped her tighter. "Then we can leave." He glared at Lady Valéry. "Not a moment before."

"Now, Sebastian—" Mary tried to object.

Sebastian started toward their bedchamber. "Now, Mary," he mocked.

"You can't have your own way about everything!"

Mary's voice was fading as they walked down the corridor, and Lady Valéry snorted when she heard Sebastian chuckle.

Mary was beaten. She just didn't know it yet. And the way Sebastian was looking at her, she probably wouldn't realize it for at least fifty years.

"Georgette." An excited, desperate, wholly aroused Burgess stood in the door of her bedchamber and beckoned. "Come back, Georgette. I have something for you."

She assessed him. He was younger than the others. Easier to train. Held some potential. And as long as she was stuck here for who knew how long . . . "All right." She untied her bonnet and removed it with a gesture of exasperation. "But try and keep up this time."

New York Times Bestselling Author

CHRISTINA
DODD

"Christina Dodd keeps getting better and better!"
Debbie Macomber